PRAISE FOR THE WORK OF JOHN F.D. TAFF

"Of the current breed of authors riding the wave of digital liberation, John Taff is a standout talent. Literary, affecting, chilling, and indicative of that old-school mentality meets new-school daring."

— **Kealan Patrick Burke, Bram Stoker Award®-winning author of** *The Turtle Boy,* **Kin** and *Jack & Jill*

———————————

"Taff's mastery is such that he can as easily induce *déjà vu* in a nightmare you've never had before, and stir your guts with *Twilight Zone* panic. Taff has the rare literary confidence and narrative skill to decide where you will feel what. It's his choice alone."

— **Erik T. Johnson, author of** *Yes Trespassing*

———————————

"Taff sketches a fresh blueprint in the canvas of existential horror, classic sci-fi and post-apocalyptic realness. Taff doesn't rely on pretense to get his words into your mind; he relies on natural talent, then laces it with a poet's wit to keep you engaged, focused, but most of all, satisfied."

— **J. Daniel Stone, author of** *Blood Kiss* **and** *Absence of Light*

———————————

"*The End in All Beginnings* is accomplished stuff, complex and heartfelt. There's an attention to character and an access to feeling that's very refreshing indeed! The best novella collection in years!"

— **Jack Ketchum, World Horror Grand Master and Bram Stoker Award-winning author of** *The Box, Closing Time* **and** *Peaceable Kingdom*

———————————

"Taff brings the pain in five damaged and disturbing tales of love gone horribly wrong. This collection is like a knife in the heart. Highly recommended!"

— **Jonathan Maberry,** *New York Times* **bestselling author of** *Code Zero* **and** *Fall of Night*

ALSO FROM JOHN F.D. TAFF

LITTLE
BLACK
SPOTS

JOHN F.D. TAFF

GREY MATTER
P R E S S

CHICAGO

LITTLE BLACK SPOTS
ISBN-13: 978-1-940658-84-1
ISBN-10: 1-940658-84-5
Grey Matter Press First Trade Paperback Edition - September 2018

Copyright © 2018 John F.D. Taff
Cover Image Copyright © 2018 Sabercore Art
Cover Design Copyright © 2018 Grey Matter Press
Book Design Copyright © 2018 Grey Matter Press
Edited by Anthony Rivera

GREY MATTER
P R E S S

CHICAGO

Grey Matter Press
greymatterpress.com

Grey Matter Press on Facebook
facebook.com/greymatterpress

THIS ONE GOES TO MY GOOD FRIEND RANDY W. KALIN.
ONE OF THE BEST MAGICIANS I'VE EVER SEEN AND PROBABLY THE
OWNER OF THE MOST COMPLETE COLLECTION OF MY WORK.
HERE'S A LITTLE SLEIGHT OF HAND OF MY OWN.

TABLE OF CONTENTS

INTRODUCTION
BY DOUG MURANO

BEFORE YOU READ THE FOLLOWING STORIES, let me give you a few words of warning: You're going to want to hang on to something.

Yeah…I know what you're probably thinking: What else is new? That's exactly the type of thing you're supposed to say about books like this one. If you're anything like me, the line reminds you of cover blurbs you've read on your favorite authors' work: "These tales will chill you to the bone!" and "You'll want to keep the lights on all night long!" or "These stories will grab you by the throat!" And so on. I know I've seen plenty of breathless, hyperbolic descriptions like those in the horror stacks.

But here's the thing—and if you're a regular reader of John F.D. Taff's work, you know this already—when I tell you that you're going to want to hang on to something, it isn't merely because you'll feel frightened, chilled, asphyxiated, sleep-deprived. Are there chills here? You bet. But there are also other, subtler, lasting delights waiting for you in these pages because Taff possesses tools and a sensibility that separate him from damned near every single one of his contemporaries and elevate his work into the rarified air that only the all-time greats frequent.

Indulge me for a moment of explanation.

I first encountered Taff's work after briefly meeting him at his table in the dealer's room at the 2015 World Horror Convention. In those not-so-long-ago days, I was a newbie editor, fresh off of my first anthology, ready to conquer the world, and eager to gab with as many authors as I possibly could. That was the year everyone (and I mean everyone) was raving about Taff's phenomenal collection of novellas, *The End in All Beginnings*, and so, naturally, catching up with him sat near the top of my list.

We exchanged pleasantries, he signed my book and, in conspiratorial tones, I brought up the theme of my upcoming project, which he listened to and expressed interest in, with the saintly kindness, patience, and grace of someone tossing a tennis ball for an excited Labrador Retriever pup who had just learned the endless joys of fetch. (That's something you should know about Taff... He's one of the nicest guys in horror. Don't tell him I said that. It would embarrass him.)

For the next week or so, Taff stunned me with the contents of that book. Reading those novellas was a revelation steeped in longing, memory, nostalgia, and unyielding horror. It was an experience not unlike discovering McCammon's *Boy's Life,* taking that first sweet sip of Bradbury's *Dandelion Wine,* or spending a hazy summer on the far edge of youth building a dam in the Barrens with the Losers' Club.

Said another way, the stories *made me want to hang on to something*: those bittersweet memories from years gone by, the last light of a late August day as September seeps into the evening air, the hand of a long-dead loved one. Hell, thinking about them now makes me want to hug my dog. Taff's work digs its claws into a deep, resonant emotional core very few authors working in horror can even sniff at, and the way he does it looks as effortless as breathing.

To my amazement and delight, he ended up taking me up on my invitation to submit a story for *Gutted: Beautiful Horror Stories,* and another one for *Behold!: Oddities, Curiosities and Undefinable Wonders* and yet another for *Shadows Over Main Street, Vol. 2.* In the three years since WHC 2015, Taff has become one of a small handful of authors I've come to lean upon whenever I have a project underway because I know what I'm going to get (a top-notch story) and how I'm going to get it (with professionalism, enthusiasm, and true warmth).

How could I do anything but jump at the chance to introduce *Little Black Spots*? How could I pass up the chance to once again wade into the amber-colored light and dive into the lavenders, indigos and inky blacks I would surely find just below the iridescent surface?

I found those hues here, folks—those and so many, many more. What strikes me most about these stories isn't the skill on display (which is substantial) or the telltale marks of an assured hand at the height of its skill (which there are), but the stunning *variety* of stories Taff showcases in this collection.

Early on, Taff gives us "The Bunny Suit," a vicious, disorienting tale imbued with a species of erotic dread and body horror that harkens back to Clive Barker's *Books of Blood,* but which is of a style and tone that Taff owns wholesale. You're going to check your lover's skin for seams after this one.

Elsewhere, he mines socio-economic injustice to produce darkly humorous gems like "Just a Phone Call Away," where a woman's new gig as a phone-sex operator escalates into horrific appetites and "The Depravity of Inanimate Things," which examines the danger in allowing our possessions to turn the tables and own us. Speaking of depraved appetites, look to the dagger-quick darkness of "Their Hands," and the gruesome "The Bitches of Madison County," which suggests that the modern age's hunger for authenticity just might be its undoing.

There's horror rooted in place, as found in "The Dark Level," a Lynchian barn-burner, full of paranoia, which expands the dark corners of the mind into an apocalyptic tableau, and also in "Everything Must Go," which ultimately reveals more questions than it answers...not that we truly want to know.

The bizarro underpinnings and imagery of "Purple Soda Hand" provide a vivid account of how a chance encounter with a mysterious object can effervesce into a surreal tale of addiction horror.

And then there are the stories that I think of as "The King of Pain" tales—the pieces that remind me of my first taste of Taff's work.

In "A Winter's Tale," Taff winds his narrative around childhood terror, troubled family dynamics, and painful memory—and, like a tightening tentacle, it'll squeeze you until you can't breathe.

Johnny Cash famously said that love is a burning thing, a concept Taff dials up to eleven in "The Immolation Scene," in which an estranged couple sifts through the literal dying embers of their relationship to see if there's anything left to ignite. The theme of lost love carries us through "A Kiss from the Sun for Pardon" as well, in a vampire tale stood upside down like an inverted cross—and one that whispers the only thing that lasts forever is heartbreak.

Through a series of vignettes, Taff shows us "The Night Moves," suggesting that, while we're all different, we're united in sin. Similarly, in "Gethsemane in Rain," a sense of unease unites disparate slices of life as dread doesn't so much build as it *accumulates,* like puddles in the driving rain.

Near the end, Taff explores the horror of what might have been. In "The Coriolis Effect (or Chiromancy for Beginners) he shows us how a single terrible moment can spiral into our lives…and into infinity. And, in the closer, "Lincoln & Booth at The Orpheum," Taff gives us an alternate history with shades of (appropriately enough) Ambrose Bierce that provides a touching send-off for the collection and to one of the greatest American presidents.

So go forth, intrepid reader! But remember my admonition: Hang on to something. Hang on to your skin. Hang on to your sanity. Hang on to the things that keep you sleepless in the small hours of the night. Most of all, hang on to these stories…the thoughts and feelings, the gorgeous imagery, the memories they dredge up from deep within you.

Yes.

Hang on to them as tightly as you can.

Doug Murano
South Dakota
August 2018

THE IMMOLATION SCENE

ASHES...

It's snowing, the flakes are red, like snow in Hell, and Corey thinks they taste of cinders. That's what spills down his throat when they melt, leaves his mouth raw.

The warehouse before him is in full conflagration, flames leaping from its roof, flicking like reptile tongues from its burst, shattered windows, between the skeletal remains of its façade. He stands apart from the chaos—the twisting hoses, the intent firemen, spinning red lights—far enough to avoid being consumed, close enough to consume it: the roar of the flames, the avid heat, the burning grit.

He can also smell the rich scent, scummy and thick on the ash-laden air, of boiling human fat. He wonders if anyone else smells it, knows what it is.

They were here tonight. The Immolation Scene. I can feel it. I'm getting closer to them.

To her...

* * *

Amy.

She had come to fix his laptop. He'd been typing at home late the night before, trying to finish a report. Nodding off, fire had squirted from his fingers, singeing the Q, W, E and R keys, melting the A, S, D and F keys.

He was still wondering how he was going to explain it when she came in.

Amy's hair was upswept in a '40s movie star style. It was red, the unnatural red of crayons, traffic lights and fire engines. She wore a dark, prim skirt and a severely plain, long-sleeved white blouse that revealed tattoos beneath its shifting edges. Each ear boasted three earrings, and there was a discreet nose piercing that glittered when the fluorescents hit it. Her heavily chewed fingernails were painted dark eggplant.

Corey was as uncomfortable with her quirky beauty as he was with the fact he had dated her for a while a few months back. The attraction had been instant, over drinks at a departmental party at a nearby bar. Their relationship was swift, torrid, the chemistry definite and mutual.

But after six months, most of which Corey thought were pretty good, she abruptly broke it off. There were arguments, tears. So many tears.

He didn't understand at the time, still didn't.

I love you, he told her. *Isn't that enough?*

Her answer was *No.*

You're not willing to really love, to give yourself to it, let it change you. You're not willing to let yourself feel anything.

It had been uncomfortable for a while, after the split, working at the same company. But the office was large enough that they didn't see too much of each other.

"Umm…hi. Someone's computer not playing nice?" she asked standing in the entry to his cubicle. She carried a small grey case before her, slung around the corner of his desk, holding it before her like a shield.

"That'd be mine, I guess," he said, blocking her view of the keyboard.

"Mind if I take the captain's seat?" she asked, flicking her gaze across him.

"Sure," and he leapt to his feet. They stood face to face for a moment; he looked into her eyes, eyes that he still saw in his dreams, eyes that were a beautiful, deep violet, the Technicolor of Elizabeth Taylor's eyes in old photos, or of bruises, of twilight.

Then she was sitting and he was shuffling behind her, gritting his teeth, wanting her to say something. "Usually I get Devon," he said, as much to fill the silence as to offer a silent thanks to the Gods of IT for sending her instead of Devon—of the too-tight pants and the body odor that smelled of equal parts Big Mac and Axe body spray.

"Well, it looks as if you fell asleep smoking at the keyboard, which is generally considered a bad thing. Not as bad, I guess, as falling asleep in bed smoking, but..."

"You know I don't smoke," he said awkwardly.

"Ummm...well, that's good, actually, because the company pretty much frowns on employees who burn up their laptops while smoking menthols. I'd probably have to report you or something."

Corey realized she seemed more nervous than he felt. He saw she was rolling up the right sleeve of her blouse, doing so conspicuously, as if wanting him to notice it and not her words. A magician's misdirection in reverse.

Her arm was thin and gracile, lovely. The skin was smooth and pale, freckled with moles. Corey was a sucker for moles and freckles.

Then he saw *them*, and he froze. His mouth went dry and he felt it— that feeling he got when it came, when the fire came.

It was a tingling, a little ticklish buzz just beneath the skin, like the first electric pulse you feel on your lips before you get a cold sore.

She had a few small, red, circular welts across the smooth inner flesh of her forearm, grouped like crop circles.

You might think they were cigarette burns, especially given her hair, the tattoos, the piercings. And you might not be altogether surprised.

But he knew her, knew what he was looking at.

And he *was* surprised.

He had seen every inch of her closely, carefully. Why had he never seen these before?

Corey grabbed his own arm, felt the first pulse of fire push outward from his skin, singe the hairs there, felt its heat push against the cotton sleeve of his own shirt.

He saw her take notice, watch a small brown pinprick of heat scorch the fabric.

Grabbing the computer, she stood, almost frantically, stepped away.

"I'll have to replace this," she blurted, pushing past him. "I'll move your files to the new one. I can get it to you in about an hour or two, if that's okay. Well, even if it's not okay."

Moving into the hallway, she turned, eyed him uneasily.

He slapped at his arm, patting the flame out, patting the flame back into his body.

"I'll call when it's ready."

Corey watched her walk to the elevators, his laptop clamped under the arm still exposed by her rolled-up sleeve.

* * *

Corey waited, but she didn't return.

He went home and sat on the couch, picked at the toppings on his frozen pizza. In his peripheral vision, the images on the television jumped and bucked, shifting colors, shifting lights.

Numb.

On his arm he coaxed a small flame into being—crisp blue at its base, yellow-white at its flickering tip. He watched it bob and weave, a tiny dancing wraith, burning his skin, tickling his mind, pleasant and unpleasant.

He thought of her, the burn marks pocking her arm.

Why hadn't she said anything before?

When he looked back, his entire forearm was ablaze. He saw the skin turning pink beneath the gaseous blue sheet of flame that engulfed it. He stared at the fire in awe for a moment, never having let it come out this far before. He felt the delicious hotness of it atop his skin, beneath it…

…in it.

It was burning him, devouring his flesh, crisping the fine hairs.

He leapt to his feet, waving his arm over his head as if dispelling a cloud of bees. Slowly the flames sputtered, faded.

Corey breathed heavily, shocked at how far he'd let the fire go. The skin was unbroken, mildly red as if sunburned. He smelled something acrid in the air, saw that all the hair on his forearm was gone, burned away.

Quietly he went into the bathroom, let cold water run over the scalded skin, then applied a daub of burn ointment from his medicine chest.

When he went to bed that evening, that skin—new and pink and sensitive, burned to life by destroying the older layer above it—felt everything.

* * *

The coffee from the café downstairs sloshed out of the Styrofoam cup. He grabbed a few napkins to keep it from touching the new laptop that sat in the middle of his cluttered desk. Mopping the coffee away, he noticed a small white envelope addressed to him in a loopy, girlish hand.

Corey took the envelope and, impulsively, smelled it. A faint air of flowers hung about it, made his skin tingle. A small card tipped into his palm when he ripped the envelope open.

IF YOU'RE STILL INTERESTED, AND I AM,
MEET AT THIS ADDRESS FRIDAY AT 9 P.M.
WE CAN TALK MORE.—AMY.

Without realizing, he rubbed the new skin of his arm beneath the sleeve of his business shirt.

It was going to be a long week getting to Friday.

* * *

Corey steered through a section of the city he'd never been in before. It was almost 9:00 p.m., and the streets were lit only by the orange glow of dusk-to-dawns perched high above the pavement.

A figure stood beside the closed door of the building that matched the address on the card. The man barely looked at him as Corey pushed the heavy door open, stepped inside…

…a carnival, for that is what it seemed.

The space was enormous, industrial, dark. It seemed to recede into shadows that were moving, punctuated by lurid, red bursts of light. People filled the space, easily one hundred or more, men and women of all ages, races and shapes.

And the smell, the smell he would associate forever with them, the Immolation Scene. Like any bar, it smelled of close bodies, stale beer, the tang of lemons and limes, cigarettes. But there was something more, something at the back of all this, behind it, yet looming in its presence.

It was heavy on the air the way a campfire or fireplace is if you're sitting too close; piney and vaporous, as if you were inhaling the soul of what had burned, a thing too tenuous to carry with it an actual aroma, only a hint.

Below this, the scum, the oily smear of *something*.

To his left stretched a bar, slick wood and dirty brass. She was there, at the bar, draped over a seat. He noticed her bare arms atop the slick, dark wood, noticed the numerous small dots of red that freckled her flesh.

Her violet eyes sparkled like amethysts.

"You came," she said, and it sounded to Corey less like surprise than a simple acknowledgment.

"Sure," he said, sidling up to her. "You thought I'd stand you up?"

"No," she said, her smile enigmatic. "I knew you'd come."

"How's that?"

She said nothing, reached to him, took his arm in her two pale hands. He shivered a little as her nails touched the skin of his wrist, undid the button of his shirt cuff, peeled it back to reveal the skin of his arm, still raw, red from the other night.

Exposed, he could feel the goosebumps she raised with her breath, the dangerous sharpness of her nails as they raked his flesh. She ran her fingers in a slow, looping curve up the swell of his forearm, and Corey nearly gasped in pleasure.

His arm twitched, and she giggled, letting loose of it so slowly, so gently he almost felt as if she were reluctantly passing its ownership back to him. He blinked, rolled the shirtsleeve back down.

"How's *that*?"

A hand drifted up, pushed at a curl of hair near her temple, toyed with it in that most common of flirtations. Corey smelled the hint of her perfume, violets perhaps...or roses, gentle on the air in the narrowness between them.

He chose to believe, for no other reason than the color of her dense purple eyes, that it was violets.

"How come you never told me, never said anything?"

She considered that for a moment, toyed with a drink on a coaster, sighed. "How come you didn't?"

A thousand answers flashed through his mind. Instead, he asked, "So, how did you know?"

Amy stirred at the slumped, yellowed ice in her glass. "Not too difficult, really. Just look for melted laptops. It's a sure sign. Besides, there were those flames on your sleeve." She nodded toward his arm. "It feels a whole lot better if you do it with someone else. Believe me, I know."

Corey's brows gathered in the center of his smooth forehead.

"Wikipedia defines spontaneous human combustion as 'the burning of a living human body without an apparent external source of ignition.' That frakked up computer, those burns on your shirtsleeve," she let her voice fade.

"Yours, too?"

She smiled. "Wikipedia also says its victims are mostly lonely people," she looked down at the bar, swirled a finger atop its pitted surface. "Are you? Lonely?"

Corey considered that for a moment. He had friends, a life. Since he'd split from her, he'd been out on the occasional date. But he also thought of the evenings at home on the couch, the cold meals, the long nights alone in his rumpled bed.

From all of these, it was her that was missing.

"So what is this place?" Corey swallowed, flexed his still tingling arm, looked around.

Amy tilted her head. "A place."

"Does it have a name?"

"Not really. It's just a place we meet. We meet at a lot of different places." She shrugged, lifting the glass and tilting a melted chunk of ice into her mouth.

"Who's *we?*"

Watching him carefully, certain that he was paying full attention, she pushed the chunk of ice to the front of her mouth with her tongue, caught it between her teeth. Another tongue, this one of fire, darted from her mouth, melted the ice cube almost instantly. A puff of steam escaped between her lips, and she smiled, giggled again.

"People who want to *feel* things, *feel* life. You know, one of *us.*"

"*One of us?* What are you? Magicians? Carnies?"

Amy laughed hard at that, taking in the dregs of her drink, and setting the glass onto the bar. "Are *you* a magician? A carnie?"

Corey shook his head.

"Then you're one of us," she said. "We're, like, made for each other." She looked up suddenly, her violet eyes dark as wounds in the dim light of the bar. "But I'm tired of the tears, Corey. So, how far?"

"How far what?"

"How far are you willing to go this time? How much of yourself are you willing to give?" Her eyes focused on him. "How much are you willing to *feel?*"

Corey blinked, not sure of what she meant, then *sure* of what she meant.

"As much as I need to, I guess."

She considered this for a minute, weighed it.

"Okay, buy me a drink and I'll show you around."

* * *

Amy led him, her arm entwined in his, and she felt soft and warm against him. The new skin of his arm tingled as she rubbed against it, maddeningly painful and sensual at once. And she seemed to know because she held her body close against him as they negotiated the crowd.

She seemed to have a destination in mind as she pushed through the crowd, leading him. As they progressed, Corey took in his surroundings.

Here, a man stood on a small platform, shirtless, bearded. A blazing ring encircled his head, forming a crown that burned white and gold. From his eyes, flames guttered. His hands were outstretched, palms facing the crowd, more flames, blue and violet, dancing atop his fingertips. He was talking, reciting poetry, his voice sonorous, enchanting over the rush of the conflagration. His gaunt appearance and blank eyes were startling, like a prophet of the apocalypse.

There, a woman, also topless, hair swirling as if caught in an underwater current. A necklace of fire crawled across her chest, her shoulders, a thin string of blue flame beaded with balls of orange the size of marbles. The whole thing moved, orbited her body, rolling across her flesh. Her face was raised, rapturous eyes cast to the dark ceiling. Corey could see their whites.

Barely visible through the crowd, a man and woman stood nude on a slightly raised dais, entwined, the entire circular platform rotating slowly, affording the crowd a changing view of the couple.

Amy's tug on him lessened, and he realized that she wasn't watching the couple, she was watching *him*, his reaction.

The couple was completely enshrouded, burning fiercely. Flames rose from their heads, squirted between their lips, followed the line of leg, the curve of hip. Rose-colored, amber, orange, jet-blue tinged with jade green, the blaze moved about them, sensuously, avidly, sinuous and alive.

Corey could feel the heat from the performance, could hear the flames crackle, the whoosh of the air that fed them like an open, uncontained furnace.

He turned to Amy, leaned into her, the sounds, the permeating smell of ash, the greasy smell of roasting flesh overwhelming his senses. She reached to touch his face.

He sensed, rather than saw, the corona of flames that surrounded her hand, felt its heat as it neared his face.

As if she had drawn it forth, a tuft of fire erupted from his cheek, guttered there in anticipation of her fiery hand.

When it came, when her enflamed hand softly caressed his cheek, the entire side of his face burst into luminous blue-green, covering it like a caul.

He watched her through these flames, watched her smile, watched her close her eyes and move in to kiss him.

Only then did he feel the heat. *Really* feel it.

He pulled away from Amy, thrust her roughly from him.

Corey brushed at the flames. The skin of his cheek stung, throbbed.

Amy's eyes searched his; something deep and pleading swam in them. He allowed her to press against him, allowed her to find his lips again. They were chapped, hot. He felt pressure building inside his skin, but willed it to stay down, stay inside.

They kissed, and this time he kept his eyes open.

They kissed and he saw the couple on the stage, now extinguished, saw them naked of their fire, saw the burns and scars and weals that covered their bodies, the raw, red skin, the charred flesh of thigh, of palm, of chest.

They kissed again, and Corey closed his eyes.

* * *

When he awoke, he stared at the ceiling for a minute, trying to figure out where he was.

Amy's place. He recognized the crack in the ceiling, the muted street sounds through the closed window of her apartment.

He felt it as he moved, the sheets sliding over his body, that tingling pain and pleasure sensation that raced electrically across him, across his new skin. *New skin burned to life from the old.*

He quietly rose from the bed and padded into the bathroom. The door closed with a gentle click, the light came on with another.

What greeted him in the mirror caused him to gasp, clench the edge of the sink.

The face that stared back was tight and shiny, red, scalded. His eyebrows were gone, his hairline scorched. His lashes, too, were gone, melted. His eyelids were red, puffy, filled with fluid.

His chest, his arms were burned, deep enough to make his skin feel stiff, drawn. The hairs on his chest, under his arms were gone as well, as neatly as if he'd shaved them. Burns trailed further down to his stomach, his groin, his thighs.

Corey gasped, not in shock, but in feeling. All of this new skin, all of this exposed skin brought with it overwhelming sensation. Over the pain, there was an almost euphoric sense of *feeling*, as if for the first time.

He felt the edge of the countertop press his legs, the shivery coolness of the porcelain sink, the stir of the air conditioner, all of them, all at once, and it was almost too much.

Trembling, hands shaking, he fumbled open the medicine cabinet, raked across its contents, sending them spilling into the sink, clattering onto the tile floor. He found a tube of burn ointment, twitched its cap open, squirted a thick dollop of it into his palms.

She pressed into him from behind, and the contact, the silken warmth of her body conforming to his, made his eyes roll back in his head, his hands clench on the sink and the tube of ointment.

It was as if someone had pressed a bare electric wire to his spine.

"What are you doing?"

He thought of the woman, the one with the flaming necklace, how she had raised her head to the ceiling, her eyes white with rapture as the fire burned her skin, burrowed a groove in her flesh.

"The burns. Got to put something on them," he gasped, pushing her away. Cool air flooded the space between them, making every remaining hair on his body stand on end.

"Why?"

Corey took a deep breath.

Was she kidding?

He turned to face her, was not surprised to see that she, too, was covered in red, scalded skin. Some of her hair was singed, her eyebrows. There were raised, red burns across her breasts, the flat of her stomach.

"We burned each other. Here, let me—"

Amy looked at him sadly, slapped his hand away, spattering the blob of ointment against the wall.

"No!" she said. "That's *what* we do, *who* we are. I'm not going to cover all the new skin we've burned off. It lets me feel so much more. It lets me feel *you*."

She stepped closer, put her palm against his red chest.

"Don't you feel it? Don't you feel me?"

He *could* feel her, the coolness of her palm, the moisture. The enlivened nerves of his new skin seemed to triple, quadruple the normal feeling of it, sent it slamming into his brain in a rush, a sensation that threatened to incapacitate him.

Corey took her hand gently, pulled it from him, held it. He saw the pads of her fingertips, the wrinkled moist palm, all red, all burnt. He thought again of the couple they'd seen at the warehouse, entwined, enrobed in sensuous, living fire. But then he remembered how they looked after—the seared flesh, twisting scars, melted skin.

"Look at us," he croaked, through blistered and cracked lips, through lungs that felt sere. "We'll burn each other to death."

"No," she said, beginning to cry, trying to get close to him, to touch his skin with hers. "No, don't think of it like that. Think of it like we're burning away the loneliness, burning away the empty evenings, the lonely nights. We're not burning to death, we're burning to *life*. A new life together."

Corey looked at her, and despite his love for her, all he could see were the burns, the angry flesh, the swelling. All he could think of was the pain, the fluids rushing in beneath the appalled flesh, flushing away dead cells, trying to heal that which had been hurt.

"No," he said. "It's too much. I can't do this."

She cried harder, her breath hitching, tears trailing down her cheeks, across her naked breasts. "You said you would…give as much as you needed to…this time."

Corey wanted to reach out, to hold her, to tell her that he loved her. But he saw his own hands, shriveled, burnt, and drew them back.

"Not this way."

She looked away. "I should have known. This is just like last time."

"Jesus Christ! You're asking too much of me. Too much!"

She stepped away, let him pass.

They did not touch.

Corey sat on the edge of her bed, put on his clothes slowly. As he drew them over his skin, each movement was a symphony of sensation. His breathing quickened, his pulse became erratic, thready.

When he was dressed, he turned to her, standing still, silent in the bathroom doorway, limned by its colorless light.

She said nothing, and her face was in shadow, but Corey heard her sobs.

"I can't do this anymore. I won't cry for you anymore." She sniffled. "This is it."

Within the darkness of her face, a small flame appeared, centered on her right eye.

It flared there, intensely bright, as violet as her eye.

Just as quickly, it went out.

He heard her gasp.

He heard a small pop!

He heard something drip to the tile floor. *Plipplipplip.*

He was horribly sure that it *wasn't* her tears falling. But he could think of nothing to say, to do.

So he turned and left, silently, carried away on the scent of violets, of burning flesh.

* * *

Months passed. Amy disappeared, quit her job, left her apartment. No new employer noted, no forwarding address left. And for a while, that was fine with Corey.

For a while.

He went back to long days at work, longer nights at home, eating alone, sleeping alone.

Numb.

Old skin had grown over the new, insulated him again from feeling anything.

Numb.

Until he thought about *The Immolation Scene.* That's what it was called on the jewel box for the movie soundtrack CD. The name fit, so Corey took it, used it for her group.

The Immolation Scene.

He watched the movie on his DVD player over and over, because that scene came the closest to showing how it actually felt.

Or maybe how he *wanted* it to feel.

In the movie, the antagonist—*or was he the protagonist here?*—sprawled atop the dark beach injured, defeated, a river of magma flowing past him like a hot line of hate, a sky of lurid, blackened clouds boiling overhead. Fire all around him, in the air, the ground, the river.

When his body erupted into flames, though, those flames came from *without*, Corey thought, not from *within*, like his own fire.

Corey always believed that his fire was something else, something different: a wick tapping into some deeper fuel, a fuel that burned only the grace from him. He could relax, not worry about it consuming him; not worry about losing himself in it.

But that man there on the screen? It didn't just consume him, it changed him, altered his soul as he lay on that black sand beach. You knew because the movies were made out of order; you already knew, going in, what the fire *did* to him, what it *made* of him.

He had thought all of this *then*, but *now*...well, *now* he knew better, since he met her, and lost her...*again.*

Now he paid more attention to the fact that the character in the movie had also let the flames make of him what they would.

And for what?

For hate.

She had asked him to do the same, but for love. And he had resisted that, misinterpreted it.

Just as that character had.

You're not willing to let yourself feel anything.

If someone's willing to do it for hate, he told himself, *you should be willing to do it for love.*

Corey thought about that as he watched a tiny bloom sputter atop the pores of his left arm, let it roll down to his hands, crawl up his fingers. The fire was white hot, radiated heat in great pulses that he could feel on his cheeks.

He had never let the fire get far enough for that, though...

...not even for her.

Numb.

No more.

He let the fire go, to make what it would of him.

To make him feel.

And he did. The heat grew until it sent tendrils of pain down his hand, into his arm. He smelled the ash, the charring skin, the cooking meat.

First one, then another of his fingers fell to the floor, sloughing embers like cigar stubs.

Corey fell to the floor, too, on his knees, weeping, *feeling, feeling it all.*

He had to find her.

He had to tell her that he *felt*, show her how he *felt*.

* * *

Glass. Shattered glass.

Corey stoops to pick up a piece that sparkles in the swirling lights, the twitching firelight. It has melted its way into the soft asphalt at his feet, like a small meteor hurtled to earth, and he must pry it from the gummy material.

How many more of these warehouse fires will I have to visit before I find her?

He needs to find her; he knows that now.

He needs to tell her; he understands that now.

It isn't sharp, jagged like shattered glass should be. Its edges are blunted, blackened. It is as smooth as a pebble worn by water.

The size of a quarter, it is egg-shaped, perhaps a broken piece of something larger, probably a window in the building that is completely engulfed. Corey turns it in his hands, his hands smudged by the black ash that slicks its surface, and thinks that it looks familiar.

He is close. So close now.

As he rubs the ash aside, Corey sees a flash of color within the glass. Perhaps the window bore a painted sign, the name of a lawyer or the logo of some pharmaceutical firm.

But it's not that. It's not a piece of a window or a cocktail glass. He realizes this as he holds it in the ash-smudged palm of his ruined hand. It pulses with deep purple light, the color of violets.

Amy's eye.

His heart lurches, his hand bursts into white-hot flame. He feels it scorch his palm, melt the glass fragment to slag, which drips to the pavement between his remaining fingers, *plipplipplip*, like the original that this glass one had replaced months ago.

Another tear, shed for him.

She wants him to find her.

He is close. So close now.

He *feels* it.

He feels everything.

THE BUNNY SUIT

I SANG THE WORDS TO HER there in the dark, nestled in the crook of my arm, my hand shaking as I stroked her cheek.

Something about spring, a warm embrace.

I loved her face, loved that it was lined with argence from the moon, lined in shadows, but no longer lined with sorrow or worries.

Or fear.

She closed her eyes, and I sang to her in the soft fall of moonlight, the dappled night protecting us.

My heart was full, gorged on the blood that raced through me, fired my veins, tripped circuits that burst before my eyes like a shower of phosphenes.

I held her, and I was full, would be full…for a while.

Later, I washed my hands, went home to my wife.

* * *

"Let's go get our Halloween costumes after dinner," she said, placing a plate onto the table before me; chill, white porcelain onto which she splatted a large metal spoonful of some brownish casserole.

I smiled at my wife Deanna.

"Leftovers. Sorry," she said, slopping some onto her own plate then sitting across the table from me.

"I love leftovers," I said, lifting a clump of it to my mouth and chewing. It was dense, tasted of cheese and potatoes.

"You're too easy," she said, laughing. "That's why I love you."

We chewed together in silence for a while. I drained my glass of water as much to lubricate the wads of casserole as to moisten my dry mouth.

"Now, what was that about Halloween costumes? Is it really that time already?"

Deanna rolled her eyes. "How could you not notice? The jack-o'-lanterns? The decorations? The fact that everything comes with pumpkin spice flavoring?"

"How soon?" I honestly didn't know.

"Next weekend, silly. Let's go to that Halloween superstore and find something to wear."

She stood next to me, behind me, over me, put her arms around me.

"But we're not really going anywhere, are we? Not anywhere we'll need a costume."

"No, I know you don't like people," she said.

"Except you," I said as she nuzzled my neck.

And it was true. She was different, always. She looked different, sounded different, smelled different from everyone else. It was something almost eldritch about her that set her apart.

Something about her *skin*.

Something *real*.

How could I help but love her?

"Except me," she repeated, her breath hot against my neck. "So let's get some costumes, just something to wear around the house for Halloween."

I hated Halloween. It was false fear and false gore and false monsters. But then I hated most holidays. There was nothing real about any of them, so little that was real about the world as a whole.

Just her and I, really.

Her tongue flicked playfully at the skin of my throat, and I felt goosebumps radiate from its touch like ice crystals spreading across the surface of a freezing lake.

"Sure, let's go get costumes."

* * *

A bunny suit.

She picked a bunny suit from the warehouse-sized store we visited.

The aisles were stocked with all sorts of Halloween crap—plastic candelabra dripping with blood, screaming witches' heads, cauldrons, bones of all sorts, skulls of all sorts.

But everything was fake, fake, fake. Too pristine, too *clean*.

It's never that clean: death.

The store was clogged with people. They moved around us like ghosts, smeary across my vision. Always too fast or too slow, always swimming out of my peripheral vision, fading away.

So unreal, so bothersome.

Deanna pulled me through all this, a smile affixed to her lovely face. She sorted through rack after rack of women's costumes—the whorish princess, the whorish nurse, the whorish maid, the whorish zombie—finally holding up a plastic package with what looked to be a square of fluffy, greyish-brown fur folded inside.

The package was sealed with a cardboard header that was simply labeled HARE, along with a lot of Chinese characters. The label showed a picture of a young Asian girl dressed in the costume, cool and gamine.

"That's a kid costume," I said, shrugging.

She opened the package, unfurled the thing, held it up against her body as if sizing a prom dress. "Looks about right."

I shouldn't have doubted, really. Deanna is built small, so much smaller than me.

It was a full-body jumpsuit kind of thing, with legs that ended in elastic at the ankles, and arms that ended in the same at the wrists. There was a zipper up the belly and an attached hoodie that pulled over the head to become a half-mask, covering everything but the nose, mouth and chin. There were even gloves of the same material, little booties.

A little fluffy white cottontail sewn onto the costume's rear end.

She folded the thing, slid it back into its crinkly plastic pouch, then looked at me.

"Now, you."

After a few minutes of searching, I chose a plain, black ninja costume; sleek, satiny material that made the model wearing the costume look like an absence, a hole in reality.

Deanna wrinkled her nose at me.

"Thousands and thousands of costumes to choose from, and you chose to look like…darkness?"

That's why I loved her.

* * *

She put the costume on as soon as we got home. And I mean as soon as we got home. I was still deep into my routine—locking the front door; checking the windows; the door to the cellar; the back door that went out into our small, pristine yard, the detached garage and the alley—when she came into the living room.

I flinched when she entered my vision, like a vaporous cloud, oozing into the room in a way that surprised me, shocked me.

The way she moved wasn't like her.

She slid to a stop before me, held out her hands.

"Ta-da," she said, then spun, giggling.

It took me a moment to catch my breath.

The costume looked as if it had been made for her, tailored to her unique dimensions, which also struck me as odd. She was so unique. That was what I loved about her. But evidently a Chinese factory worker hunched over a sewing machine in some dank factory sewed this to fit only Deanna's body and hers alone.

The thin layer of grey-brown fake fur hugged her curves, stretched taut over her breasts, pinched at her waist, slid down her thighs in a way that was both erotic and disconcerting at the same time. The sleeves and legs were just long enough, ending at her delicate wrists and ankles, disappearing seamlessly into the gloves and booties she wore.

And the hoodie, well, that was what disturbed me most, I guess. Not the only thing, mind you, but it made me shiver when I looked at it.

It swooped over her head, fell over her face like Batman's cowl. Two ears perched atop her head, furred outside with smooth, garishly pink material on the inside. One thrust straight up, the other bent in the middle, draping over itself.

Somehow the hoodie, too, seemed fitted specifically to her, with no gaps or bulges. The fur conformed to the shape of her face, cupped her cheekbones, closed tight below her chin.

Only the cupid's bow of her mouth and the very tip of her nose showed. And her eyes, her soft, grey eyes, almost the eyes of a rabbit already.

Now they were hooded, literally, by the strangely real grey-brown fake fur, which dipped into each delicate eye socket, clung around the edges of her eyes.

I shivered again, said nothing.

"Well, what do you think?" she asked, twirling before me again, her little cottontail giving a saucy flounce as she flexed on the balls of her feet.

My mouth felt dry, my tongue like a shriveled sponge. The costume was perfect, absolutely stunning in its fit.

And because of this—because of things that were deeper, so deep inside me it made me slightly dizzy to contemplate them—it deeply discomfited me

"I…um…love it, honey," I said, hearing the falseness, the unrealness of the words that left my lips and hating the way they sounded, the way they made me feel.

I saw the uncostumed corners of her mouth gather into a frown. "Well, that's hardly confidence inspiring," she said in a huff. "Aren't you going to try yours on?"

"Nope," I answered. "Not right now."

The frown lines deepened on Deanna's face.

"Party pooper," she pouted, then came to me, stood close, put her arms around me and stood on her tiptoes to kiss my cheek.

I think she felt me shudder, because I did.

Deanna stepped back, stepped away from me, but turned to give me a quick backward glance, a measuring look that I'd seen plenty of times, on plenty of others.

Never on her.

"Well, I'm going to bed. Lots of stuff to do tomorrow. Busy day. You coming or is my night owl puttering?"

I found enough moisture in my mouth to answer.

"Yeah, puttering tonight, babe. You head on up. I'll slip in later."

She headed for the steps that led up to our master suite. Again, she turned.

"I love you," she said, then, laughing, hopped up the steps one at a time.

I found my breath had stopped, the sight of her in the bunny suit, the wan light of the living room playing on the fake fur as it rippled and stretched across her body, the way the ears flounced as she hopped up each step.

Before I left, I turned the lights out, stood there in the dark staring at the ceiling, listening to her breathing upstairs in bed. I imagined I could see her there, sprawled out across the king-size mattress, taking up her space and mine, the covers twisted around her.

And where the covers gapped, where they should have showed her smooth, naked skin, I saw grey-brown fur. I shivered fiercely, as if gripped by an ague, and stumbled back down the stairs, out of the house.

* * *

When I returned, the night was old and weary, and the half-lidded sun was somewhere just below the horizon, creeping slowly upwards.

I took off my soiled clothes, dropped them into my personal hamper—she insisted we do our own laundry, and I was fine with that—and took a long, hot shower. When all of the darkness had swirled down the drain and I was as clean as the gritty bar of Lava soap that I now dropped into a small Ziploc bag, deposited in the small bathroom trashcan, I went into the darkened bedroom, naked.

The windows were open, and the cool October air rifled the sheer curtains, the bed sheets.

I stood at the end of the bed and felt alive, gigantic.

It was like this a lot when I returned home.

I felt engorged, charged with power, as if everything inside me had increased tremendously in size, all pushing outward, making me feel larger, taller. I stared at my hands, scrubbed clean of their stains, and saw them glow in the moonlight, as if made of chrome.

Several deep breaths, and I went to my side of the bed, pulled the covers aside.

Deanna slept soundly, not roused by my showering or padding through the bedroom, nor my climbing into bed beside her. It was one of the many reasons our marriage just worked.

But as I reached over to touch her, my hands stroked slick, silky fur, not the smooth skin I had expected.

Then I remembered.

The costume.

She'd worn the damn thing to bed.

I lay awake for much of the rest of the night, just a sliver of it anyway, staring at her lump under the covers.

What was she becoming?

* * *

I left her in the morning, curled into a small, furry ball beneath the covers like the cat we'd once had. I showered again, dressed in clean clothes, went off to do my day job, to sleepwalk among the sleepwalkers, push computer keys and send unreal numbers out across the unreal ether, to spill across other displays in places so far away they had to be unreal.

When I returned that night, I could smell dinner cooking even as I went up the front steps to the porch. The house was ablaze with light, warm and soft inside, inviting. I drew the door open, inhaled the warm air of the furnace, the acrid smell of the fireplace, and something rich and inviting in the oven.

As I shrugged from my coat I caught Deanna in my peripheral vision, an attenuated shadow slinking down the hallway, coming toward me.

It startled me, the more so when I realized that she still wore the costume.

"Did I spook you, honey?" she said with a laugh, throwing her arms around me. I could feel the soft fur slide over the back of my neck, could feel her tight, hard body beneath the jumpsuit conform to mine.

She lifted her face, sought my lips. I kept my eyes open, searching her face. Her grey eyes were open, too. They peered from where the mask curled around her brows, cupped her sockets from below. There seemed to be no boundary between the dusk-colored fur and her smooth, pink skin.

I laughed nervously, but I could also feel the sweat leap from my pores, slick my own skin. I returned her kiss but tasted only her lip balm and something else. Something bloody, like kissing a slice of raw liver.

Pulling away, I licked my lips in an attempt to rid them of her taste.

"Well, only because...I mean...have you been in that costume all day?"

She turned, scampered back to the kitchen. Silhouetted in the doorway, she turned, gave me an impudent shake of her little rump.

"So what if I was? I love this thing. I feel so…" her voice trailed away into a guttural growl, and her body gave a tremendous shake.

"Put on yours," she said, bringing the package from where she'd hidden it behind her back.

I hadn't seen it since the other night, and I really only bought it to please her. I had no intention of wearing it.

"No," I said, shaking my head. "Why?"

"Because," she said, coming over to me, the packaged ninja costume between us, its plastic crinkling as she pushed against me. "It's you…and kinda sexy."

With that, she pressed the costume into my hands, bounced back into the kitchen.

I stood there holding the thing, feeling equal parts aroused and ridiculous.

Then, shaking my head, I tore the thing open, pulled out the costume. It was a silky, basic black, form-fitting tunic with tight black pants, a wide black fabric belt. Slick, satiny black gloves and a black cowl that exposed only the area around my eyes.

Dutifully, I put it all on over my clothes and, curiously, found that I liked it. It made me feel powerful in a way, lithe and graceful and dangerous.

Dressed, I went slowly into the kitchen, and it was…well, it was a mess. She'd basically used nearly every pot and pan in the kitchen to cook whatever it was she'd prepared. The kitchen was staggeringly, dismayingly cluttered, and it wasn't just the mess that bothered me.

This wasn't her, wasn't Deanna. She wasn't messy, didn't cook like this. It was one of her hallmarks, one of the things I loved about her.

But here we were, with dirty cookware and utensils piled in the sink, soiled towels scattered everywhere, dishes and all manner of bowls piled teetering on the counter.

I found it all a bit hard to take in, a bit hard to breathe.

I turned to her standing in the dining room, watching me, smiling, the one erect ear of her bunny suit bobbing amiably.

"Great. You dressed. Come in, I've made you a fantastic meal."

And she had.

I walked to her on numb legs, and she spread an arm out over the dining room table.

As messy as the kitchen was, the dining room was immaculate, ordered, just as it always was. Two place settings were atop the table, at her seat and mine. There were two candles, their flames flickering brightly, and the single centerpiece: a glass bowl filled with blown glass balls.

Atop my plate was a gigantic strip steak, easily over a pound, nicely charred yet oozing pinkish serum across the plate. A side plate nearby held a baked potato the size of a child's head, split open, steaming, dripping with butter and sour cream. A wine glass held a globe of dense, dusky red wine.

"Your favorites," she chirped, motioning me to sit. She sidled around behind me and I felt—*heard*—the fur of her costume squeak against the polished wooden back of my chair, setting my teeth on edge.

She sat as I did, pulled her plate close.

There was no steak on her plate, no baked potato.

Instead, there was a handful of greens so scraggly they looked as if she'd uprooted them from the front lawn.

And that was it.

"No steak for you?" I asked, looking from my plate to hers, then up to her masked face.

Her eyes shone from within the furred folds, smiling even more than her mouth did.

"No, the steak is for you. *Your* favorite. I wanted us to have a romantic evening," she said.

"But you like steak. You love it, in fact," I said, picking up the sharp knife in my gloved hands, holding it familiarly.

She stared at me, contemplated what I was doing, what I'd said.

"This just seemed...*right*," she answered, almost absently.

I drew the knife across the seared flesh of the steak. The meat parted around the blade, exposing its soft, yielding interior. Thin red fluid welled up and out of it, and I fought back a frisson of delight. She watched me spear the sliver of meat, lift it to my mouth, chew.

"Good?" she asked after a minute.

"Yes," I said, nodding. "Fantastic."

That was the way dinner went for almost twenty minutes. She watched every cut I made, every bite I took, watched my throat as I swallowed, watched me decant the dark, dark wine into my mouth. She punctuated each of these moments by lifting a green leaf to her own mouth, sliding it through her lips to be torn up and mashed by her sharp, perfect little white teeth.

I found myself sweating, breathing hard.

And then I felt something on my leg, pressure on my thigh.

It was her gloved hand, sliding up my inner thigh.

I looked up in surprise, saw her leaning in toward me, felt her breath hot and moist from across the table.

Her fingers dipped beneath the waistband of the thin black pants, tripped across my zipper, fumbled playfully with it.

"Done?" she asked, her voice deep and sounding as if from a distance.

I wasn't done. There was at least half of the steak left, bleeding out deliciously on my plate, and I hadn't even touched the baked potato.

But her voice, her touch, well, we hadn't been together much as of late, with me working during the day and pulling long hours at night away from home as she slept.

"Yeah," I croaked, and I let her stand, coax me to my feet, lead my upstairs. I watched the taut curves of her ass sway back and forth as she ascended the steps, her flesh jiggling within the costume in ways she knew excited me.

When we lay in bed, her legs entwined mine, pulled herself to me.

Every muscle in my body spasmed when I felt the slick hairs of that costume slide against my leg, press against my chest.

My hands shaking, I reached out, fumbled with the zipper at the front of the bunny suit.

She pushed my hand away, playfully.

I found the zipper again, and this time she lashed out, almost instinctively, slapped my hand.

"Are you kidding me?" I asked, rolling away from her and finding it difficult not to leap from the bed.

"What?" she asked in an earthy, breathy whisper, her hands coming out from the darkness to grasp me, pull me back.

Her gloved, furred hands.

"We're not going to wear our costumes while…I mean…"

'Yeah, we are," she breathed in a voice that didn't sound like Deanna, but sounded like need. Like need personified. "Are you going to tell me that's a problem?"

The tips of her fingers tickled at my chest, scrabbling down my abdomen, finding me, finding *it*, urging me back.

It wasn't a problem.

It wasn't because…well, because…*reasons*, that's why.

Those fingers slid across my costumed skin like a team of trained ice skaters, finding the right places, setting those nerves afire. I found myself rolling to her, atop her, kissing her exposed face, her swollen, torpid lips.

I tasted her and she tasted green: like lettuce and leafy, growing things.

She ground into me, beneath me, pushed me, pulled me, clawed at me.

I went back to the zipper one more time and she grabbed my hand, tugged it down until it was between her legs.

My mind didn't have the free neurons at the moment to debate her or wonder at the viability of what she seemed to be asking me—*demanding* me—to do.

So, I thrust my hand down, away from hers, slid it across the flat of her stomach, pushed it between her legs.

It was hot here, like sticking your hand into a warm winter glove.

But it was also damp, as it shouldn't—*couldn't*—have been, and my fingers felt wetness, matted hair.

And then a cleft, smooth skin, warm, wet. My fingers penetrated this, and I was inside her.

This I knew the feel of. This was Deanna.

But how?

Had she cut a hole in the costume?

I felt along the edges, and it made no sense. What my fingers communicated to me made no sense.

There was no hole here. The wet, tangled hair had no gaps or boundaries that I could feel.

The fur simply faded to flesh.

But I was given no time to contemplate this.

She pulled me roughly to her, and I grasped her hips

There was no similar hole in my tight black pants, so I peeled them down, slid into her.

What followed was everything I remembered about her, except for the costume. I could feel her muscles clench and release beneath the fur, but it didn't feel like a costume anymore.

It felt like skin.

I didn't last long. She cried out, thin and reedy, breathless. Her furry legs wrapped around me, tightened convulsively, threatened to snap my spine, then released.

I pulled from her, rolled off, but by the time my head hit my pillow, she was asleep, curled away from me, breathing in little gasps.

I lay there stunned, trying to figure out what was going on, what had just happened.

Who she was.

What she was becoming.

Daylight saving time, and the 8:00 p.m. room was already like midnight. Stars glittered in the unadulterated sky, and the moon had already risen, bathing everything in its ghostly glow.

I swallowed, rolled over onto my side, spooned with Deanna.

She murmured something, scooted into me.

I draped a hand over the rise of her hip, felt her warmth, felt her pulse through the fur.

And as I lay there, staring at her costumed body in our bedroom, I saw *something…*

…something *moved* beneath the grey fur, something that undulated just under the costume, slithering up from between her legs, looping across her ribs, then fading, diving deeper as it progressed up her slumbering form.

It pushed the costume's fur ahead of it, like the wake of a ship passing through water. *But it didn't seem to be between the costume and her skin.* Rather it seemed as if the costume *was* her skin, and this moved beneath her flesh.

A hump of whatever this was passed underneath my hand like a diving sea serpent, and I leapt from the bed, repressing a horrified shout.

I stood there for a moment, watching as this thing, whatever it was, disappeared down into her body, leaving a ripple that moved through her like a shudder.

Quickly, without quite realizing why, I pulled the ninja costume from me, tossed it aside.

What worried me most, as I stood naked beside the bed, was that she was becoming more and more unreal to me.

Like *them*. Just like all of *them*.

I knew that I'd have to, eventually I'd have to, remove that costume.

But that would need to be later.

I had things to do that evening.

* * *

In the moonlight, I sang softly, so softly that the words were like whispers breathed into the ear of the night.

Something about a rose, something about the charm of spring.

I became something.

And so I did, and she did, too.

But I was so distracted that night, distracted about what was going on at home, what was becoming of Deanna, that everything was rushed, a mess.

I lowered her gently to the ground.

I was black in the moonlight, glistening, slick, sticky.

It took a while to hide her

A while to clean up and get dressed.

A while to decide what to do.

* * *

It is late. It is early.

It is that time of the night when everything is still, quiet, quiescent, poised between the easing down of the evening and the winding up of the coming morning.

I walk home through the territories of Halloween, that most ridiculous of holidays.

Houses draped in cotton cobwebs. Styrofoam tombstones in front yards. Limp inflatables—huge jack-o'-lanterns, skulls, creatures, hearses—drooping across darkened lawns like used condoms.

Deanna loves this holiday, but I loathe it, with its cute costumes and fake candles and candy and fallen leaves. Its nodding, mocking acceptance of death.

I know death. *Intimately.* And there is no part of it that is cute and cozy.

It is cold and slimy, hard and sharp, sweating and itchy, breathless and unbreathing. It is frenetic, panicked, oozing fear.

Then it is motionless. But, for a moment, calm and serene.

It is screams and low moans and bubbling sighs. It reeks of copper and salt and piss and shit. It is sad and profound and mysterious and it aggravates me—infuriates me—that it would be mocked by this shallow holiday.

I enter the house quietly, as I always do. Tonight, though, the air inside is dense and aggrieved. As if I've made some serious *faux pas.* As if I've entered somewhere I'm not allowed, aren't meant to be.

I shut the door behind me, lock it, go through the usual routine of checking windows and doors, testing locks. I leave the lights off. I always do. I know my way around the house intimately, with every light extinguished, with my eyes tightly closed. I sidestep ottomans, swerve around the corners of a bookshelf, the outthrust footrest of a recliner.

Up the steps now and the air, already thick downstairs, congeals as I near our bedroom. It's as if the very breath of the house is scabbing over, coagulating like old blood.

In the doorway to our bedroom I pause, my hands grasping the lintel as if trying to prevent me from being sucked inside.

I can hear the subtle snapping and popping of the structure's hidden bones, the ticking of the furnace in the basement, like one of the house's secret hearts. I can hear my own breath, my own heartbeat.

There is a smell here within the room, dense and unpleasant, of musk and sweat, like the reek of an animal, cornered, imprisoned in its den.

It's not Deanna's smell, I realize.

And then I realize something else.

Deanna had no smell, not *before.* She wore no perfume, didn't smell of soap or moisturizer or shampoo, at least not that I ever noticed.

But now, now she smells, and her smell fills the room like a miasma.

I know it's the smell of two things.

The bunny suit.

And *fear*.

The suit has to go, has to be removed.

It's still dark outside, and the room is a shadow box.

I step inside, and the floorboards creak under my weight.

She stirs in the bed, moves, and the pearlescent light catches the fibers of the fake fur, shimmers across it.

Unreal.

I peel my clothes off, climb into bed by her, but I can't bring myself to curl up to her, to fold my body around hers.

My side of the bed is safe but cold.

Real.

I fall asleep.

I don't know what I was thinking.

* * *

In the morning the sun pours into the room exultantly, filling every corner, pushing out every shadow, obliterating every darkness.

Groggy, I reach out to her side of the bed, but my hand encounters only rumpled sheets. The indentation in the mattress where she laid is no longer warm.

She is not in bed, not in the room. I listen for the shower, but there is nothing but silence.

Nothing disturbs the dust motes that swirl in the beams of almost solid light that penetrate the room.

Suddenly, with only the vaguest of panic, I sit up in the bed. The covers fall away from my body.

I'm wearing only my underwear.

My clothes!

I look to the side of the bed, where I stepped from them last night.

Stupid. Sloppy. Why didn't I put them in my hamper, like I always do?

I swing my legs off the mattress, stand.

There they are, draped over the foot of the bed.

Nothing much: a shirt, a pair of pants, a pair of socks.

They are extravagantly, exuberantly stained with blood.

You'd think I'd be nervous about this, anxious, fearful.
You'd be wrong.
I know exactly what I have to do.

* * *

She's in the kitchen when I come downstairs, sitting at the table, her head slumped forward, forehead resting on the cool wood. The furred hoodie covers her entire face, takes away everything that is Deanna from her.

She's weeping.

I don't say anything, because there's nothing of any meaning left to say. Everything has become so...*unreal.*

The kettle is on the stove. I fill it with water, wait the uncomfortable minutes for it to boil. From the cabinet I grab a chamomile tea bag, a cup. I unpackage the tea bag, float it into the mug of steaming water.

From the higher cabinet, the one she can't reach, I bring out a small, unmarked tin, pry the lid open.

It's filled with sparkling white powder. I contemplate how much, decide on one heaping teaspoon, which goes into the tea. I replace the canister, close the cabinet door.

One teaspoon of sugar, too.

I put the cup onto the table before her without saying a word.

After a moment, she raises her head, looks at me.

The eyes that peer through the fur are red-rimmed, puffy.

She says nothing.

I assume she knows.

Just as I do.

She takes a deep, quivering breath, pulls the cup to her.

Lowering her head again, I can hear the sounds of her drinking it slowly, lapping it with her tongue.

The house fills the silence with all sorts of creaks and groans and ticks.

I go to the living room and sit in a recliner.

And wait.

* * *

A sound roused me.

I must have dozed off. It was a long night, and I hadn't slept much.

I looked into the kitchen, and she was slumped on the kitchen table.

She was still breathing, I could tell, slow and shallow.

I stood, went to her, carried her small, limp body upstairs, to the bedroom.

It was night again, covering and protective. Outside the windows it was still, peaceful. I had no idea what time it was, how long I'd slept, but there were no cars moving, no sirens in the distance, no dogs barking.

I placed her on the bed, arranged her limbs so they were straight, comfortable.

It was time for the goddamn costume to come off.

It was time for things to be real again.

I slipped the knife in gently, so gently. Gentler than sex, gentler than love.

I thought I moved the knife between her and the costume, but there seemed to be no space separating the two.

Blood is the fluid of the unreal, and it bubbled up through the fur, spilled over the bedsheets.

I tried to staunch it with my hand, but it gurgled through my fingers, coated my skin.

Now it was my turn to weep.

Is anything—anyone—real anymore?

Or is it only me?

Am I alone?

As I stood there over her in the dark of our bedroom, I looked down.

One hand was slicked with her blood, black in the blackened room.

The other hand, too, is bloody, though not nearly as much.

A closer look reveals a cut, a slice along the plump part of my palm, down across the heel of that hand.

The cut is thin, but blood oozes sluggishly from it, twists and turns down my wrist as I hold that hand up to contemplate it.

Blood.

My blood.

The tears come stronger now, blinding.

How can this be?

* * *

So I stand here in the moonlight, singing.
Something about running, something about what she's done to my heart.
Time for me to remove my costume, see what is beneath.
Am I real or not?
The bunny suit lies limp on the bed in a pool of midnight, as if drained of everything that kept it inflated.
The knife slips in like a whisper, and there isn't even a hitch in my song.
And there is blood, so much of it.
Surprised, I look around the room.
There, there is the ninja costume, where I'd tossed it the other night.
I am wearing no costume.
Rain patters to the floor beneath my feet, and I am.

THE DEPRAVITY
OF INANIMATE THINGS

THE MOVIES.

That's where they started, you know?

The voices.

I watch a shitload of movies. Pretty much every movie that's released. From the box office smashes to the stuff that's so bad you can tell the actors are wondering how they managed to land in such a piece of shit. All of 'em: cartoons, weepies, chick flicks, period dramas, sci-fi, horror.

And I watch them all, from opening to end credits.

Nick, that's my name.

Everyone knows it.

Every *thing* knows it.

I work for a living, naturally. You could say I distribute movies. Yeah, that's good. *Movie distributor.* I make sure that some of the less fortunate among us get to see shit like *Iron Man II* and Harry Potter, either in a theater or in the comfort of their own homes.

Being a movie distributor lets me dress like I want and live like I want. So what if I'm not wearing fuckin' Armani suits and driving a Ferrari? I still have money for a house, a sweet whip—one of those new Chevy Camaros, black, tinted windows, leather seats, deluxe audio package, nav system—nice clothes, kicks, a little bling. And, yeah, plenty of money for the ladies.

No, dickhead, not *those* kind of ladies. Nice ones. Well, nice looking anyways. Got enough money to get them presents every once in a while, take them to dinner, to the movies.

Yeah, the movies.

Anyway, it was one of those superhero movies. I can't remember which one, they all look the same to me. Some fruity guy in a cape flouncing around or some punk-ass kid in spandex pajamas CGIing all over the screen. Whatever. Not my cup of tea, you know? I like horror movies, axes and blood and shit. Yeah, give me a good splatter movie where a guy gets his shit chopped off and fed into an industrial meat grinder any day over a fucking superhero movie.

I was getting ten clicks for this one, after just racking up fifteen clicks for that last Harry Potter flick. It was shaping up to be a good summer for me.

There I was, in my seat, planted, ready to sit perfectly still for two hours.

Don't understand, do ya? Well, let me instruct you in the ways of movie distribution.

You see, our friends in Asia account for more than half of the population of the planet, probably more like three-quarters or something. But they also account for only about two percent of its wealth. Yeah, I'm making this shit up. What do I look like, Google?

But these people want the same stuff we all do—the Chevy in the driveway, the nice house, the high-def TV, the G.I. Joe with the kung-fu grip. They want to see *The Hangover Part II* and *Twilight* just like everybody here in the good old US of A. Trouble is, they don't have money like we do.

So, my employers pay me to go into a theater, a nice one here on the East Coast where most of the operators aren't on the lookout for guys like me. I buy the overpriced, watered-down sodas and the stale popcorn in the giant tubs.

I take a seat, adjust the ball cap I'm wearing. Under the hat is a small, high-def camera with a very sophisticated mini microphone and an even more sophisticated wireless device. I tether this to my *very* smartphone, for which I have a pricey, unlimited data plan. I check the phone's touchscreen to make sure the movie screen is centered and nicely framed and in focus. I make sure the microphone is picking up.

Then I sit perfectly still, perfectly quiet, and watch a movie for two hours. I don't eat, I don't drink, I don't fucking move or blow my nose.

As I watch, it streams over Wi-Fi in real time to some servers in Chicago, and from there it goes, well, who the hell knows? It goes to a lot of places I ain't never been and ain't never gonna go, depending on who's paying me.

When they get the feed, it's downloaded, cleaned up and burned to DVDs. In a couple of days, literally, what I just watched in an air-conditioned theater in a cushy suburb of Boston winds up on the streets of Islamabad and Manila and Macau, in Phnom Penh, in Hyderabad, in fucking Moscow.

Huh?

Yeah, I think I'm doing the world a service. Fuck those guys in Hollywood with their fucking Interpol warnings and shit. They've got enough money as it is. And they couldn't care less about my customers.

Yeah, I provide a service that helps people. So what if I make a few bucks doing it? Who am I hurting? Arnold Schwarzenegger? George Clooney? Steven Fucking Spielberg?

Okay, so there I was, sitting in that fruity superhero movie, not paying much attention, when the worst thing for someone like me happens.

Kids.

I try to avoid 'em, choose midweek matinees and shit when I know they'll be in school. But there they were, right in the row in front of me.

They start whining about something or other. Probably had to take a piss, what do I care? Except they were cluttering my audio, and I'd have to stay and watch the fucking movie again.

Again, with the capes and shit.

So I, trying not to be too loud, to move too much, shushed them.

That got me a dirty look from the mother or the babysitter or whoever she was.

Worse, though, she turned around to deliver it, turned around and rose in her seat, her head in frame, completely ruining the shot.

And that's when it happened.

Hit her with me. I'm hard. If you turned me on edge, I think I could knock her out, maybe even draw blood. And if you hit her with me a couple of times, well…

Clear as day, like it was coming from someone sitting in the seat next to me.

My phone's screen, lying on my thigh, was on, lit.

Confused, I lifted it to my ear.

"Hello?" I whispered, but there was no one there.

The bitch in front of me took this opportunity to sharply remind me that cell phones were a no-no in the theater.

"I know that," I said, rising in my seat and digging my hands into my pockets for the car keys.

You could stab me through her eye, deep, deep into her brain.

You could kill her with me.

I heard this voice as clearly as I hear yours now.

I stared down at the keys in my hand.

"What did you say?" I asked, looking at the keys.

"Sit down!" someone hissed from behind me.

So, yeah, I left. Fucking left. I knew I'd have to come back again, but not this time. This shot was ruined, and I was freaking out.

When I went outside, I took my hat off, turned off the camera, the mic, the Wi-Fi. I tossed it onto the passenger seat of the car. My eyes were still dark-blind from the theater. I stood there rubbing them, the car door open, black heat rolling out in waves.

Then some fucker honked at me, wanting to get into the space next to mine.

My car talked to me.

Hop in, it said. *Hop in, back out, and we'll run him down while he's walking through the parking lot.*

If that weren't enough, I heard four little voices after that, all talking together.

Yeah, yeah, let's run him down, grind him into the asphalt. Let our treads drink his blood.

I stood there for a few more minutes, like a fucking retard, until the guy just pulled in around me. He got out, slammed his door, flipped me the bird, walked away.

That shook me, and I got into the car quickly, fired it up and pulled out.

Because, just for a moment, I thought about listening to those voices.

* * *

So, I went home, to crash and drink. I figured maybe a few beers would calm me down. I had a couple tallboys, followed by an entire bottle of Cristal I had in the fridge from the other night.

Anyways, there I was, lounging on the couch, getting my drink on, scratching my dog Max's head, when I get a call from my current girl-friend.

I'm talking to her, and she's pissed about something or another. They're always pissed about something, aren't they? It's like God didn't hang the sun right from the beginning, as far as they're concerned. Right?

So there I was, pretending to listen, and then she notices. Because they notice sometimes if you slip up and really aren't listening. If the "yeahs" and the "okays" and the "uh-huhs" you're throwing out don't exactly line up with what they're saying, they get all pissy.

She knew I wasn't listening and called me out.

Before I could answer, though, I heard the voice.

Nick, it says. And now it knows my fucking name, is using my name like we're best friends or some shit.

Nick, it says, and I know it's the champagne bottle, don't ask me how. I just know.

Nick, it says, *why don't we just go round and you can bash me upside her head, break me against her stupid skull. Once she's unconscious, use one of my sharp edges to slit her throat.*

I gotta tell ya, my blood iced up. I dropped the bottle, and was a little surprised that it didn't make a noise when it hit the floor.

That it didn't say anything. Anything *else*.

"Nicky!" she shrieked in my ear, rattling the little speaker in the cell phone. "You're not fucking listening to me now, are you?"

"What did you say?"

But I wasn't talking to her, get it?

I was talking to *it*.

The motherfucking champagne bottle on the floor, empty.

I shut the phone off, more to stop her chirping in my ear than any-thing else, tossed it onto the coffee table.

It rang and rang and rang, but I didn't pay any attention.

I gotta tell ya, I stared at that champagne bottle for a long, long time before I fell asleep on the couch.

When I woke I felt like I'd been skull-fucked, probably from the Cristal. Max was curled up on the opposite end of the couch, on top of my feet.

I sat there with my head in my hands and the phone rang, making me jump like I'd been goosed, sending a jolt through my head.

I fumbled around the coffee table for it, answered it.

Yeah, it was her again. I held the phone away from my head as she yelled at me. I caught words, mostly names she was calling me. Max even sat up and stared at the phone.

I tried to put the phone back to my ear, but she was shouting now, and crying I think. Yeah, I think so. Makes me feel miserable now, but then it made me mad. I mean, Christ, I didn't do anything, leastways not to her.

Leastways not then.

But as she went on yapping, I heard other voices over hers, nearer, all around me.

I looked at the glass bong I kept on the shelf next to the plasma TV. Yeah, a bong. So, arrest me. Hah!

Break me against the wall and slice me across her stomach and watch her guts spill onto the floor, Nick.

I looked at one of the throw pillows on the couch.

Put me over her face, Nick, and hold down hard, until she stops kicking, until she stops breathing.

At the books on the shelf, mostly King and Koontz and Straub.

Hit her head with my spine, Nick. Hit her head hard, over and over, until her brains spatter everywhere.

At the rug under the coffee table.

Nick, use me to roll up her dead body and take it to the dump.

At the empty beer bottles, the wine opener, the lamp, the fan, the fucking TV.

All talking.

Use me.

Cut her. Hit her. Hurt her.

Kill her.

I couldn't take it. I jumped up and yelled, "Stop it! Shut the fuck up!"

Scared the shit of out Max. That was about it.

The voices faded but didn't stop.

I saw my car keys on the table, the same keys that had wanted me to kill that woman in the theater just the day before. I grabbed them, clenched them tight in my fist like that could stop them from talking.

I took the car back to the theater, found the movie that those fucking kids had ruined yesterday. It started in twenty minutes, so I grabbed my hat rig and hot-shoed it inside, bought my ticket, my bushel of popcorn, my gallon of Coke, took my seat.

Then I realized that I didn't bring my phone. Without the phone, all the high-tech stuff was worthless. I couldn't check the framing, couldn't connect the Wi-Fi, couldn't download the movie.

Fuck yeah I was pissed. But, I thought, what the hell, ya know? Maybe sitting here alone, in the dark, watching this stupid movie would take my mind off things, quiet the voices.

It didn't.

About a third of the way into the movie, the big guy who plays the hero in the fruity cape, you know, the blond guy, what's his name? Anyway, he's macking on the lead actress chick, getting ready to super-score or something, and suddenly he's talking.

Nick, buddy, listen, the best thing you can do right now to get some relief is head over to her house and smack her around a little. Or a lot, if you know what I mean.

"Huh?" I asked, and a few kernels of popcorn fell out of my mouth.

Ever strangle someone with a phone cord?

"A phone cord?"

Oh yeah, cordless phones. Well, how about a bath towel? A big one, rolled up, then looped around her neck. Pull it tight from behind her and bingo!

"A bath towel?"

Someone in front of me turned around, shushed me loudly, but the two on the screen were still talking.

Bath towels and phone cords? said the female lead, the one with the dark brown hair and the big, dopey eyes. *Ugh. Leave it to a guy to screw that up. Just be direct. Push her out of a window. Or toss a toaster in the bathtub.*

Well, that's fucking stupid, he said. *Ever heard of ground-fault interrupters? That won't work.*

Your ideas are any better? Bath towels? I mean, Christ, what's he gonna do, dry her to death?

You know, you're a bitch, and the entire crew knows you're screwing the producer.

Yeah, well, your breath is awful. And I read in the rags that you're gay.

Suddenly, I was on my feet. The giant soda sloshed to the floor, spilling down the slanted concrete. The popcorn flew in the air.

The guy in front of me, a lover of superhero films if there ever was one—you know the type, middle-aged, fat, pasty faced—turned and shushed me again.

I ignored him, lurched out of the row and stumbled down the darkened aisle to the exit.

As I left, I could hear the two stars still advising me.

That asshole who's shushing you? Just a short, sharp jab upwards with the heel of your palm against the bridge of his nose. Drive the shards of his nose into his brain.

* * *

I went home and drank about a six-pack. Thankfully they didn't talk to me, so I went to bed. The voices didn't start in until right as I was drifting to sleep, so I didn't pay any attention to them. Just jammed my head under the pillows and let the beer carry me off to sleep.

About three in the morning I woke up about to piss my diddies. Forgetting everything else, I danced over to the bathroom and drained the lizard right before it ended up going down my leg.

As I stood there in the bathroom, though, they came back.

Jam me into her mouth and just keep pushing until you hear bone, said the toothbrush.

What am I here for, anyway? Slit her throat, said my razor.

Hold her down and force her to eat every fucking pill. Don't induce vomiting and don't call poison control, said the open, super-size bottle of ibuprofen.

Roll me into a ribbon and strangle her with…, began the towel hanging near the shower, as if it had been to the same fucking movie I saw earlier.

"SHUT! THE! FUCK! UP!" I screamed, and it was loud enough that I actually hurt my throat.

From there it was about a solid week of mostly sleeping, taking stuff I had around the house—Darvocet, Percocet, OxyContin, anything—anything I had to take the edge off, to numb me, to let me sleep in silence.

Because every time I got out of bed, to take a leak or a shit, to eat something, to scratch my nuts, I heard them. All of them. It was like every fucking thing in the house had suddenly found its voice and wanted to talk to me nonstop.

I couldn't figure out why, still don't know.

And I don't know why they were all so fucking *angry*, so filled with hate.

So filled with murder.

I'd get the mail, and the umbrella stand near the door wanted me to run out with an umbrella and *shish kabob* the mailman.

I'd get a phone call, and fifteen things within earshot were all offering themselves as a way to off the poor bastard who called.

I'd spot a neighbor when I looked out the window to see what time of day or night it was, and the curtains wanted me to strangle him with them. Or the window wanted me to shatter it and slice the guy up. Or the cord to the blinds wanted me to…

Get the idea?

By about day three of this, I was pretty loopy.

By day seven, I was fucking crazy.

She came over on day ten.

* * *

Yeah, Stacey. The girlfriend of the moment.

Yeah, the one on the phone.

I was still asleep, nice and peaceful, when I heard Max suddenly go apeshit.

Someone was at the door, knocking.

Why did I ever give her a key?

That key, that motherfucking key ruined everything.

And it never had to say a word.

Max came bounding into the room just ahead of her, circling and yipping, tail going a mile a minute.

He was excited.

She, definitely, was not.

"Nick!" she yelled at the top of her lungs at the foot of my bed. "What the hell's going on? I've been calling and calling and you don't answer. You don't listen to your messages? You don't return calls?"

I was awake by then—who wouldn't be with that going off right in your bedroom—but I lay there with my head under the pillow.

Lay there *waiting*.

She smacked the pillow covering my head hard, and I heard her bracelets jangle, her nails claw the pillowcase.

"Nick! Nick? You awake or dead?"

You know how a southern accent, like from Georgia or Alabama, sounds so hot on a girl, so smooth and silky? Yeah, well, let me tell you that a South Boston accent is just the opposite. It's like fingernails on a chalkboard. Especially when they're pissed.

I took my head from under the pillow.

"Hey, Stacey."

"Don't you 'Hey, Stacey' me, motherfucker," she said. Sweet, ain't she?

I opened my mouth to reply, but they started.

All of them.

Everything in the entire house, all at once.

Cut her, Nick.

Bash her, Nick.

Smotherherstabherdrownherslashherpushherhither.

I couldn't stand it anymore, you know? It was too much, too much.

I was tired, freaked, strung out.

Afraid.

So, I jumped out of bed and grabbed her.

To shut them up, you know? Just to shut them up.

She was too surprised to do anything.

I wrapped my blankets around her like a cocoon, knocked her to the ground.

I could hear her screams, muffled, distant, drowned by the other voices.

I grabbed the clock radio, I think, and bashed the covered lump of her head until its plastic casing cracked. Tossing it aside, I saw my golf driver leaning next to the closet door.

A few tee-offs with that, and I dropped it, bent and useless.

The voices were louder now, insistent, gleeful, manic.

A book, a lamp, a knife from the kitchen, a baseball bat, an electrical cord.

I was sweating, panting when it was over.

Max was sitting in the corner of the room, watching it all with his dark, dog eyes, confused, wary.

The voices were dull now, as tired as I felt.

But still there, like whispers from the row behind you in a dark theater.

The lump—*her* lump—lay on the floor before me, still wrapped like a mummy in my sheets, in my comforter. There were a lot of tears in the fabric. Jesus. Blood, blood soaking through it all.

She didn't move, no noises.

I remember swallowing, and it tasted like my tongue took a shit in my mouth.

I remember hearing a single voice above the others, and I tripped through the house looking for it.

It was my cigarette lighter.

It told me what to do.

And I did it.

To shut them up.

* * *

That's when it happened, the fucking thing that drove me over the edge, that pushed me right over.

Yeah, wise ass, I wasn't *already* over the edge.

As I stood there watching my house burn down in front of me, feeling the heat of all of the things inside it press against my face, I felt something rub against my naked ankle.

I looked, and there was my dog Max. Good old Max.

I reached down to absently scratch the top of his head, and as I did, he looked up at me.

About time, he said to me, tilting his head toward the burning house. He spoke as matter-of-factly as if we talked every day. *She was just like all the rest of that shit in there. They just couldn't shut the fuck up, none of them. It got so bad, I couldn't hear myself think.*

THE DEPRAVITY OF INANIMATE THINGS

Yeah, that's it. That's what did it.

Having a little chat there in the yard with my dog, with the house burning.

That's when I fainted.

I didn't want to hurt her. Do you get me? I didn't want to hurt *anyone*. But they wouldn't leave me alone, not for a minute.

They wouldn't shut up about it, not even after I did it, what they said.

Eventually even that didn't shut them up, so I burned the fucking house down.

I just hope to Christ that worked.

* * *

Can we take a stretch now? Can I get a Coke or something? I'm getting a little thirsty from all this talking.

I haven't talked all that much lately, if you know what I mean. Kind of like the silence.

Sure, I can sit here by myself for a minute, no problem.

No, you don't have to worry about me. Go ahead.

* * *

Jesus Jumped-Up Christ!
Finally, you're back.
Your goddamn pencil.
You left it here, on the table when you went out.
I guess you figured I was handcuffed, what could I do?
And you were right.
But you wouldn't believe the shit it said.

For my friend, T. J. Lewis.

A WINTER'S TALE

DAVID'S MOTHER CUFFED HIM as he walked out the front door. Nothing too hard or angry, nothing that left another mark or drew blood. Just something to remind him that she was still around and that she didn't particularly care for him.

It didn't hurt all that much, but David flinched anyway. He found it sometimes placated her, thinking he was more hurt or more afraid than he really was. Sometimes it made the hitting stop.

Sometimes.

"Make sure you keep an eye on 'em," she slurred, holding the beer bottle in one limp hand and a smoldering cigarette in the other.

He'd gotten them both for her yesterday, twelve bottles of beer filled at the Tullamore Lounge on the corner. Then pulling his battered Radio Flyer, the bottles clinking together convivially, across the road to the general store to pick up two packs of cigarettes. One for his mother, another to sit on the scuffed Formica kitchen table with a book of matches and a plate of food covered in foil for his dad when he got off work.

His dad whom he never saw, seldom even heard these days. Sometimes, late at night in the small bed he shared with his brother and sister slumbering on either side of him, he might hear his dad come in from wherever it was he worked, clatter and clomp around the kitchen. He might hear the bone rattle of his knife and fork against the china plate, the hiss of one of those beer bottles being opened, the rustle of the cellophane around the pack of cigarettes, the huff and exhalation of his father's smoky breath.

David might see shadows underneath his door, oozing through the jaundiced light from the kitchen. He might hear his mother's voice, as thin and papery as his father's cigarette breath. Her voice always seemed low, tense, as if urging him from some course of action.

Sometimes, just as sleep curled at the edges of his consciousness, he might hear his dad's voice, softer than his mother's, liquid and almost... *bubbly?* Or maybe it just seemed that way. Maybe his sleep-filled brain, exhausted from the day's chores his mother imposed on them—but mainly him, being the oldest—warped the words and even the rhythm of his father's voice before simply smothering everything in darkness.

Sometimes, he swore his father opened the bedroom door, slid softly into the children's cold bedroom, came to the side of their bed. David had usually fallen too far into sleep when this happened to open his eyes fully, to say "Hello, Daddy" or register his father's presence in any way. Still, he could feel the man there in the nighttime room, hear his gentle breathing, smell the ashes on his breath, the sea-tang of his cologne.

Not often, but sometimes, feel a caress from him, soft, oh so soft, smooth and cool and sinuous on his forehead, ruffling his hair. The smacky sound of kisses bestowed on Maggie and Howie.

Then his father would recede, the door would close, and the kitchen light would snap off.

Sometimes he would hear his parent's low voices whispering in an almost musical way, their words strange, the cadences unnatural and tripping.

Sometimes he only heard the tinny voices on the radio in the sitting room, playing the swing music his mother loved or the radio shows his father liked to listen to—mostly comedies like Eddie Cantor and Ed Wynn.

Sometimes his father's laughter would ooze through the house, soft, squishy, like mud swirling through water.

These ghostlike manifestations of his father were some of David's best memories, and so he never begrudged it when his mother sent him to the tavern, the general store, despite the sour looks he got from Mr. Beeker who drew the beer taps at Tullamore or Mrs. McGillicutty behind the counter at the A&P.

Their disapproval and silent reproach, even his mother's disdain and coldness, were somehow made manageable by these rare, brief night visits from his father.

Now, though, his mother stood framed in the warped doorway of their house, stood in her ratty bathrobe, her hair disheveled, her lean, pinched face looking expectant yet somehow distressed. She took a pull off the beer bottle, a pull off the cigarette.

David dimly thought it was early in the morning for beer, but it never seemed too early or too late for beer, at least for his mother. He honestly couldn't remember her drinking anything else, not even a glass of water or a tumbler of milk on those rare occasions when she had the money—or even the thought—to buy some.

"Can we get a pop?" he asked her, standing on the stoop and looking at her almost evenly. He'd grown over the last year, shot up as the neighbors said, despite the haphazard care he'd received, the haphazard nutrition.

Ms. Novacek had told him he looked as thin as an alley cat after he'd mowed her grass for a nickel earlier that summer. She'd felt so badly that she'd taken him in and fed him, nothing special, just a bologna sandwich with bright yellow mustard and a glass of sweet tea. She offered him a thick slice of lemon cake, too, but he begged off eating it right there at her table. Instead, she wrapped it in a square of wax paper for him to take home. He was careful to hide it from his mom, even as he handed over the nickel he'd earned.

He brought it out from the dresser drawer that night when Maggie and Howie and he were in bed. They shared it, cooing and ahhing so excitedly that their mother came to the bedroom door and snapped at them to shut up.

David held a finger to his lips, only realizing afterward that the room was too dark for them to see this gesture. Still, they fell silent. When their mother's footsteps receded into the house, they gobbled down the rest of the cake quietly, licking their lips and fingers until they fell asleep.

He couldn't see them in the dark, but he liked to think they did so with smiles on their faces.

"A pop?" his mother snapped in surprise. "It's freezing cold out. Why would you want a pop on a day like today?"

David shrugged, but it was hardly noticeable through his thick winter coat. It was too big and threadbare, donated by the ladies of the church. He couldn't understand why they gave clothes to his family—his mother had never taken them to a church of any kind—but he was glad to have them. His mother had sent them out on many a winter's day with simply the clothes on their backs. David had spent many cold afternoons hunting for newspapers to stuff into their pants and shirts to keep as much of the icy wind from their skin as possible.

"Just a pop while we're out," he persisted. "We're hungry."

"Oh, hungry are you?" she asked, wrinkling her face in disgust. "You three are nothing but a burden on your father and me. Like weights, dragging us down. We're in a depression or haven't you heard? And what do you think? I'm made of money? That I've got all sorts of money to throw around for you three? Is that it?"

"No," David said. It was pointless to argue with her, so he turned and descended the steps to the street where Maggie and Howie waited.

"Oh, all right," their mother sighed, then muttered, as if to herself. "It's the last time, I suppose."

When David turned his mother held out a single nickel, as dingy and battered as she looked.

David smiled at that, and for an instant—a brief, almost unrecognizable moment—a smile played on his mother's lips, too. Fleeting, leaving no trace of its presence after it faded.

"Can we go to the pond?"

Suddenly, she looked alarmed. "No! I've told you about that before. Stay away from the pond."

"But we wanted to play on the ice."

"You can go to the river. The ice'll be thicker there, safer. And don't come back until supper," she said as he plucked the coin from her fingers. "Don't stray."

"We won't, Mother," he said.

"Just keep together, okay?" she said, taking another shaking puff from her cigarette. "Be together at the…"

David looked at his mother in confusion. She seemed not herself this cold January morning, fretful and somehow sad. *Sad?* He'd never seen her sad. Angry, yes. Annoyed, plenty. But sad? No. And about what?

He opened his mouth to say something, but his mother faded back into the darkness of their home, closed the door behind her.

The mouthful of frigid air he'd inhaled to ask her if she was all right floated from his lips, clawed its way back into the grey, closed sky.

He turned to his brother and sister, took their hands in each of his, and went down the street, feeling the cold disc of the nickel in his pocket against his thigh

* * *

They did stop by the A&P and picked up a bottle of Coke from the fancy new dispensing machine Mr. McGillicutty had installed that summer. His wife wasn't in the store just then, and Mr. McGillicutty was a more sympathetic presence. Though he was baffled at the children's desire to have a cold soda on such a chilly day, he showed them how to use the contraption, how to open the soda on the conveniently built-in bottle opener. He even threw in a paper straw for them to use when it became apparent they were going to buy only one bottle.

He kept up a line of chatter with the kids, the only people in the store, asking them about their mother, their schooling. She was fine, they'd never attended school, but what David thought was most strange was the fact that Mr. McGillicutty never asked about their father. Not once.

He asked them if the one soda would be all for today, and David nodded solemnly. The shopkeeper asked them if they might want a lollipop or sugar stick or maybe even a fine apple. David politely told the man that he had only the one nickel, that was all.

David watched the man study them. He knew he was measuring them, their scrawny, wind-chapped faces, their worn clothes. David knew he should, in some way, be embarrassed by this, but he wasn't. It was simply the way things were, and David had grown accustomed to it over the years. He was glad, though, that his brother and sister were both too young to understand.

The shopkeeper considered this, came to a decision. He nodded toward the barrel sitting out on the floor near the shelf lined with candy jars. "Why don't you and your brother and sister each pick an apple from the barrel, on the house. They're not going to last long anyway. You'd be doing me a favor taking them off my hands."

He looked around the shop warily, and David knew he was making sure his wife wasn't within earshot.

"Quick now," he said, shooing them off good-naturedly. "Before I change my mind!"

David thanked the man, and the three kids scampered across the wooden floorboards to the barrel. He slapped their hands away from pawing over the apples piled inside and selected three nice, shiny apples, passing one first to Maggie, then another to Howie. His little brother took his and immediately took a huge chomp from it, then turned to Mr. McGillicutty and said between chewed apple and missing teeth, "Thanks, sir!"

Mr. McGillicutty patted the air between them, urging them to be quiet.

When David fished the nickel from his pocket, pushed it across the worn wooden counter where the fine, ornate cash register sat, the shop owner seemed to hesitate. He almost looked as if he didn't want to accept their money, but he finally did, covering the coin with his wrinkled hand, scooping it up and dropping it into the cash register's open drawer.

"You children keep warm, you here? And stay out of the woods," he warned. "Stay away from that pond. Too many children lost out there, falling through the ice or just plain disappearing. You want my opinion, you three should just turn around and go home. Too cold for the likes of you to be out in this weather anyway."

The three kids looked at Mr. McGillicutty with wide, somber eyes, said nothing in return. The old man clucked his tongue, shook his head, then drifted off to restock a shelf or dust a display.

David pushed the apple into his coat pocket, then helped the little ones with their gloves. Howie complained it was hard to hold the apple with his mittens on, but David told him he'd have to figure out a way to make it work. And he did. Maggie didn't complain at all, and hadn't taken a bite of her apple yet.

"Aren't you hungry, Mags?" he asked.

She looked up at David. "I think I'm so hungry that I'm not hungry right now," she said in a very serious tone.

"Fine. Want me to put your apple in my pocket, hold it for you?"

"Yes. You promise you won't eat it. Right, Davey?" she asked. His brother and sister were the only two allowed to call him by that name. He would have let his mother, too, though she never seemed interested in addressing him even by his real name, much less a diminutive. And his father was never around to speak his name at all.

"I promise."

"Okay."

"My coat is really heavy, Davey," Mags told him.

"I know. It's supposed to be, to keep out the cold, Mags. You'll be happy for it later."

He pulled out his own gloves, slid her apple into his other pocket.

Once they were on, the three kids held hands, and David led them back out into the cold, the store's bell jingling clear and crystalline on the air as they left.

* * *

When they went back outside, it was very cold, but the sky had cleared. It was the kind of January day where the unclouded sky was the deep blue of glaciers. The sun dazzled in the air, but offered little warmth. Smoke from the brick row houses all up and down their street billowed into the air like the children's breath, dissipated quickly.

David kept hold of Maggie and Howie's hands as they walked. Maggie was quiet, content to simply go wherever it was David took them. Howie, though, jabbered incessantly between bites of apple.

"I'm cold," he told David for the dozenth time. "Where are we goin', Davey?"

"I told you, Howie," he replied. "I dunno. How about the park near the river?"

"Oh," Howie said. Then, after a minute, "How about the pond? Can we go to the pond instead?"

"Mother said not to. She said to go to the river instead. Besides, lots of kids go missing near the pond. Didn't you hear Mr. McGillicutty?"

"But the river is so much farther. I don't feel like going that far," Howie protested.

As David made to answer, he felt Maggie's small hand squeeze his.

So, instead, he turned to her. "What?"

"She told me I could go out onto the ice."

David frowned in confusion. "Who told you that, Mags?"

"Mother."

David frowned, and the way his face stretched made his cheeks sting. It seemed like a strange thing for their mother to say to any of them, much less Maggie. David knew that the other kids' parents generally told them to keep away from both the pond and the river, and to especially stay off the ice.

"She said I could lie down right in the middle of the ice an' make a snow angel."

"You want to go to the pond, then, Maggie?"

His little sister nodded enthusiastically.

Their mother never checked on them, never seemed to care where they went, except where the pond was concerned. But how would she ever know where they'd been anyway?

It was cold, and the park was a lot farther away.

"Okay," he shrugged, having nowhere else in mind to go. Besides, they had all afternoon. They could always go to the park later.

"Let's go to the pond."

* * *

The pond was nestled in a span of trees at the edge of the neighborhood. Their small town had not yet expanded in this direction, and these woods were ancient, pristine, stretched all the way to the distant river that twisted lazily through this section of the country.

A declivity in the land sloped gently down from the city into the forest, providing a gradual entrance into its dark, sheltered domain; dramatic, almost operatic in its effect

Normally, the trees and brush created a natural screen that rose up like a green wave within a dark sea, frozen in places by forces that seemed atavistic. Stepping down into this forest was like stepping into another world, a more primitive one, where even the air felt ancient and weighted with knowledge.

Though the woods were teeming with dangers—poisonous creatures, deadly plants, and even adults with questionable motives—their mother never made it off limits to them. Nothing, no place was off limits to them, ever. Their mother never seemed concerned about their comfort or even their safety when she kicked them out of the house on these day-long expulsions. Normally, they would have chores to keep them busy, but on the days she didn't assign them tasks, she gave them no boundaries, set no limits.

The only rule was don't come home early.

David had only made that mistake once, before either Howie or Maggie was born. He'd been about five years old, and his mother had shown him the door on a cool spring day. David remembered standing on the same stoop, his mother drinking and smoking as usual. But she'd seemed so much younger then, so fresh and even beautiful. Still angry, yes, but it only made her beauty more terrifying to him.

As always, she'd taken his arm, squeezed it roughly and told him not to come back until it was dark outside. David remembered the kids playing out on the street, the sound of the organ grinder somewhere in the neighborhood, peddling his fruits and vegetables out of a rickety cart pulled by an ancient donkey.

He marveled at the immense freedom he was given, the unbelievable ability to go and play wherever, with whomever, for however long he wanted. His young mind boggled with the possibilities, and it seemed he'd have no problem at all filling the time. But this was early in the day, and he was little.

By midday he was exhausted and hungry. And though he knew there was little to eat at home, his bed was there, and he longed to be in it, taking a nap. So, waving goodbye to the neighborhood kids whom he'd played stickball with, he set off for home, just a few blocks away.

When he arrived he climbed the front steps, put his hand on the doorknob and turned it.

The door opened a crack and pale, violet light spilled out, fell in a thin, venous wedge onto the front stoop. Where it met the sunlight already there, the strange glow sizzled and roiled, especially at its edges.

As David looked on with curious wonder, he heard his mother shriek. Not just a scream, she shrieked, a combination of pain and surprise and rage.

David jerked his head up to look inside the house.

"Get out! Shut the goddamn door and get out of here!"

She lurched toward him, her form partially obscured in swirling mist the same lavender color shot through with a nauseous green. Her arms were outstretched, dripping steaming ichor from her elbows. Her fingertips twitched and clawed at the air as she approached.

But her eyes, oh her eyes were the worst. They glowed in the afternoon murk of the house, glowed a strange nacreous emerald that seemed to emanate from far, far deeper than the insides of her head. They were flat and unrecognizing, taking in nothing but the opening of the door, the transgression of her command not to return home until dark.

David gasped, his hand still on the doorknob.

As his mother came near, he saw she was naked, completely without clothes. He'd never seen her naked, and the sight was just as shocking to him as everything else.

More, though, a snake-like form slithered around her, across her breasts, between her legs. It was connected to a form that loomed in the striated, glowing mists behind her.

Her mouth opened and she released another shriek on a burst of mottled grey-green froth that spattered his face, his clothes.

"Go!"

David's hand twitched on the doorknob, and he pulled it closed, hard, held it there as he felt her body collide with it, her weight shuddering up his arm.

Her fingernails scrabbled against the wood, then he heard her footsteps finally lurch back into the house.

He took a deep breath, stepped away, letting loose of the doorknob.

There was no more sound, no more mist, no more violet light. Just the cool spring day, the calm blue sky and the radiant sun overhead.

David backed down the steps, his eyes locked on the door, afraid she would yank it open and come hurtling down the steps, stark naked, green venom spilling from her lips, screeching his name.

But she didn't.

As he stood there, he smelled a rank odor, like stagnant water or rotting plants.

He looked down and saw mucousy ropes covering the front of his shirt, ribbons of grey-green slime with small, dark spheres inside.

Scraping the stuff off, he fled his yard, walked for a long, long time, only returning home when it was good and dark.

His mother, for her part, never acknowledged seeing him or that anything had happened.

Sometime after, his brother Howie was born.

* * *

"Should we go out onto the ice, Davey?" Howie asked as they passed through the copse of trees at the top of the shallow incline leading to the pond. It was irregularly shaped, probably no more than two acres in size, cupped within a hollow in the woods to the south of their neighborhood.

The weeds and rushes and vibrant green growth that normally ringed it were gone, replaced by the relentless browns and greys of winter. Dead trees with the grey lightning of their branches, stalks of cattails jabbing up from the dank, frozen mud along the banks, clumps of papery, dead weeds and grasses like corpse hair framing a blank and lifeless face.

The pond itself was sealed tight, capped with a thick layer of dense, opaque ice that reflected the bright blue sky as a dull, almost steel grey lens. A cataract atop a frozen, pallid eye.

The three children stood at the top of the rise, hand in hand, the steam from their breath clotting in the air above them.

"I dunno," David said, considering the question. "It might not be safe."

"It's pretty cold," Howie said. "It should be thick enough."

"Okay, but if it starts to crack, even a little bit, we get off. So if I say to get off, you have to listen. Right?"

They both nodded at him and, still holding hands, they descended onto the ice.

* * *

"Why aren't Mom and Dad ever together?" Howie asked as Maggie twirled in tight circles on the ice, hands held out. She sang little nonsense notes into the cold air—*La-ma-na-oh-ki-no-ba-da-dee*—eyes closed, breath corkscrewing into the sky.

"Whaddaya mean?" David asked, absently plunking stones into a slushy pool of brackish water that formed a hole in the ice near the shore on which the boys stood watching their sister. A single filthy sock lay in the frozen muck—discarded, lost, child-size—and it made David uneasy, remembering all the neighborhood stories of the children who'd disappeared in these woods.

He tossed another rock and it struck the small sock, carried it down into the murk. He'd been doing this for a few minutes, waiting for the perfect *ker-ploosh!*

"I mean how come we never see both of 'em?" Howie asked, selecting rocks from his own stash held in one mittened hand and tossing them in after David's, trying for the same sound but producing just small splashes. "Donnie's parents are together all the time. And Roy's. And Mikey's…"

"Because our dad works hard," David answered, *ker-plooshing!* another rock into the smaller pond within the frozen one. "He has to work real hard, in order to feed us. Pay for stuff."

Howie turned to David, wrinkled his forehead. "But we never have any money, Davey. If he works so hard, how come we don't have anything?"

David balled his fist around his remaining rocks, hauled off and punched Howie in the shoulder. Not hard, but hard enough.

"Oww," he yelped in surprise, dropping his rocks into the water, where many of them made a satisfying, though ignored, *ker-ploosh!*

"Don't say that. We've got enough. We got a house and a bed and clothes. We got food."

"But we're always hungry."

"No we're not."

David was getting cross. He went back to launching rocks into the water.

"Yes we are. I am."

"Well I'm not."

Ker-ploosh!

Howie turned to him, cocked his head. "Yes you are. But mom isn't. She never is."

The rock David threw next missed the water, hit the ice, skittered across its surface toward where Maggie spun in slow, loopy circles.

"She's always got beer. And cigarettes." That last vice was said breathlessly, as if he couldn't quite believe he was uttering its name out loud.

It wasn't as if Davey hadn't thought of these things before. The ten cents he paid over to Mr. Beeker at the Tullamore almost every other day for a wagon-full of beer bottles. The money she gave David almost as regularly for her cigarettes. She always had money for those things, Depression or not.

But money for food—a sack of flour, some lard, buttermilk, potatoes, perhaps a hank of bacon or ham hocks if she felt indulgent? That was given sparingly, grudgingly, if at all.

Often Davey was told she had just a few boiled potatoes to spare for them, when he knew she'd sent him to get a whole chicken or some pork neck bones earlier in the day. He supposed they ended up on her plate… and their father's plate. But there were never any leftovers the next morning, not even bones. The only thing left was the tantalizing aromas of roasted meat, simmering beans or greasy bacon that hung in the early morning air of the kitchen. In all this, she offered them only a piece of toast with a thin smear of butter or a small bowl of oatmeal.

Was he hungry? Yes, all the time.

Despite all this, despite how supremely indifferent she was—even how downright mean she could be—she was their mother. David found it hard to work past that one roadblock, to get around it to feel legitimate anger for her.

David loved her.

Didn't he?

He shook his head to clear it.

"Shut up and eat your apple, Howie."

Howie turned a sour look back at him.

"I finished it before we got here."

* * *

When the last of the rocks had been thrown, David clambered down the bank to join Maggie. She lay prone on the ice, spread-eagle, scissoring her arms and legs against the thin veneer of snow, trying in vain to make a snow angel.

David lay beside her, as close as her flailing arms and legs would allow. Howie stood on shore, glaring at the two of them silently.

Maggie was still singing nonsense syllables, babbling in her light, high voice.

"What are you singing, Maggie?" David asked.

Her eyes were closed, but she opened one and looked at him with it.

"I dunno."

"Well, then why are you singing?"

"I dunno," she said. Then she stopped moving her arms and legs and lay as still as if she'd frozen to the ice itself. "Momma told me to."

She smiled at David, closed her eyes again.

David closed his, too, felt the hard, cold surface of the ice push up against his back, its coldness seep through the padding of his coat.

Maggie flipped herself over to lay on her belly. She cleared the dusting of snow from the surface directly beneath her face, breathed against it as if it were a piece of glass.

"Whatchya doin'?" Howie shouted from the shore.

"Seeing if I can see through the ice, down to the bottom," she said. "Maybe see some fishes."

David flipped over, cleared an area of ice in front of his face, fogged it with his breath, then cleared it with the sleeve of his coat. The ice was cloudy, streaked with air bubbles and mud.

"Can we go now? To the river?" Howie asked.

"I thought you wanted to come to the pond," David replied, staring down into the ice.

"Momma said we should go to the river," Maggie said, humming that tune again. "She said for me to go out on the ice there and sing my song."

"Please!" Howie whined, but David ignored him.

Why would she say that?

"What song, Maggie?"

"*Od j'zanth R'yleh tak. Cor soc d'pren N'yog-Sothep jek Carcosa…jek Carcosa…*" Maggie sang, her voice barely audible, lilting and atonal.

"Maggie?" David asked.

Somewhere behind them, near where Howie stood on the shore—where that hole in the ice was—David heard water sloshing, lapping. He felt a shift beneath him, as if the ice had undulated atop the water.

Staring through the cloudy lens of the ice, he saw something large and shadowy move in the frozen depths, twist serpentine and sensuous.

The ice bucked a terrific *CRACK!* like a gunshot echoed within the little hollow that cupped the pond. David pushed himself up on his elbows, looked down at the ice.

Cracks had erupted across the glassy surface, twisting like a skein of electricity, radiating from one central point.

Just underneath his sister.

David rolled toward her, hand extended, grasping at her own mittened hand.

The cracked ice fell in and gave way around them with a sound like shattering glass.

And water, so much water.

So cold it literally drove David's breath from his shocked lungs. His heart shuddered in his chest as the water enveloped him, then settled into a racing, quivering beat that shivered through his entire body, palsied his limbs.

His fingers fluttered against his sister's, then they were gone, floating away, sinking as he was into the impossibly frigid, impossibly dense water.

Above him, the light of the sun was little more than a wan, gray ceiling, shattered and broken, floating across his vision in pieces. Something large and dark blocked the light, and David heard muffled shouts and screams.

The jagged shards of that gray ceiling broke into even smaller pieces, and a shadow entered the water.

Howie.

David reached his heavy, trembling limbs out to catch his falling brother, but he was too deep now, farther away than he'd have thought possible. His arms were leaden, barely flexible, as if frozen by the water. He continued to fall deeper and deeper into the dark, face upward, back bowed down, limbs cupped. As he fell, the cold became warmth, the anoxia became euphoric, and the darkness became a million-billion pinpricks.

David felt the urge to gasp, to draw in a breath to feed his burning lungs.

But then something slid around him, encircled his teardrop-shaped body, slowed his descent, stopped it. It was something solid, a coiled cord of muscle that moved through the water easily, with purpose. It wound around him, curled him in a powerful embrace, drew him through the water. Not down now, but sideways.

He felt he was approaching something, a sizeable mass, a dark, misshapen accretion of shadows floating free in the icy waters. As the muscular coil drew him towards it, David opened his eyes. Even though the water burned them, even though the pond was dim and murky, what David saw took the remainder of his breath away.

There, as if floating within the depths of space, was a creature so unexpected, so at odds with reality, David might have gasped had not the water held his breath hostage. A thing of spirals and curlicues, a fluid twist of shadows and lumps of things even darker, a beast that seemed both sedentary and at motion, winding about itself, uncurling a vast number of limbs through the water. And all about it, emanating from within it, was a deep violet glow, as if it bruised reality.

Before David passed out, before the lack of oxygen squeezed his eyes closed, his heart and lungs motionless, his brain into a peaceful torpor, he saw something else, felt something else. An eye—a great, singular eye—as big as a dinner plate, its fathomless pupil ringed in gold turned to him, rolled to him, widening in a shock of its own: recognition.

A caress—soft, oh so soft—smooth and cool and sinuous on his forehead, ruffling his floating hair.

Then darkness.

* * *

When David awoke, he opened his eyes onto a dark blue expanse, mist rising up into it. He lay still for a while, too stunned to move. He felt blood coursing through him, warm and exhilarating. He felt cold air enter his lungs, expand his chest. He felt his heart beat, and he moved his arms, his legs.

Faces appeared against the blue, his brother and sister. They smiled down on him, jabbered excitedly as he tried to sort through where he was, what had happened.

Then another face, a face he didn't remember seeing before, but knew instantly. Older, weathered, bearded, with gold-ringed eyes.

"Father?" David croaked, propping himself up on his elbows, reveling in the fact that not only was he alive, but he was also dry and warm, despite still being outside on the cold ground.

His father held out a hand to him, and David took it, clasped it, let it draw him to his feet. He stood, a bit shakily, but he stood before his father, then fell into him, embraced him.

His father was tall, dressed in ordinary clothes—a long coat, work pants, a simple cap on his head. A dark beard jutted from his chin like the frozen spray of a waterfall. He felt solid, and yet as David squeezed him, he felt squishy and squirmy underneath that muscle.

"Children," he said, and his voice was soft and mellifluous, higher-pitched than David might have imagined, but calm and soothing to hear. "What are you doing here? Surely you've been told that the pond, these woods, are forbidden?"

"We were bored," Howie said, standing to the left of him.

"The river was so far away, Daddy," Maggie said, clinging to a fold of his coat, looking up at her father with a broad, loopy smile.

"What were you doing out on such a cold day?"

"Mother sent us out," David said.

"Out? But why?"

"She always does. Every day. We're not to come home until sunset."

"Every day? What are you to do? What are you to eat?"

The children went silent without so much as a shrug.

"You look thin, slovenly. Does she feed you? No, no. I see the truth of it in your faces. But why here? Why the pond?"

"She told me to go to the river today," Maggie lisped. "Told me I could go out on the ice and play. But it was so far, Daddy, and I was cold and tired. But Mr. McGillicutty gave us all—"

"The river?" he boomed, and his voice rang in the hollow of the pond. "She sent you to the river? To *him*?"

The children cowered at the sound of his voice, and for a moment their father seemed to fill the bowl that held the pond, seemed to expand into that same sinuous, shadowed shape that David remembered in the water.

"Let's go to her," he said, and the gold of his eyes flashed as he turned them to David.

"Take me to her now."

David took his father's smooth, powerful hand and was pulled by him up the banks sheltering the pond, through the woods and back into the neighborhood.

He felt a powerful surge of love for this man, so long absent, as they moved quickly through the streets, passed the houses of the city they'd lived in, mostly without him.

As they sped toward home, David looked up at his father, seemingly possessed of something strong and powerful.

He felt his father's grip on his hand, tight and secure.

And he swore, though it couldn't have been, that his father held the hands of each of his three children in his own as they walked.

* * *

They paused at the foot of the steps that led up to their door.

It was twilight, the sky blushing a beautiful pale rose tinged with burnt orange and a deep violet that David recognized from his time beneath the waters of the pond.

"Wait here," his father said, letting loose of Maggie's hand last, bending to receive a kiss from her. "Just a minute or so," he said to them, one foot atop the steps. "Then I will return and we will go to your new home where you will never be cold, never be alone, never awaken or go to sleep hungry."

He squeezed David's hand before he walked to the door, opened it without knocking, closed it without a look back.

The children huddled together on the street, listened as their parents voices rose into the night, watched as nacreous purple and green lights burst through the windows, flashing off and on, cycling faster and faster.

Just as the lights built to a crescendo, their mother's voice rose above, a wailing keen that cut through it all, up through the lights and then was gone.

Water burst through the windows, shattered the glass and founted onto the front stoop, spilled down the steps, freezing as it gushed. Water tore the front door off its hinges, flattened it, sent it down the steps and out into the street. More water gushed from the house, freezing in elaborate arches and silvered fountains.

On one such wave rode their father, as calm and cold as the night. It carried him onto the street and he turned, clasped his children in his dripping arms. David marveled that he had so many of them.

"All is well now," the man said, gathering them together in an embrace. "You will come and live with me!"

"But where is mother?" Howie asked.

"Where she won't trouble you anymore," he replied. "I should never have left you with her. Forgive me. I made the wrong sacrifices for you, I see. But no more."

And he drew them away by their hands, back through the neighborhood, back into the forest, back to the edge of the pond from which he'd come.

* * *

Underwater, David saw the void his father had come from, where he and his brother and sister would all live now.

There were castles within the violet light…and parapets.

THEIR HANDS

IT WAS JUST THEIR HANDS. In the end.

Their hands.

No matter what was said after, on the news, on the Internet, by the pundits and bloggers, psychics and psychologists, police. Always trying to make everything more complicated than it actually was.

It was simple.

He'd seen them at the campground, at the pool.

He'd seen them in their Old Navy bikinis and their dollar store flip-flops. With their jeweled cell phones and sparkling purses and tubes of lip gloss.

He'd seen them and then, almost, unseen them, as he'd unseen everyone else.

Almost.

They were trailer park thin, with angular, boyish hips, long boyish legs. They were country pale with high cheekbones and dark, sunken eyes with too much blue eye shadow. They were cousins, maybe sisters; too similar looking to be just friends. Maybe they were half-sisters; perhaps the same father, perhaps the same mother. Stuff like that happened out here beyond the suburbs.

He'd stretched on his perch at the pool, a spot he'd scoped early that morning. A clean towel—he always brought a clean towel; his momma had warned him against germs—lay over the lounge chair, soaking up his sweat.

The towel smelled like bleach, acrid in his nostrils.

His sweat smelled like coconut suntan lotion, and the sour dread of its anticipation.

Its demands.

When the girls came, he'd already dismissed everyone else. They were all talking too loud and pointing here and there and laughing. They throbbed in his head, like a hive of agitated bees. They made his head hurt, his eyes twitch. He dismissed them all immediately.

So he sat in the sun, smelling his sweat and the towel, his eyes shaded by sunglasses.

And waited.

Then the girls came in. They entered the pool area quietly, glided across the hot concrete in a tight, cool envelope of silence.

Except.

He sat up in his chair, the towel momentarily sticking to his slick, bare shoulders, then peeling away like a layer of discarded skin, drifting back to the lounge.

His breathing quickened, and he fumbled with his sunglasses. They were the big, dark aviator kind that made him look cool in the little mirror of his little bathroom in the little, ramshackle RV he lived in, rode in from nameless place to nameless place.

They were slippery in his oiled hands, and they dropped to the chair, clattered to the ground.

Their hands.

Silent as they were, their hands fluttered in the air before them like tethered birds, captured in their orbits. They soared and dipped, fingers circumscribing arcane shapes and symbols in the air.

He stared, not at them anymore, but at their darting hands, at the air in which they swooped. They left silver streaks like the contrails of jets against a blue, blue sky. These incandescent arcs and spirals floated before them, between them, and faded, faded slowly into silver spangles that shone in the air, shone in his brain like faery dust before disappearing.

For a moment, it subsided within him, the demands, hypnotized into its own silence by their hands and the occult letters they spelled out onto the very slate of the air.

And then it was back, thrumming through him with a power that rippled the taut muscles of his stomach; that vibrated every cell in every blood vessel in his body.

For a moment he sat there, his body trembling, his mouth agape, staring at them, at the air around them.

And then he was back, noticing them notice him.

Smiles, small and flirtatious, clung to their immobile lips.

Their hands danced subtly before them, sharing thoughts and feelings that he saw in silver flourishes.

Because of their silence, because of their hands, they were beautiful to him, shining, different.

Seen.

Suddenly his head felt better, the pressure decreased, and he felt washed in cool air, as if enveloped in the shell of the rarer atmosphere they seemed to inhabit.

He smiled back at them, smiled with the full force of his demand, and they hesitated, smiled back.

His smile broadened, then, broadened because, in looking at their hands, their right hands in particular, he saw his answer.

Each wore on her wrist a black silicone bracelet, popular these days and usually imprinted with a slogan, like LIVE FREE or HOPE. He didn't care what the bracelets said, not really. He cared more for what they *showed* him.

For what they showed him was how they demarked those hands from the rest of their bodies, like a boundary drawn by a surgeon.

A surgeon.

That thought made his smile grow even larger, and then the girls did start giggling, but silently, with their eyes sparkling and their mouths drawn wide and their lungs hitching in air.

He thought, then, to remember that look on their faces.

But he knew he'd see it again, under much different circumstances.

"Hey, girls," he said, careful to pronounce the words succinctly, moving his mouth in an exaggerated way. "Are you as hot as you look?"

Their smiles grew larger, but they remained motionless, smiling at him, appraising him.

"I've got AC and cold soda in the RV. I was heading there now. Wanna come?"

They giggled again, silently, and their hands, their beautiful, airy hands, leapt out before them and made incantations, more for each other than for him since they nodded in response to his question.

So, they walked back to his RV, arm in arm. The one's right arm wrapped around the other; the other's right arm wrapped around him. But his arm, thrown over both, never touched them.

* * *

Later, and far away, a trucker saw him haul two large, suspiciously shaped plastic trash bags off the side of the interstate and dump them in the weeds along the shoulder.

What was left. After.

There were police when he stopped, questions, searching, finding what he'd kept.

Their hands.

It was just their hands. In the end.

JUST A PHONE CALL AWAY

CYNTHIA HAD LOST CONTROL.

Home seemed foreign to her, a place she wasn't supposed to be on a weekday morning. Her small apartment wore the air of a person awakened too soon: groggy and grumpy and put upon.

"Get used to it," she mumbled, shivering in her underwear at the kitchen table. She took another sip from the heavy ceramic mug that read DON'T ASK ME I JUST WORK HERE, a memento of her recently ex-job.

Cynthia was not ready to get out there and look for another job. She was 44 years old. Her long brown hair was pulled back, showing off a pretty, if somewhat heavy face; a face her mother called "handsome." She wore the best clothes she could afford, but they were old; too tight in the wrong places, too loose in the wrong places.

Cynthia hadn't been the office romance type, either, but that hadn't stopped her. She wasn't the self-assured, tight young college graduate; the naïve, even younger secretary; or the older, yet still sexy vice president with the failing marriage.

She may not have had the body, the age, or the power to attract lovers, but Cynthia had the voice. And she had learned long ago that her voice was as sexual as any breast or butt or leg.

It was deep, raspy, but not grating or harsh on the ear. It was a husky, resonant, breathy voice reminiscent of whiskey and cigarettes; of Lauren Bacall and Kathleen Turner; of sex in candle-lit rooms on beds with rumpled sheets and the smell of sweat dewing the air.

Without a doubt, it turned men on in ways her body alone never could.

It had been what had attracted her boss, what had kept him in her bed for eight months, had kept him *laid*.

It couldn't, however, save her from being *laid off*.

For the record, it had been a company-wide housecleaning, not just her. So there was little her former lover could do to save her—the economy and all. But this single act left her feeling powerless, not knowing quite what to do. So with a couple weeks' severance, a last lunch with the remaining staff, and a parting, bad-dog-eyed goodbye from her ex, she left, with no prospects and fewer ideas.

Another punishing draught of hot coffee and she flipped the newspaper open, scanned the want ads. Down the columns, through administrative assistants, receptionists, secretaries. She circled those that appealed to her. There weren't many—the economy and all.

Her eyes drifted across SEX-CAM PERFORMERS WANTED and she snorted, almost gagging on her coffee. Sex on a webcam? She looked down at her rumpled, faded T-shirt, the frayed waistband of her panties. She thought of her wrinkles, her droops, her veins, her... No, no way possible she could seriously consider doing anything live on a camera, streaming through the Internet to God knew where.

But the phone.

She wryly remembered what Ralph in accounting had told her on her last day.

"Well, Cynthia," he had laughed, his voice dropping. "With your voice, I bet you could find a great job in the phone sex business. You'd make a fortune. Hell, I'd pay you two dollars a minute for you to talk dirty to me."

"Ralph!" she said, her protest half-game, half-flattered.

Suddenly though, cold and depressed and in her underwear on a Monday morning, Ralph's idea didn't seem so ridiculous. With the phone company contacts she'd gained through years as a receptionist, a little research on her part, and a little money borrowed from her retirement fund, she could swing something like that. *Couldn't she?*

But a voice at the back of her mind—her mother's, no less—whispered to her exactly what she was thinking of doing.

Talking dirty to men on the phone.

Not just men, but men she didn't know.

And not just dirty, but explicit and, well, X-rated.

You really aren't going to go through with this, her mother's voice chided.

There was really only one way to tell.

* * *

It amazed Cynthia how quickly it all came together.

She secured a business license, got a tax number, made the necessary arrangements with the phone company. Her liaisons there were more than eager to help her get a 900-number line installed in her apartment.

While she waited, she visited the newsstand outside her building. There, under the silent, curious eyes of the old newsman, she self-consciously bought a few of the seedier men's magazines.

Back in her apartment, she sat in the little space she'd cleared for an office and flipped through the magazines, intending to go straight for the classified ads at the back. Her curiosity, though, demanded she scrutinize the first several books carefully. She turned pages quickly, the photos taking on a surreal look, so tightly focused she was sure even a gynecologist would have difficulty identifying what she was seeing.

She was able to cobble together pieces of the ads she liked into a small ad of her own that she scheduled to run in several of the magazines she'd reviewed and a few local alternative newspapers, as well as some of the less seedy websites she'd visited.

Now all she needed was practice.

* * *

"Hello?"

"Ralph. Hi, this is Cynthia."

"Cynthia?" he asked, lowering his voice. "*Cynthia Johnson?*"

"Yes," she purred into the receiver. "And do you know what? I'm sitting here totally nude." She paused, hitched in a deep breath as her stomach fluttered. "And I'm really wet."

There was stunned silence on the other end, and Cynthia, her face burning, her heart thundering so loudly she feared she'd be unable to hear Ralph's response, put her finger on the cradle of the phone, prepared to hang up. She heard the tinny sound of a television somewhere on Ralph's end. She almost laughed, imagining him standing there in his kitchen listening to her as she sat in a T-shirt and jeans with no makeup.

Not nude, and decidedly not wet.

"My wife is here, for Chrissakes!"

"Ralph," she moaned so low that the phone vibrated in her own ear. "Oh, Ralph. I've been thinking of you ever since I left. I've been very naughty, touching myself."

"Dear Lord."

"I took your advice and started a phone sex business. You're my first customer. But don't worry," she said with a throaty giggle. "This one's on the house."

"Can I call you right back? I've got to get to—"

"No. We've got to finish. Right *here*, right *now*."

And he did.

After that, Ralph became her first paying customer.

* * *

The phone rang at 3:00 a.m.

Cynthia didn't bother to turn the lights on as she picked her way to the chair by the phone. In the three months she'd operated the service, she'd walked this path many times in the dark, more asleep than not.

The men who called at this hour were more lonely than horny, a bit more sincere, sweeter and desperate for simple human contact. Cynthia found she could talk to these men about things other than sex: jobs, hobbies, problems. Sometimes these callers became so engrossed in their conversations with her that they never made it to the sex part.

Cynthia plopped into the chair near the phone, answered it without even clearing her throat. These men wanted to feel they'd roused her from bed. They wanted to hear her raspy, sleep-filled voice. It lent an air of intimacy to what they did, as if they'd rolled over and awakened a lover curled beside them.

"Hello, honey. This had better be good."

"Hello." The man's voice was rough, hoarse and whisper-quick.

With one word, Cynthia sized him up. His kind would say nothing more, only respond to questions or ask short, wheezing queries. In this situation, very few men wanted to take the lead. Better to be led.

She preferred it that way.

"Does your mommy know you're up this late calling me? 'Cause if she doesn't, you go tell her it's $2.99 per minute."

"She's not here."

"Good. Neither is mine."

"What are you wearing?"

"Nothing, baby." Actually, she was wearing a pair of panties, but otherwise this was accurate. "I sleep naked. You never know when the opportunity might...*arise*. What are you wearing?"

"I'm not wearing anything, either."

"And I bet you've got quite a handful, don't you?"

"You could say that," he said, laughing. That laugh raised goosebumps on her arms. It was disturbing, confidential and low, like a rusty engine slowly turning over. She heard a sound from his end, distant, maybe the squeaking of bedsprings, the rustle of covers. "Tell me about yourself."

"Down to details. My kind of man. I'm five-eight, 130 pounds, brown hair and eyes. Twenty-eight years old, 38-26-34. Like to fuck. How about you?"

"What do you *like*?" he asked, breathing a kind of hazy weight into his last word. "I mean *specifically*."

"I like it all."

"You haven't been doing this long, have you?" he asked, his tone changing as if he were an actor stepping outside character. "That's the *easy* answer. The *pat* answer. But what do you really like? More than anything?"

Cynthia rolled her eyes. Obviously the guy was looking to talk to someone who liked the particular kink he was into. And he seemed intent on making her guess what that was.

"I like to be spanked," she said, and that *was* a safe answer. Kinky enough to satisfy the more perverted, not so perverse as to disgust the milder men.

"You do?" he said, lapsing into his previous hushed tone.

"Yeah," she said, relaxing. "Do you?"

"Yeah, sure," he answered a bit distracted. "Sure, sure."

There was a moment of silence.

She thought she heard him lick his lips.

"So, you like...*pain?*"

"That depends on who, what and how much." She fumbled for her cigarettes, sensing that control was coming back to her.

"I like pain."

"Great." She inhaled on the cigarette. "You liked to be spanked, whipped, bitten—"

"*Cut,*" interrupted the voice from a great depth. "I like to be cut."

Cynthia hesitated. "Cut?" she repeated, crushing out her cigarette, struggling to keep her voice neutral. "How?"

A deep, rattling sound from the other end.

"A sharp knife. A razor. A piece of glass. It doesn't matter."

If that litany was not unsettling enough, he did something then that almost made her drop the phone. He moaned, soft as a caress.

"What are you doing?" She swallowed, hoping to change the subject.

"Stroking myself."

"Are you hard?"

"Yes. And so is *it.*"

"Is what?"

"*My knife.*"

"What are you doing with a knife?" she asked, unconsciously covering herself with a blanket, sliding her feet underneath her.

"Cutting...myself," he said, his voice rapturous. "Little lines across my chest...my abdomen...around my nipples... *Ohhh!*"

She felt the shudder in his voice.

"Keep talking to me. I like your voice," he said.

"Are you going to keep doing that?" she asked, her stomach folding in on itself.

"Oh, yessss."

"Doesn't it hurt?" she moaned, biting a finger.

"No! *Yes!*"

"Stop!" she screamed, leaping up, the blanket falling forgotten around her feet. "Please stop!"

"Jesus! OH! OH MY GOD!" he yelled, his screams descending into broken sobs.

Cynthia stood, her hand cupped over her mouth.

Neither said anything for a minute.

Neither hung up.

"Are you okay?" she whispered, her hand still not far from her mouth.

"I cut off my nipple."

"Oh my God," she groaned, her eyes fluttering back in her head.

"I've got to go now. I've got quite a mess here. But you were wonderful. I'll call again."

With a creaking of bedsprings, the receiver clunked into place.

* * *

Cynthia sat upright in bed the rest of the night, wrapped in her quilt, staring at the phone. It rang several times, stopping at around 4:30 a.m., but she did not answer it.

She'd heard many things over the phone in the last three months: things that were exciting and intriguing, rude and disgusting, uncomfortable and unpleasant. But this had gone far past those other calls.

Too far.

Into territory within herself she found unfamiliar and frightening.

Cynthia replayed the conversation over and over in her head. Each time, the feelings surged back, as strong and as vivid as they had been during the experience. Strangely, even though they had never talked about sex, the call left her with an overwhelming sense of being used.

Being out of control.

She hadn't experienced that yet. Up to now, she had always been in control on the phone. This man, though, had played her as deftly as she had played other callers.

There was something else that disturbed her even more; something that clung to the borders of her conscious mind, hid in the shadows.

Cynthia caught only a glimpse of it, but that was enough.

Excitement.

She'd been *excited* by the conversation, by the man hurting himself.

Unable to think of another explanation, unwilling to accept this one, she sobbed herself to sleep just as the sun poked through the slats of her bedroom blinds.

And the phone rang.

* * *

Two days later, Cynthia felt well enough to begin taking calls again.

Passing the jangling phone late in the afternoon, a soda in one hand, cigarettes in the other, she picked it up on impulse.

"Hello?"

"I didn't frighten you, did I?"

Cynthia stiffened, fumbled a cigarette.

"I can hear you *smoking*," he said, just as she exhaled. "I'm sorry if I upset you. I've been trying to call back for days."

She exhaled another cloud of thin smoke, took a drink of soda, sat down. She was going to make sure she was in control before she answered, even though her heart was vibrating inside her chest, her mouth bone-dry.

"I really enjoyed our conversation. It was the best I've—"

"Did you really do it?" she asked.

"Good, you are there."

"You really cut...it...*off?*"

"It only hurt for a little while."

"I can't believe you did that to yourself," she said, her own nipples beginning to ache with imagined pain. She crossed an arm over her breasts, crushed them to her as if to reassure herself they were intact.

"Why not?

"Is that a serious question?"

"Sure."

"You're not going to do it again...are you?"

"Who says that I'm not doing it right now?"

That stopped her. Of course he was doing it right now. That's why he'd called.

"You are, aren't you?" She puffed, keeping the cigarette perched close to her lips.

"You don't even know if I really did it or not. It excited you, though, didn't it? Even if it scared you, repulsed you?"

Blood, hot and angry, flooded her cheeks.

"That's just sick. *You're* sick. You're a fucking weirdo!"

"Ohh... Ummm... I love your voice. It tickles my ear."

"Stop... Stop it! Whatever you're doing, stop it."

"I've got my knife again."

"No! I'm hanging up!"

"I'm...ahhh...making three or four...ahhahhh...little cuts along my dick. There!" he breathed. "Yeah, that's great."

"Oh my God!" she shrieked. "*Stop!*"

"Ohhh," he groaned. "Just enough to get a little blood. It's nice. Warm. A great lube. If it doesn't dry out. Gotta...keep it fresh."

"Please," she was whining now, twisting and untwisting the phone cord. "Please stop."

"So hard now. It stings. Need...ahhhh...another cut. Talk to me."

"No. Stop. Just...please stop."

"If you don't want to listen, hang up...awwww—"

"Don't do this. *Please.*"

"But it feels so good. Stings a little, but...ahhh!"

An image of him appeared unbidden in her mind; a vague face grimacing, a nude body writhing upon white sheets at the center of a Rorschach test of blood. The straining, swelling thing he held in his closed fist was a deep, dark red; the warm, secret interior of a cherry pie.

Warmth spread in waves from within her, even as her stomach shivered.

Cynthia found, perversely, that her own disgust only heightened the arousal she was fighting. It was illicit and forbidden, and she hadn't felt that since sex with her teenage boyfriend long ago while her parents were away from home.

"You still with me?" he asked, his voice tight and distant.

"Yes."

"Good. So good."

"Yes." It was the tone of defeat and remorse, edged with the instinctive desperation of sex.

The caller's voice hissed through clenched teeth as he redoubled his efforts.

"Do you want me to finish?"

"Umm," she breathed in assent, plopping onto the chair near the phone, her fingertips brushing lightly down her belly, pulling her robe apart, her panties to one side.

"I'm feeling a little...faint...gotta hurry. Talk to me!"

"I want you to finish." And her voice was low, commanding. Cynthia threw her legs over the arms of the chair. "Finish now."

"Yeah, okay. Ahh…"

"Right now. Do it!" she urged, using her shoulder to clamp the phone to her ear, freeing both hands.

"Ahh! Yes! Oh…God…yesssss," came his reply, panting close to the phone. Then, abruptly, not breathing at all for a few moments

Cynthia lapsed into silence as an orgasm, painful in its intensity, flashed through her. One of her legs spasmed, lashed out, knocked a lamp off the table near her. The light bulb popped as the lamp shattered. Suddenly the afternoon room was engulfed in darkness.

"Did you…"

"Yes," she panted. It had happened so fast that beads of sweat were only now forming on her forehead. Her aching arms twitched loosely.

"So did I. Are you still wet?"

Cynthia brought her fingers close to her face, rubbed them together. "Yes."

"So am I," he laughed. "I always have a mess to clean after I talk to you."

The image of him sprawled atop his sheets like an ink blotter after a spill returned to her.

In the shadows, her own wet hands were slicked with darkness.

And a smell drifted from her fingers, imagined.

It was a flat, arid smell, metallic. The smell of dirty metal and copper pennies.

Blood.

Her stomach, which she had ignored, leapt uncontrollably. It was all she could do to drop the phone and lower her head before she vomited.

As she shook and gasped, the man's voice chirped from the receiver on the floor. "Are you still there? Are you all right?" But she could not answer, could not even pick up the phone, her hands shook so badly.

She stumbled into the bathroom, vomited again into the open toilet, fell into the shower.

There, she checked her fingertips.

They were unstained.

Cynthia stayed in the shower until she had obliterated the phantom smell with soap and water.

* * *

It was dark again when she awoke, the covers curled like shed skin around her naked body. She inhaled hesitantly, expecting the blood odor, but all she smelled were the warm, clean sheets with their stolen scent of fabric softener.

Her stomach rumbled, loud enough to hear, and she realized she hadn't eaten since getting sick yesterday. The mere thought of food brought a rush of saliva.

Swinging her feet off the bed, she stood, wobbly and stiff.

She grabbed the robe hanging from the bedpost, thrust her arms into it, pulled it closed and knotted the tie.

The kitchen was flooded with the moon's translucent silver light until she snapped on the harsh fluorescents, whose light seemed to ooze from the fixture, creep across the countertops and the white tile.

An omelette sounds really good right now.

Soon she was beating eggs, pouring them into a hot skillet.

The refrigerator held grated cheddar cheese, mushrooms and a tomato. She gathered them, set them out on a cutting board. Her movements were as spare and unconscious as any cook working in a familiar kitchen.

Until she opened a drawer to get a knife.

The knives gleamed, long and tapered like razor teeth.

Cynthia reached tentatively for one, as if the drawer might snap closed around her hand like a hungry mouth. Snatching the knife out, she slammed the drawer shut with her hip.

She'd grabbed a paring knife. It was slim and delicate, curving to a point like a miniature scimitar, its gentle, upward angle not unlike that of a…

Shaking her head, she thrust the knife into a tomato, cored it, divided it.

She didn't even realize she'd cut herself until she dropped the tomato into the bubbling center of the omelette and washed her hands.

Under the water, blood welled from the cut, hair-thin but deep. Cynthia, grimacing even though it didn't hurt, pulled its edges apart. It opened to reveal a moist, red interior.

The cut made her finger feel warm, her body a little faint.

Is this what he feels?

Her gaze drifted back to the cutting board, to the knife that rested there on the damp, red wood. Her fingers curled around it, tickled the back of her other hand with its tip.

Behind her, the tomatoes melted into the mass of the omelette.

Her robe slipped open, and she pressed the flat of the cold blade against her breast, the sharp edge circling the nipple. It became hard immediately. She flicked the blade's tip to her other breast, traced its curve to her nipple. Goosebumps rushed in a wave up her abdomen, across her collarbone, down her arms.

The knife's blade grew warm. A momentary sensation of heat swept across her like a dry, scouring wind. Then a sudden cold that made her cry out. She orgasmed, her legs buckling beneath her.

Her free hand caught the counter as she fell to her knees, gasped for breath. Beneath her, bright red pennies dripped unnoticed to the kitchen floor.

In the pan, the omelette burned.

* * *

Cynthia cleaned the kitchen, scouring the charred egg, cheese and tomato from the pan. She mopped the floor, trying not to distinguish between the pulpy tomato drippings and the spots that were thicker, redder.

The bandage she had applied chafed the sore, raw nipple it covered. She had already changed it twice, but blood still oozed from the wound, soaked through the bandage, her T-shirt.

When she had first gone into the bathroom, blood dripped from her nipple, trickling down the curve of her breast, beading on her stomach like water on a finely waxed car. With hesitant, probing fingers, she discovered the sharp little paring knife had nearly sliced off her entire nipple. It hung from her breast by a small flap of skin. When she touched it, it swung like an opening door, exposing bright red tissue beneath.

She quickly closed it.

Amazingly, it took nearly an hour for it to begin to hurt; first in a tentative, stinging way, then in great, pounding throbs of pain that made both breasts ache in rhythm with her racing pulse.

Once the kitchen was clean, she poured herself a glass of soda, gathered her robe around her, sat in her chair near the phone. She did not cry, and her stomach ached only in a vaguely threatening way. She felt she now understood him better, as if they had bonded in some secret, bloody pact. She felt she could handle him better when he called next.

She felt in control again.

The phone on the table next to her rang shrilly, and she set the glass down, answered it.

"Hello? Hi, Steve," she said to one of her regular callers. "Is your wifey asleep? Great. Yes. Uh-huh. I bet you are hard, Stevie. I've got something that's hard, too."

Steve stayed on the phone, angry at first, then scared, then weeping.

When she finished, he asked if he could call her again.

And she had another mess to clean.

* * *

The phone rang, as it did more and more often these days.

So many calls, so many callers.

Many times, they didn't like what Cynthia wanted to offer.

With most, though, it only took a phone call or two to turn them on, just as it had been for her.

But it was getting harder with each caller.

It took more and more of her to keep that control.

Cynthia grunted, fought to pull herself from the sticky, crusted bed-sheets. She spent most of her time in bed these days, the phone now moved to her nightstand where it was within easy reach.

Cynthia was naked, as she was all of the time. She found clothing of any kind, even a loose silk robe, chafed the many wounds on her body, some still oozing fluids, some scabbed over, some covered with thick, ropy scars.

There were far too many to worry about Band-Aids.

It was now difficult for her to walk. She was weak so often, and it was hard to maintain her balance without toes. The neighbors had started to complain— first to her, then to the building manager—about the screams, the moans, the strange, unpleasant smells coming from her apartment.

"Cynthia?" The voice on the receiver trembled through her.

Her ex-boss. Her ex-lover.

"Hello." Her voice was hard and hoarse. It had suffered the most over the last six months, through all the shouting, the shrieking, the crying. The toll of that stress was as apparent in her voice just as it would have been in the wrinkled, saggy body of a burned-out topless dancer.

For a moment she felt like she had when he'd fired her, when the man who cut himself called her the first time.

Out of control.

Pushing that thought aside, she fumbled for something just out of reach. It sparkled in the low light of the room as she brought it around, settled back into bed.

The knife was awkward to hold these days. All the fingers on her left hand were gone, and on her right hand only a single finger and thumb remained. This, she found, was the minimum number of digits necessary.

"Ralph told me to call you."

"He did? What else did he say?"

"That I'd never forget it."

"Ohh, you'll never forget. I'll make sure of that. You'll never *forget.*"

"What are you doing?"

"I'm stroking the tip of my knife over my skin," she whispered. "Wishing it was you."

Clumsily, she moved the knife, trembling a little each time the blade skipped over a scar, slid through a wet, raw patch. She sought something she had given to no caller yet; some part of her body that was whole and unscarred to offer.

To control him with.

He made a noise that sounded as if it were ripped involuntarily from a place deep inside him.

"Ummm. It feels nice, doesn't it?"

"Yes." He hesitated briefly when he heard something underneath her heavy breathing. The corrugated sound of metal cutting into something soft.

The knife moved against her, into her.

Warmth spread within her, upon her.

What remained of her voice cracked with pleasure.

"Good...*so good...*"

She screamed, her hips bucking uncontrollably, shuddering with the powerful waves that crashed through her, the warm liquid that spattered over her.

Through everything, she heard him on the other end, gasping through the spasms of his own pleasure, his breathing as intimate as if his mouth were pressed directly to her ear.

She smiled fiercely as her vision dimmed.

It came out with so little difficulty, and she held it glistening and dripping in the blackness of the room. She was surprised by its smallness—no bigger than her fist—and the fact that it still shuddered timidly.

The receiver slipped away, dropped to the bed, the still-beating heart squirted from the ruin of her other hand.

But, oh, Cynthia was in control again…

THE DARK LEVEL

WITH ONE HAND, Jim pulled the yellow flyer from beneath the windshield wiper of his car.

"What now?"

Over the last few months, the parking garage had raised its rates and had restricted the number of available spaces to accommodate employees of the insurance company across the street. Parking was at a premium these days. With the construction boom in full swing and tourism at an all-time high, developers just couldn't seem to put up garages fast enough.

Since Jim didn't work for the insurance company, his space kept moving deeper into the bowels of the structure as the owners carved additional parking spaces for their largest tenant.

Draping his coat over his arm, he scanned the flyer.

ATTENTION.
Effective June 1, the Market Street Garage will become
the corporate parking structure for
First Mutual Indemnity Insurance Co.
Only employees and guests will be allowed access to the garage.
Any outstanding balance should be paid in full by that date.
We have appreciated your business.

"Shit!" he exclaimed loud enough for the word to echo off the low ceiling in the subterranean chamber.

That's Monday, for Chrissakes! Thanks for the notice.

He crumpled the flyer into a little ball and tossed it. His eye fell on several other balled or torn up flyers. Evidently others had received the news with as much grace.

Jim climbed into the car, slinging his briefcase and jacket onto the passenger seat. He ran down a list of the garages he knew, but quickly discarded them all. They were obvious choices, and he was sure the other evicted parkers would be exploring them, too.

He glanced at his watch. 6:15 p.m. The traffic wouldn't be too bad at this hour.

Backing from his space for the last time, he decided to drive around the city for a while to look for another garage with vacancies.

* * *

The city blocks transitioned from offices and restaurants to storefronts and apartments to dilapidated tenements and vacant, weed-choked lots. Upon reaching one particularly distressed warehouse district, Jim decided he was out of luck.

Litter blew down the streets, and grey weeds thrust through the pavement. Across an empty lot he saw three lean dogs with dull, matted hair and feral eyes that followed his car.

Turning onto a side street, he began a U-turn when he noticed a large sign from the corner of his eye, bright and clean and incongruous with the rest of the scenery.

PARKING $7 DAILY.
VACANCIES.

"No," he laughed, looking through his rearview mirror. "I can't be this lucky."

The garage was set out a little from a squat, one-story building, long and narrow, that fronted the street. The building seemed new compared with its tumbledown neighbors, and Jim could see car bumpers gleaming within, like metal teeth in a dark, smiling mouth.

He smiled back at it, pleased with his good fortune.

The sign was attached to a large, metal cabinet with hundreds of tiny, numbered compartments. A smaller sign at eye-level instructed him to either see an attendant or leave a business card in one of the open boxes along with a check for the monthly charge.

Jim searched for an attendant, but couldn't find one. With only a little hesitation, he wrote a check, folded it around his business card and tucked the parcel into the box marked 1103, closed the tiny door, which locked.

Feeling happy with himself, he climbed back into his car and pulled away in a swirl of dust and garbage.

* * *

Monday morning came, and Jim wondered why no other cars entered the garage with him. And yet, as his car swirled down the ramps, he noticed almost every parking space was filled.

He'd gone slowly down three levels looking for space 1103 before it became so dark he was forced to turn on the headlights. He barely made out a 321 in dirty yellow numbers on an empty space to his left between an Audi and a Kia.

As he wound deeper into the building, his eyes adjusted to the dim light. Still, he did not see a single person; no one pulling into a space, climbing out of a car, filing toward the bank of elevators.

Motes of dust sparkled in his headlights as he swept through the aisles. The parked cars wore the dust like sequined dresses.

His car curled around the last corner, and he barely saw the numerals painted onto the dingy wall as his headlights raked across them.

Level 11.

Jim cruised slowly down the aisle until he found 1103. He sighed in relief when it appeared, as much at its existence as at the fact that it was, indeed, unoccupied.

When he doused the headlights, though, darkness, complete and utterly impenetrable, surrounded him. He sat for a minute, debated starting the car and leaving. But go where? This was, quite simply, the only garage where he could park.

He opened the car door, throwing a wedge of pale light. But this weakened quickly, and he was able to see only bumpers, the glare of other windshields.

Grabbing his briefcase, he looked back to where he'd seen the elevators. He thought he could just make out their vertical shapes.

He let the door slip closed cautiously, unwilling to relinquish the light, as feeble as it was.

Jim immediately moved off toward the elevators, his briefcase held before him.

The air was cool and slightly damp, heavy with the odors of gasoline and metal, gritty with cement dust. It was quiet, with none of the sounds normally associated with a parking garage: the hollow WHUMPH! of car doors slamming, tires squealing around corners, the sudden ululation of an alarm.

All he heard was the quiet ticking of a single car engine, cooling in the encompassing murk.

* * *

After five minutes of stumbling around in the dark—and sharply bumping his shin against the fender of a motorcycle—he reached the far wall. His hand, splayed out along the wall, found the button.

Smiling, he pressed it once, hard.

The elevator gave no indication that it heard his summons.

He stabbed the button several times in rapid succession. Nothing.

He would have to walk the eleven stories up to the mouth of the garage.

He found his way back to the ramp more quickly than he had thought. A handrail guided him and made it a bit easier to walk in the dark.

By the time he'd walked up four levels, he'd broken a sweat and was fuming mad.

If there is someone up there when I get there, they're going to get an earful.

Another three levels, and he could feel streamers of sweat run down his back, soak into his shirt.

And it was still dark, as dark as it had been on the levels below.

Jim paused on what he assumed to be the fourth floor, hesitated.

Driving in, the lights on this floor had been on.

He could barely see the useless fixtures hanging from the pipes and conduits. No light was visible, either, as he looked up the ramp to the next level.

By now, there should be some light leaking in from outside.

For a moment, he thought of returning to the car, if he could even find it. But, now, so close to the entrance, going back seemed ludicrous.

Two more levels up, and more confusion.

Where the fuck am I? This should be the first floor.

The far wall was just visible past a row of cars, a ghostlike number painted on it. Cursing, he moved toward it, passing between two cars.

He set his briefcase down, brought his face close to the wall's surface.

A big, red 1 was painted there, its outline hard to see against the dirt and grime.

And next to it, he saw, was another 1.

For a moment, it refused to register in his mind.

A sound, sudden and distant; scraping, soft and barely audible.

Like something moving across a cement floor, grinding tiny rocks and other debris.

Coming toward him.

"Hello?" he said, hearing his voice rebound flatly off the concrete.

The crunching ceased.

Jim decided it was time to find his car and get the hell out of the garage.

The concrete scraping began again, a little louder, and his pace quickened with his pulse.

Down the row quickly, his briefcase swinging at his side, the only sounds that of his own footfalls and the gentle, sliding crunch behind him.

A shape stood out from all the others in the darkness, the familiar outlines of his car, and he ran the last few steps.

The key came quickly out of his pocket, poked at the door handle several times before seating itself and slipping in. He turned it, but it didn't budge. Nervously, he jammed it in tighter, twisted it again, jimmied it back and forth.

Then he noticed the car itself.

There wasn't enough light to make out its exact color, but Jim could narrow it down to black or brown or blue or green.

His car was *white.*

The slow crackling movement neared, stopped before him.

Jim stood still, his hand on the key yet in the lock.

Suddenly, the horn of the car he'd been trying to get into went off, and he jumped back from it as if electrocuted, reeled into the car beside it.

His briefcase was flung into the darkness, clunking onto something metal and clattering to the floor.

Then, every horn in every car in the garage was blasting simultaneously, reverberating off the walls, the low ceiling.

Jim covered his ears against the clamor, ran back to the ramp.

Still, the horns bellowed, a continuous, unwavering harmony that resonated in his brain, made his teeth chatter.

He ran until he struck a cement pillar head on, sprawled to the ground.

Lights erupted in the darkness, pressed down upon him, and he lost consciousness.

* * *

From blackness onto blackness, he opened his eyes.

He felt the cool air wash over him, the floor press up against him.

For a brief moment, disoriented and sore, he couldn't remember where he was.

It came back to him on the smells of gasoline and rubber, and he lay there for a time, took stock of his situation as best he could in the dark.

There was a knot, tumid and warm, throbbing on his forehead above his left eye. His suit was torn at the elbows, and the heels of his palms were scraped and bleeding.

As he drew himself up, he had the disturbing sensation of *sinking* into something gummy.

At first, he thought he'd fallen into a patch of tar or asphalt. But he followed the contours of the warm, tacky substance with his fingertips. It felt vaguely organic and conformed perfectly to the shape of his prone body.

It was as if the floor itself had melted beneath him.

Springing to his feet, he brushed at the front of his jacket, which felt unusually warm in the cool, moist air. The jacket fell apart under his hands, buttons clinking at his feet. He rubbed through its material, which powdered at his touch, to his business shirt.

Where the dust from the desiccated suit touched his raw palms, there was a tingling, then a burning sensation. Wincing, he rubbed his hands briskly on his pants, peeling a strip of cloth from the front of each leg.

He now felt the burning on his legs, too, so fierce that his eyes teared.

He heard a tinkle, paused.

It was high-pitched, varying in intensity.

As he listened motionless, it became a gurgle, a rush.

Water.

Either the light had increased since he'd lost consciousness, or his eyes had finally adjusted. Whichever, he could see ahead of him a broken pipe angling from the ceiling, water spewing from its severed end.

Its sound filled the confines of the garage, echoing within like a secret grotto, and he went to it.

The cold water splashed upon him, seared into him. His muscles tightened, his teeth gritted as he brought his hands into its flow, let it scour his abrasions.

Thirsty, he drank it, so cold he didn't mind its flat, metallic aroma or the acrid, bitter aftertaste.

Soaked, he turned away from the stream, sloshed to a nearby car and squatted on the fender. He shrugged out of the remainder of his coat, tore his tie off, dropped them both to the ground.

A profound fatigue penetrated him, and he did not even attempt to stifle the head-splitting yawn it produced.

Gotta lay down for minute.

So tired.

Jim was barely able to stagger around to the passenger door of the car he'd been sitting on.

The door whooshed open without a key, and an odor forced its way through Jim's haze.

Sweet, sticky, sticky sweet.

Overpowering, it flowed from the car's interior in waves, each one stronger than the last.

As he pondered this, his left foot rose over the lip of the rocker panel, descended. It kept descending until it was lower than his right, still on the pavement, and he began to fall after it into the car.

Inside, he had a glimpse of a dark, deep chasm, whose sides pulsated, glistened wetly in the nether light. At the bottom was a shallow pool of thin, brackish liquid from which poked bones—a skull, several femurs, a hip, a hand waving jauntily.

Wrenching himself around, he scrabbled at the doorframe, threw himself backwards.

He rolled down the side of the adjoining car, spilled to the ground.

The door snapped shut.

Although his heart thundered blood through his body, the lethargy within him grew stronger.

The part of him that mattered simply wanted to slump to the concrete and sleep. But he remembered how the ground had earlier dissolved underneath him. Hauling himself unsteadily to his feet, he stumbled away, found another car.

Locked.

Two, three more. All locked.

He remembered his suit turning to powder, the bones at the bottom of the pit.

I can't fall asleep out here.

Another car, and the handle worked.

Fumbling the door open, Jim had the presence of mind to reach inside first, feel along until his hand contacted the cold vinyl seat. He bent, meaning to slide in, but his eyes closed as the wave of exhaustion rolled over him, and it became a collapse.

Half in and half out of the car, Jim was asleep before his head rebounded from the vinyl.

* * *

The dark was a familiar thing when next he opened his eyes.

His right cheek was stuck to the vinyl, and he pulled it away with a sound like peeling tape, noticed that he was now entirely inside the car with the door shut.

He scratched his head, swallowed, felt the urgent desire to pee.

Then the seat moved, as if collapsing from the middle.

Jim scooted to the left side of the car, his back pressed against the door, fumbled with the handle.

The door wouldn't open, even though it wasn't locked.

There was movement again in the car, and this time Jim saw the entire back seat, floorboard and all, descend slowly about two feet, then drop from sight.

A *SPLASH!* came from somewhere below.

The front seat sank a little more, and Jim grabbed the steering wheel.

Thinking back on the science films he'd seen in grade school, Jim remembered one particular film that showed a fly sliding down the inside of a pitcher plant, flailing for purchase until it drowned, then being time-lapse dissolved by liquid at the bottom of the bowl.

He turned, pulled at the door handle, beat at the window, screamed.

The door didn't move.

Something tight and metallic snapped beneath him.

The middle of the bench seat sagged, there was a thick, ripping sound, and it fell away.

His section now inclined precipitously into the growing maw of the dark pit, and he scrambled to keep his balance, locking his arms around the steering wheel and praying it would hold his weight if necessary.

Acting on an impulse, he lunged for the glove compartment, opened it, grabbed whatever was inside: gas receipts, papers, maps, tissues.

He tucked these between his legs, fumbled across the dashboard.

Pushed in, it popped out a few seconds later.

He pulled it out, a baleful red eye.

Acting quickly, he retrieved the wad of paper, pushed the cigarette lighter into its center.

After a second or two, it flared into flames.

He waited until he was sure the fire had taken.

Then he dropped it into the pit.

It fell like a meteor, sloughing embers as it tumbled.

In the wavering light cast by the projectile, he could see it had landed on the vinyl seat far below, which began to burn.

Suddenly the whole car shook, and a noise—almost a moan—rose from the pit.

Thick, oily smoke rolled up from the hole, filling the car's interior.

Jim chanced a leaning glance below, saw the back seat engulfed in flames that licked at the smooth, wet walls of the pit. Black weals scarred them where the fire touched, and the shriveled material it revealed underneath looked decidedly green and plant-like.

The car shuddered again, followed closely by another groan.

Beneath him, the small section of seat on which he sat shifted, plummeted.

He hung from the steering wheel, coughing in the heat and smoke, his legs pinwheeling above the pit. With his free hand, he tried the door handle again. It moved, grudgingly, and he strained all his weight against it. The door sprang open, collided with the adjacent car, rebounded. Jim caught it, braced it.

The flames were now tickling his feet, and he felt the steering column begin to soften, to droop. He swung toward the lip on the driver's side, caught it with both hands, hoisted himself out. As he did, the door slammed forcefully, and a loud rumbling emanated all around him.

The car's windows, lit a lurid orange, shattered.

Jim leapt up, scrambled out of the way.

The pavement gave way like mud, and the car sank crookedly about three feet, smoke and flames belching from beneath it.

He fled to the nearest car, staying well away from the capsizing, burning wreck he'd crawled from.

As he approached the door, he heard a soft but meaty *KA-CHUNK!*

He tried the handle.

Locked.

He turned to the next car.

KA-CHUNK!

Up and down the row, and off into the distance, he heard the sound repeated dozens, hundreds of times.

"You son of a bitch!"

As if in response, the building shook with another low, throbbing roar.

In the fitful light cast by the burning car, he found an old Dodge, covered with dust, unlocked.

As the door swung open, the car's headlights snapped on, the horn went off, as did all those of the cars around him.

Although startled, Jim pressed on.

Ignoring the wailing alarms and flashing lights, he searched the car for any paper or clothing.

Anything that would *burn.*

Everything he found—from rags to clothing, from paper to gasoline cans—was piled in the middle of the row. When he finished, he regarded it with grim pride.

Gathered near the pile like acolytes were two gas cans. One was emptied quickly, dousing every car he could before running out. The contents of the other he used to soak the material he'd gathered, then he threw both empty containers onto the pile. The smell of gas, formerly a ghost, was now a physical presence in the building, floating on the air, cloying at Jim's senses.

He stood before the pile, flipping a book of matches over and over in his hand. In case this didn't work, he held the lighters in reserve.

He pulled one of the matches off, struck it.

Light suddenly flooded his senses, and for a moment, he thought he had ignited the gas in the air. He braced himself against a rush of heat, a blast of air.

But none came.

Instead, daylight sparkled off glass and metal and chrome, spilling gold into dark recesses, blotting out shadows.

The entrance of the garage beckoned to his right, up just one level of the ramp.

He'd been on the second floor all along.

Jim felt the sun warm his clammy, half-clothed body, felt its tug.

But he had never heard of a pitcher plant releasing its prey.

"Forget it," he said out loud, flipping the match onto the mound.

It erupted even before the match touched, and Jim felt the air around him sucked toward it.

An enormous fireball mushroomed to the ceiling, feelers racing along the floor toward the fuel-covered cars.

The garage shook again, a pained, high-pitched squeal, as the cars burst into flames.

Jim dashed toward the exit, passed through it, blinked and teared at the sudden onslaught of light.

The first thing he saw when his vision cleared were the three dogs standing together in a loose group about twenty feet away. They ignored him, though, their fearful canine eyes taking in the fire.

Thick, black smoke poured from the structure which had already begun to fall in on itself, sagging here and there. It seemed to melt, though, more than collapse the way Jim supposed a real building would.

Then again, it wasn't a real building.

Several muffled explosions punctuated the fire as cars exploded within. They, apparently, were real enough.

His had been.

He stood there for some time, in his dirty business shirt and underwear, black socks and dress shoes, and watched the fire burn. Smoke drifted toward him, and he smelled gasoline and burning rubber.

Something else smelled of sweetly burning green wood and sugar.

The smoke rose high into the air, blotting out an entire section of the sky.

He surveyed the vacant lot around him, littered with paper, soda cans, over-large beer bottles and kicked an area clear and sat. He noticed a large weed poking out of the dry, hardscrabble ground.

He yanked it up roots and all, pulled a lighter from his breast pocket, roasted the plant. He didn't notice something burst open on the roof of the now completely engulfed garage.

Didn't see the hundreds of tiny, furry spheres it released into the hot, swirling air.

Didn't see how they were caught by the wind, carried aloft, east toward downtown.

EVERYTHING MUST GO

"I'VE NEVER SEEN THAT SHOP BEFORE."

Brian stopped short in front of the store, the cardboard Starbucks cup—still mostly filled with the sickeningly sweet peppermint mocha Kaylie had talked him into buying—paused halfway in the trashcan's maw.

Brian had never noticed the shop before, which was unusual since he stopped by the Starbucks just a few doors down practically every morning, sometimes in the evenings, often on dates like this one.

The shop was tucked between a Hasidic tailor and a locksmith. There was a tattered, dirty green awning over its door. The awning had no number. The windows were darkened, painted over on the inside. A few playbills from some off-Broadway production were slapped over the outside.

But no name, no address, no phone number. Nothing to tell what went on inside. Was it a sex parlor? Bakery? Mob front? Who knew?

Under the canopy, in a tall director's chair whose canvas back and seat were the same drab green as the awning, sat a bored-looking woman of indeterminate age. She wore a look of intense discouragement and a stained down jacket that had seen better days. She engaged none of the passersby on the busy sidewalk, and no one other than Brian seemed to notice her or the shop at all.

Behind her was what really interested Brian, though. A single metal frame door was wedged wide open, but just past it thick, black curtains that looked to be made of velvet blocked any view of the interior. He couldn't see any light, hear any sound come from behind those curtains.

The curtains went from floor to ceiling, totally covering the doorway. And though it was cold outside, there was no hint a furnace filled the space inside with enough hot air to ruffle the material. The curtains were as motionless as a black wall.

Brian felt a prickle on the back of his neck, pressure against his bare cheeks, heat. It was as if something behind that curtain generated an enormous amount of power; something that made the air thrum like a plucked guitar string.

Kaylie's face screwed into a mask of annoyance. She looked at him, then looked at the storefront. "No, I'm not from around here, remember? Why?" Her tone made it plain that what she really meant was "You weren't even listening and you interrupted me for *that?*"

"I haven't either. Strange," he said, letting the coffee cup finally fall into the trashcan with a splash.

"What's so strange about that?" Kaylie asked, and Brian instantly knew that the date was over. "I mean, stores come and go all the time on these streets. Who gives a fuck?"

Brian, who'd been trying to catch the eye of the woman seated in the shop's doorway—as if her eyes might give him some clue as to what was going on behind those curtains—winced. Kaylie's carefully constructed veneer, applied as thickly as her make-up, had cracked. The rough Bronx accent—the one she'd probably spent years speaking in front of a mirror trying to bury—honked through with that single *fuck*.

Tearing his eyes away from the woman sitting in front of the mysterious store, he looked at Kaylie. "Sorry. Didn't mean to interrupt what you were saying. I was just curious about—"

"Whatever," she whispered, turning away from him, stepping back into the flow of people hustling in either direction on the sidewalk. "I think I'll just head home now, take the train. Thanks for a fun afternoon."

Brian narrowed his eyes in frustration, at Kaylie's sarcasm and at the shop. The first was just annoying; the second nagged at him like a sore tooth.

He shook his head, sighed, stepped toward her. "How about I walk you back to the train?" He held his hand out to her, but she looked at it as if he'd offered her a turd.

Instead, they walked silently back to the train station a few blocks away, where they said awkward goodbyes. She didn't ask him to call her and he didn't offer. She made her way down the steps, cursing silently.

As Brian watched her go, little pellets of snow began to fall, making whispery noises as they struck his coat collar. He took a deep breath, let it out in a grey cloud, turned to look back down the street. He couldn't see the green awning from here, but did see the Starbucks just a little ways past it.

Something about the strangeness of the shop, the fact that he'd never noticed it, bothered him. He didn't know quite why it should, and that bothered him, too.

Before he could rationalize it away, he set off back in that direction. As he walked, he knew he'd get a real cup of coffee, knew he'd try to engage the woman seated out front of the shop in a conversation, try to figure out what lay behind that propped open door, those dense, sepulchral drapes.

But she wasn't there when he got back.

* * *

The metal door was closed, and its glass, like the windows, was blacked out. Again, there was nothing on the door, no street number or business name.

Brian shrugged his way through the early evening crowd to stand under the awning. As he stepped beneath it, a curious thing happened. The streets were noisy. A mixture of sleet and snow was falling now, and it made a background white noise, like static, that lay under the crunch of car tires, the bleat of horns, the wail of distant sirens.

But stepping under the awning was like stepping into a rarified envelope of air. There was a smell to it, electrical, clean-smelling and full of ozone. It tingled against his face, pulled at his hair, even the hairs on his arms.

And the street sounds vanished. Not completely, but as if they were muffled, heard from a distance. Replaced with a hum so deep, so low in tone that he felt it more than actually heard it. It thrummed up through the soles of his shoes and made his teeth vibrate.

Looking around, he saw that no one passing on the street paid him any attention. So he pushed his face against the door glass, tried to find a spot where the paint had been scratched or rubbed away.

But there was nothing. He stepped back, looked around the small area covered by the awning. No intercom box or mail slot. Nothing. He took another step back. The tailor shop he noticed earlier was closed, but its address was clear in the window: 8315. The locksmith on the other side of the unknown space also clearly noted its address: 8313.

Brian frowned at that. On this side of the street, there shouldn't be anything between these businesses. The address 8314 should be across the street. This heightened the mystery for a moment, but he finally dismissed it. Street addresses in this part of the city were almost laughably haphazard as buildings were torn down, put up, subdivided and whatnot. For all he knew, this shop's address could be 8313A or 8315B.

Feeling a little foolish now—and understanding how his strange behavior had irritated Kaylie—he stepped back out onto the sidewalk, shaking his head. As he passed from underneath the awning, the street sounds returned, the smells of the city rushing at him and eliminating any vestige of the clean, quiet, almost purified air he'd breathed just a few seconds ago.

The crowd parted around him as if he'd been dropped midstream into it like a rock. A few people muttered curses under their breaths, reminding him of Kaylie. He thought, for a fleeting moment, thought of stepping back under the awning, but quickly dismissed it. It was getting late and darkness fell over the winter city early.

Giving the shop one last look, he stepped into the flow of pedestrians, walked the eight or so blocks back to his apartment.

* * *

The next morning, he wondered fleetingly as he brushed his teeth in his cramped bathroom if the shop would be there at all when he passed by on his way to the Starbucks.

If it would be there at all.

That seemed a curious way for him to put it, he thought, as he surveyed himself in the mirror. Shrugging at his reflection, he snapped the light off, grabbed his winter coat from the hook by the door, left for work.

Another *venti* latte and he shuffled through the dense line in the café and out again into the brisk, cold morning. The air seemed compressed and grey here in the canyons between the buildings. No sun to make the air crisp and invigorating. Everything felt cold and sodden, as if a murderer's hand pressed a rag of wet, grey wool over the city to smother it.

Yesterday's brief spray of ice was still crunchy underfoot, hadn't melted during the night. So the sidewalks had a deceptive slickness to them that made people walk a little more slowly, more carefully, especially over the ubiquitous metal grates and sidewalk doors.

Brian made his way as quickly as he could down the street. He saw the locksmith, and he felt a little disappointed that the shop next door was still closed, still dark, still lacking any sense of what it housed.

He paused briefly before it, took a sip from his coffee, then dismissed the notion already growing in his mind that he should step under the awing, take hold of the door handle and see if it would open. He knew it wouldn't.

Oh, well. Taking another swig of hot coffee, he made his way to the office and started his workday.

* * *

Brian made it to about 10:15 before he started searching for the missing address. His first stop was Google, inputting a variety of versions of the street address the shop might have had. Page after page of businesses scrolled by, but nothing looked promising.

Then Brian remembered Street View on Google Maps. He clicked over, looked around to make sure no one was peering into his cubicle, and input the address of the locksmith. The page came up, and Brian clicked on the little yellow person icon, dragged it to the map. A bright summer's day picture of the street flashed onto his screen, and Brian rotated the view with his mouse.

Frowning, he rotated it again, an entire 360 degrees.

There was the locksmith. There was the tailor.

But there was no store between them, just a blank stretch of wall: no door, no windows, no awning.

That couldn't be... Can't be.

He stared at the blank wall between the two buildings. Just a plain, battered city wall with graffiti and handbills of all kinds plastered over it.

Nothing unusual or out of place. He finally decided that, perhaps, this particular photo had been shot *before* the store had arrived.

Arrived?

That's a funny way to put it.

On a whim, he typed another search into his computer, picked up his desk phone as the information came up. He called, in quick succession, the chamber of commerce, the street department and the post office. Each time, there was a pause as he related his question, another pause as the person on the other end of the phone did some kind of search, then a cool, detached voice telling him that the given location didn't exist before hanging up on him.

Didn't exist?

That wasn't possible. It was there. He'd walked right past it, green awning and all.

His thoughts were interrupted by the phone ringing, which startled him. On the other end was Sandra, the ex-girlfriend who'd set him up with Kaylie, wondering what the hell he'd done to screw up the date so badly.

Brian listened to her for a moment, reached over and clicked to close the search window.

* * *

A few days went by, and Brian tried to forget about the oddness the shop represented. He walked by it several times each day, and it was always closed unlike it was the first time he'd seen it. But it was *there*—blacked-out windows, the green awning, the featureless door—right between the locksmith and the tailor.

* * *

The weather was getting colder as winter set in. On Tuesday a few weeks later, Brian was wrapped in his heaviest winter coat, a hat and a scarf topping this. He came out of the Starbucks, one hand holding his coffee, the other trying to re-wrap the scarf to protect the maximum amount of his neck and face.

The streets were crowded, a vast throng of black- and gray-clad people moving in clumps, head down to avoid the wind that swirled through the streets. Most of his view blocked by the scarf and the hat pulled low over his head, he merged into the crowd, let it carry him down the street.

As he passed the shop, he gave it the same cursory look he'd given it a dozen times before, expecting to see nothing. But the woman was back, seated atop her rickety director's chair, swaddled in her dingy, threadbare down jacket.

Brian slowed, stopped. A person walked into him, jostled his coffee, muttering as he walked away. Brian instinctively thrust the cup away from his body, so that if any sloshed out it wouldn't spill on him.

He wound up pointing directly at the seated woman.

And she moved her head, took notice of it...*of him*.

Brian felt a chill as her eyes fell on him. He was close enough to see they were colorless; not just grey but completely devoid of color. They seemed almost cataractic when the light struck them.

But it wasn't just the strangeness of her eyes. The simple act of her noticing him in the crowd sent some pulse—*of energy? electricity?*—through the air. Whatever it was penetrated the layers of Brian's clothing, found his spine and raced up it, making him shiver like a dog throwing off water.

When he'd composed himself, he stepped out of the flow of the crowd, walked to her. The woman didn't turn or move in any way, simply watched him come forward. Behind her, the door was open again, the black curtains still and impenetrable. Even though the wind was fierce this morning, even though the shop had to have had a furnace running, no breeze, hot or cold, stirred those dark drapes.

But now, closer, Brian could see a gap in the curtains, a small sliver of *something* that peeked through from behind. Squinting, he could see shelves that receded into the darkness. Empty shelves. A single fluorescent fixture winked through the gap in the curtains, and its light had a disturbing, oozy quality to it.

Brian paused before the seated woman, close enough to see her clearly. She had seemed strangely ageless from a distance, and now, close up, that perception was underscored. Her ash-colored hair was clean and vibrant, her face relatively unlined, but there was something about her that expressed age—*tremendous* age. Perhaps it was her curious, sallow eyes, the tilt of her chin, the way her hands sat palm flat on the tops of her legs, unmoving but seeming to writhe when Brian looked away from them.

The woman said nothing as he approached. But as Brian decided to step around her, to widen the gap in those curtains, to peer into what was beyond, one of her hands shot out, clutched Brian's left wrist and tightened until his bones creaked.

He stopped moving, his eyes widening at her unnatural strength.

"It's not for you." Her voice was smooth but deep, not exactly feminine. It sounded almost artificial, like something uncoiling within her dark, open mouth had made the sounds. After uttering the words, her mouth closed, lips compressed into a tight line.

Brian noticed there was no cloud of vapor, no hot breath that escaped from between those lips to be carried away on the cold wind.

She released her painfully tight grip on his wrist, and Brian pulled his hand back quickly, hid it under his right arm. Once released, she turned away as subtle as a dismissal, and her eyes lost the force of their focus on him.

Licking his dry lips, Brian cast one final glimpse back at the shop, at the scene unveiled by the curtains, then stepped away.

The woman ignored him, didn't seem to even see him.

Brian noticed he was shivering as if suffering from exposure. The cold was so great it felt like heat, heat pulsing between his skin and the clothing he wore. That heat centered on—radiated from—the circlet of pain around his wrist where the woman had grabbed him.

Feeling dizzy and nauseous, Brian turned back toward his apartment, went home, called in sick to work. He unpeeled his winter clothes, kicked off his shoes and practically fell into bed.

A greasy, slithery kind of sleep wrapped itself around him, pulled him down.

* * *

Brian didn't return to work after that. He never called in and quit, he simply never went back. He felt changed somehow, alien in his own body. He was wobbly when he walked, as if the bones in his legs had softened, becoming so malleable they weren't able to carry his weight.

While his legs were jellifying, his skull seemed to be expanding, thickening, hardening. It pounded day and night. Phosphenes played at the edges of his vision; bright, bursting bubbles of pain that ate deeper into his field of view every day. Conversely, his teeth jiggled in their sockets, threatening to tumble from his gums.

He spent hours standing before the mirror in his bathroom, searching his features in the cold, antiseptic light of the single fixture that spat its illumination onto the room from its perch over the mirror. His fingers explored his loose scalp, the curve of his skull back to the nape of his neck, the soft, pink foundation of his gums.

Each day without fail, despite his rubbery legs, his throbbing head, he dressed and walked to the shop. Since the day the woman had grabbed him, spoken to him, the place had remained shuttered as tightly as if holding its breath.

Brian no longer went to the Starbucks. He'd found a diner across the busy street, and now he took his coffee there, sat at a window seat and stared out. The shop's darkened windows seemed like a corpse's eyes, empty.

But the door, that single, ordinary door, blackened just as the windows were. That door radiated wrongness, a pulsing corruption that erased the street noise, filled the air with waves of heat.

He'd stood by it a few times since the woman had spoken to him.

It's not for you.

When he did, the pounding in his head receded, faded to a background hum that cycled in harmony with whatever energy was communicated through the door…lay *behind* that door.

And each time he grasped the door handle, slick and metal, pulled. But it was as tight in its frame as an impacted tooth, hot with infection.

Always he forced himself to leave, to return home, where he did little but sleep.

Even that was becoming a horror. He dreamt. He knew that, felt it, but couldn't remember anything of his dreams, other than they were powerfully disturbing. He could only recall images, disjointed, incomprehensible. Curled shapes slithered across his vision; dark, glittering appendages twisted and writhed, sheened with a wetness that was repellant and disturbing in its beauty.

These images meant nothing to him, but left him feeling as if a strange, alien sinuousness had taken up residence in his brain; was even now devouring the soft, pink hillocks of that organ, driving him slowly, inexorably mad.

It's not for you.

What had she meant by that?

He had to know.

* * *

Two more weeks went by. Brian had stopped answering the phone. The calls—from friends, family, his coworkers—meant little to him now. The last time he'd spoken to Sandra she had wanted to come over, demanded to know if he was on drugs, or off them.

But he ignored them all. None of it mattered. Nothing mattered except the strange store, the woman in the director's chair, the glimpse of something hidden behind those black-out curtains.

Brian had stopped bathing. He ate little, slept little. His clothes were rumpled, unclean. His beard had grown out and his hair poked from his head in spikes and curls, matted with grease and dirt.

Most days he sat in the diner across the street drinking bottomless cups of coffee, as he did today. He drank and drank and stared through the plate glass window—through the lines of pedestrians on both sides of the street, through the traffic—at the shop, closed as it generally was.

The diner staff mostly tolerated him. He was quiet, didn't disturb the other patrons, and he usually bought food throughout the day—a piece of pie here, a burger there—even if he didn't touch it.

There were a few complaints about the smell, the soft muttering, but it was the big city. If you can't put up with a little body odor and some crazy muttering, you need to move out to flyover country. At least that's how the diner's manager felt.

That day Brian huddled in a booth near the door, swaddled in his heaviest winter coat. He shivered each time the door opened, followed it with a mouthful of warm coffee. A piece of cherry cobbler sat before him, leaking a thin, red fluid like plasma onto the white plate. A fork rested amiably atop it, but hadn't cut into it yet.

It was early, just a bit after 6 a.m., and the morning crowd was just starting to come in. It was grey and dismal, still dawn-dark.

As the waitress refilled his cup with black coffee, there was movement across the street.

Brian froze.

He saw the door of the shop open. The woman in the tatty down coat pushed her chair through the curtains, set it forcefully just outside the area covered by the green awning. Satisfied, she sat, face forward with her hands flat atop her thighs.

She was looking right at him.

Brian let out an audible groan that attracted attention from the people around him. He sidled out of the booth, rushed to the door.

"Hey, buddy," called the manager. "You gotta pay for that stuff before you leave."

Brian, his hand on the door handle, fished into his pocket, pulled out a number of crumpled bills, tossed them behind him as he darted out. Straight across the street he barreled, pushing aside indignant people, squeezing between cars and taxis whose drivers blatted their horns, shouted imprecations at him.

On the other side of the street, he came to a panting halt before the woman. She said nothing, regarded him with the slightest of indifference.

Behind her, the black curtains parted, this time by a foot or more, and Brian saw motion there. A man—slender, perhaps 30ish, carrying a leather satchel, a topcoat covering a grey twill suit—was fighting, trying to push his way through the drapes, out of the place.

Others wrestled with him, restraining him, attempting to keep him inside the shop. They were short, clad in what looked to be blue denim uniforms of some kind, like coveralls. These figures weren't just short, Brian realized, they were little people.

But their faces...

Their faces were curiously flat, pushed in. Their skin was dark, swarthy, and their heads were covered with hoods. Their eyes were as black as anything Brian had ever seen, and they fumed with anger.

They looked *pissed.*

There were at least four or five of them, hands grappling at the man's legs, his arms, trying to bring him back, keep him from fleeing. Brian caught a glimpse of the man's face. He was wide-eyed with panic. His mouth moved around inchoate words.

And behind him, behind the man and his strange captors, there was something else.

Gone was the vast stretch of empty shelves Brian had seen the last time, replaced by a clot of swirling fog the color of bruises—deep violets, bursts of yellow, blues and dark greens. This miasma roiled upon itself, spun like a mandala, folded and spiraled and spat, reached out tendrils toward the struggling man. And though these wisps had no features, they communicated avidity more clearly than anything Brian had ever seen.

Brian could feel the thing's power on his exposed skin; more than power, though. It bled a potent sense of wrong across his senses, as if it were a violation of reality itself. He knew that whatever it was, it was the force he'd sensed when he'd stepped under that awning.

Suddenly, the little uniformed men overwhelmed the man, dragged him down. A pair of small hands grasped the drapes on either side, yanked them closed.

When they met, it was like something, some geas had released Brian.

He sagged against the woman's chair, breathed heavily.

He remained there for a second or two, until he felt her hand gently pat his own, clenched around the chair's armrest.

Turning, he looked into her young, curiously aged face.

She smiled. "It's not for you...*yet.*"

He pulled himself from her, a trail of spittle dribbling from his mouth, spattering his coat, dripping to the ground.

"Who are you?" he breathed, absently wiping his mouth against the sleeve of his coat. "What is this place?"

The woman's smile grew wider, deeper, and Brian saw teeth there. Rows and rows of teeth that faded in perspective down the black gullet of her open mouth, like the empty shelves he'd seen behind the curtain. They weren't long or sharp. There were just so many of them, row upon row; a vast army of teeth.

"You noticed it. You shouldn't have. Because in noticing it, it noticed you," she said, a little primly. "Now it *knows* you. Now it *wants* you."

"What?" Brian whispered.

"Everything must go, eventually," she said, cackling just a little. "But not you, not yet. Check back later."

Brian pushed away, stepped back to the trashcan that, weeks before, had received the mostly full cup of coffee he'd dropped into it. Somehow, feeling this substantial thing, this real thing under his hands, brought him back a little.

He looked at the woman whose smile had disappeared, subsumed into her laconic trance, ran down the street and back to his apartment, bolted the door behind him.

But he didn't go to bed this time. He peeled off his coat, sat on the couch.

Now it knows you. Now it wants you.

Not yet.

If not yet, then when, he thought.

Then when?

Rising, Brian went to the small desk under the bedroom window, took out a pen and some paper.

.   * * *

Brian waited a day or so. He awoke early on a bright, clear morning where the sun spilled across the tall glass buildings and dribbled to the streets like golden syrup. He showered and shaved, dressed quickly in his best clothes.

Down the elevator, out onto the street, he strode briskly and people parted before him. Within minutes, he stood in front of the shop.

She was there, seated on her chair as he knew she would be. She smiled enigmatically at him. Brian walked past her toward the open door, confident, no hesitation at all.

As he approached, several small sets of hands drew the curtains fully aside.

Before him was the swirling mass of indigo smoke, already sending arms out toward him, beckoning him.

The woman's voice called out behind him. "It's for you today."

Brian stepped forward.

The curtains closed behind him.

* * *

Sandra stopped on the street, pursed her lips. There, just as Brian had said in his letter, was the tailor, the locksmith. Reaching into her purse, she extracted the envelope, removed the single sheet of paper. She scanned the few lines of the letter, looked back up at the storefronts.

Brian had said there was a shop here, some kind of strange place that he'd noticed months ago, that he'd been staking out, studying for weeks. It was right between the tailor and the locksmith, a small, nondescript space. He described a green awning, devoid of name or address, arched over the single door, which was, like the windows on either side, blacked out.

But there was nothing here.

A flat, plain expanse of brick wall, perhaps a dozen feet or so in length, stretched between the two stores that were there. Nothing lay between them except this wall.

Sandra refolded the letter, slid it back into its envelope, back into her purse.

When her phone calls were never returned, she sent the police around. But they didn't find him. So, she used the key to his apartment he'd given her during their abortive period of dating, before they became friends instead of lovers. He'd forgotten he'd given it to her and she'd never returned it.

She had found the letter addressed to her on his small kitchen table. Everything else in his apartment was untouched. His wallet lay on the nightstand near his bed. His clothes were all in his closets. Food rotted in the fridge, a stack of mail spilled off the counter and onto the floor. A pile of filthy clothes, a dirty winter coat lay in a ball on his bathroom floor, discarded.

Sandra had taken the letter, opened it and read it sitting on his couch.

The letter told her that he'd seen this shop that no one else seemed to see. A woman sometimes sat on a chair outside it. No one seemed to know about it except him. It didn't have an address. It nagged at him, became an obsession. Once, he'd seen a man trying to escape from inside before being wrestled to the floor by overall-wearing midgets.

Then there was the swirling purple cloud.

She wondered what had happened to Brian, where he'd gone. How could someone go nuts in such a short period of time? How could she not have seen it?

Now, standing on the street where he'd apparently seen a phantom shop, she wasn't sure what to do. Call the police, she supposed, let them do their job. Hopefully, they'd find him somewhere, get him the help, the medicine he obviously needed.

Sandra looked around the street. She'd come down here hoping to find him, hoping that he'd still be down here keeping watch on his apparition.

What had he meant, in the letter?

I think it's finally for me.

She decided to grab a cup of coffee and clear her head before she called the police. She walked to the coffee shop, went inside. The morning crowd had already been through, and she was served quickly.

She took her small cup of coffee outside, hesitated. Perhaps one more loop of the block to ensure that Brian wasn't there, huddled in some dark alleyway needing her help.

She walked back slowly, her eyes searching everywhere, inside every store, every restaurant, scanning every face as it approached her. Finishing her coffee, she found a trashcan, went to it, threw her cup inside.

Turning, she saw a woman seated in a director's chair outside an open door between the tailor shop and the locksmith.

Underneath the green awning, the black drapes were tightly closed.

PURPLE SODA HAND

PURPLE.

The liquid in the glass bottle was swirling purple, deep and indigo, turning dark black near the bottom. Tony had found it in the weed-choked culvert that nuzzled the side of the street he'd pedaled his bike down that summer afternoon.

It was obviously a soda bottle of some sort, looked to be about a liter or so. Tightly sealed with an unbroken aluminum twist-off cap. Whole, uncracked glass. Strange in this land of plastic this and that. No torn label or scuffed imprint either. No logo on top of the cap, no little bar of computer printing with a UPC code or the ubiquitous BEST BY date.

Nothing to show where it had come from, what it was, how it came to nestle amidst the weeds and direct-mail flyers and the single, discolored Converse sneaker that swaddled it almost protectively.

Tony hefted the bottle, jiggled it in front of the blazing afternoon sun. The purple fluid inside moved and frothed like soda, seemed to have the body and thinness of that liquid. But it was so dark. So opaquely, mysteriously violet like the unknown medium within those Magic 8-ball toys.

It looked like a soda bottle, too. It had the same curves, the same wide base tapering to a thin neck. The same kind of screw-off cap a soda bottle had.

Tony tilted it back and forth, the sun eclipsed by the dark liquid, rising from it.

What the heck was it?

He stood there contemplating it, a thirteen-year-old Hamlet addressing a purple, liquid Yorick.

Yes, he contemplated drinking it.

Here's the thing. Well, actually two things.

First, Tony was hot. *Very* hot. And sweaty.

He'd been riding his bike all morning, through his neighborhood, through the park, up to the little strip mall with the used bookstore, the Vietnamese nail salon his mom went to, the discount smoke store where his dad got cigarettes—and the occasional cigar, though thoroughly disapproved of by him and his mom—and the deli where Tony spent the lunch money his mom had given him that morning.

Second, and let's be polite here, Tony was chunky.

At thirteen years of age—his birthday had been just two weeks earlier—Tony was a big boy. He already stood about five-foot-ten, and weighed in at close to 200 pounds. He enjoyed playing sports, and that alone probably kept his weight under 200. High school football coaches were already eyeing him with great interest, but his first love was basketball. His team, the Golden State Warriors; his player, of course, Steph Curry.

But here he was, standing near his bike, holding this sealed bottle of purple soda, hot from riding on this sweltering St. Louis day, nowhere near anywhere he could stop and get a drink, and with only a measly thirteen cents in the pocket of his Nike shorts left from his lunch money—he'd splurged and bought the extra meat on his Italian sub at the deli.

Simply put, Tony was thirsty.

He looked around, up and down the street. No houses nearby, no one out who might see him. The culvert along this side of the little-used road snaked down to a thin stream of dubious origins. The creek wriggled along the boundaries of an easement near the back of his neighborhood. It skirted a wide, flat plain where the power lines ran from one Eiffel-shaped tower to another, receding into the distance like an art school forced-perspective exercise.

Tony eyed the bottle, licked his dry lips. He felt sweat trickle from his armpits, drip down his chest and back, soaking the waistband of both his shorts and his underwear.

He shrugged his forearm over the front of his face, the plain white T-shirt he wore under his Steph Curry #30 jersey soaking in most of the sweat, at least for the moment.

Telling himself he'd just take a whiff once he got it open, Tony twisted the cap.

It split with that familiar tiny, metal rasping sound, and the liquid inside hissed as the air rushed in.

Tony pulled the cap away, lifted the bottle to his nose.

He could hear the faint, staticky fizz, and as he brought the bottle close, its aroma hit him, forcefully.

Sugary, an almost overpowering grape scent, muscular and unsubtle on the hot summer air. It smelled of grape juice and cotton candy and Skittles and lemons.

Tony's mouth watered as the smell permeated his brain, the little glands in the corners of his cheeks puckering, almost stinging as they prepared for this liquid to flood over them.

It looked like grape soda, smelled like grape soda.

What harm could there be in taking a small sip?

It's in a bottle that was sealed.

And he was hot, so hot.

He lifted it to his lips.

Lukewarm liquid poured past his teeth, over his tongue, saturating those stinging glands. Tony almost had to take a breath at the punch of its flavor.

It was wholly unlike anything he'd ever tasted.

It had hints of grapeness, to be sure, but not artificial or chemically at all. It tasted of the essential essence of grape, something that nothing came close to, at least for him, except for actual grape juice.

It tastes like grape juice times a thousand!

It also tasted like the sweetest candy ever, of sunshine and citrus and some kind of delicious earthiness he couldn't quite place. The flavor exploded in his mouth, and Tony found himself almost swooning from it

He realized, after a second, that he had actually planted his feet to steady himself.

That he'd closed his eyes as he drank.

And that he'd taken at least four or five good swigs of the soda already.

It also came to him that he was standing on the side of the road, drinking from an unlabeled bottle that he'd found in a ditch.

His mother would knock him upside the head if she learned of this.

What on Earth is wrong with you that you'd do something stupid like that?

That realization made him open his eyes.

What made him stop drinking, though, what made his throat close, was not his mother's voice in his head, but the hand.

There, floating in the remaining purple ichor in the bottle, small and disembodied, was a hand.

* * *

Tony stood there, stunned, fixed as if the bottle he held up to the blazing sun were a spike skewering him in place.

The hand floated in the ethereal liquid, pale, tiny fingers flexed, severed at the wrist. The violet soda accentuated every whirl of skin on the five digits, every wrinkle across its palm, every knurl of flesh encircling each knuckle.

It was small, but it was definitely *not* a baby's hand. It wasn't as chubby or stunted as that. It was fully formed, fully in proportion.

Tony immediately thought it must be a joke, a gag. Perhaps that's why it was discarded, left where it was as a trick on whatever poor slob found it.

The hand inside was probably from an action figure or a doll.

But...

It seemed a bit too large for that. And as the appendage swirled in the liquid—which in a moment he would realize was still trickling into his mouth—he saw the stump of its wrist. Saw the purple-stained meat, the whitish glare of bone within that severed disc of flesh.

Convulsively, his lips pushed away from the neck of the bottle, and he sprayed what was still in his mouth out into the air in a purple mist.

More of the liquid sloshed out, and the tiny hand spun crazily inside the bottle, its upraised fingers slightly cupped in a way that made Tony think of the Queen of England's hand as she waved impassively to the crowds.

Some of it dribbled down to soak into the bright white of his basketball jersey, and he absently brushed at it, hoping it wouldn't stain.

To prevent any more liquid from spilling, he slapped the cap back onto the bottle, twisted it fiercely, tightly shut.

All the more so, he thought, to keep that hand in, too.

Then, it dawned on him that he had swallowed gulp after gulp of the very same stuff in which the little hand twirled.

The severed appendage had steeped for who knew how long in that soda.

What he'd drank had bathed that severed wrist, that nub of white bone, that disc of exposed meat.

Suddenly the delicious soda pooling in his stomach seemed to curdle, threatened to climb back up his throat and spatter onto the hot asphalt. But bending over a bit at the waist, somehow he was able to keep it in.

When the last waves of nausea finally subsided, Tony was able to stand again, wipe more sweat—this not wholly from the sun—from his forehead.

He contemplated the now quarter-empty bottle, thought about tossing it back in the culvert. Instead, he slid it gently into the deep right pocket of his basketball shorts, climbed gingerly onto his bike, pedaled quickly back home.

With each thrust of his leg, he felt the bottle bump against his thigh, reminding him that it was there.

Reminding him that he really, really wanted another drink.

Needed another drink.

* * *

The bottle was full again by the time he got home.

Tony skidded his bike to a stop outside the garage, leaned it against the brick wall. It was still a little early for either his mother or father to return from their respective jobs, so he let himself in with his key, bumped the front door closed with his hip as he raced inside and into his bedroom.

He closed the door there, too, jolted to a halt near the desk that fronted his bedroom window. Carefully, he slid the soda bottle from his pants and set it atop the cluttered desk.

His room was silent, only the distant *whoosh* of the air conditioner, the flutter of the curtains. He stood staring at the bottle as if it were not the very same one he'd jammed into his pocket just minutes ago.

He frowned, reached out, testing it to see if it had lost any of its solidity or realness on his pell-mell ride home.

It hadn't, of course.

How could it be filled with soda again?

He knew he'd drank at least a quarter of it. Knew it, could still taste the electric grapeness of it on his tongue, in the puckered glands inside his cheeks.

Then how…?

Tentatively, he gave the bottle a little jiggle.

The purple soda swirled and eddied inside, and as it did, the pale palm of the tiny hand was exposed, careening inside like a leaf caught in a tornado.

Tony took a step away from it, fell back onto his unmade bed.

He stared up at the posters of Lebron, of James Harden, of his man Steph.

There was only one thing to do in a situation like this.

Tony called his best friend, Mike.

* * *

His parents did not think Tony was old enough for a phone just yet, something that proved a continual source of irritation for him. Many of his friends had their own phones. Maybe not iPhones, but phones.

Mike had an old flip phone, passed to him from his father. He couldn't surf the net with it, but he could call and text. Tony, on the other hand, was reduced to either using the cordless in the kitchen or an older, corded phone that his dad had finally agreed to put in his bedroom as a way to placate his suddenly teenage son.

Tony looked over at the digital clock near his bed, twirled the kinked cord of the phone. His parents would be home in less than an hour, and Mike's phone rang and rang.

Just as he thought Mike's message would play, there was a clatter, a spray of noise on the line.

"Hey, what's up, man? Where you at?"

"I'm home. Where're you?" Tony asked.

"Up at the b-ball courts at the park. Come on down and shoot some with me, why don'tchya?" Mike huffed.

"Nah, man. You got to come to my place. Now. I found something weird… Seriously weird."

"Like what?"

"It's just… You gotta come here. Now."

There was silence for a second. "Okay, on my way. Give me a few."

* * *

Tony yanked the door open, grabbed Mike's arm and pulled him inside the house.

"Come on, man."

"Crap, bro, give me a minute, I freakin' raced over here," Mike said, stumbling inside, sweat pouring off him. "I'm dying, man. You got something to drink?"

"Shit, yeah," Tony said, pulling him along. "Come on!"

He led Mike down the hallway festooned on both sides with family pictures that never seemed to hang straight, jerked him into his bedroom, slammed the door.

"Yo, man. Easy, easy," Mike said. "What's up your ass, anyway?"

"This," Tony said, pointing to the bottle of soda on his desk.

Mike nodded. "Great! I'm parched."

He pushed past Tony, grabbed the bottle, lifted it.

As he twisted the cap, Tony said, "Better take a look at that stuff before you take a drink."

Mike already heard the refreshing hiss of the soda, already started lifting it to his lips. He turned, the bottle partially raised, and looked at his friend.

"Huh?" Mike lowered the bottle slowly, peered at it.

"Give it a little shake."

Mike did so, and the purple liquid fizzed obligingly.

There, within those violet currents, the pale hand tumbled and twisted.

"What the f—" Mike said, pushing the bottle as far away as his arms would reach.

"Shhh," Tony said. "My parents'll be home soon."

His mother and father didn't much like Mike anyway, and they were not fans of cussing.

"What the hell, man? What kind of joke is that?" Mike said, thunking the open bottle back onto the desk.

"No joke. I found it like that on the side of the road down near the power lines."

Mike eyed the bottle warily, turned to his friend.

"You found a bottle of soda with a tiny hand it?"

"Yep. And it was factory sealed, man."

Mike took that in, then his eyes narrowed.

"Why'd you open— Aww, man, did you actually *drink* some of it?"

"Well…I mean…shit, man, it was sealed!"

Mike looked incredulously at his friend.

"Let me get this straight. You find a bottle of something on the side of the road with a hand in it, and you take a drink? That's messed up, dude. Seriously."

"I didn't know the hand was in at first," Tony argued.

"Hand don't matter, bro," Mike shot back. "Why you drinking from a nasty bottle you find in a ditch?"

Tony hesitated, sat down on the edge of his bed.

"It's fuckin' delicious, man. I mean, I've never tasted anything like it."

Mike looked unconvinced. "So? Who knows what it is? Bong water. Crack juice. Meth-a-lade. How you know?"

Tony shrugged. "Take a drink and see."

Mike looked at the unsealed bottle on the desk, looked back to his friend.

"I ain't drinking outta that. Who knows what diseased crackhead drooled into it? And what about that fuckin' tiny hand?"

Tony prepared to answer, then heard the front door open and close.

"Anthony?" his mother called. "You home?"

Tony flashed a look at Mike, who turned to the desk and gingerly recapped the bottle.

"In my room, Mom."

"Okay, I'm starting dinner in a few." A pause. "I see by the bike outside that Michael's here."

"Yeah, Mom."

"He staying for dinner?"

Tony turned back to Mike, who shrugged in return.

"I guess so, if that's okay."

Tony's mother didn't answer.

* * *

After a rushed dinner with his parents, Tony and Mike returned to his bedroom. Atop the desk, just as they left it, was the bottle of purple soda.

Even from across the room, they could see the pallid hand, resting near the bottom like some tiny deep-sea creature.

Tony closed his door, sealing off the sounds of the evening news from the living room. Mike went to kneel by the desk, examining the bottle without touching it.

Full and a little tired, Tony collapsed on his bed. He lay on his stomach, his head at the foot of the bed, watching Mike.

His friend moved the bottle, turned it here and there, jiggled it a little. He studied the foam this produced, watched the tiny hand swirl and spin within its lavender depths.

"And you drank some of this sh—stuff?" he corrected himself. "You actually drank from it?"

"Yep. I told you."

"But the bottle's full. You can't have drank much."

"I drank about a quarter of the bottle. I'm telling you, by the time I got home, the bottle was full again."

"Bullshit!" Mike snapped, then clapped a hand over his mouth.

Both boys waited to see if Tony's mom had heard this exclamation, but no loud voices came from outside the bedroom.

"What's it taste like?"

"The best grape soda you ever tasted," Tony said, sighing in contentment. "I've never had anything like it."

"Could you taste...*it?*"

"The hand? Nah. I mean, I dunno. What's a tiny hand taste like?"

Mike didn't respond, as there seemed to be no real answer to the question.

"Why don't *you* taste it?"

Mike, still kneeling, swiveled his head to where Tony lay.

"You kidding? That's effed up, man. I ain't drinking none of that. You don't know what it is, where it came from."

"Take a whiff of it. You'll change your mind."

"I doubt it."

Mike turned back to the bottle. The liquid inside had settled, and the hand spun lazily near the murky bottom.

"Whatevs. Hey, you wanna spend the night? We could stay up late. Dad just got NBA 2K18 for the PlayStation. Long as we keep it down, they won't care how late we play."

Mike stared hard into the soda. Tony wondered what he was thinking. If he was considering taking a swig from it.

"Sure, okay," he finally said, standing. "I'll have to go home, grab some clothes, tell my dad."

Tony nodded, and Mike gave the bottle one long, last look, then left the bedroom, closing the door behind him. Tony heard him tell his mom and dad goodbye, thanking them for the meal, telling them he'd be back.

Tony could hear the thin veneer of disapproval on his mother's voice even through his closed bedroom door.

For a while, he lay there looking at the bottle, too. He remembered how hot it had been outside, how parched he'd felt. And how good that lukewarm grape soda had tasted, how it had electrified his body.

And then, the hand that floated inside it.

As he thought of this, he stared at the bottle.

The tiny hand inside had come to a rest, its wrist against the thick glass bottom of the bottle, its palm splayed out flat against the inner wall, fingers spread.

Stop!

* * *

Two a.m.

Mike sprawled over the couch in the living room, his head on one armrest, his huge, sock-clad feet propped on the coffee table in defiance of all of Tony's mother's rules.

Tony lay on the floor, his own socks pointed toward the 60-inch television on which computer-generated NBA players ran and twisted and shot. Even though the volume was turned way down, the roar of the animated crowd buzzed through the darkened house.

They'd been playing since about 10:00 p.m., when Tony's parents had retired to their bedroom. His mother admonished them not to stay up too late, not to make too much noise and not to eat them out of house and home. She'd ruffled Tony's hair as she passed him on the way to her bedroom, her nails tickling over the fade she'd only just allowed him to get. Mike's head was shaved, something Tony had wanted to get, too, but Tony's mother was not Mike's father, as she reminded him. The fade was as far as she was willing to go.

On the screen, Harden, his beard magnificently rendered, thundered toward the basket and laid it up. The ball dropped through the net, a buzzer went off, photo flashes popped in the stands.

Tony yawned, dropped his controller onto the floor.

"Man, I gotta take a piss," he said.

"Tony!" Mike whispered, mock-horrified.

"Sorry. I gotta go wee-wee," he said, standing, stretching, then padding toward the bathroom. But he made a quick detour into his own room, opening the door quietly, closing it behind him. He listened for a second to make sure that Mike hadn't followed him.

When he was sure, he crept to the window. The room was mostly dark, only the small desktop lamp was on. Near it sat the soda bottle, a cylinder of compressed, liquid twilight.

It was full again.

Tony's thoughts were no longer troubled by the mystery of this. He'd been in his room like this three times tonight, each time sneaking in on his way to the bathroom or to change into his bedclothes.

Each time, he tiptoed to his desk, unsealed the bottle and drained the purple soda down to a level where the tiny pale fingertips jutted from the liquid.

Each time, he let the grape soda fizz into him, scouring his throat. As it pooled in his stomach, he shuddered in something approaching ecstasy.

And each time, he sealed the bottle, left the room as quietly as he'd come.

This time was no different. He drained the soda, quivering like a dog shaking off water, recapped the bottle and went to the bathroom.

What he didn't know—didn't even consider as he lifted the toilet lid to empty his bladder in anticipation of all the purple soda he intended to drink tonight while everyone slept—was that Mike had been doing the very same thing.

* * *

The boys collapsed in Tony's room at about 3:00 a.m.

Tony feigned sleep until he heard Mike's rhythmic breathing, then he slid from his bed, drank from the bottle until he was sure he felt the tiny fingertips tickling his lips.

Or maybe it was just the fizz from the soda.

* * *

Twenty minutes later, as Tony lay deeply asleep, Mike rose. Looking furtively at his sleeping friend, he raised the bottle, gulped down the liquid inside. He tried hard, vainly at first, to keep his moaning quiet.

Oh, god, but it's soooo good.

* * *

Purple bled into their dreams.

* * *

Mike dreamt of his mom, who'd left a few years back, headed out to the coast. Though Mike's dad hadn't told him this, Mike knew she'd left with her boyfriend.

Didn't much matter. They weren't married, and Mike's dad had other girlfriends, too. Wasn't much of a change in his living arrangements, either. Mike's dad simply moved more of his stuff into the empty space left by his mother's departure.

Though his mother had her problems, though she may not have been the best or most attentive mother ever, she was his mom. And he missed her.

Oh, he missed her quite a bit.

In his dream, Mike awoke in his own room, in his own bed. A hazy, violet glow came through the crooked, broken plastic blinds. The multi-colored Christmas lights he'd framed his window with blinked crazily. On his stereo, Kendrick was telling someone to sit down, sit down over a thumping bass and minor piano keys.

But from somewhere else in the apartment, outside his room, there was different music, another voice, softer, insistent.

Mom!

Mike went to throw his feet off the side of the bed, dash out of the room and find her, even though he was still mad at her for leaving, still mad at her for abandoning them. *Him.*

But he couldn't move, couldn't operate his muscles. He was frozen to the bed, stuck with his head on the pillow, his arms by his sides. He looked around wildly, at least as much as he could with his neck immobile.

There, on the cluttered stand that held his television and game consoles, was the soda bottle from Tony's room.

How did it...?

Its purple light filled the room, gave everything an eerie, otherworldly indigo sheen. He could even *taste* the light on his tongue, at the back of his throat—like ripe, ripe plums and Starburst candies and something sharp and acidic that made his mouth pucker.

The sound of his mother's singing slowly grew closer. She used to wake him for school in the morning by coming in and opening the blinds. She'd sing while she did this, songs by Lena Horne or Etta or even Whitney. Sometimes she'd even remember to make him breakfast or—rarely—fix his lunch.

He heard the doorknob to his room click, turn. Footsteps soft on the carpet.

A shadow in the purple light fell across his bed.

At last.

A figure hovered over him, bent toward him.

He couldn't make out her face, but recognized the shape of her shadow, the cut of her hair.

Mom!

It bent to him, stopped singing.

He could smell her shampoo, her perfume, the Juicy Fruit gum she chewed, sweet on her breath. Almost *too* sweet.

"Hi, honey," she drawled. His mom had been born in Vicksburg, and some of that Southern accent still hung at the edges of her speech. His father had told him that twang, as he put it, was what had first drawn him to her.

"'Bout time to get up from bed, ain't it?"

She pulled away, spun toward his window, yanked the blinds up a bit too forcefully. The cheap, plastic things snapped, fell away from the window, exposing the sky outside.

A nightmare tableau of roiling purple clouds, twisting and folding in on themselves. Vivid streaks of bright, violet lightning jagged across the sky like cracks in the firmament.

Things flew within those clouds. Strange, many-legged things with gossamer wings that shimmered. Things with drooping limbs and distended bellies, with snaky arms covered in bristles.

And mouths.

Open mouths with rows of teeth and articulated purple tongues that weaved imprecations on the soda-colored air.

Mike's mother spun back to him, hunched over now. She crept up the bed, over him, until her face hung above his, so close he could smell her breath.

It smelled of the purple soda, thick and sweet and cloying.

"Well past time to get up, ain't it, sweetie?"

She came in close, he thought to kiss him, and Mike tried to turn his head away.

But she didn't want to kiss him.

As her lips met his, her eyes snapped open, and it was like two sets of shades rolling up. Behind those shades, as if they were covering mere holes in her head, were the same roiling, violet clouds he'd seen outside his window.

Then, purple soda came gushing from her mouth. The impact of it forced his lips open, and the soda sprayed against his face, glurted down his throat.

It was more than he could take, more than he could swallow. And it showed no signs of stopping or even diminishing.

He couldn't breathe, and still the liquid poured into him, soaked his hair, the bedsheets.

Mike couldn't move, couldn't draw in any air, couldn't stop the soda from flowing into him.

As his vision squeezed from purple to black at the sides, he could see the soda bottle sitting atop the shelf. It glowed with the same crazy, lavender light that oozed from the clouds outside.

And the tiny hand?

It was pressed flat against the glass of its container, palm forward, three fingers and a thumb crossed, one finger raised high toward him.

Flipping him the bird.

His vision fading, he couldn't make out much more than the shape of his mom's head pressed against his.

Somehow, as she regurgitated more soda into him, he could hear her still singing.

Aaaat laaaaaast…

* * *

Tony dreamt of being on his bike, gliding down smooth roads, around gently banked turns. No cars to threaten him, no hills to wear him out. The air was smooth and cool as it brushed by him.

And overhead, a coruscating amethyst sun that pulsed in the sky like a beating heart.

That great, grape sun gave everything a purple cast, like looking at the world through violet sunglasses. The grass, the road, the trees, his own hands on the chrome handlebars. All purplish.

But he paid little attention to this. He just rode and rode.

It was exhilarating, the freedom of riding, of cutting through the silk of the air with no destination in mind, no schedule, nothing to really do or see.

All that was interrupted by color, something alien in this purple-shaded landscape.

Blue. And red.

Tony's heart gave one great, tremendous beat, and then froze.

The cops.

Here?

But he didn't hesitate. He did exactly what his parents had taught him.

He pulled the bike over to the side of the road, dismounted and stood in front of it with his hands splayed wide, empty and visible.

And he waited.

A car came over the last rise, and Tony blinked.

The car was entirely purple, from its slick lavender paint to its dark, indigo windows.

Lights spun atop it, blue and red, the only things other-colored in this strange dream.

The cruiser came to a lurching halt just behind the bike, sat idling for a full minute before the driver's door cracked open.

Out stepped the strangest police officer Tony had ever seen.

His uniform was entirely purple, from head to toe. The material was of the same color as the car, and his boots and belt and gloves were of a slick, shinier violet. He had a gun strapped to his hip, and his face was entirely covered by, of all things, a mirror-visored motorcycle helmet.

He crunched the gravel between his car and Tony, stopped a footstep from him.

"You know why I pulled you over, son?" he asked, in a voice not unlike The Rock's.

It was all so ridiculous, so outlandish that Tony wanted to laugh. But so deeply ingrained in him were his parents' warnings that, even in an absurd dream like this, he didn't dare shake them.

"No, sir."

The cop's mirrored face reflected Tony's own back at him, funhouse-fat and grape-colored, like Violet Beauregarde's from that old Willie Wonka movie.

He made a sound beneath the helmet, as if he were *tsking* Tony's answer.

Tony watched, eyes widening as one of the cop's hands fell causally to the butt of his holstered gun.

"You took something, kid. Something that didn't belong to you."

Tony began to panic. His fingers clenched the cold metal frame of his bike. His legs felt weak.

Took something? Took what? He hadn't taken anything from…

As he looked around, he noticed that where they now stood was a purple approximation of the road along the perimeter of the power field. The culvert that snaked along behind him was where he'd found it earlier today.

The purple soda bottle.

Tony snapped his attention back to the officer.

"He says he left it here, but it isn't here anymore," the cop said, nodding his head to indicate someone behind him.

Confused, Tony looked back at the cruiser.

It seemed as if, just for a moment, the reflective shine of the windshield cleared, revealing…someone sitting in the cruiser's backseat, behind a metal grid.

Tony couldn't make out many details, but it appeared to be a man, nondescript, no features visible.

As Tony stared at him, the man raised a hand and waved familiarly. *But it was just a wrist. The man's hand was gone. Missing...*

Tony's legs wobbled beneath him, and he stumbled into his bike.

"Hey!" the cop warned, stepping back, drawing his gun from its holster. Tony watched as he fell to the ground in a tangle with the bike.

"No!" Tony shouted, but it hardly mattered.

The purple cop took another step back, raised the weapon with one hand, steadying it with the other.

"No, please!"

"Return it, and we'll call it even," the cop shouted, then pulled the trigger.

Tony braced his dream self to receive the weapon's rounds, but instead from the barrel came a stream of purple liquid that fizzed as it struck his face, his chest.

He wanted to laugh then, but realized the cop wasn't laughing. That it might be a bad idea.

So he lay there in that ditch, sprawled atop his bike, and let the purple cop soak him with grape soda.

It went on for quite a while, the handless man waving at him the entire time.

* * *

When Tony awoke, light filtered through the drawn curtains of his room. Even with the AC on, that shaft of weak light falling onto the foot of his bed warmed his socks enough that he shuffled his feet together to peel them off, kick them from the bed.

He lay there, still sleep muggy, thinking that he'd get up, take a quick leak, then come back in, drink some more of the purple soda without waking Mike. Then he'd go in and start the day right. Big bowl of Cinnamon Toast Crunch, glass of OJ, another game or two on the PS4. Then out for some biking. Maybe a pick-up game with Mike.

As he considered all this, part of last night's dream came to him, and he opened his eyes, sat bolt upright in bed.

The soda bottle, which had been sitting atop the desk by his window, was gone.

So was Mike.

Tony looked around the room. There was no sign of his friend. It wasn't unusual for Mike to rise earlier than him when they stayed over at each other's house. It wasn't unusual for Mike to even wake up here and go home without waking Tony.

But something about the dream last night. Something about the bottle being gone worried Tony.

He suddenly felt the overwhelming need to put that bottle back exactly where he'd found it yesterday.

Peeling off his pajamas, he slid on shorts and his Steph Curry jersey, stepped into his shoes, dashed out of his bedroom.

The house was quiet and empty, his parents having both gone to work.

Had his mother come in and found the bottle, wondered why he'd have a bottle of soda in his room? Might she have put it into the fridge?

Nope. He knew before he even opened the door. The refrigerator held a couple bottles of Faygo Orange, even one of Grape, but no unlabeled bottle of purple soda with a tiny hand floating inside.

Mike.

Tony grabbed his keys off the kitchen table, ran from the house without even checking to see if he'd locked the door behind him.

* * *

After twenty minutes of riding, he found Mike shooting hoops at the basketball court in the park. It was only around nine in the morning, but it was already hot, more than ninety degrees. And humid as only a St. Louis summer can be.

Tony was drenched in sweat by the time he saw him shooting lay-ups on the court. The rest of the park looked empty, with that drowsy, early morning summer haze hanging in the air, the buzz of insects droning over everything like white noise.

He'd been to Mike's apartment—no one home—the 7-Eleven they sometimes hung at, the GameStop at the little strip mall where he'd bought his lunch yesterday before finding it: the purple soda bottle.

As he crested the hill and saw Mike's tiny figure running back and forth, tossing the ball, catching rebounds, he thought he also saw it sitting there next to his backpack, a small, dark bottle.

Why'd he take it?

Had he... Had he secretly drank from it last night?

If he did, then he knew. He knew about its sublime taste, the way it made his cheeks sink in at its sour grape electricity.

The way it called out to him to drink more and more.

The way it even played on his dreams, called out to him even there.

Tony paused atop his pedals, shivered in the heat at that last thought.

That purple cop in his purple car. The purple gun firing at him.

Tony shook his head, mashed the pedals, careened down the hill into the park.

* * *

Mike looked at him nonchalantly as he rode onto the court. His best friend was crouched at the free throw line directly before the basket, sizing up his shot.

Tony skidded the bike to rest, stepped off as he laid it onto the asphalt.

"Whatchya up to?" Mike asked, putting the ball over his head with both hands, pushing it away with one. The beat-up old orange Spalding arced overhead, lined up perfectly with the rusted, chain link net of the basket, swished in.

Mike trotted over to retrieve it.

Tony noted all this only peripherally.

Because there in the overgrown grass at the edge of the court, laying atop Mike's brown backpack, was the bottle of soda. It glowed with an almost radioactive violet in the morning sun.

It appeared to be full.

"Did you take my soda, bro?" he asked, walking toward it.

"Didn't think you'd mind," Mike said, dribbling the ball back to center court.

"Thought you weren't interested in drinking any of it," Tony said, stopping near the bottle and turning back to Mike. He watched Mike's eyes move from the bottle to him, back and forth.

He shrugged. "I took a few hits last night while you were screwing around, going to the bathroom or whatever. It was...pretty good."

"Then you know."

"Know what, man?" Mike turned back to the basket, dribbled the ball a few times, pretended to not pay attention.

"That it keeps refilling somehow, no matter how much you drink."

Mike squinted into the sun, which had risen above the trees directly behind the basket, shot the ball. Again, it sailed in a perfect arch, swooshed through.

"Noticed that, too."

Tony prodded the bottle with the toe of his sneaker.

Nothing had changed since he'd found it. Except now he was having to share it.

He found, standing there looking down at the bottle nestled amiably against his friend's backpack, he didn't like that.

Didn't like that one bit.

Didn't seem fair that he would have to share this with anyone, even as close a friend as Mike.

Then he remembered he wasn't here to share it, he was here to put it back where he'd found it.

That didn't seem exactly fair either.

Bending, he snatched it, held it up to the sun, which sparkled purple-blue through the liquid.

The bottle had heft. The glass was slippery smooth in his hand. And when he cracked the top, when that little *hiss-puff* of carbonated air escaped, he found his mouth watering, flooding with saliva, even before the smell of concentrated grape floated into his nostrils.

He lifted it to his mouth, took a deep, deep swig. Then another. And another.

When he opened his eyes, he saw that he'd drained most of the bottle. That the tiny hand, pallid and flexed, was slumped in the remaining purple pool.

He remembered the handless man from last night's dream, waving, waving.

Mike appeared next to him, looking on with narrowed eyes. "Hey, man, don't drink the whole damn bottle," he said, reaching over to snatch it away, the business end still stuck between Tony's lips.

Tony tightened his grip, pivoted away as if protecting a stolen ball.

"I want some," Mike shouted, his hands suddenly all over Tony and the bottle, pawing at him, at it, trying to wrest it from his grip. "If it keeps filling up, there's plenty for both of us!"

As if on cue, the bottle, still jutting upward from Tony's mouth, began re-filling. Tony watched, mesmerized, as purple liquid gushed into it, seemingly from nowhere, swirling in from the glass bottom pointed toward the sky. The soda sluiced into his mouth, tasting every bit as effervescent and grapey as if he'd just cracked it open. He gulped four or five more jolts of the stuff, spinning as he did so to avoid Mike. As fast as he drank it, though, new soda filled the bottle, frothing and foaming.

Tony continued to pivot away from Mike, guarding the soda. But as he did, two things happened. Mike's fingers slipped across its smooth, un-labeled surface, not grabbing it, but gaining enough purchase to dislodge it from Tony's grip.

Tony's thirteen-year-old feet, in their gigantic, ungainly sneakers, tripped over each other. Falling, he watched the bottle spin out of both their hands, sail into the air, flashing silver and purple, spraying froth from its neck as it spiraled to the ground.

Tony hit the ground first, instinctively reached out to grab it. His hands, though, were nowhere close to where they needed to be.

The bottle clinked to the asphalt, its glass bottom taking the impact, sending a fount of soda out through the neck before it tumbled over.

Tony didn't breathe. Neither boy said a word. Neither moved.

The bottle spun lazily, more soda frothing from it.

A jagged crack appeared in the glass, running the entire length from its wide base to its tapered neck.

"Shit!" Mike yelped.

Tony scrabbled to his knees as Mike leapt toward it.

Soda now poured into the bottle as fast as it leaked out onto the hot blacktop.

Mike reached it first, righted it so just some purplish flecks pushed from the neck. Inside, the tiny hand seemed stuck against the glass, fingers clenched as if trying to dig in for purchase.

Tony hauled himself upright, lowered his head and prepared to rush his friend. He stopped when it was apparent Mike didn't seem to care. He'd raised the bottle to his mouth, let the purple soda flow into him.

The heat, the sight of Mike slurping down the soda, the crack in the glass, and even the tiny hand inside all seemed to be mocking Tony, egging him on.

One thing rang out above it all.

He'd found that bottle. It was his.

All the soda inside, even that tiny, maddening hand. It was all his. And if he didn't want to share it with Mike, if he didn't want to put it back where he'd found it, then he didn't have to. Besides, for all their friendship, he was bigger than Mike. Thicker. Stronger. Feeling his scalp crawl with anger, he lurched over to his friend, clamped his hands on his shoulders, spun him around.

Mike, still drinking, tried to clothesline Tony, but even though Tony was bigger, he was agile. He reached past Mike's outstretched arm, grabbed the bottle, yanked it from his grip. Soda sprayed from Mike's mouth, from the bottle.

"Hey, bro, share. There's plenty—"

"No!"

Tony tore it out of his hand, twisted it to one side. He upended it, held it like a club, swung it around. Hard.

The bottle landed squarely on Mike's temple with a dull, fleshy *CLUD!*

Mike stumbled, but somehow managed to stay on his feet, then launched himself at Tony. His momentum carried them both to the ground. Mike landed atop his friend and the impact tore the bottle from Tony's grasp, sent it skittering across the blacktop. Before Tony could react, Mike's fists lashed out, pistoning into him with great rapidity and even greater force.

The ferocity of the blows, the anger, the hatred, stunned Tony. Sure, they were teenage boys. They'd known each other since kindergarten. There'd been fistfights aplenty, but nothing like this. The fury this rain of blows exhibited screamed of some deep well of antagonism for Tony, of chafing at his family, his friendship. Something unspoken, tamped down until now.

Several of his punches landed squarely, rocking Tony's head against the basketball court. He was able to buck Mike off him, send him sailing away with a powerful kick of his legs.

Tony was dazed, looking up into the blinding ball of the sun, blinking. When he licked his lips, he tasted copper pennies. When he wiped his forehead with the back of his hand, it came away smeared red.

He propped himself up on one elbow, looked across the court. To one side, Mike sprawled, looking back at him wide-eyed.

To the other, the cracked bottle, still spilling its purple contents.

The little hand sat crabbed near the neck, as if trying to plug the leak. Or pointing at him.

He scrambled to his feet, wiped more blood roughly from his face, strode toward Mike. On his way, he reached down, snatched up the purple soda bottle. Inside, the hand flopped to the bottom on a froth of suds.

Mike, perhaps thinking his friend was coming over to make peace, reached up with one hand. Tony swatted it aside, straddled Mike's body, swung the bottle in a high, gleaming arc over his head. It whooshed down in a violet comma, separating the part of the sentence where Tony understood what he was doing from the part where he lost all sense of who he was.

The bottle struck Mike's right cheek with a curious, twang like the sound an aluminum bat makes when striking the leather hide of a softball. A streamer of stuff flew out from that impact. Silver and purple and red, red in the bright sunlight.

Mike fell back to the asphalt, eyes closed.

But Tony didn't stop.

He fell on Mike, his full weight atop his chest. As the bottle reached the top of its arc, he brought it back down, smashing it into the bridge of Mike's nose. There was an awful CRACK!, and purple soda and bright, red blood burst in the air, spattered Tony's shorts, his Steph Curry jersey.

Tony might have stopped there, seeing the ruin of his friend's face beneath him. Except he saw that Mike was licking his lips, drawing in not only blood that flowed from his nose, but flecks of purple foam. As beaten as he was, he was still lapping up the purple soda through his own blood.

Tony struck again.

And again. Shattering Mike's cheek bones, opening cuts on the boy's forehead, his temples. One last blow and the bottle shattered, unable to endure any more of the violence it was being used for. Glass sailed into the weeds at the edge of the court, and Tony ended up holding just the neck of the bottle, with a jagged half-cup of glass like a bouquet.

The tiny hand was nowhere to be seen, freed at last.

Tony looked down at his friend, his ragged features. Blood and purple soda were everywhere.

Mike's lips moved, saying something.

Tony leaned in.

"Mama... Mama..."

Tony reared back, whipped the arm holding the broken bottle down at Mike's face. Its jagged crown dug in around the socket of his eye, and Tony twisted savagely. The bottle's teeth cored Mike's eye, scooped it out like a melon baller, hurtled it into the weeds with the rest of the broken glass.

Tony collapsed onto his friend's chest, breathing hard, sweating.

It was so hot and he was so thirsty.

He pushed himself off, rolled onto the gritty, sticky asphalt, felt it burn the skin of his legs and arms. But all he could think of as he opened his eyes and stared into the bloody hole in Mike's head was the effervescent, sugary taste of that grape soda. How good, how refreshing it would taste right at this moment.

* * *

That's where they eventually found him later that morning, sprawled next to Mike's dead body on the basketball courts. There were people and screams, and Tony noticed he still held the neck of the broken bottle tightly in his blood-covered hands. Noticed it when the police officer shouted at him to *drop it, drop it!* Tony did so, fainting as he imagined the officer spraying him with grape soda from his purple service revolver.

* * *

Renee wasn't supposed to be at the basketball courts. Her mom had made it clear that what had happened there a few weeks ago was still very, very much at the top of her mind. It wasn't any place for a young girl to be playing.

She'd tried to tell her mom that she hadn't known either of those boys. They were a little too old for her anyway. She was only nine, and they were teenagers. The gulf in ages was unthinkable, but her mom would have none of it. If something like that could happen down there, then it was no place for one of her kids. Off limits.

But summers in the city could be boring. There weren't a lot of girls her age in the neighborhood, and Miss Trammel—who watched her during the day while mom was at work—was sure not going to let her walk all the way over to her friend Kim's house.

So, instead, while Miss Trammel snoozed in the living room watching *The View*, Renee scooped up the pink and purple WNBA basketball she'd got last year for her birthday. Closing the front door softly, she dribbled down the front steps, across the street and down three blocks to the park where she could shoot hoops for about an hour, then hightail it home before Miss Trammel even woke up.

The day was warm and bright, and the fact that Renee was out in it, doing something she wasn't supposed to, made her happy and light.

Turning the corner, she strode past the park's entrance sign, the run-down bathroom building with the verdigrised water fountains.

She was already thirsty, and wished she'd remembered to bring a bottle of something from the fridge. The water fountains never seemed to work right, often not working at all. But even when they were, the water was thin, hot and tasted, she thought, of loose change.

Oh well.

The courts were empty, as she'd hoped they'd be. Evidently other moms also felt uncomfortable letting their children play somewhere a boy had killed his best friend.

Renee dribbled up the court slowly when something caught her eye, sparkling in the brush at the side of the court. There was usually plenty of trash there: crumpled chip bags, Micky D's wrappers, cigarette butts. So it might not have drawn her interest.

But it sparkled a deep rose, winked at her from the weeds.

She set the ball down, walked over to it.

It was a soda bottle, smooth and unlabeled. Sealed tightly.

The liquid inside was a deep, deep, fruit punch red, fizzed a bit as she shook the bottle, peered into its depths. She plucked it from the grass, held it up in the sunlight. The sun shone through it, and as the red stuff inside swirled, something circled into view, orbiting the inside of the bottle. It was a single, complete eyeball, its brown iris dilated, trailing a streamer of veins and connective tissue behind it like a jellyfish swimming in a rose-colored sea.

Despite this, or—terrifyingly, *because* of this—Renee was suddenly overcome with thirst...

For my friend, Josh Malerman

A KISS FROM THE SUN
FOR PARDON

THIRSTY.

Or is it hungry?

He can't tell. The two emptinesses—each pressing, clamoring for his attention—seem sharp, each taking precedence moment by moment.

He can't keep anything down. He's tried, for three days now he's tried. Not even water.

But he stumbles to the bathroom anyway, turns on the squeaky, rusty tap and water spills into his cupped palms. He wets his lips, splashes his face, a smeary reflection in the mirror. He swallows a handful of the strongly chlorinated water, feels it slip coolly, deliciously down his throat. The moment it hits his stomach, though, he's retching into the cracked and stained toilet, which has *not* been sanitized for his protection.

On hands and knees, he makes his way back to the bedroom, pulls himself to the window. He parts the curtains the tiniest bit, to see where he is, what time of day it is, and the sun slaps him like a spurned lover, knocks him back. He holds onto the curtains, but his knees give way. His ass hits the threadbare, cigarette-burned carpet and he sprawls there for a moment.

He wonders what drug, what drugs he's taken, what drugs he's addicted to.

What drugs he's suffering withdrawals from so he can buy some more, take some more to feel better.

But he doesn't know, doesn't know much at all—not where he is, not who he is.

All he knows is that, right now, he is tired. Hungry or thirsty and tired. But, right now, tired more than anything else.

He sleeps a while there on the floor, awakens suddenly, still feeling awful. Maybe a shower will help.

He wonders when the last time he's had one.

Back in the bathroom, he strips, steps into the gray-scummed bathtub and lets the lukewarm water dribble over him from the encrusted showerhead. It feels fantastic.

Dressed again, even his dirty clothes feel clean, and he draws the flimsy door carefully open…

…onto night.

He stands on a concrete balcony that stretches the length of the second floor of the fleabag motel he's in and looks over the wrought iron railing across the parking lot, across the city.

What city? He has no idea, but it drapes over the horizon, its lights twinkling like a thousand—a million—small fires.

He inhales a carnival of aromas, so heady, so rich. There is the tang of gasoline, the crisp ozone of approaching rain. There is freshly mowed grass and a mixed perfume of flowers.

The smell of people, of hot bodies, of electric sweat and desire.

He lurches down the stairs, across the parking lot. He doesn't know what to do, isn't sure where to go. Is the hotel room he just left paid for? For how long? Does he even have a key?

His hands go into the pockets of his pants. His left hand comes back with the wad of paper money. A jingle of coins rains down onto the concrete at his feet.

His right hand comes up with two things. The first is a small plastic card, embossed with various sigils, and a name in raised letters: STEPHEN EMIL COCTEAU.

That name resonates briefly, sends weak ripples into the dark well that is his brain. While these stir the sediment, nothing rises to the top.

The other thing his hand has fished out, though, does.

It is a scuffed matchbook, half of the matches torn away.

On its black cover, two words, in red: BAR SANGUINE.

* * *

The taxi drops him off at the front door of the place.

It is after 10:00 p.m., and the street is alive with cars, lined with bars and restaurants that are teeming with people, stuffed with people.

A vast, empty feeling of loneliness cuts through him deeply.

Also a hollowness, a hunger that makes his stomach growl, flip queasily.

Like a rock in a stream, he stands on the sidewalk outside Bar Sanguine as the flow of people part around him.

The outside of the place is subdued. A single sign hangs in a heavily draped window. The door is a thick wooden Gothic arch, banded with iron across its polished boards.

Two men stand there, one on either side like columns. They are clad in black jeans and black T-shirts, muscles bulging beneath the fabric. They pay him no attention.

He draws the door open, steps inside the space revealed. An antechamber, big enough to hold about a dozen people, cordoned off with heavy, black velvet curtains. A red-haired, heavily tattooed girl wearing a black corset stands behind a podium at the rear of this space.

"Mr. Cocteau," she says. "How pleasant to see you. If I can just see your card, the services of Bar Sanguine await."

Stephen fumbles in his pocket and brings out the card. She plucks it from his fingers, does something with it below the top of the podium, hands it back to him with a smile.

She parts the curtain behind her, and he sees lights, people.

Skirting around the podium, he pauses in the opening she has created.

"Are you meeting someone?" she asks, still parting the curtain for him.

"Ahhh, no. It's just—"

"You want to speak to Mr. Rood," she says. It isn't a question.

"I suppose so, yes."

"I'll let him know you're here."

Stephen slips through the black velvet, which closes behind him with a sound as soft as a sigh.

Bar Sanguine is a club, but a club in the older sense. A private place where people of similar proclivities, similar social strata come together, mingle. There is a bar, polished dark ebony with the appropriate choir of liquor bottles behind it, lit dimly by tapers, glimmering like jewels. A few people sit on the padded leather stools, nursing drinks.

Paneled wooden hallways lead off from this main room. The decorations are subdued, tasteful, Old World: burnished wood and thick carpets and tasteful paintings. He can hear music, low and barely registered.

After a moment he decides to make himself easy for the manager to find, so he takes a stool at the bar. The bartender is older, thin, with slicked-back hair and a bow tie.

"Mr. Cocteau," he says, wiping the bar in front of Stephen with a rag. "How nice to see you this evening. The usual?"

Stephen doesn't really want anything, knowing what effect it's likely to have on his stomach. But maybe the taste of his "usual" drink will bring back something, some dim memory.

"Mr. Cocteau will skip the usual, Martin," says a thin, silky voice from behind him as a spindly hand falls onto Stephen's shoulder.

Stephen turns to face a man who is taller, even thinner than the bartender. His eyes are dark, set in an oval face that is divided by an aquiline slice of a nose, underscored by a thin-lipped, pinched mouth.

"How are you this evening, Mr. Cocteau?" he asks. "Carmelina told me you wanted to speak with me. I am Mr. Rood."

Stephen stands, offers his hand, which Rood looks at for a moment before taking. Rood's hand clenches Stephen's with a strength that belies its delicate appearance. His skin is cool, papery. He shakes Stephen's hand once, unclasps it with a definitiveness close to dismissal.

"Thanks for seeing me," Stephen says, aware he has no idea what he wants from this man.

"Of course," Rood says, then nods to Martin behind the bar. "Mr. Cocteau needs a Tepes water, Martin. Have it brought to the East Salon, will you?"

Martin nods, and Rood guides Stephen down the hallway to a small sitting area. There is a fireplace here, a divan, a few overstuffed arm chairs, a bookcase.

"Have a seat, Mr. Cocteau," Rood says, going to the fireplace and stirring the logs with a poker. "I suppose there are questions."

"Questions?" Stephen laughs. "Sure, starting with who am I?"

"That, at least, must be clear by now. You're Étienne Cocteau or, if you prefer, Stephen Cocteau."

Just then a woman enters the room bearing a drink on a tray. Rood inclines his head fractionally toward Stephen. The woman steps towards him, lowers the tray. Stephen takes the drink, which is in a tall, slender metal cup that looks like a vase.

He lifts it toward his nose as the woman leaves. The liquid inside is dark; its smell is flat and mineral.

"What is this?"

"How long has it been since you've eaten?" Rood asks.

"I can't keep anything down, even water."

"Of course, but how long has it been since you've *eaten*?"

Stephen stares at him, unsure how to reply.

"You're going to subsist on this until your body re-accommodates to its new form."

Stephen hesitates, and Rood raises an eyebrow.

Mentally shrugging, Stephen takes a sip of the drink. He expects something alcoholic, strong. But what he gets is something metallic, carbonated; like drinking soda water steeped with copper pennies.

He spits it back into the glass.

"What the hell is this?"

"Tepes water," Rood says, slurring the first word into a fading "shh" sound, like the end of a whisper. "It's the only thing you can have for at least a few weeks."

"Why?"

Rood's face, his whole demeanor, changes. The brittle civility falls away, and the full force of his disdain fills the salon.

"Because you're no longer *vampir*, Mr. Cocteau."

"What?" Stephen hears the word Rood has said, but it is, again, curiously slurred.

"Drink!" Rood snaps, and Stephen puts the rim of the cup to his lips, closes his eyes. Its contents are drained in four large gulps, leaving a tinny taste in his mouth. Grimacing, he places the empty cup onto a side table.

He feels the liquid descend into him, spread inside him. It makes him feel warm, sated. It clears his head.

"What is it?"

"Blood. Beef broth. Seltzer. A few exotic herbs. A squeeze of lemon. Your body still can't process mortal food. Its need for blood isn't entirely gone. This fills the transition."

"What?"

"You are *dhampir*, a fading *vampir*. Soon to be fully human again."

"I am…*was*…a vampire?" Stephen doesn't protest. Somehow, this explanation feels right. "I remember nothing."

Rood draws a hand casually along the length of the mantle, regards his palm. "I know your name. It has been on the member rolls for…well… many decades. How you were turned and by whom and where? Who knows? All I know is that you are no longer *vampir*."

Stephen takes all this in, his head swimming, his mouth tasting of raw meat.

"How?"

"This happens sometimes when the one who turns you is killed," Rood says. "Usually, you die. But distance lessens this effect. The one who turned you must be far away, perhaps not in America. His death, while not killing you, has left you without memories."

Rood turns to him. "You can retain your membership here until the change is complete, if for no other reason than to take the Tepes water. After, you will no longer be welcome."

"Wait," Stephen says, standing. Rood pauses at the entrance to the salon. "How will I know when that is?"

Rood smiles. "When you stop smelling like one of us and start smelling like…*food*."

With that, he turns and leaves.

Stephen slumps back into the chair, lets out a long expulsion of breath.

Quietly, a woman enters the room. She is full-bodied, almost ridiculously so, with a cascade of hair that is so blonde it's almost white. Her eyes are dark, her lips full. Her fingers end in perfectly manicured, unpainted nails. She wears a tight, shimmering white silk cocktail dress.

"Étienne?"

He doesn't know her, doesn't know how to tell her this.

"Benoit is dead. I don't know how," she says, stepping into the salon, toward him. "I thought you were…might be…"

"I'm sorry, I don't know who you are. Not really sure about myself, for that matter. My name is Stephen, though."

"Oh, Étienne," she says, throwing her arms around him, running those nails across the nape of his neck. "Of course, you are Stephen, too, in America. I'm Abrielle…your wife."

Her body feels strange against his, hard and unyielding, especially where it should be softest. Her skin, her hand against his cheek, is smooth and satiny.

She is cold, too, as cold as plastic.

Stephen swallows, steps from her embrace, backs towards the leather chair and falls into it.

"This is worse than death," she breathes. "You really have no idea who you are, who I am?"

Stephen shakes his head. "Mr. Rood was kind enough to—"

"Rood!" she growls. "He's nothing but a…glorified *consigliere*. He's not even that. He's just a club manager."

"He kicked me out."

Abrielle kneels at his side, takes his warm hand in her cold one. "This can't be happening. Not when we'd already made the decision."

Absently, Stephen puts his hand onto her head, strokes her hair. It is fine, luxurious, slips through his fingers like flax, like a doll's hair.

"The decision?" he asks, distracted.

"To end this."

Stephen's fingers stop, and the strands of her hair fall one by one back into place.

"You are *vampir*," he says, trying to give the word the same intonation Rood had used.

Abrielle nods. "Just as you…*were*. You turned me only days after Benoit turned you. We have been *vampir* for almost three centuries. Do you not remember?"

"No," he says. "I don't. I'm sorry."

"Soon, you'll be human, and we'll be separate. You'll bear this because you won't remember. But how am I to bear this? All I have are memories. That's all a vampire's life is, in the end. Memories."

She sniffles a little, turns away.

"We had planned…well, now it doesn't matter, I suppose."

"What had we planned?" He spills from the chair to kneel on the floor beside her, takes her cold, hard body in his arms.

"Once, we were weary of the isolation, the fear, the feeding. The coldness, the apathy, the dim, grey world we inhabited," she says.

"And so we wanted to become human once more?"

She laughs at this, laughs as one might at something a child has said.

"No, that is why we became *vampir*, so long ago. So foolish now. It took a while, a century or two perhaps, but we realized that the *vampir* life doesn't offer anything more. It doesn't make things better. It is one lived in memories."

"Memories?"

"Everything we do as *vampir* is simply our memories of our lives. What we do, what we wear, what we like, where we choose to live. Memories of when blood ran warm through our veins. We remember what things looked like in daylight, how birds sounded, how food tasted. All just memories. Even the night is but a dim memory of the day.

"The longer we lived, the more these memories crowded us. So, we decided to end our lives as *vampir*; to receive a kiss from the sun and go wherever it is our souls go. Together," she says, and begins crying.

Stephen cups her face with his warm hand, wipes away her pink tears with a swipe of his thumb. They leave red smudges like commas under her eyes. He kisses her cheek, and it is like kissing a mannequin.

"What would you have me do?"

Abrielle turns her face to his. "You will be human soon, and I...I will take my kiss and leave."

She moves her head, brings her mouth to his. Her lips are as cold and hard as marble, but he gives himself to them. His tongue moves into her mouth, slides gently over sharp teeth.

"I would end my life, whatever it is I am right now," he whispers, their faces close enough for him to realize that she isn't breathing. "To be with you."

Abrielle was the only clear memory he had; the only touchstone that he had to relate his life to, to define it, give it depth. Suddenly, he couldn't bear to be without her.

"No! Who knows where my soul will go? Now that yours is cleansed, it won't go to the same place. We'd still be separate. No, dearest, you have gained a bittersweet reprieve; a second chance to live your life. Grab it, claim it."

"But, how can I—"

"Shh," she whispers into his ear, kisses him again. "Take it, just as I once took yours."

Stephen swallows. "What I did to you…was a gift?"

"Yes, to be together, forever. At least that's what we thought. How were we to know otherwise? But, yes, a gift nonetheless."

"I should apologize, for doing this to you. I should beg your forgiveness."

"Oh, love, of course it was a gift. But flowers wilt and cakes spoil and all gems lose their luster eventually. You needn't apologize for giving me something I desired more than anything."

"Still…"

"Then accept this gift as my pardon, if you want. It is the last I can give. To be human again, to live again, once more under the sun. To begin again, with an unsullied soul. To build a new life. To make new memories." She strokes his cheek. "If only I could build them with you. If only you could remember me, the centuries we shared. If only you could carry me in your memories."

He wants to tell her he will. He wants to tell her that hers is the now the strongest memory of the very few he has. He wants to kiss her again, hold her, but she pulls away, draws him to his feet, leads him from the salon.

Down dark, wainscoted hallways she leads him. Past others of her kind who look on them with, he thinks, a mixture of pity and contempt. They pass through doors that unlock at the touch of her hand. They glide through midnight rooms where heavy curtains block the outside world and furniture squats like cowering beasts.

A final door opens onto a winding staircase, and she leads him up, up, up.

He finds that he is breathing hard. It is a curious sensation to him, to feel the air burn in his lungs. He feels burning, too, in his legs, his thighs as they press ever upward. She shows no sign of fatigue, no sign of slowing.

Many, many floors later, she pushes open another door, and they step out onto dark, graveled tar paper, the bowl of the sky curving over them.

Abrielle turns to him, smiles wanly, pulls him gently out onto the roof of the building.

Above them, the dawn spreads across the sky in roses and violets and fading blues that take his breath away with their beauty.

Below them, the city awakens. Its lights glimmer more strongly now, surpassing the weakening stars that fade overhead.

The wind here is cool and languid, swirls the hem of Abrielle's dress. She holds his hand as they walk across the roof, pausing only to remove the high-heeled shoes she wears.

At the eastern side of the building, she turns, draws him in, kisses him again, lowers herself to sit on the ledge, her bare, white feet dangling hundreds of feet above the city.

She looks up at him, pats the ledge near her.

Feeling dizzy, he squats, swings his legs over the edge, sits beside her.

She puts her head on his shoulder, closes her eyes.

There are no words for this, and so he says nothing, simply puts his arm around her, squeezes her to him.

The sky's roses-and-bruises hue gives way to a band of gold at the horizon. He almost sees curls of fire at the edges of this white-hot layer as it spreads upward, diluting the night as it seeps into the sky.

Abrielle trembles as the first rays of sunshine lance over the rim of the earth, striking the tall buildings and casting shadows that are like the night, but not nearly as dark.

He begins to tremble, too, as the first arc of the sun's sphere pushes into the air.

He kisses her forehead as its light begins to fill the sky, washes over the roofs of the buildings like warm water.

There is nothing dramatic, nothing like in the movies. There is no bursting into flame, no crumbling ashes.

Abrielle simply lifts her head into the light, winces as it strikes her skin.

She turns to him one last time, smiles bravely.

And then she dissolves, fades in increments until she is nothing more than a smudge in the air, a heat mirage, a ghost through which the weight of his arm slips.

He sees, at the end, he sees her lips move in words that he cannot hear. *Vivre, mon amour.*

* * *

Stephen sits there as the sun climbs the sky.

He feels hollow, like an empty vessel whose contents have been poured out. He wonders if he will ever be able to fill it again.

After a while, the sun's warmth becomes too much, and he climbs to his feet, walks back to the stairwell. He retraces his steps down, down, through rooms and chambers that are still dark, but now empty.

At the bar, Martin is there, alone. When he sees Stephen approach, he goes to work pouring liquids into a chalice.

Stephen sits, and Martin pushes a steel vessel toward him.

"Is this what I think it is?"

Martin nods.

Stephen lifts the metal container, tips it in acknowledgment of the bartender, drains the liquid in the glass.

He slams the empty glass onto the bar.

"Anything else, sir?"

"No. I guess I'll be leaving," he said, turning toward the curtained doorway. "But I'll be back, at least for a few weeks,"

"Where will you go, if I may ask?"

Stephen stops, lifts the velvet curtains that lead to the exit, to that other world.

"Back into the world, to learn how to be human again, I suppose."

He passes through the veil, out to receive his pardon.

Hers.

THE BITCHES
OF MADISON COUNTY

DONALD HARMON STEPPED OFF the private jet and onto the dull grey tarmac of the metropolitan airport.

One word, grim and dead in his brain, lay just as lifeless on his tongue. *Home.*

Harmon was not a large man, a fact that had lent itself well to his chosen profession and had saved his life on innumerable occasions.

Still, he carried with him an undeniable air of power, of self-assuredness; not aggression nor belligerence, but rather self-containment, as if no opinion or judgment could pierce the shell of his carefully constructed personality.

Arranged on the tarmac around him was everything he owned—two trunks of camera equipment, a few mementos from his travels, a ridiculously few articles of clothing stuffed into two duffel bags. And in one of those bags was an envelope; cream-colored and slightly textured, a gold embossed rectangle near the return address, his name carefully typed on its front.

Within that envelope was the reason Harmon was here, in the city he'd left, for good he thought back then, more than thirty years ago.

> *Dear Mr. Harmon,*
>
> *Although the investigation into the unfortunate incident in Kisumu has proven, thus far, inconclusive, we regret the necessity to cancel your current project and its funding. We have enclosed a check that should cover your expenses to-*

*date. Our contacts in the Kenyan government have told us
that they wish you out of their country immediately--before
they change their minds.*

*Please accept this with the best possible wishes. We will
contact you when another suitable project arises.*

Yours truly, etc., etc., etc.

An over-large check and a plane ticket on a chartered jet rounded out
the envelope's contents.

He found out quickly how empty the words in that letter were.

Clutching those bags, staring into the hot orb of the sun as it tried to
melt the asphalt and metal, he wanted to tear that letter and the check up
into tiny pieces.

But this was a passing desire, just as this sun was a weak counterpart to
its African companion.

To Donald Harmon, life was seen through a lens.

Which meant, of course, that life was a narrow circle of reality, surrounded on all sides by darkness. Only the things at the center of this
circle concerned him. Anything outside this focused sphere of realism,
anything within the darkness—or beyond—he did not really see.

His camera had taken it all in during its 30-year partnership with him.

His paychecks bore the best of credentials: *National Geographic, Smith-
sonian,* The Discovery Channel, the BBC, PBS, The Learning Channel,
Mutual of Omaha's Wild Kingdom. Yes, he'd shot for them all; everything—color, black and white, slides, motion picture film, video, even
infrared and night-vision.

The things his camera showed him, he showed the world.

And it brought him money, and security and a kind of life that seemed
adventurous and romantic, but in the end was as little connected with
reality as he was.

* * *

Whispering Pines Condominiums was as upscale as such develop-
ments come. It was complete with lighted tennis courts, three pools—one

indoor and heated—a clubhouse, laundry facilities and a large population of single women.

In other words, his surroundings were teeming with the kind of life Harmon wanted to study.

His first subject was Cindy Barbett, a thirty-five-year-old divorced accountant who left for work early each morning and usually came home late in the evening. She lived in the apartment downstairs from him, and so made an easy subject.

For the first few days, he did not photograph her at all, as was his habit. Instead, he made copious notes in a three-ring notebook. He spent Wednesday affixing reflective film to all of his windows and the glass sliding door that led to his deck so that no one would be able to see into his apartment.

Across the flooring of the deck, he spread a length of black theatrical scrim cloth so that Cindy would not be able to look up and see the pencil-size camera he had aimed down at her lounge chair from a space between the boards.

He began principal photography on Thursday as she left for work, driving away, coming home. Harmon worked feverishly, eating little, living on coffee and cigarettes. He stayed up long hours, lest she should come or go without him knowing.

And he began to see the patterns of her life, as if looking at some grand design from a higher ground. She stayed late at work on Mondays, Wednesdays and Fridays. She had six nice outfits that she wore in varying combinations so as not to repeat them too often.

She did laundry on the weekends, laid out on her deck to sun herself, drank Diet Pepsi seemingly by the gallon. She read *People* and *Us* and *Cosmopolitan* and *Vogue*. She backed from her parking place without looking, usually hit the curb when she pulled in.

Cindy never had any visitors, male or female, so her sex life was null as far as he knew.

As notebooks and slide sleeves filled, Harmon slowly lost interest in her. He realized that, much like the weaverbirds, Cindy's life was a series of uninteresting activities strung together in a predictable routine that, though possessing the illusion of complexity, was truly boring.

So, he began to look for a new subject

This was the pattern he repeated over the next two months, finding another woman in the complex to study, untangling the seemingly complex strands of her activities, finding himself uninterested when the knot finally dissolved and the line of her life sprang taut and predictable.

Just as his attention wavered, however, a new subject presented itself to his lens.

Jayne Fletcher was a rather severe woman whom Harmon had seen several times when he was picking up his mail or taking the garbage out. Maybe forty years old, maybe older, but her body was trim and fit.

She lived across the parking lot from Harmon's apartment. In fact, their apartments were on the same level, and their bedroom windows opened on one another.

It was, in fact, one morning when Harmon was walking past his bedroom window on his way to shoot another day in the dreary life of one of his more boring subjects that he really noticed Jayne.

He'd seen on several occasions that she left her bedroom window shades up, but he'd been too busy with Karen, his current subject, to see why.

This morning, Jayne sat perched on the edge of her bed like some exotic and magnificent bird. Her hair was down and it was long and radiant and luxurious. She wore a pair of stockings that clipped to a garter belt around her narrow waist.

And nothing else.

Harmon stood transfixed as he watched her reach to someone else in the room.

When her hands came back, they were attached to the paper boy. For the next hour, Harmon forgot about Karen, refocused on Jayne. It was a study in physics and energy the likes of which he had never seen before. Twice the paper boy prepared to leave, but each time the woman dragged him back and put him to work again.

When he finally did leave, at 9:17 a.m., he wobbled away on his bicycle as if just having completed the Tour de France.

* * *

Unlike Cindy or Karen or the dozen or so others he'd watched previously, Jayne presented Harmon with an interesting array of activities—and not a few challenges.

She was always punctual and neat, and Harmon slipped into her routine with little problem, photographing her in action with nothing to get in his way.

Her sexual proclivities proved ridiculously easy to document. The quiet Ms. Fletcher was conspicuously, voraciously active, with a marked taste for young men. In addition to her encounters with the paper boy, Harmon captured her seductions of the pool boy, several neighbors, countless pizza delivery boys and even a Jehovah's Witness.

One morning when he was sure of her schedule, he waited for her to leave for work, walked to her apartment. He carried a large metal toolbox with him. Setting this down on the stairs, he looked at her door from various angles and sightlines before deciding where to position the tiny video camera. With this, he'd be able to study how she answered the door.

Not to disappoint him, Jayne ordered a pizza that very same night, and it came attached to a rather sturdy young dark-haired boy who wore about him the air of a man on an important, desirable mission.

She didn't even smile as she took his hand, drew him in.

Harmon saw the pizza box spill to the ground just as the door closed.

He soon realized that she was as much exhibitionist as nymphomaniac; he was only able to photograph her during these activities because she wanted to be seen, though she didn't really *know* that she was watched.

But Harmon felt the need to see beyond what she presented. His experience in the jungle, on the savanna demanded it.

To capture the moment with a lion, he had told other photographers, you must think like it.

You must act like it.

You must live with it.

* * *

On Monday morning, when the knocking of Jayne's car faded as it turned from the entrance onto the main road, Harmon slowly dressed in blue coveralls, carried a few boards and a toolbox over to the door of her apartment.

He'd watched her enough to know that she hid an extra key on the top of the light fixture outside her door. Reaching up, he found the key amidst the dust and dried bodies of insects, brought it down to unlock the door.

Replacing it, he creaked the door open, pushed his head inside.

It was dark and well ordered, a little warm and stuffy.

Seeing that no one had noticed him, he picked up the boards and the tool case, stepped inside, locked the door behind him.

* * *

This was the apartment of a spinster, despite what his cameras had already shown him. Couches and chair were stiff and prim, covered in fabrics that would stain and rip if allowed to. Cabinets and shelves were crammed with tastefully arranged bric-a-brac: vases, porcelain figures, silk flowers.

A china cabinet squatting impressively in the dining room held silver and crystal and heavy pieces of china with a florid rose print adorning the serving side. Harmon bet they'd never once been used.

Tables in the well-appointed little living room bore brass coasters, dried flowers, neatly stacked magazines: *Reader's Digest, Architectural Digest, Vanity Fair, National Geographic.*

Smiling, he bent to flip quickly through the last one's cool, slick pages.

An article about Albania caught his eye.

Photos by James Hendrickson.

Snorting, he turned the pages. The photos were dark and cold, the people alternately apple-cheeked and smiling or grim, dirty-faced testaments to poverty and Third-World hardships. Yet at the core of each was something that bothered Harmon, had always bothered Harmon about his colleague's photos.

They were posed, *false*. The photographer hadn't captured a true moment in the lives of these people, this country. Instead, each face in each photo screamed, *I know you can see me!*

And that, to Harmon, was the antithesis of photography, of the moment.

The moment was a stolen kiss, the silent capture of the secret essence of the thing photographed.

Like the primitives, Harmon believed—believed with all the fervor of a religious zealot—that a photograph should strive to trap the soul of what it captured on its unblinking strip of film.

It should steal the moment, trap it in its shuttered heart, blast it forever onto the thin strip of celluloid.

And the person photographed should never know, should never be aware.

Hendrickson, by becoming a participant in his own photos, ruined what he shot.

He subverted the moment, the very thing photography should strive for.

As far as Harmon was concerned, Hendrickson proved himself little more than a wedding photographer or a bumbling uncle at a family picnic.

Shaking his head, he closed the magazine, straightened the stack on the coffee table.

* * *

Jayne's bedroom was simple to the point of austerity, and yet not in a way that testified to any particular design philosophy. It was not filled with the curved, blonde lines of Danish furniture, not the chrome and black of Modernism, not the clean ascetic of Japanese design.

There were four doors: the one he had just come in, the one leading to the bathroom, and two more that opened onto a standard closet. He opened this and found a fairly sparse collection of dresses, skirts and blouses, shoes stacked neatly on the floor, sweaters, T-shirts and various purses and makeup cases folded and piled on the shelves above.

Harmon pushed the hangers aside, found the rear wall. He knew this wall backed to a similar closet in another unit. This unit, as luck would have it, was unoccupied. He'd checked at the office of the complex, under the pretenses that he was interested in switching units.

Harmon looked at his watch, a gift from the magazine he'd given more than half his life to, and took a deep breath.

Seven hours and twenty-five minutes until Jayne returned home.

He had a lot to do.

* * *

Seven hours and two minutes later, Harmon exited the vacant apartment, closed the door behind him, locked it. One of his projects that day was to replace the lock on this door with one of his own purchase, so that he'd have a key to get into his blind whenever he needed.

Picking up the toolbox, he walked around the corner, past the front door of Jayne's place, smiled. He crossed the parking lot, walked up the steps to his own unit, whistling quietly.

Inside, he cracked open a beer from the fridge, washed down a few Advil, then went into the bathroom and took a long, steamy shower. When he was finished, he slipped on a pair of boxer shorts and a white T-shirt. He crumpled his dirty clothes into a ball, a fine dust of white drywall powder and sawdust billowing from them, and plopped them into the washing machine.

A visit to the fridge for another beer, then Harmon sat at his computer. He placed the beer beside the keyboard, fired up a program. The screen sputtered like a TV tuned to a bad channel.

Harmon had cut through the adjoining wall from the empty apartment's closet directly into Jayne's closet. Through that hole, he had introduced two remote control pinhole video cameras, a digital still camera and an infrared camera, to see her when the room was totally dark. Discrete, they attached to the inside of her closet door, looked out between the narrow slats into her bedroom.

The remote control equipment he left in the closet of the empty apartment, connected to an old laptop of his with a wireless Internet connection. He could control the laptop from here, and thereby control the cameras without being in the apartment.

He fired up one of the small video cams, panned it around the room. Excellent. The connection was working, the camera tracking and transmitting good images.

Jayne did not disappoint that evening. Her date for the night was dressed in a suit and a tie. A young man, a junior executive at the software developer Harmon knew Jayne worked for.

Harmon took a pull from his beer, his face lit by the flicker of the computer monitor, settled in for the evening.

* * *

Two weeks later, Harmon was not so sure about the effectiveness of his blind. Jayne had not spotted it, had not given any clue that she knew her watchers were now not limited to what she chose to show through the bedroom window.

Her activities were just as open, just as numerous and just as energetic as they'd been before Harmon had planted the camera.

And that was the problem.

Harmon was not so much a pervert as a pragmatist. He existed to capture that one moment, the place in time where a person exhibited something real and true. But this could take place only when that person didn't know he or she was being watched, filmed.

Sex was usually that one time people forgot about themselves, forgot about their surroundings, lost themselves in the moment.

Not so with Jayne. Her sexual romps were, as he finally figured out, controlled and almost choreographed. Jayne knew what she wanted, and used the willing young men she brought into her bedroom as props; things to be used for a purpose, then put away.

Jayne was not uninhibited in the bedroom tableaus she unwittingly created for Harmon. She was not her secret, private self. Not a single one of these young men would see Jayne brush her hair, put her makeup on, make breakfast, read a book, paint her fingernails, make coffee.

Too many of the tiny details of Jayne's life were occurring off camera.

Perversely, it was those tiny, myriad details of her life that she hid—and it was these intimate moments that Harmon found himself wanting to see.

That was where Harmon would find his moment.

* * *

To capture these moments required Harmon to reenter the unoccupied apartment, remove the back of Jayne's closet, so neatly cut out and put back earlier by him, its seams perfectly concealed. He'd have to find places to secrete more tiny cameras: in the living room, the bathroom, the kitchen. When Jayne drank her morning cup of coffee, did her laundry, tweezed her eyebrows, read her latest *National Geographic*, Harmon wanted to be there.

So one morning after Jayne went to work, Harmon checked his tool-box, prepped three additional small video cams and their control units, prepared to make another house call.

Before he left this time, something—his training in filming other animals from blinds, a premonition—made him dig through his own closet.

He pulled away a few boxes, mostly papers, old slides and old camera bodies, until he found the long cardboard tube. He wrestled it out of the closet, set it on the bed, pried open the cap at the end.

Gently, he inclined the tube until something slid into his waiting hand.

The rifle was long, its barrel thick and gleaming dully in the light of the bedroom lamp. It kept coming out of the cardboard tube, longer and longer until it seemed like a trick, a clown's gun drawn unendingly from its holster to the delight of the crowd.

But this was not a clown's gun. The barrel finally came to an end in an oversized stock of dark wood—ebony perhaps—that was carved with all sorts of little figures of romping antelope and plodding elephants.

It was an elephant gun, ironically, given to Harmon by the chief of a Hutu tribe in Rwanda in the late 1970s, two decades before those people descended into genocide against their neighbors, the Tutsi. The gun was a run-of-the-mill .500 caliber rifle that took shells nearly as thick as Harmon's wrist.

The gun was heavy, and he needed two hands to close it. He slid it back into the tube, shouldered the cardboard cylinder as if it were the rifle it concealed.

* * *

By 11:14 a.m., Harmon had pried the back wall of the adjoining closets out and had entered Jayne's apartment. He'd placed the cameras in the living room and the kitchen, and was now taking his time placing the camera in the bathroom. It presented some problems, but he'd finally decided to clear a small hole in the silver backing of her mirror and place the eye of the flat lens behind this.

He was finishing this when he heard voices outside the front door.

Harmon froze.

He heard the metallic click of a key entering the lock of Jayne's apartment, the wet sounds of kisses, the roll of the tumblers.

LITTLE BLACK SPOTS

Acting quickly, he flipped the lights in the bathroom off, sidestepped into the bedroom, closed the door. He bet that she wouldn't bother with the bathroom, that she'd take some time to get into the bedroom.

Harmon nudged his toolbox into the closet, stepped in and drew the door partially shut. He backed into the darkness as far as he could. Besides Jayne's dresses and clothing, a five-by-four section of drywall leaned askew in the closet.

And his gun. He'd taken it from the tube, left it loaded and cocked leaning in the closet should he need it.

Instinctively, Harmon wrapped his right hand around the barrel.

What was she doing home?

Harmon took a long, deep breath.

He could hear their voices again, closer now, whispery.

"Wine?" came the reedy voice of a young man. "Isn't wine at lunch against corporate policy?"

There was another sound. She was removing his tie. More wet kisses.

"Well, if you're going to break corporate policy, you should do it in a big way."

A zipper revved down.

"Oh," she cooed. "And I can see you are."

This was followed by a tangle of bodies that as much fell into the room as entered it. Her partner was a thin and bespectacled young man. He fell onto her, into her, guided by her deft hands.

Experience made him patient. He assumed this was an afternoon quickie, and that they had to return to work shortly. He could wait them out. He'd waited longer in blinds on many occasions.

* * *

He'd seen this played out many times before, so even the voyeuristic thrill of what was occurring mere feet from where he stood left him cold. He leaned on the rifle, and his thoughts drifted away.

A sound pulled him back. A hand on the closet door in front of him. A voice.

"Oh, you like dress up, do you?" said Jayne. "Well, I've got an outfit in here that I'd be glad to slip—"

Her voice fell away on a puzzled note.

Harmon, rather than leaning back into the dark, moved forward, put his eye to the crack between the wall and the closet door.

The dim afternoon light illuminated the room clearly, and Jayne was right before him, looking down.

Footprints in the carpet.

Drywall dust.

Harmon didn't have time to curse.

Jayne opened the closet door.

His hand closed instinctively on the barrel of the rifle standing at his side.

Her eyes started at the floor, moved up.

Harmon leaned back then, used both hands to bring the gun up.

Jayne was inches from the gun's muzzle.

"Who are y—"

There was a flash, a brilliant, deafening detonation of light and sound in the small room.

It smothered all sounds from Harmon's ears, but his eyes recovered quickly. Quickly enough to see Jayne's body fall backwards in two pieces. The bottom half landed between the young man's splayed legs. The other half slumped to the floor at the foot of the bed, flipped and disgorged its contents like a spilled grocery bag.

The guy, his mouth open in horror, was spattered with blood from the soles of his feet to his forehead.

Harmon stepped out of the closet, shouldered the rifle.

It was heavy, long and unwieldy, and difficult to aim.

The young man turned to leap from the bed, the beginnings of a long, high-pitched scream pushing past his lips.

Harmon tracked him with the gun, pulled the trigger.

Another roar and blast of white, obliterating light.

His head tumbled end over end like a poorly thrown football. It struck the wall above the headboard, rebounded with a sound like a steak being slapped onto the butcher counter, rolled onto the floor.

The previously bland and colorless room was now festooned with a mass of red streamers and polka dots, like a room decorated for Carnivale or a Haitian voodoo ceremony.

Harmon stood in the middle of the carnage for a moment, breathing loudly. His mouth was dry and hanging open.

He'd ruined his blind, blown his cover, had to put his subjects down before they turned on him. It happened before, to be sure. But it never prevented him from doing his job as a photographer.

From capturing the moment.

And it wouldn't now.

* * *

It took until the next evening. When neither Jayne nor her partner returned to work or showed up the next morning, an alarm was raised. Calls were made. Harmon saw a few people park their cars near Jayne's, go to her apartment and knock on the door. Harmon's door camera was working, and he could see their concerned faces and hear their earnest voices.

"Jayne?" they called. "Ms. Fletcher?"

Another knock, then more hesitantly, "Tim? Tim Pratt?"

Three people made this trip, knocked, spoke similar words.

Three people left with knitted brows.

In the evening, the police arrived and the scene changed.

Three squad cars, an ambulance, a station wagon bearing the seal of the county coroner, and a homicide van all crowded the parking lot. People milled all over—residents from the complex, cops, reporters trailing cameras and wires and lights.

Harmon even saw the young night manager, standing in his baggy shorts and sandals, one hand atop his head, his mouth agog as they wheeled out one of the stretchers with a lumpy and misshapen body bag atop it.

* * *

The mortuary was locked. But really, who wants to break into a funeral parlor? It didn't even have an alarm system.

She was still in one of the parlors. The room was draped in cloth and dotted here and there with brass urns and tasteful accessories. Her casket was nearly lost in a spray of flowers that formed a corona of multi-colored blossoms.

It was a peach-colored bronze, and Harmon wondered if this color was a personal favorite.

Standing before the casket, he spent what he figured to be an appropriately respectful period of time. Then, he opened its top half. Her hair was up in a tight bun, and her face looked secretive and pinched. He opened the lower lid.

The upper half of Jayne's body terminated abruptly at the waist, artfully disguised by a drape of white lace and satin. Where the lower half of her body was supposed to be, though, was a white satin bag, tied at the top with a cord. Through its sheer cover, he could make out the shape of her legs.

He hefted this out, a surprisingly heavy and awkward package, and took it to the lobby, found what appeared to be a janitor's closet just off the main office and stashed the bag there behind a stack of orange traffic cones, cleaning supplies and boxes of window stickers that read FUNERAL.

Returning to the parlor, he took stock once again of the supplies jostling around in his vest, checked the seating of his lens on the camera body, closed his fingers around the loose extra batteries.

He was set.

This was where being a small, slight man paid off, just as it had in the jungles.

He climbed into the casket, his head opposite Jayne's. He lifted the padded batting she lay upon, scooted his legs underneath, straightened them all the way out. Even so, they came to just about Jayne's shoulders. *Plenty of room.*

He sat up, rearranged the pillows and veils on Jayne's end, made sure his feet weren't showing or knocking what was left of her body out of level. He closed the upper end first, then closed the lower end.

* * *

It had been dark a long time now, and it was difficult to breathe.

Harmon had heard the early morning rustling, the lid of the casket opening and the mortuary attendants prepping Jayne. He'd listened to the muffled words of the service, felt the casket tip and sway when the pallbearers hefted it into the hearse.

He felt the casket lowered, lowered, slowly, until it thumped onto the ground. Then the concrete shell settled over it, and the distant patter of earth that fell upon it, the sinuous twists of dust that squeezed through the space between the two lids.

He heard it all, but paid no attention.

The camera was to his eye, his hands grasping it lightly, his finger slick with sweat, pressed gently on the shutter button.

And he waited.

As the air thinned and his shirt soaked with his own sweat, he waited.

He waited for the moment, the one place in time when he could be sure she wasn't aware of his presence, that she was her one, true, private self. There would be no brushing her teeth now, no making waffles or washing dishes.

Only this.

So, he put the camera to his eye and waited.

All was darkness circled by darkness.

But he could wait. Oh, yes.

He could wait for it. The moment.

He could wait with the best of them.

THE NIGHT MOVES

IT IS A FLUID THING, a thick thing. A tangible, frangible thing.

It moves, it moves like water—dark, thick water. It covers and it hides. It envelops and surrounds. Buoys you on its rippling back.

And in its anger, drowns.

We move within it, and it moves within us, too.

Some say it is an absence; the lack of warmth, the lack of light.

But it is, in its truest form, a presence; the abundance of stuff too tenuous, too tenebrous to sustain itself in the presence of light.

But it is there, there with us, all the time.

Oh, the night. How it moves...within, without.

Always...*everywhere*.

* * *

He walks the streets of the city, a city, any city.

It is that time of year when the air itself is edged, wet and cold like the lips of a woman's open, expectant mouth held ready for a lover's deep kiss. It presses against him from all sides, the air does, stirs the edges of his great, black coat as he walks, long, long strides, his legs scissoring.

Twilight spreads across the sky like a bruise; the sun the color of a dropped peach. And he walks, he strides his long strides through the city.

And he smiles, smiles a wide, inviting smile that shows teeth, that shows dimples on either side of a set of pink, sensuous lips. Eyes that are direct, focused on something ahead, just out of sight, just out of reach.

The people, the other people of that city who pass him, notice him as they notice almost nothing else. For them, all of them, he stands out from the background noise that is the buildings, the cars, the rain-glazed pavement steaming like an overheated beast, the plate glass windows fogged with the breathing of those inside, the puddled sidewalks, the swirl and eddy of the wind.

They see, these people, his smile, fleeting as it is as he strides by, the flapping of his great black coat like a raven's wings, visual punctuation to the grace note of that smile.

But it, his smile that is, is like the flash of a knife, a white-hot knife that sears across their vision, slicing at the wounds within each of them, exposing them, cauterizing them.

Later they will remember that smile, only that smile, but not the look of the man, his hair, his eyes, even the long, billowing black coat.

* * *

She, there, the woman with the supple Coach briefcase and the Manolo Blahniks, she loses her stride, the definite forward momentum she has maintained since exiting the subterranean depths of the Metro. Without thinking, she throws out a hand to catch herself, an error, a *faux pas* in this city, any city. Her hand closes on a shoulder, clenches, touches, actually *touches* a stranger.

And she remembers her college roommate, the theft of a term paper years ago, not thought of since. A simple thing, a stupid thing. But the roommate was a better student, a better writer. She could afford to take a zero on it, even though it was a mid-term. That was the thought, at the time, her thought, for what it was worth.

But the zero wedged itself into the cracks of her roommate's already crumbling life, split it apart. That zero she never recovered from. First it became a C, in that class, then spread like a cancer into the very tissue of her life. She lost her scholarship, dropped out, disappeared. And never knew what had become of the paper, that her roommate—her friend!— had stolen it, had done the thing, the small, stupid thing that sent her life cascading out of control.

And this woman, who stands here on the street, her Coach bag limp, one Manolo Blahnik hanging askew from a slightly raised foot, still clasps the shoulder of a stranger, clenches it with a shaking hand to keep from falling.

She falters, closes her eyes against the tears she feels burning behind her lids.

A small thing, a stupid thing.

* * *

He, there, the man with the grease-smudged coveralls, the dirty denim coat thrown open, the very tip of a dagger tattoo visible, its haft descending his sternum, its blade disappearing under the stretched collar of his gray T-shirt, he pauses, drops the clipboard he is holding. It clatters to the ground at his feet, its multi-colored papers fluttering like the wings of an exotic, tropical bird.

He, too, lurches to a standstill in the man's wake, but retains enough presence to stand on his own.

The memory flashes in his brain with a force that snaps his head back on his neck.

The feel of its fur held tight in his calloused hand. The writhing mass of muscle that twisted and squirmed and spat and hissed. The flash of claws raking through the air, vainly trying to reach him, to dislodge the hand, to draw blood.

He sees the face of his ex-girlfriend—*the bitch, the cunt*—smiling, somehow like the man who strode by.

He sees, in his memory he sees, the flash of the knife across its throat, the spray of warm, dark blood. The hissing, mewling turning to a bubbling, gurgling.

The frantic movements fading, lessening.

He sees the face of his ex-girlfriend—*the bitch, the cunt*—after, as he'd never actually seen her, red and puffy, tear-streaked as she kneels over its body, weeping as she sees herself reflected in the pool of its blood.

And he knows, knows for the first time, that she never knew, never suspected that it was him, had been him, his knife, his rage.

He swallows this knowledge whole, burning, bitter in his mouth, his throat. It falls with an almost audible plop into the pit of his stomach, and there it begins the slow progress of eating a whole through his gut.

A small thing, a stupid thing.

* * *

He, there, the boy with the Godsmack T-shirt and the ruffled formless hair, the metal belt that is actually a bicycle chain, the low-hanging jeans and untied, high-top Converse sneakers, black but discolored from walking through puddles, he pulls his pale, shaking hand from inside the long, black duster he wears.

He stops, buffeted by people on all sides, people still walking, people who do not see the smile, the slash of the smile, the fierce, cutting beam of his smile.

With one hand, one pale, shaking hand, he wipes his forehead slicked with rain but also with salt sweat. It is a damp, chilly day in this city, any city, and yet he sweats beneath his thin Godsmack T-shirt and the open, expansive, covering folds of the black duster.

Inside the shadows of that great coat, tucked into pockets, secreted in zippered pouches and mesh sleeves, snuggled along the long, thin bones of his nearly meatless body, are guns. Four guns. Each loaded, each jostling amiably against cardboard boxes of ammunition. Each box of ammunition is special to that one gun: a box of .22 bullets, a box of .38 bullets, a box of .45 bullets and a box of 9 millimeter bullets.

Each box of ammunition is particular to each gun, because each gun is particular to each victim. It is a symmetry he likes, has spent time thinking about, planning for. The .22 for his younger brother. The .38 for his older sister. The .45 for his mother.

The 9 millimeter, oh, that is for his father, only for him.

And each bullet within each of those cardboard boxes, carefully constructed to keep each bullet upright and tightly packed and safe as eggs in an egg carton, each bullet is marked, in his mind at least, with the name of the person he will put them into. Each bullet. *All* of the bullets.

That thought, each bullet blooming from the gun, blossoming in slow motion from the barrel of each gun like a magician's trick bouquet, that thought now makes him sweat, where before it had given him a kind of cold pleasure.

Now, after the smile, it just makes him sweat. Sweat and a yawning emptiness within him, inside him that makes him feel, curiously, that he is standing on a pit, on the edge of a pit inside himself. That he is in danger of falling into some bottomless pit inside him. *Of* him.

But it is a pit filled with nothing, containing nothing.

And that is the thought that makes him sweat; that within him is a vast, bottomless chasm of nothingness whose edge he must find a way to creep from, ever so slowly, to avoid falling into.

To avoid losing himself *within* himself.

When he recovers, he bends forward like an accomplished actor just finishing the role of a lifetime, bows and vomits his lunch of a cheeseburger, fries and a chocolate shake from McDonald's onto the slick and steaming pavement. The crowd keeps moving like fish inside an aquarium herded by the tapping of a finger on the outside of the glass, parts around him and the spray of his vomit, pink and congealed on the sidewalk.

When he recovers—the burning slash of that man's smile, his smile lingering in his brain—he stumbles off down the street, unconsciously following the path of the now wholly gone and mostly forgotten man. He comes to a bridge over the river that bisects the city, any city, parts the dark folds of his coat and hurtles the guns and the cardboard boxes of ammunition over its side.

The guns flash on and off in the peach-colored sunlight as they tumble end over end down and into the water. The cardboard boxes open, disgorging their ammunition, which spreads across the air over the river, sparkling like fireworks.

For a moment, a moment that opens inside him, opens as wide as the dark pit, he considers following them, climbing atop the battered, graffiti-covered railing and simply falling into the river.

But he doesn't.

He knows, somewhere inside of him, that he wouldn't sparkle in the sunlight like the guns, like the ammo. He would flop like a shadow into the water with no lights to carry him there, to welcome him there.

Just water. Dark, encompassing water.

He goes to leave, turns back to the river and sends the black duster, wadded into a ball, into the water, too. It falls in his place, unfurling like a dark parachute before it slides to the water, sinks, sinks, sinks.

A small thing, a stupid thing.

* * *

He, there, the boy with the Godsmack T-shirt and the ruffled, formless hair, the metal belt that is actually a bicycle chain, the low-hanging jeans and untied, high-top Converse sneakers, black but discolored from walking through puddles, he puts his pale, shaking hands into the pockets of his jeans, heads for home.

* * *

The smiling man, though, he has moved on, left these people in his wake.

Moved on, as the night does, as the night moves.

As the night moves through the city, a city, any city.

But it is there, there with us, all of the time.

Oh, the night. How it moves…within, without.

Always…*everywhere.*

Heavenly shades of night are moving, falling, starless.

And we, finally free, rise to greet it.

Always…*everywhere…*

GETHSEMANE, IN RAIN

I. THE DAUGHTER

The sign on Missouri Highway 94 welcomes visitors to Gethsemane, population 28,756 according to the census of 2000. In the finest tradition of Midwestern pronunciations—"Kay-ro" for Cairo, "Versales" for Versailles—the town's name is pronounced "Jeths-man-e," with a long "e" at the end. Newcomers inevitably mock this peculiar pronunciation, but soon they are gently correcting those who come after them, in whispers, as if passing along the town's hidden name, its secret heart.

Gethsemane may seem a strange name for a small Midwestern town, but the stolid settlers of the plains dove into the Bible many times to find names for their pleasant, dust-blown little villages—Bethany, Canaan, Salem, Gilead, Jericho, Bethlehem, Jerusalem. Gethsemane, the garden in the hills of Jerusalem where Christ was betrayed after the Last Supper, struck someone at some time as just the right name for this pleasant town.

And no one disagreed.

Inarguably, Gethsemane is a lovely town, as lovely in spots as a garden. And to be sure, there are many, many people who have been betrayed in this Gethsemane. It is a lovely town nonetheless.

That other Gethsemane, being a garden in the desert, felt little rain within its boundaries. The most meaningful rain its dusty soil received was the blood sweated from Christ's brow before he was led off to be crucified.

This Gethsemane, though, does receive rain. And in this rain, Gethsemane is as lovely as a town gets. Like an aging actress filmed through gauze, the city's harder edges are fuzzed, blurred; not so much softened, though, as made vaguer. Like squinting at a scene that is perhaps not the most beautiful, the lack of focus and the falling rain bleed detail and color together like a hastily done watercolor.

In the rain, the town's green hills look like the glistening humps of some enormous serpent rising from the depths of a dark and mysterious sea.

In the rain, the town's buildings seem diluvian, twisted and fluttering in a strangely beautiful way. Like strands of kelp undulating on the currents of that same mysterious sea.

In the rain, the town's inhabitants move amongst each other like fish, flitting here and there amidst the grey background, the rain making everything seem transparent and insubstantial. The citizens don't interact. Rather, each seems locked in his or her own fate, going through motions that have within them a feeling of deep familiarity. They're fish constantly testing the transparent walls of a great aquarium.

In Gethsemane, the dead interact more than the living.

* * *

Jim Monroe hates the rain, hates the way the city glows in it, flaunts it. He hates the *k-thip, k-thip, k-thip* sound of his wiper blades, hates the way the water beads on the hood of his freshly waxed car. He hates the umbrella dripping on the floor behind his seat, hates the squeak of his shoes against the sodden carpet of his aging Buick. He particularly hates having been made to go out in this rain, as drivers in Gethsemane, in his opinion, lose any of their driving ability in the rain.

Jim drives to Feel-Rite Pharmacy to pick up a prescription for his wife, who has taken to her bed in the grips of some illness that has gotten worse over the last eight hours or so. Jim has patiently waited on her for three days now, not complaining, not begrudging her the time in bed or the dozens of little requests she makes of him: hot tea, water, soup, another pillow, another blanket.

Though Jim is not a patient man himself—and even though Jim is the kind of sick person who prefers to crawl away and be left alone to either recuperate or die—he takes care of his wife with worry and compassion.

Until she makes him call the doctor to get a prescription.

Jim is not a believer in anything stronger than aspirin or a glass of Alka-Seltzer. Prescription medicine, in his mind, is yet another way for companies to bilk money from older people. Jim isn't yet retired, but he is sixty-three, and the insurance from the accounting firm he works at isn't the best.

He himself has managed to weather illnesses without a single visit to the doctor in more than eight years. And that lapse only because a kidney stone caused him to pass out and be taken against his will by ambulance to the hospital, where he spent three very expensive days in an uncomfortable bed being fed sixty-dollar aspirins.

So, when Gwen, pale and shaking, asks her husband to call the doctor and have him phone in a prescription, Jim is not happy. But he can bear his own pain. He cannot bear his wife's. He sets his teeth and calls their physician, who calls the Feel-Rite Pharmacy to order something he assures Jim will help Gwen.

Of course, when he learns that he will have to go out into the rain to pick the medication up, well, Jim fumes and fusses—all to himself.

But here he is now, out amidst the other fish swirling obliviously in the rain. Except for Jim, that is. He is vigilant, aware of every movement of every ill-driven car near him.

Ahead, down an insubstantial smudge of dark grey he knows to be Main Street, Jim sees the pulse of red lights turning the rain on his windshield into thin drops of blood. Without thinking, Jim slows, not to lollygag but to take even more caution against the other drivers who are, no doubt, lollygagging themselves. A second of attention taken from the road to see the accident, Jim knows, would result in another.

Drivers ahead of him stab at their brakes, their own red lights adding to the crimson on Jim's windshield.

As he approaches the wreckage, the traffic slows to a near standstill. Jim, almost idle, takes a moment to look out his side window.

Through the glass smeared with pulsing red, he sees the outlines of two cars T-boned in the oncoming lane. The accident looks serious with at least four police cars, two ambulances and a fire engine crowding the scene. Plenty of dark-suited people mill about here and there, wraith-like through the rain.

A snide shake of his head joins a snide thought about how right he was about his fellow citizens' lack of driving skills as he turns back to see what is in front of him. The traffic is completely stopped.

Sensing he might be there a while, he shifts the car into PARK.

A light flashes not on the window, but in his head; a light that calls his attention to the left, out the side window.

Turning slowly, he scans the accident scene, the emergency equipment, the line of road flares that cordon off the area, the people that flit here and…

…*there.*

A single figure stands amidst the chaos, within it, yet not of it. Immune to it.

It is smallish and very white, aglow with some inner brightness that causes it to leap at him from the overall darkness of the wreckage as sharply as the warning light that fired in his brain.

He gasps, brings his hand absently to his chest to clutch the area over his heart.

His other hand fumbles with his glasses, which he had not bothered to put on for the drive. He rakes them across his numbing face, pushing them roughly over his eyes.

That same hand then, still trembling, flicks at the switch to lower the electric window of the Buick.

As soon as there is a gap of an inch, rain pelts in, striking cool against his warming face, speckling his glasses.

The window whirs down and the scene comes into stark focus, like a lens snapped into place.

Jim Monroe's heart *moves* within his chest, as if unsure of its place anymore; rousing itself like a thing that has been asleep overlong.

He swallows, tries to form her name on his lips, to cry it out to her.

She stands in what seems to be a tear in the space around her, as if seen through a hole in a photograph. Dark violet light, the color of fresh bruises, edges this wound in the air. She is stock still, her back to him, her white dress radiating light, the rays of which seem to fall on Jim and only Jim. Neither the rain nor the red emergency strobes touch her fair skin, her blonde hair or even the vaguely pulsing purple aura clinging to her.

Although he can't see her face, he knows it is her, knows it in his lurching heart.

Jim wipes at his glasses with a shaking hand. When that doesn't clear his vision, he wipes at his eyes.

Replacing his glasses, he notices she has turned to him. As he watches her small, beautiful face—the recognition of which, after so long, blows doors within his mind cleanly off their time-rusted hinges—her mouth opens wide, then wider, forming a huge perfect O.

Slowly, she raises her right arm, points back in the direction Jim has come, her face alarmed, beseeching.

His breathing having stopped moments earlier, Jim strains to hear her words over the patter of the rain, the emergency personnel and their equipment.

And then, in another blast, a single word erupts in his brain. His teeth come together hard on his tongue, which brings pain and the taste of copper into his mouth.

Go!

The white light clinging to her form erupts then, bursts from her in a soundless, hugely loud blast that detonates over Jim in a furious, blinding concatenation sounding strangely of trumpets. It sweeps the violet light before it, seals the wound from which she emerged.

Fumbling, his eyes filled with exploding phosphenes, he clumsily throws the car into REVERSE, backs up at an angle to the alarmed honking of the car behind him. Without looking, he completes his three-point turn, lurches crazily into the oncoming lane, not stopping to look for other drivers.

Luckily with the traffic stopped, there are none, and he fishtails into the distance, his departure marked by policemen and firemen shaking their heads and silently cursing his impatience.

Jim drives through the pouring rain of Gethsemane; drives as he hasn't done since he was a wild boy of seventeen. On the way, he isn't sure if he takes a single breath or if his heart makes a single beat.

At home, he finds Gwen half in and half out of the bed, her face strangely slack and a thin line of drool connecting her lips with the phone that lies on the floor. He hoists her gently into bed, dials the ambulance.

The sound of trumpets fades in his light-deafened ears.

* * *

Three days later, Gwen comes home to their same bed, following treatment for a heart attack that also brought with it a mild stroke. Jim dotes on her as he brings her home, makes her comfortable.

He never does explain to her what had brought him home so soon, breathless and wild-haired and without the prescription. Nestled in her bed, with a cup of tea and a good book, she does notice something that makes her wonder.

There, on the dresser and the bureau and the hope chest, on the wall and on her bedside table, are photos of their only child Kelly. Thirty years ago these pictures had disappeared from the house, taken down by both parents separately, quietly, as if by some unspoken agreement.

Gwen reaches over and lifts the photo nearest her. Kelly is about nine years old in this photo, wearing the white Easter dress she loved. A penumbra of white light spills from the sun behind her, gives her form a radiant aura.

Jim comes in as she holds this picture, soaking in its details.

He sets the cup of chamomile tea on her nightstand, gently takes the photo from her and replaces it beside the teacup.

"When you're feeling better…up to it…you know," he stammers at her, looking at his feet like a schoolboy asking for his first date. "I thought we'd go out there, see her, you know. Maybe take some flowers."

Gwen nods imperceptibly, as if the stroke still holds sway over the muscles of her neck.

"That would be nice," she answers, suddenly wondering if she can remember just where the tombstone is.

Gwen looks at her husband, eyes still lowered, and knows they'd never find her in the light of the sun.

II. The Living

The chair comes in on a Wednesday. It is a simple Louis XVIII, prim and uncomfortable looking. The old upholsterer chuckles to himself when he sees it, knowing the old saw that people look like their pets was truer about people and their furniture.

Before he rounds the corner of his back room, where he'd heard the tinkle of the little bell over his door, he guesses the chair's owner will be a pleasant but stately matron, perhaps widowed, perhaps not. A blue-haired doyenne with at least one room in her house where people—the *grandchildren*, particularly—are not allowed, certainly never on the furniture.

The little man is glad to have a customer during the day. Walk-in business these days is rare. Reupholstering furniture was becoming a rare need and an even rarer skill, especially in a sleepy little town like Gethsemane. What business he has comes through word of mouth and small ads placed in the local newspaper.

He comes around the corner wiping his hands. He'd been staining the arms of an oversize Mission-style rocking chair, and his palms are brown and sticky and redolent of varnish.

The chair's owner is partially blocked by the chair itself, sitting atop the man's front counter, near the ancient cash register. The upholsterer comes to the counter and places his hand on the chair.

"Hello," he says, his voice cracking. There is a touch—just a touch—of an accent in it, which he hates but has learned to live with. The accent is soft and vague enough to be misconstrued for just about anything, and he is cheerfully as vague when asked about where he is from. As far as he is concerned, fifty-plus years in this country qualify him as a native, just as the same amount of time in his profession qualifies him as an upholsterer.

Not to mention all the hard work he's had to do. Everything he's had to give up.

Who he was before this, what he did is meaningless.

"Oh, hello," comes the voice from behind the chair. "I need some help."

The upholsterer freezes at the sound of the voice, takes his hand away from the chair as if burned.

Against his will he begins to tremble, and he leans some of his weight against the counter to steady himself.

Run, you old fool, his mind shouts.

But where to go. And why now, now after all these years?

The man pushes the chair to one side and presents himself to the upholsterer. It is raining outside. The man is brushing water from his shoulders. He is a tall, powerfully built, good-looking man in his late 30s or early 40s. His short, neat hair is plastered to his head, and water trickles down his temples, soaks into the collar of his Oxford shirt.

His face is blandly unlined, as if he has never crossed anything in life that has crossed him in return. He is full of what the shopkeeper has learned to accept among most Americans: a kind of vacuous, all-purpose friendliness that is as infectious as the common cold and just as long lasting.

Swallowing, he stretches his face into a pliable smile again.

"Well, if you need help with this chair, I might be able to help, sure."

The man does not notice, or chooses not to notice, the upholsterer's shaking hands, the slightly too-stretched smile on his face. "Well, I'm friends with the Monroes. You know, Jim and Gwen. You reupholstered their couch and chair a few months ago, and you did a great job. They gave us your name and recommended you highly."

The shopkeeper closes his eyes and tries to focus. "Ahh, yes, the Monroes. Yes, nice people," he says, remembering both pieces of furniture and the work he did. He had recovered the couch in a chocolate and pink material that, while very stylish in its colors, did not appeal to the husband. To compensate, the wife had let him recover the chair in a buff-colored micro-suede that *did* appeal to the husband.

Internally, the upholsterer shrugged. Not his best work, but adequate. *If only they knew what I am capable of doing at my best*, he thinks. But the thought is fleeting, easily dismissed. Does one ever know what another is capable of doing at his or her best?

"Yes, well it was nice of them to recommend me," he says, trying to avoid looking at the man's face.

It was close, so close. Close enough to make the upholsterer's heart hurt.

"Well, we had a little accident and ruined the material," the man says, tilting the chair so the shopkeeper can see the seat.

The material is a slick, lemony-yellow cotton, patterned with alternating thin and thick lines of white where the material was stitched to look like lace. It is spattered with darkening spots where raindrops have soaked into the fabric. He wipes at these spots distractedly.

Across this backdrop is a large, fan-shaped stain, narrower at the end toward the chair's back and expanding to the front edge of the seat. It is made up of strange runners of dried material, ribbons and snakes of the stuff that twist across the fabric like a Medusa's head.

The stains are brownish and slightly faded, as if the owners had tried many remedies to remove it. All their efforts had managed to achieve was a slight fading of the stains, and a mottling of the delicate yellow of the fabric.

"What is the stain?" the upholsterer asks, still peering closely at it.

Wine? Chocolate ice cream?

"Blood," the man blurted, seemingly glad to get it out quickly.

He looks up at that, peering intently at the man.

Blood? he says, but it is only in his mind. *Please, God, no.*

"Well," the man says, clearly relishing the story. "My wife was pregnant, and…well, you're not going to believe this. She went into labor last month at home, and I ended up delivering the baby myself right in this chair. Tied off the umbilical cord myself. *With my shoelaces!*"

The man smiles his idiot smile, and the shopkeeper blinks, takes a deep breath. He lowers his head again to the fabric, touches it softly with his aged hands, calloused now from handling so many yards and yards of material, sawing and joining wood. He strokes it as if he can feel something more through it.

"Your wife, she is okay?"

"Oh, sure. Both of them are doing fine and back at home."

"That's good, ya?" the upholsterer says, absently slipping a little more deeply into his accent. "And the baby?"

"A beautiful baby girl, Maria Anne."

"Maria Anne," he repeats, tears he cannot afford to spill gathering in the corners of his eyes. "A beautiful name."

"A little too Old World for me, but it was her mother's name. She never knew her mother, so I guess it was a way for her to, I dunno, honor her or something."

The shopkeeper ducks behind the chair, still pretending to examine it. He draws the rough back of his hand, the varnish there still tacky, across his eyes, clearing them of tears.

"How did she know her mother's name if she never knew her?"

"She's adopted. Been trying to find her real parents, but with no luck. She's only been able to find out her mother's first name, but not her maiden or married names. So, can we fix this?"

The upholsterer blinks again, stands. "Does your wife have a fabric preference?"

"She just wants something as close as possible to the original. It doesn't have to be an exact match, just close."

He considers this, hand on his chin.

"I think I can find something similar."

He quotes the man a price and gives him an estimate of how long it will take to find the fabric, get it, and repair the chair.

Shaking hands, the man accepts these terms and takes a business card from the upholsterer. They say their goodbyes, and the man turns to leave.

"Give little Marie Anne a kiss from me and say hello to Ellen, too."

"I will," the man answers, follows with a cheery wave, then disappears into the rain, into his car.

The little bell tinkles again, and the door closes behind him.

The upholsterer watches him climb into his car and drive away. The man didn't react when he mentioned his wife's name, though the man hadn't brought it up in conversation.

And what if he had? the shopkeeper asks himself.

What if he had reacted?

What if he'd asked why? How?

He sighs, lifts the chair and carries it to the back room. He sets it onto the floor and clears an area on his workbench to accommodate it.

He gathers several tools, then goes to work immediately. He already knows where he can find the fabric that is a close match to this. He will call the supplier tomorrow and order several yards. It should be in by Monday. Tuesday at the latest.

Until then, though, he removes the stained material from the seat, carefully lifting the seat itself from its base, then using a pair of needle-nosed pliers to yank out the staples holding the material to the thin piece of wood.

When the final staple is removed, he peels the fabric away, exposing a few layers of cotton batting and the foam pad underneath. He pushes the chair aside and snaps the fabric out to its full dimension. It is a rough circle, perhaps three feet in diameter. The fabric that had been tucked in and stapled underneath is noticeably more colorful and vibrant than the perfect circle of material that had been exposed as the seat.

The stain is visible through the back of the fabric and, he notices, on the batting and foam padding. Gently, he takes this stained piece of cloth and pins it to a bulletin board hanging over the coffee pot that is the one piece of comfort he has in his neat and tidy workroom. He arranges the piece of material so the stain flows downward.

The upholsterer steps back to admire it, and the tears start again, rolling freely down his craggy features, slipping into his trembling lips.

III. The Dead

Help.

Gerald holds the note gently, unfolded in his palm like a stricken bird.

He stares at it for a full minute, taking in the torn edges of the paper, ripped from a larger sheet. The handwriting is in ink, the letters large and loopy. The letter P in HELP is blurry, smeared by some liquid.

A tear?

Gerald closes his hand. He is standing beside his mailbox, a smooth, plump box of green plastic that looks as if it has been extruded from the earth. His house sits behind him, and those of his neighbors stretch to the left and right, across the street and into the distance. For Gerald, there is a comforting, enveloping sameness to them, as if they were dropped by an exacting baker like pre-measured cookies on a sheet.

It is a modest neighborhood, but fine for him. It might seem unusual to have bought a house in a new subdivision for a man his age, but it is exactly what Gerald wanted. He wanted something known, something not challenging, something calmly ordinary.

Gerald, you see, is dying.

Not merely because he is seventy-nine, though this certainly doesn't help in any way, but because he has inoperable liver cancer. The disease is in what his doctors euphemistically call its *terminal phase*, with perhaps no more than six months until it runs its final course and terminates his— and its own—existence.

Only eighteen months ago, Gerald took his remaining money from various investments and retirement plans and spent it on a house in which he could be comfortable during his last days.

Gerald just wants to see the neighborhood kids go off to school, the housewives sweep the front porches and sun themselves in the backyards.

He wants to see dads mowing the lawns and washing the cars and grilling out on the weekends.

This is preferable to living in a skilled nursing facility or a retirement village or whatever other test-marketed, flim-flam name they give old folks homes these days. More preferable than sitting across a Formica table watching women named Agnes and Ethel and June gum their grey mashed potatoes or play canasta or churn out ridiculous crafts meant to vie for shelf space with distressingly similar items made by their grade school-aged grandchildren.

He doesn't want to watch others of his generation slowly dying. He doesn't want to be any more reminded of his own impending departure than is absolutely necessary.

He wants to know, wants to see that life does go on, that life will go on, even without him.

In choosing this kind of end to his life he makes himself a target of gossip and discussion from neighbors who look at him with curious suspicion.

Gerald doesn't speak much to his neighbors. He is more an observer, not a participant. Most days he is too weak, too sick to go outside and chit-chat. Often the only time he's able to go outside, the only time his neighbors are likely to see him, is to retrieve the mail. It isn't much, but he insists on going every day to collect it, which, these days, is little more than credit card offers and coupon mailings.

And, ironically, the occasional mailer from a mortuary or cemetery.

So, he tells himself still standing there at the mailbox, *the person who left this note knows enough about me to know that I get my own mail.*

But who?

Who left this note in my mailbox?

Who needs my help?

A sharp flash makes his tired heart lurch a bit. He feels a twinge of guilt at his mood being lifted by someone's need.

But it makes him feel useful for the first time in many a year.

The question is *who* needs his help?

And *what* do they need?

And why?

Gerald scans the houses nearest his, first left then right, then across the street.

In the house directly across from his there is a young couple with two children, a boy of eight and another of about six, if memory served. The wife works part-time at a bakery in a nearby strip mall, while the husband is some sort of creative type. Gerald surmises this, rather than knows this, because the man leaves for work each morning in a golf shirt and jeans. Times may have changed since Gerald was last in the workforce, but he doubts if a banker would leave the house dressed this way even today.

Holding the crumpled note, he turns slowly to the house next door. It's a mess. The grass is a little too long, bikes are sprawled in the front yard as if there has been a massive motocross accident. Trashcans, empty now, stand by the curb from Wednesday's pickup, and here it is Friday. The screen door hangs askew on its hinges, giving the house the comical appearance of a person with a single crooked tooth.

Behind his house there is a grungy apartment complex that hangs on the border of the subdivision like a barnacle, grotty and unwanted. Gerald automatically dismisses that it could be someone from there, though he supposes that anyone who lives there probably does need help.

To his right, then, is a house in which a new couple has recently moved. They are a little older, quiet, keep to themselves. He's seen them a few times. The woman is small and furtive, nervous as a bird. The man is large and moves with aggression, his face smooth and curiously bland, his eyes dark and as depthless as a shark's.

More often than not, all of the shades in their house are drawn, but sometimes at night, backlit perhaps by a small television or table lamp, Gerald has seen strange shadows play across these closed curtains. Curious, serpentine shapes that undulate across the flashing indigo light.

One morning just a week or so ago, Gerald saw the husband wrestle an upholstered chair into the back of his pickup truck. He could have sworn the seat of this chair was stained with blood.

Help.

Could she need help? Help to get away from him?

Perhaps she is in there now, hiding, cowering, thinking of how she might escape him, his words, his anger. His fists.

Gerald stares at the little slip of paper and suddenly, the entire weight of his seventy-nine years falls onto him.

Thirty years ago, even twenty years ago, he might have been able to provide the kind of help this woman apparently needs.

But now? Nearing eight decades of life, with a poisonous liver, bad knees, flabby muscles, poor reflexes and a disconcertingly bad sense of balance, what help could he provide?

His mind drifts for a bit as he tries to recall something, something small, something packed away in a plastic tub in his basement.

It comes to him eventually, standing there holding someone's cry for help in the palm of his hand, and he thinks that, yes, perhaps there is something he can do.

He closes his hand tightly, crumpling the note.

Raindrops fall around him as he hobbles back into the house, makes the long, arduous journey down the basement steps.

The tubs are moved carefully, slowly.

He finds it nestled in a tub marked CHRISTMAS, enfolded in old stockings.

It gleams darkly at him, invites him to lift it, hold it.

Upstairs he sits at the kitchen table, several fingers of bourbon poured into an orange juice glass. The bourbon is fire in his mouth, falling down his throat, but it gives some heat, some life to his frail legs, his arms.

It almost steadies his shaking hand.

He doesn't think to wonder if the note is real, if it is directed at him, if it is from the neighbor woman.

He doesn't think to wonder why anyone would chose him to come to their rescue; what aid they might reasonably expect to get from a dying seventy-nine-year-old man.

He doesn't think to wonder what might happen to him when he opens the front door to his house and lurches into the rain.

He thinks only of how this part of his life has been about waiting: for visits from his family, for the drugs to kick in, for the results of the next test.

Waiting to die.

He's tired of waiting.

He wants to do something.

So, he stands, feeling the weather in his knees, his hips.

Outside, he is soaked by the relentless rain before he reaches the end of his own driveway.

The gun gleams dark and oiled with each flash, as if a photographer were capturing every moment, searing it into the slowly unraveling fabric of Gerald's life. Each flash of lightning is another memory, a burst of life, a benediction.

And Gerald is *alive*.

IV. THE SON

The lost boy peers from the single window and wonders how he came to be here.

The window is small, uncleaned. It is guarded by blinds and a thick layer of curtains that he must dig through to gain the outside.

Rain falls from a sky that is rendered even greyer as seen through the filthy window. Outside is the half-empty parking lot of the apartment complex. Those cars still there—rusted, dented, dirty—huddle together like wounded beasts.

How easy it would be, he thinks, *for me to walk down there—walk down there with no fear, smash a window, hotwire the car and drive away.*

Away.

But to where?

And, no fear?

Who am I kidding? There's always the fear, even if it sleeps now, stirring only occasionally.

Still there.

Besides, if I wanted to go, I could do it far easier than boosting a car.

I could ride my bike.

I could walk, for that matter. Open the door wide, stride out and walk to the police station, walk right in and tell them who I…who…

Fear.

No, just as it prevents him from taking a car, it dismisses the bike, warns against taking off on foot.

It leashes him here as effectively as chains.

No, more so, because it affects his *desire* to leave, his *need*.

This is home.

Here.

With *him*.

Now, not *before*…

But there is no *before* anymore. Not with him. There was, of course, but best not to think of it.

Because the *before* hurts him, oh, how it hurts him.

And the *before* that was even *before* that hurts him even more.

He closes the heavy curtains, seals the light out of the dirty apartment.

I could go outside, leave this place.

The door is unlocked.

He's very sure, my new father. So very, very sure…

He can be gone from the apartment or even just sealed away in his room, the off-limits bedroom with the locked door, from beneath which deep purple light oozes across the scruffed carpet.

Either way, he's very sure the lost boy won't leave.

Instead, as he usually does, the lost boy turns to the TV, to the video game console and the stack of games there. Pulling one from the stack at random, he glances at its cover illustration of guns and explosions, nods as if in agreement, slides it into the player.

His movement sends a flutter of tiny slips of paper to the floor, unnoticed at first. Each has one word scrawled carefully on it.

HELP.

When he sees the little fall of papers atop the dirty carpet at his feet, he rakes it under the couch with the heel of his tennis shoe, forgets it.

Sinking into the sagging couch, he takes a controller and mindlessly pushes buttons as the game flashing on the TV tells him where to go, what to do, how to feel.

Because, in the end, it is so much easier, so much less painful than doing these things himself.

Briefly, he remembers his new father telling him that he's damaged goods.

No one wants something back after it's been broken.

So, he saves the game, moves to the next level.

And leaves *before* where it is, where it has been since his new father took him.

Lost.

THE CORIOLIS EFFECT
(OR, CHIROMANCY FOR BEGINNERS)

PHRENOLOGY IS FOR IDIOTS, beginners, charlatans.

What's so hard about reading the bumps on someone's head?

I'll tell you the secret of this useless talent, and it's a small secret, indeed.

Be the person who *makes* the bumps, then you have no problem reading the meaning supposedly hidden in them.

But a person's hands, their palms, oh, that's a different thing altogether.

The palms reveal every difficulty, every setback, every bad decision, *everything*. All exposed by the lines crisscrossing there, intersections between every bad path their bearers have ever taken.

The lines show all, including the future, if you know how to read them, to decipher their secret codes, their byzantine structure, their arcane minutiae. Every tiny crack and every miniscule furrow is a story, an encounter, a soul trapped in a thin layer of skin, telling its story over and over, to be read by the fingers of another like the most intimate of braille.

In a way, they are like roadwork. Or, better yet, a map. Like a Rand McNally atlas of a life, showing all the routes, all the highways and old roads, the gleaming interstates and the dusty, gravel byways branching out almost infinitely from them.

Yes, they tell their stories to those who *will* hear them. To those who *can* hear them. From beginning to end.

For stories always end. *Always*.

One way or the other, everything ends.

It's all in the way, the *direction* they spiral in that's important.

* * *

Where?

I don't know where it started. But then again, yes, I do. I can see that path on my own palm, trace its delicate length, a straight arc, a slash across the flesh from the mound of my own thumb all the way across the palm to the meat of its heel.

It started there, always there, back there.

And it's all about how I got here from there. Because, ultimately, it's never about the starting point or even the ending, for that matter. It's always about the trip, the path, the journey. You know, the stops along the way, the seemingly random decisions, the haphazard obstacles, the unseen off ramps and diversions.

The things that lie buried along the way.

I wonder, as I stare at my own palm, I wonder about *his* palm, *his* lines.

I wonder if my brother's palms look anything like mine.

* * *

I held my mother's hand right before the mortician wired them together across her deflated bosom. I checked her palms, and it was a helter-skelter mess of intersecting lines, careening from that initial one, as familiar to me as my own.

They buried her, at my insistence, with her palms wired together, shut. Stephen, too, thought this was fitting.

They thought it nice, as if I wanted her praying.

Not it, not it at all.

I wanted those lines pressed together for eternity, caught in an eternal loop, endless beginning and ending, so there was no clear start, no clear finish anymore.

Just peace in eternal repetition.

Even now, when I think of my mother, I think of her hands folded there in the dark, beneath the earth, and the infinite twist created by the joining of all those lines, like a closed electrical circuit.

* * *

Stephen came along, oh, in '68 or '69. My parents even then were sailing obliviously into their eventual divorce. Everyone seemed to know it except them, even me, and I was only five.

My father worked long hours for an aeronautics company, back when our country did cool stuff like send people to the moon. What he did I'll never really know, because he died back in '85, before he thought either Stephen or I was old enough to discuss it. Oh, it was nothing secret, I'm pretty sure. Just something technical and teeth-numbingly dull, like him.

But I digress. Let's see, mom was a housewife, and so she did lots of interesting stuff like make meals and launder clothes and grocery shop and coordinate what relatives' houses we'd go to on what holidays. Evidently something every bit as complicated as determining lunar insertion orbits, or so she constantly told my father.

Anyway, dad was working lots of hours those days, in the twilight of the Apollo program. It was the late summer of '72. School had begun. The Republicans had nominated Nixon for a second term. Jane Fonda toured North Vietnam and was photographed sitting atop an anti-aircraft gun. George Carlin was arrested in Milwaukee for performing his Seven Words You Can't Say on Television act in public. Eleven Israeli athletes were murdered by Arab terrorists during the Summer Olympics in Munich.

All this, and my brother and I saw our first naked man, who came to us at our bedroom window, his face encased in pantyhose, and tried to pull me outside through it, take me with him.

Kidnap me.

That was where it all started, the lines that snaked throughout our lives, the beginning of so much of the... But I'm ahead of myself.

First, we have to discuss my mother's funeral.

* * *

My mother had moved out to live near me after her second husband passed. She bought a small bungalow, something easy for her to get around, easy for her to maintain. Just a few minutes away. She sold the house we grew up in—the one she received in the divorce from our father—to Stephen, who kept it, but never moved into it, never lived in it. He had his own house about an hour from where we grew up, and he said he preferred to live there.

Too many memories in that old house.

Then why buy the place? I asked.

Too many memories in that old house, he repeated, smiling.

I think I knew what he meant.

Anyway, she died suddenly, and he flew in on a warm, blue September day. I picked him up, embraced him awkwardly, then loaded his suitcase into my car. Though we'd spoken often, Stephen hadn't been to town in a few years. He was a little greyer at the temples, a little leaner and rangier, but looked good. I told him so, and he mentioned the need to stay fit, eat healthy. He glanced at my little gut, raised his eyebrows.

"Trying to stay fat so he won't be able to pull you out the window?"

We laughed at that, but it made me feel a little self-conscious in a way that I didn't particularly care for.

We chatted casually on the way back to my place, where he stowed his luggage, freshened up a bit. After he had rested a little, we climbed back into the car to go make the funeral arrangements. That trip was mostly silent.

At the mortuary we feigned interest as a thin, twitchy little man pored over catalogs, walked us through choosing a suitable casket, suitable music, suitable flowers. I'd brought a dress from my mother's neat and tidy closet, something I'd seldom seen her in but knew that she'd liked. Oh, and suitable shoes, though who'd ever see those?

When the funeral director left the room with the dress and shoes, Stephen turned to me.

"Familiar, huh? I guess you always have to assume that at some point, you're going to have to bury your parents. But still... Right?"

I sighed deeply. "I suppose. I guess we had to put all the experience we gained burying dad to good use somehow."

It was a horrible thing to say, an even more horrible thing to laugh at, but I did both.

But Stephen didn't laugh, didn't smile. His face, in fact, registered no emotion at all.

"But dad's not dead, not really. I know he lives on inside me. I think he lives inside you, too."

My mouth went dry, and my hands shook a little at that observation, on the surface so fitting for the situation, so touching in a way. But Stephen's smile looked like a snarl, and the one I returned must have looked like my twisted innards.

"They never die, any of them. Right? They live on in here," he said, tapping at his temple and not his heart.

"Like the naked man. I bet he never died for you, did he?"

I remained silent until the funeral director returned with the news that the brushed bronze rose casket we'd selected was in stock, so we were good to go.

I was preoccupied when I shook his hand, as Stephen and I drifted back to the car, drove home through a hard, driving rain that made the storefronts and homes we passed as insubstantial as apparitions.

Preoccupied with a space, deep in some woods quite a ways from my house. A quiet place, a private place I'd purchased some years ago in the literal middle of nowhere. Over 100 acres, densely wooded. My retreat, my sanctuary, my…

Reliquary comes to mind. *Aumbry? Cache?*

Other words, too, more specific, more accurate, but somehow less poetic, less appealing.

Preoccupied, too, with shovels and the sound they made piercing the dirt.

The smell of freshly turned earth, the way it crumbles between your fingers.

The muffled screams.

* * *

The road trip was Stephen's idea.

Going back to the old family house, helping him clean it and get it ready to sell. As I said, he kept the house, though didn't live in it. With our mother's death, he'd come to realize it was best just to let it go.

So, after finally placing our mother to rest in the ground, after we dealt with the mourners and well-wishers, after we scraped the macaroni and cheese and chicken tortilla casseroles into the trash, we made new arrangements. We sat in my living room, ties askew, shoes kicked off, and planned a road trip back to the house we'd grown up in. Over cups of coffee, we used an old road atlas to plan the route, then Stephen, always more technically minded than me, entered it into Google maps on his phone.

I watched Stephen's hands as he traced the delicate lines of the road atlas, so much like a web of veins draped across the outline of the country. The backs of his hands were smooth. His palms, though, were as crosshatched as my own.

I flinched when I saw that same arc, curving across the cup of his palm, that same arc that crossed my own.

When we were finished, he stood, stretched, said good night. He disappeared into the guest bedroom, closed the door. I heard the lock click, and after a moment or two, the light snapped off.

I sat in the easy chair for a while staring at the bottom of the door, the little gap between it and the floor. I waited to see if the light would come back on, but it didn't.

I gathered my keys quietly, crept from the house. I left the car lights off until I'd backed into the street.

* * *

I came to in the woods.

I had no idea what time it was, but clearly it was very early in the morning. The sky was cool blue, and the stars shivered within the hold of its darkness. My breath came in tiny, cumulus cloud-puffs that coagulated atop the air.

It was my spot, my quiet place. My safe place. I recognized the shadows of the trees that stood around us like silent witnesses. The ground was soft, spongy, and the air smelled of dirt and damp and mold. I was slick with sweat despite the chill in the early fall air, and I wondered why.

I had no recollection of the ride here, the walk from where I usually parked my car.

I had a hazy, fuzzy-edged memory of stopping at a diner, small, uncrowded, too brightly lit. Flirting casually with a young woman who'd stopped mid-country to grab a late dinner before pressing on.

Something about kissing her in the parking lot, getting slapped.

That's all.

I looked over in the blue-black darkness, saw a shovel leaning against a tree, and my stomach lurched. Whatever I'd eaten at the diner came out, covering the mildewed smell of the woods with something sharp and acidic that steamed like a living thing.

There was a long walk back to the car, a longer drive home.

I pulled the car into the driveway just as the rising sun painted the horizon a lovely pinkish-blue.

No sound or light from beneath my brother's door, so I crept into my own room, shut the door quietly, collapsed in my bed without removing my clothes.

* * *

"Do you remember the naked man?" Stephen asked, fussily smoothing out the hamburger's paper wrapper atop his thigh.

I clenched my own burger still half-wrapped in its plain, white butcher paper, tore bites from it as I drove. We were somewhere in the middle of the state, so removed from polite society that there were no McDonald's or Burger Kings around, just some roadside hamburger stand called Ed's where we gassed up my Impala. The place served plain old hamburgers and cheeseburgers, Royal Crowne instead of Coke or Pepsi, French fries and onion rings. All across an old linoleum counter, orders jotted down on a plain pad of paper with a nub of a pencil, and all of it uniformly delicious.

Once we were back on the interstate, I chewed my burger, stuffed a few fries in my mouth as a kind of chaser.

"Yep," I said around a wad of greasy food.

Of course I did. Of course I remembered the naked man.

"How could I forget when you never let me?"

Stephen smiled at me, thin and totally lacking in humor. "Yes. How could you?"

It had happened long ago, so long now that much of what I did remember seemed made up, a fantasy, or maybe a skit from a sitcom of the era.

When everything, even my memory, was colored all corduroy browns and golds, like in a '70s Polaroid.

As I remember it, I was maybe ten, and Stephen was about five. I was deep in grade school; he'd just made the move out of kindergarten. It was late summer, when school was only just back in session, but before daylight saving time ended. I remember the exact day: Saturday, September 14, 1974.

The day still stretched until nearly eight o'clock, so some kids were allowed to stay up, stay outside until the sun went down, even on a school night. Not Stephen and I, not even on a weekend. We were in by 6:30, baths taken, pajamas on. Maybe a little television before we went to bed, promptly at 9:00 p.m., no later.

Stephen and I, hair slicked back from our baths, munched popcorn in the living room watching *The Carol Burnett Show* on the huge black-and-white console that had been passed down by our grandparents. I even remember the guest star: James Coco. Not one of her better shows.

At any rate, we got into some kind of altercation, the kind that normally happens between brothers. He took the kernel of popcorn I wanted or I looked at him strange or something equally as stupid. A brief tussle ensued, followed by my mother rushing in, separating us and putting us to bed.

The sun was still out, and the weather was still warm. Our bedroom window was open, with the screen in place so that we could see the neighborhood outside.

It was torture.

There were people still outside, kids riding bikes, running around, doing stuff. Kid stuff. My mother had tucked us in with the strict admonition to stay in bed. But I was up soon after the door closed to the room we shared, face pressed against the screen.

I remember scenes within this memory with perfect, almost crystalline clarity. The cool twilight air, with its slight aroma of the mosquito fogger that had just driven past the house, noisily belching out its strangely appealing fog. The green-gold sun slanting through the tall trees on the edge of the woods ringing our subdivision. I remember the *skree-skree-skree* of crickets, the shouts of the neighborhood kids still outside, the distant roar of a jet overhead.

I'd climbed up the bunk beds we shared to lay ramrod straight atop the covers, protesting being shooed to bed, mad that mother had basically assigned the fault of all this to me, since I was the oldest.

Stephen stirred beneath me, jouncing the thin mattresses we slept on with whatever he was doing.

"Stop shaking the whole bed, retard!" I whispered.

"I'm not doing nuthin'," Stephen responded. "And don't call me that. I'll tell mom on you."

I muttered something, I'm sure, then launched myself out of the bed, alighting in bare feet onto the carpeted floor with as little sound as I could make.

Stephen curled back into his space, put his feet out to kick me, as I'm sure he thought I'd come down to give him a punch or two.

But I didn't, just dropped to my knees at the window, rested my forehead against the screen and sighed. I wasn't really even looking, just not at all tired, not at all wanting to go to sleep while the sun was still in the sky.

"Whatchya doin'?" Stephen finally asked, uncurling from his defensive position long after I'd lost any interest in him.

"Nothing. Go to bed."

"Are you sad?"

"What?"

"Are you sad?"

"What kinda stupid question is that?"

"I dunno. You just seem sad. Everybody seems sad."

I turned to him, frowned.

"Like who?"

He shrugged his thin shoulders. "I dunno. Everybody. You. Me. Mom."

"What about dad?" I asked, a lump forming in my throat and rolling down to my stomach like a snowball, gathering mass and momentum as it moved.

"Dad seems *mad*."

I didn't say anything to that. Dad *did* seem mad these days. *Really* mad. He was as likely to take a swat at you as say good morning or good night. He spent a lot of time away from home, particularly at night. And when he was home, there were arguments, shouting coming from my parents' bedroom late at night, when they thought we were well asleep.

Once I'd gone downstairs to the laundry room looking for a shirt to wear to school the next day and found a paper shopping bag tucked away near the dryer. I opened it, and was struck by several odors as soon as

I exposed what was inside—the sour tang of sweat, the musty smell of earth, something bright and metallic, and something underneath all this, something flat and base and smelling both good and bad, as some things do. Like spoiled chicken soup or weak bleach.

I reached inside, tentatively, and lifted one of my father's white shirts, darkly streaked with dirt, brightly streaked with blood.

I licked my lips, pushed the T-shirt back inside its bag, crumpled the top closed, placed it carefully back where I'd found it.

When I asked my mother about it her eyes flew wide, and she uttered a little shriek, then slapped me, almost reflexively, told me to leave it alone, forget about it. Told me to stop snooping around in the laundry room.

I wanted to tell her about the shirt I was looking for. Wanted to ask her if my dad was all right, if he'd been injured.

I was worried about him. Over the last month or two, I'd seen him twice when I was out and about, probably where I wasn't supposed to be. And both times had deeply confused me.

The first time I'd swiped some spare change from Stephen, who had set it down somewhere preparatory to feeding it into his piggy bank. Not a whole lot of change, but in those days it didn't take a whole lot of change to buy what kids wanted: a pack of baseball cards with their waxy, chalky bubblegum or a pack of Laffy Taffy or Lik-M-Aid.

I'd raced to the Quik Stop to grab a few things I could jam into my face, eating the evidence as it were. After making my purchases, I'd pedaled to the other end of the strip mall, sat on the curb. Across the street was another strip mall and from this vantage, I could look down the alley behind it, where the dumpsters were.

Searching through those dumpsters was my dad. Our car was parked nearby, and there was my father, stripped of his shirt, climbing into each dumpster, rooting around, throwing cans and bottles. When he was finished, he scrabbled out, looked around, then placed the cans and bottles into separate bags.

Big whoop, right? I mean, I'd seen plenty of kids do the same thing, to sell them for a few cents for the important purchases of candy and soda and comics. I'd done it myself.

But this was my father.

I sat there, planted, heat from my cheeks making me blink. I didn't move for fear he'd see me, someone would see me.

Or worse that someone would see *him*.

But he never turned toward me, just climbed into the car, the same car that sat in our garage at night, and drove slowly up to the next grouping of dumpsters.

As soon as he was in the car, I hopped on my bike and fled home. Didn't even come out of my room to eat dinner that evening.

The other time I saw him was with a girl. A young girl. No one I knew. No one I ever saw again.

Well, that's not precisely true, is it?

I saw her picture in the paper once.

* * *

We pulled off the highway in a little burg called Entreaty Pass. There were no major chains in this town, just a small, roadside motel. We weren't terribly picky. We'd been driving all day, and both of us were looking forward to climbing into a bed—in separate rooms, of course—and getting some sleep.

He signed in first, going through the entire process, handing them a credit card, getting a key with large plastic fob. When he was finished, he stepped away, let me up to the counter where I repeated the same process with the tired, disinterested young clerk.

As she ran my credit card, I looked down and saw the sheet of paper with my brother's room information. I noticed he'd signed in, given them a credit card under the name Orin Scrivello. That made me laugh as I took back the credit card from the young lady, got my own printed receipt for a room under the name Gern Blanston.

Swirl left, swirl right.

* * *

"Did it have any effect on you?" Stephen asked, standing in front of the door to his room, key in hand.

"What?" I asked, stepping inside mine, yanking the key from the doorknob.

"The naked man," he shrugged. "What happened."

I backed into the shadows of my room so he couldn't see me frown.

"Good night, Stephen."

* * *

Do you know what the Coriolis Effect is? I know, sounds like some Italian thing, like the weight of a meatball based on its volume or the density of Gigi's gravy. But no, it's a force that interacts with a rotating system, dictating which direction that system will spin.

In effect, it's about how things swirl in the direction they swirl in. Like cyclones or the water in a toilet. Or fingerprints.

Or lives.

My whole life is a testament to this force.

As was my father's.

As was my brother's, I came to understand.

I lay awake in that cold, spartan little motel room, the air conditioner wheezing and panting cool air that smelled of must and mildew. Over the sound of its laboring, I heard cars whoosh by on the state highway. I heard the *skree-skree-skree* of the crickets outside, the hoot of an owl every minute or so.

I also heard my brother's door open very late, close softly.

Later, I heard the trunk of the car open.

* * *

"For some reason, these ended up with me last night."

I smiled at him, pushed the car keys into my pocket, slid the motel key with its plastic fob across the counter.

A television hanging askew on the wall behind the young lady blared the local news. The crawl across the bottom of the screen read, in capital letters: LOCAL WOMAN FOUND DEAD, MISSING HANDS.

Stephen went outside to wait for me. When I opened the lobby door the air was heavy and already warm.

"Drive all the rest of the way today or stop tonight and head in tomorrow?" I asked.

He looked at his shoes, so I did, too.

They were spattered with mud.

Stephen was a bit of a neat freak, so this surprised me. He was like that even as a kid, when we shared a bedroom. We were the odd couple, my mother always said. Stephen folded his own clothes and put them away in the dresser we shared. I took mine from the laundry basket, jammed them into my drawer any way I could and still get it closed.

"We're two old duffs, so let's play it by ear," he said, his tone easy and amiable.

Stephen opened the rear passenger door as I sidled around to the trunk to put the luggage away.

"Let's just put them back here," he said. "They're easier to get in and out."

I shrugged, opened the rear door on my side, slid my suitcase in.

We were on the road after a few minutes.

* * *

The first hour or so was quiet. The early morning sun slanted over the hills, bright and buttery, promising a warm, steamy day. We drove through gently rolling farmland, still heavy green with corn and soybeans.

A few times the Amish slowed our progress, horses clopping as fast as they could, drawing their tightly closed black carts behind. The man or boy inside—it was hard to tell with the beard—steadfastly remained looking forward, not turning to question or even glare at the procession of cars that passed him in the oncoming lane.

It came back to me there as I passed the stoic man, shooing his horse along as fast as he cared to go.

Anger. My father had seemed consumed by it. As I thought back on that time, he leapt into focus clearly only when I acknowledged this, admitted it to myself. He was angry, pissed at his spouse, his kids, his job, his lot in life.

When I fit this lens across my view of him, he sharpened in my mind. Yet still the image I conjured of him steamed and smoldered with heat, as if he were an ember, glowing, ready to burst into flames at any time.

And maybe he did. Maybe he did just that.

Certainly when five-year-old Stephen had asked me, or rather told me that dad was angry, it didn't register. How could it? Admitting he was angry meant admitting what he was angry *about*. Even if I'd understood what that was, it would have meant admitting how little we all meant to him.

As I sat there staring out the late summer window of my boyhood bedroom, I certainly was not prepared to do that.

How could I, then, be prepared for what I was about to see that evening?

As Stephen blah-blah-blahed about something in his reedy little five-year-old voice, I squinted, pressed my face against the screen.

Coming across our lawn in the violet twilight was a man.

A *naked* man.

I'd never seen anyone naked, outside myself and Stephen. But there, coming toward me, was a naked man, not even wearing socks. He had a dark, blurry bush, and a disturbingly large penis that flopped from side to side as he approached.

I tore my eyes away from his swinging dick, up to his face.

At first, my horror grew by leaps and bounds. His skin was grey, his face hideously contorted, blunt and smashed, with a squashed nose and twisted, leering lips. I could hear his labored breathing, his naked feet as they crunched over my father's carefully mowed zoysia grass.

He came right to the window, and I could smell him, the sweat of him, the meat of him, through the screen. I saw that his face wasn't deformed at all, just contorted under the pantyhose he wore. The sheer material compressed his features, the remaining leg dangling behind his head like a ponytail.

I sat there transfixed, unable to move or speak. I just stared at him, unblinking.

"Let me in," he whispered, his voice low and throaty.

Unable to answer since my mouth had gone desert dry, I shook my head, leaned away from the screened window.

I looked over to Stephen, and he lay huddled in his bed, smashed into the farthest corner, eyes wide, thumb jammed into his mouth.

The naked man put his hand on the screen—such a thin layer of metal separating him from us—and pushed until the frame bent inward.

"Come on, kid."

Nervously, I bent forward, pushed in the two little tab locks along the bottom of the screen. The naked man removed his hands, stepped back slightly.

I slid the screen open about four or five inches, and that was going to be all, except that his hands shot into that opening, grabbed my wrists.

Pulled.

I lurched forward, smacked into the windowsill with my mouth, instantly seeing stars and tasting something warm and salty flow from my nose.

Before I could cry, before I realized that tears were already squeezing from my eyes, he yanked at me again, this time succeeding in pulling my arms completely out the window. My head pressed against the screen at an awkward angle.

I remembered turning back to look at Stephen, still curled into a ball on his bed, his fist now in his mouth, plugging whatever screams he'd been likely to make.

As I looked back at him, bracing my knees against the sill to prevent the naked man from pulling me out, Stephen uncorked his fist, a long, viscous line of slobber draping between it and his wide open O of a mouth.

"Dad!" he cried, turning the short word into a long series of wavering syllables.

At Stephen's call for our father, the naked man turned, the nylons only partially obscuring the panic on his face. He gave one final, frantic tug on my arms, then pulled away, raced off across the lawn, disappearing between the neighbors' houses across the street.

I fell back into the room, tumbled against the edge of the bed where Stephen still sat curled and screaming.

My mother burst into the room, angry at first, then bewildered, then calming, just calming.

She closed the window screen, then the window. She took me into the hall bathroom, wiped the blood from my nose and mouth, pressed the cool cloth to my forehead and cheeks.

My father finally showed up while we were in the kitchen, my mother getting Stephen and me cookies and milk, the naked man even then fading into memory.

I remembered Stephen calling out for our father and how mad I was for years and years that he hadn't come when I'd needed him most. Remembered how that anger, that hatred had swirled within me for years, shadowed me, how it had eaten away at the edges of my psyche like acid.

Until years later, in college, when I realized that I'd gotten it wrong, almost from the beginning.

Stephen hadn't been calling for our father.

He'd *recognized* him.

* * *

We pulled into a 24-hour Sunoco station at around midnight, about sixty miles out from our hometown. Stephen asked if I wanted anything from the store, and I told him a Coke Zero would be great. He said he needed to use the restroom and that it might be a minute. I told him to take his time.

I slid out from under my seat belt, got out of the car and started the pump. As it filled the car's tank, I looked back into the brightly lit store. A single person was behind the counter, a single person stared at items in a rack. Neither of them was Stephen.

Heartbeat increasing only slightly, I walked to the back of the car, used my keys to open the trunk. I didn't root around or search through anything inside. I just looked, for a few seconds I just looked.

Two hands, palms pressed together, blue-tipped fingers intertwined.

Their wrists were dark, as if they wore something with heavy, red sleeves.

Slowly, I closed the trunk, went back to the pump.

A few minutes later, as I slid the nozzle into its cradle, Stephen returned.

He climbed into the car, passed me my Coke Zero. I sat it in the holder, noticing the lid wasn't secure on the plastic cup. Stephen watched me as I pressed the lid down firmly, lifted the cup, took a deep, noisy drink.

Seemingly satisfied, he turned away, rested his forehead against the inside passenger window and closed his eyes.

Of course, because of that, he didn't notice that I let the liquid drain from my mouth back into the straw, back into the cup.

* * *

The house swam at me out of the darkness, frozen in the beams of the headlights like a person caught doing something untoward. I punched at the brakes and the car lurched to a stop on the street. Stephen came awake as the car jounced, looked at me with bleary eyes.

"Home," I said, trying not to laugh.

It was about midnight, but I could see the house clearly, probably as much in memory as in real life. It was smaller than I'd always pictured in my mind, but I guess that's the way of all childhood things seen as an adult. The tree that had stood in the front yard was gone and there was a new row of bushes in front of the porch, but otherwise it looked the same. The house was the same color, whitewashed brick with black shutters. Even the mailbox at the end of the drive looked to be the same.

There was the large front window that opened into the living room, closed off tightly now with curtains. There, to the left, was the window into the bedroom Stephen and I shared when we were kids. The window the naked man had tried to pull me out.

Nothing had changed.

I backed my car up, pulled into the driveway. Stephen surprised me by pushing a button on his key fob and raising the garage door. We'd never had a garage door opener, at least in all the years I lived there

"Pull it into the garage, if you don't mind," he said.

So, I did.

We sat there for a minute as the garage door closed behind us, unwilling to get out, to break the moment, to complete the journey. When I finally did open my door, the atmosphere in the garage flooded into the car, warm and heavy with the ghosts of gasoline and motor oil and old grass and older wood.

The garage was empty aside from a row of tools hanging neatly on a side wall: a few shovels, a rake, a pick. One plastic trashcan sat outside the door from the garage into the house, its lid tightly closed.

Stephen climbed from the car, stretched.

"I figured we'd just stop here for a moment," he said. "You're curious, but you're probably also tired."

"Yeah," I said, stretching exaggeratedly and allowing a very real, jaw-popping yawn. "I'm pretty tired. Like to get to bed."

"Soon," he said, and he almost skipped around to my side of the car.

"We'll just pop inside and take a quick peek, then we'll be on our way."

He slid a key into the lock, opened the door and motioned me inside.

The house was dark, but it was as I'd remembered. Even though the air was dusty, it still smelled of me, my family. Of countless greasy breakfasts and my mother's laundry detergent. Of real Christmas trees and fake air sprays and Ivory soap and barbecues and that smell of the electric furnace the first cold night it was turned on.

It was our smell: my brother, my mom, me. And my dad.

We stood there on the landing for a second. I knew that, to the left were the steps going to the basement. To the right, a sliding wooden door that led to the kitchen.

Stephen's hand reached around, found the light switch there at the top of the steps, clicked it on.

The staircase lit up, the bare concrete floors beyond.

"Go downstairs first. I have something I want you to see," Stephen said.

"Okay," I responded.

I descended slowly. Ahead, at the bottom of the steps, I saw a shovel leaning against the handrail, underneath another light switch.

Stephen followed a few steps behind.

I heard him rustling with something in his coat.

I took the last three steps almost jumping.

One hand found the shovel handle, the other, the switch.

The lights snapped off, pitching us both into darkness.

"Okay. Funny, funny," I heard him say from the black just above me. "Now turn on the lights before I break my—"

"I know you killed mom."

My words sailed into the interior night, struck Stephen. I heard his sharp intake of breath, heard him take one, two, three tentative steps down.

I closed my eyes, wound the shovel behind me.

Flipped on the lights...

I heard him gasp again, caught a brief glimpse of him throwing his hands up to shield his eyes from the sudden light.

Something fell, clattered to the concrete floor.

I flipped the lights off quickly, swung hard, careful to make sure I led with the edge of the shovel. It contacted something hard that shivered up through its wooden handle and into my arm.

There was a groan, the sound of him collapsing onto the floor.

I tapped the shovel around like a blind man with a cane until it contacted something that yielded. Stepping around this, I turned the lights back on.

At my feet, Stephen lay crumpled, blood streaming from a flat, deep wound that started at his right temple and went jaggedly into his hairline. It was nearly as deep as it was wide, and white showed beneath the blood.

I prodded him with my foot, but he didn't stir, didn't make a sound.

I knew in all probability that he was at least semi-conscious, aware of what was going on, what I'd done. Taking stock of the situation, what he might be able to do.

Measuring me.

It's what I'd do in his situation. What I might have been forced into had things played out as he'd planned.

If I'd drank the Coke Zero he'd brought me earlier that evening.

But I hadn't.

I stood in the basement of our old house, surveying this unfinished space that had held our laundry room, our furnace. Where we'd played as kids when it was too rainy or snowy or cold outside. Where we'd ridden our Big Wheels, built forts out of concrete boxes. Where I'd found that bag with my father's bloody shirt.

The space was still unfinished, and there was still a washer and dryer down here, though much newer models than those we'd had decades ago.

The only other new things, though not entirely unexpected, were the mounds of broken concrete here and there, perhaps six or seven of them scattered across the floor. Giving Stephen's body another look, I strolled over to one. A little hillock of debris, dirt mixed with broken concrete, maybe eight or ten inches high.

Roughly a person's length.

I looked over to the washer and dryer. A nearby shelf held laundry detergent, cheap stuff bought in bulk and kept in plain cardboard boxes, stacked one atop the other. Row after row of bleach bottles, the smell of which brought back so many memories.

Sitting close by in the corner of the room was a concrete mixer, stacked bags of cement.

I heard Stephen stir and went back to him, knelt out of reach. I'd found the knife he'd dropped, and I held it so he'd see I had it.

"You...you didn't drink your soda, naughty boy," he breathed, probing the edges of his head wound with shaky fingers.

"No, Stephen. I didn't."

"How'd you know?"

"Because I knew you'd killed mom."

"Question still stands."

I thought back to when he'd first come into town after mom died. I'd caught a brief glimpse at his printed itinerary before he'd stuffed it into his backpack. How that trip into town was the third part in a three-leg journey, parts one and two occurring just a few days before mom died. Part three was for him coming into town for the funeral. There was no part four, because...

He looked up at me from the floor. Blood had pooled in his sockets, and his eyes looked as if they were rising from great depths.

"I knew you'd killed dad," I whispered. "I figured it'd just be a matter of time until you killed mom."

He got angry at that, fumed, his face turned nearly as red as the puddle under his head.

"I did *not* kill dad," he replied.

"Of course you did, Stephen. I've known if for a while. The naked man affected us both, it just spun us in different ways, that's all."

"I did not kill dad, you fucking idiot," he said, ignoring what I'd just said, spitting the words at me, flecking the concrete between us with blood.

"Mom did."

I squatted there for a moment as his words careened around in my skull.

"Mom? Did?" I squeaked.

"Mom did, yes. I thought you knew that."

"No."

"Mom knew. I don't know how much or how soon, but she knew. She figured it out. She knew you'd figured it out, too. Though you might not have known it at the time."

I hadn't.

"She killed him to protect *you*. To protect *us*."

I couldn't fathom what he was saying, what he was telling me, how it fundamentally shifted the foundations of my world.

I'd assumed that my mother had known, from the time I figured out my father. And I hated her for it, hated that she'd saved me—maybe had saved Stephen—that night when the naked man was outside my bedroom window, but hadn't bothered to save anyone else.

Now I knew that my mother had saved us all, *everyone.*

From my dad.

"Then why kill her, Stephen?"

"You want the trivial answer or the real one?" he gasped, his words tinged with as much blood as the air from his lungs.

"Both."

"Because he wasn't hers to take. Because he was one of us. And she knew that about him, about me. About you."

He took a deep, rattling breath.

"Why'd you just try to kill me, then?"

"Because it's what we do…"

He lay his head back onto the concrete, his cheek in the puddle of his own blood. His voice became slurred, quiet.

"All those years ago he really did pull you out of that window. Completely. All the way. But he left me alone, left me here…"

He fell silent, and I waited there a long, long time, until my old knees hurt and my thighs burned from kneeling. When I was sure he wasn't going to move again, *ever*, I crawled to him, wriggled his arm from beneath his body, spread the cold fingers, uncovered his palm.

I stared at it, tracing that same line I knew so well, from the mound of his thumb to the heel of his palm, starting there, ending here.

* * *

I buried my brother in the basement of our childhood home, with whomever else was already interred there courtesy of either him or my father.

I stayed a few days, smoothed over those other mounds with the bags of concrete and the mixer. When I was finished, the basement was pristine, clean, with a smooth, immaculate new concrete floor. Stephen would have been very happy.

I left in the middle of the night, drove home across the country roads and state highways we'd taken just a few days earlier. I even stopped at Ed's and had a burger. It was just as good.

When I got back to my place, I brought in my luggage, and Stephen's bag, too. I went through its contents: his printed airline itinerary, a few articles of soiled clothing, some carefully folded clean clothes, toiletries, a small kit bag containing two prescriptions—one for high cholesterol, same one I'm on, and another for blood pressure—and an unmarked amber bottle half filled with a granular white substance.

I burned it all, except for the bottle of powder. That I kept.

Oh, and I kept one more thing.

His hands.

The same starting points, the same ending points. A myriad of different points in between.

Amazing how much they can tell about a person, really.

LITTLE BLACK SPOTS

LINCOLN & BOOTH
AT THE ORPHEUM

ABRAHAM LINCOLN'S HEAD HURT HIM savagely as he walked down the sandy verge of the beach. It had been that play, that damnable play they'd stayed out to see last night at the theater. *Our American Cousin.* Mary had insisted on it. He groaned to remember, and the jealous eye his wife had cast at the pushy actress who clutched at his hand before the curtains rose.

They'd left before the play ended. His head threatening to burst, and the play holding little interest for him.

It could have been worse though, he thought, much worse.

As chance would have it, General Grant and his wife Julia were in town, too. Lincoln had invited them to the theater, but the general and his wife had rather hurriedly declined. Everyone was avoiding Lincoln these days, so it wasn't surprising that the Grants would snub him. Why would the Union's losing general want to be seen out with his losing commander-in-chief?

The Union, he laughed to himself. *The Union.*

Probably for the best, though, that the Grants had not attended. Mary had years ago thrown an ugly fit in front of Julia, for supposedly snubbing her and making eyes at her husband, and neither woman had been comfortable around the other since.

And now he was the ex-president.

Ex.

The thought of losing re-election, so long ago now, caused him to rub at his temples as he stared out at the crashing waves.

The "ex" before his title meant that now everyone was finally allowed to snub him as they'd always wanted to, ignore him. Even the new president, Horace Greeley, the one who'd beaten Grant when Lincoln's drunken vice president had been passed over by the Republican caucus, had urged Lincoln to go west, had practically exiled him here.

Ex-president or no, he had a rip-snorting headache, one that caused him to squint even more than the bright, nearly tropical sun overhead. The headaches began around the time Sherman was killed in Atlanta, and they'd gotten progressively worse since. When he heard of Grant's capitulation at Appomattox, he sequestered himself in his darkened office all day, holding his head in shaking hands.

Best to let all that remain in the past now that he was here, standing at the edge of the Pacific Ocean. He'd always dreamed of seeing it, and the dreams gained life in lockstep with his headaches. But it calmed him now to actually stand upon its beach: the smooth, undulating expanse that clung to the grey-green strip of water lapping at his feet, so unlike the dishwater grey of the Atlantic.

Bedside him, quiet now, was Mary, her heavy black skirt skittering across the sand. She clucked at it fussily, squeezed his larger hand with her smaller one, wrapped in a blindingly white silk glove.

He turned, smiled at her, his face large and dark, lined and deeply cragged.

"Mother," he said softly, "wouldn't you be more comfortable without the gloves?"

She harrumphed softly, careful not to disturb his good mood with an equally bad one of her own. "I do not want the sun to ruin my hands," she said. "It's bad enough I left my parasol at that abominable hotel."

Lincoln's smile broadened, and he stopped his long legs from scissoring their way down the beach to turn and stare at his wife. So much had happened in so short a period of time; so much good, so much bad. He desperately wanted to forget the bad and concentrate on the good, but it always seemed to him that his beloved wife was unable to make that leap with him.

Ignoring the comment about the hotel, the tall man bent at the waist to peck his wife's cheek. She blushed, as she still so often did, when he showed her any form of affection in public; secretly grateful for it, but outwardly embarrassed by it. He had long ago accustomed himself to these little eccentricities of hers, and it caused him no annoyance as it once had. Besides, there was no one on the beach at present for either of them to play to.

They'd come out early, avoiding the press and crowds that hounded them all the way from Springfield to San Francisco. They'd even dodged the two huge Pinkerton guards Greeley had grudgingly assigned to protect them, to Mary's worried displeasure and Lincoln's relief. Truth be told, he wanted to do this without Mary, but she clung to him like ivy these days, unwilling for any separation, be it in space or time.

She had, he knew, been separated from far, far too many of those she loved in her life—Eddie, Tad, Willie, even Robert. No, he would let her cling a while. She needed it from him.

He wanted to be alone, though, to be truly alone for even a short time. For eight years, he felt as if he had carried a nation on his shoulders and in his heart. Its blood stained his hands and its cries sounded in his mind for too long, louder now that their chorus blamed him for the dissolution of the beloved Union. And he ached to be rid of them. All of them, the living and the dead.

He knew he never would be.

But something about the Pacific, the mystical, unseen Pacific, made him believe the gentle lapping of its waves on the far shores of his country would calm these voices, provide a much-needed balm to his weary, battered soul. So he had come out here with Mary, traveled by train and by coach across the unimaginable vastness of the western United States. Across plains teeming with Indians, across mountains and deserts and then finally, finally coming to the edge of the world, or so it seemed.

The Pacific Ocean.

Mary, sensing something deep within her husband, deeper than she could go—or was willing to go—tugged at his hand. "Come, Father, let's finish this walk before the beastly sun comes up. Besides, your Pinkertons will be wondering where you've gone."

Lincoln heard her voice as from a distance, drowned somewhat by the pounding of the waves, the pounding of his own blood in his ears.

Finish it. Yes, of course.

* * *

Something was wrong.

He knew it even back then, sensed it somewhere within him where even he could not lay a finger on it.

Well, ever since Sherman's death something had faltered, something fundamental in the world had shifted, overturned.

It wasn't right, and yet he couldn't tell what it was.

It was dark now, cool. He stretched in the bed, relieved that the hotel could find a bed to accommodate his long legs. The covers were thick and soft, proof against the cool San Francisco night. He would have liked to have opened the windows, but Mary, snoring beside him, would not hear of it. The sea air, she had pronounced, would not be good for either of them. He had muttered some half-hearted disagreement, but had ultimately acquiesced, knowing that he would open the windows when she was asleep.

He needed to hear the surf again, needed to smell the sea.

He knew what he had to do, and felt all the more foolish for it.

Throwing his legs off the bed, he gently left it, resettled the covers around his slumbering wife.

Carefully, quietly, he drew off his night clothes and laid them over a nearby chair, clothed himself with a dark suit, white shirt and tie.

Pausing at the door, he thought for a moment about bringing his stove-pipe hat, which hung on an elaborate rack near the door of their room.

"A gentleman does not go out without a hat," he could hear Mary's voice say in his head. "Scandalous."

Scandalous he would be then.

The hat stayed on the rack and he left the room, drawing the door behind him quietly and locking it from the outside.

The hotel corridors were very quiet, with only the slight hissing of the gas lamps to disturb the silence. He tread softly, lest he should disturb the sleeping Pinkertons, ensconced in rooms on either side of his own.

Taking the stairs to the lobby, he nodded perfunctorily to the night desk manager, strode past his questioning face to the door, then out into the cool air.

It was about 2:15 a.m., and there were certainly no carriages available at this late hour. Lincoln faced the direction of the ocean, breathed in deeply. The tang of the air, at once both salty and fishy, soothed his pounding headache somewhat.

He would walk there tonight, walk to the ocean and stand a while on its shores again.

Maybe, just maybe he would hear God's voice in the waves, in the wind.

God would tell him what was wrong and how to make it better.

And it would be a different solution than the one offered by his dreams.

* * *

The walk was brisk and pleasant. He had the streets to himself the entire way, which made the trip almost dreamlike. Lincoln was a big believer in dreams. He remembered them, wrote many of them down, had regaled his cabinet with retellings of them.

Many considered these retold dreams as thickly spun as some of his other tales from his life in Kentucky and Illinois, but they were just as Lincoln remembered them. They were neither embroidered nor enlarged, but told just as they had unfolded in his sleeping mind.

He was laid out in the Capitol, his casket atop a catafalque draped with the colors of the Union. Soldiers guarded his corpse as mourners filed past, thousands of them in a line that stretched outside into the cool, grey spring Washington day.

Or he was a spectator in a large crowd watching a train huff its way slowly down the tracks. A short train, an engine and just a few cars, all draped in black bunting with just a few hints of red, white and blue.

"Whose train is that?" he asked in the dream.

"President Lincoln's," said the young boy standing beside him. "He gave his life to save the Union, and now he belongs to the ages."

Just dreams, they had assured him—Chase, Seward, Stanton—just dreams.

He hadn't given his life.

He hadn't saved the Union.

Dreams. Just dreams.

But they haunted him still, even after it was all done, all over, all lost.

He was still here, disgraced in a sense, while the Union was dead, fractured at the Mason-Dixon Line. Two new republics had been birthed to its south: The Confederate States of America and a newly liberated Republic of Texas. Three bickering, disagreeable siblings where once there had been a shining, unique whole.

And he was the midwife.

Still he had the dreams of his honorable death, still the dreams of his sacrifice, still the dreams of leaving behind a Union that was whole, united.

It seemed a punishment of sorts, a torture for no discernible reason.

Wasn't the mere fact that he was still here while the Union was not punishment enough?

No, evidently not.

So, he suffered through the dreams and the headaches.

There was something about the Pacific, though, the warm, mysterious, green-blue waters that stretched from his nation's still intact West Coast all the way to the even more mysterious Orient. Something about it calmed him, soothed his nerves, stroked away the worry and the pain from his deeply wrinkled brow.

By the time he looked up, he had passed the wharf district and the docks. There were a few more people out here: sailors, stragglers, dock workers overseeing midnight loadings or unloadings of cargo from the shadowy ships that lay in berth. But no one paid him any attention as he glided by, a tall, thin sliver of a ghost. He was glad he had not brought his trademark hat.

Farther from the docks, the rugged landscape of San Francisco took over again: the craggy hills, deep crevices and ragged trees. He came to a beach of sorts, not the same as he and Mary had visited yesterday morning, but he could see the dark swell of the ocean, could hear it crashing onto the sand, could smell the seaweed and the salt and the distinct fishiness of the cool, moist air.

Walking to the edge of where the waves became an ebb of water, Lincoln paused, facing the water, and closed his eyes. He drew in a breath, let it out. With it went a pulse of pain from his head, and he let his shoulders slump a bit, felt some of the tension wash from his weary muscles.

"Lincoln?" came a voice from nearby, and the tension returned in a burst of pressure that raced up his nerves. "Abraham Lincoln?"

The tall man sighed, turned.

"I cannot believe, of all people to come across here on the edge of the United States," the voice continued, and Lincoln noted two things before he even opened his eyes to see who it was.

This voice was loud and clear, stentorian and deep, with an artificial melodiousness to it that sounded as if the person were singing the words to unheard music.

And the words "United States" had been spoken with an edge of clear contempt.

Slowly, he opened his eyes.

"You have the better of me, sir," Lincoln responded, squinting to make out the figure. A dark shape, all shadows and absences, walked toward him across the beach, limping a bit through the damp sand, favoring his left foot.

The man was shorter than Lincoln by at least half a foot, wirier. A hat topped his head, a casual-looking dark slouch hat, and curls of black hair, nearly ringlets, spilled from beneath it. His face lay in the shadow of the hat, but Lincoln could make out dark eyes, a dark mustache and beard. He could also smell alcohol on him, a sweet reek of grain atop the salt air.

The man made no attempt to shake Lincoln's outstretched hand—a habit from campaigning—and just stared at him.

"I know you from somewhere," Lincoln muttered, searching his memory for that face, that voice.

The figure snickered. "I should say so. Mine is probably the most famous face on the continent."

Lincoln could not bring to mind who he was, though, and the smaller fellow harrumphed in annoyance. "John W. Booth, sir. Pre-eminent star of the stage, wherever that stage may be. In the Confederate States of America, the Republic of Texas or even...the United States."

Again, the theatrical emphasis, the derision heaped on those last few syllable. Only now, they made sense. Even before the war was over, even before it was clear who would win, Booth had been a well-known southern sympathizer. Full of whiskey, Booth would tell anyone and everyone what he thought of the Union, of Grant and even Lincoln.

"Of course, Mr. Booth," Lincoln said, offering his hand again. This time, the other man cast a disdainful glance at its owner, then slowly—very slowly—took it in his own firmly, shook twice, then dropped it.

"I remember seeing you once back in Washington, at…at…" Lincoln rubbed his temples. "Well, you will excuse me. I can't seem to remember. Headaches, you see. They rob me of my sleep."

"'Tis nothing, Mr. Lincoln," Booth replied. "I daresay I have tread the boards so many times that I often cannot keep track of all my roles. But at least I was correct in saying you know me. I am *assured* of that."

"Yes," Lincoln chuckled. "You are correct."

They stood side by side for a few moments in silence. Lincoln closed his eyes again. The throbbing in his head, which the rhythm of the waves had soothed, had returned, pounding all the more in Booth's presence.

"You know, of course, my feelings for you. For the Union. For the war?"

Lincoln smiled, but did not open his eyes. Yes, he'd had some whiskey. That much was clear.

"Yes, I believe you've made your views generally known."

"And you feel no anger. No hatred. No sense of danger being with me this evening on a dark, out of the way beach all alone?" Booth nearly whispered. "With no Pinkertons in sight?"

Lincoln opened his eyes, turned. "I suppose if you'd wanted to kill me, you'd have had plenty of opportunity when I was president."

Booth waved a hand through the air absently. "Yes, of course, you're right. Absolutely safe now. Why need Macbeth kill Duncan if he is no longer king?"

Lincoln, no actor but a keen fan of Shakespeare, replied, *"For murder, though it have no tongue, will speak with most miraculous organ."*

Booth snorted, actually laid a hand on the taller man's shoulder, squeezed amiably.

"Now, you mix works, my dear ex-president," Booth laughed. *"Hamlet* does not go well with *Macbeth.*"

"No?" Lincoln asked as the actor's hand fell away. "Do they not both involve murders?"

"One, sir, involves revenge. The other guilt."

"Are they not different sides of the same coin?"

Booth snorted again, this time lower. He understood.

"I suppose so, sir, yes. I had never looked at the two in contrast before." Booth sketched a brief bow, comically, perhaps even insultingly dramatic.

Lincoln tipped his hatless head, smiled thinly.

"What brings you to San Francisco, Mr. Booth?" Lincoln asked, turning back to the dark ocean. "I would have supposed that you'd have eagerly sought those southern audiences whose views you so championed. To bask, as it were, in their glory."

Booth stiffened.

"It is not as you think, Mr. Ex-President," he said, his voice thinner now, edged. "They have turned on me. Oh, not loudly, to be sure. But turned nonetheless."

"How so?" Lincoln asked, his hand absently going to his temple.

"They avoid me, sir. I am no longer booked in the larger cities, asked to the better theaters. I am no longer begged to make an appearance at the best parties and balls. Even the women, the dear southern belles, no longer seek my company, sir. Me, John Wilkes Booth, defender of the Confederacy and the best living actor on the entire continent."

"Why is that? One would think they would be lifting you on their shoulders, filling every seat at your performances."

"No, sir. They avoid me because they wish peace with the United States. They wish a return to those sacred bonds of brotherhood they enjoyed when both countries were one thing and not just brothers. They are embarrassed of me, sir. They wish to forget me and my views. No one in the United States, either, wants me anymore. For exactly the same, if stronger, feelings."

Lincoln nodded, massaging his temples and trying to let the crashing of the waves do their magic. But it was as if Booth's presence aggravated his condition.

"So, I was forced to come out west, to play in cattle houses in Texas and bordellos here in California. Have you ever attempted King Lear in front of Mexican barons?" Booth shook his head ruefully.

"Are you performing here in San Francisco, Mr. Booth?"

Booth sighed. "*You.* Of all people to meet out here on the Pacific, I meet *you.*"

Lincoln cleared his throat rather than repeat the question.

"Yes, yes," Booth answered, impatiently nudging the sand with the tip of his boot. "At The Orpheum. My engagement begins tomorrow and runs until the end of the month."

"What is the piece?"

Booth angrily kicked a clod of sand toward the black wall of the ocean.

"I am reduced to small plays and comedies, doggerels and pantomimes," he replied. "It's become impossible for me to assay a Shakespeare or a Bacon."

"The piece?"

"*Our American Cousin*," he whispered, embarrassment emanating from him in waves that were, for a moment, as strong as those of the ocean.

"As it turns out, I am familiar with that play. It is relatively new, isn't it?" Lincoln asked.

"New? Yes, relatively. Oh, it's a trifle to be sure," Booth said, ignoring or not hearing the compliment Lincoln tried to pay him. "And most come to see Laura Keane, the darling of the stage."

Booth's tone was unabashedly jealous.

Lincoln took a deep breath, straightened.

"Will you be performing tomorrow night?" he asked.

"Yes, why?"

"I believe that Mrs. Lincoln and I would like to attend."

Booth's eyes narrowed, and he glared at the president.

"Come to one of my performances? Whatever for? It played for two weeks in Washington several years ago, and you never bothered to come and see it."

"Were you in it then?" Lincoln asked, an unexplainable shiver rippling through his body.

He wanted Booth to say yes, because, for some reason, it would make sense. Something about that play and Booth.

Something about Laura Keane.

Something about these awful headaches.

But Booth shook his head.

"*Our American Cousin*?" he laughed. "I think not. At that time, I was still on top of the world. I wouldn't have gone to *see* it, much less *be in* it. But now, well, now my circumstances are somewhat straightened."

Lincoln closed his eyes and Booth's words faded away, washed from his senses on waves of pain.

"I come, then, to see your performance, Mr. Booth," Lincoln said. "I come to see destiny."

Lincoln closed his eyes against the throbbing pain in his temple.

Beside him, nearly invisible in the dark sea spray, Booth smiled.

* * *

"Why, Father," Mary said as she drew on a pair of elbow-length lace gloves. "You seem positively nervous tonight. I have never seen you so excitable. Is something bothering you?"

Lincoln shrugged himself into his long, dark coat, fidgeted with his tie.

"No, no, Mother," he said, forcing himself to smile, relax his hands. "Just anxious to step out with my sweetheart on my arm and lose myself in the theater."

Mary narrowed her dark eyes at him, took his hand in her plump, enlaced hand.

"If you'd rather, we can skip the play and have a private dinner instead," she said, squeezing his large hand and reaching up to stroke his craggy cheek.

Lincoln smiled crookedly. Sometimes she was so lucid, so discerning that it disarmed him, reminded him that the deaths of their children hadn't caused her to completely lose her mind. There was still something of the 20-year-old Mary Todd he had simply wanted to dance with so long ago.

He took her hand cupping his cheek and kissed it gently.

"No, Mother, I'm looking forward to going tonight."

"But, *Our American Cousin?* It doesn't seem your type of play. It's not Shakespeare."

He laughed, released her hand and smoothed the lapels of his jacket.

"You make me seem so high-browed, Ms. Todd," he chuckled, "when you know I'm just a rough, homespun country boy. Besides, tonight I wish to laugh."

Mary smiled, a smile that could still light her haunted, hollow features.

"Then, laugh you shall, Mr. Lincoln."

* * *

The carriage bounced and jittered down the pockmarked San Francisco streets toward The Orpheum. Lincoln held Mary's hand, stared out the window at the buildings, the people he passed.

Ghosts. All of them, he thought.

Ghosts.

People who had shape and color, but no solidity, no reality. They existed here, but here was not where it was supposed to be, not what it was supposed to be. He felt it, but didn't know why he felt it, didn't know why these people failed to register on his senses.

The play's the thing, he thought. *The play's the thing.*

For some reason, he believed that a minor farce written by a minor playwright would give him the answers he needed to make sense of what he could not make sense of in any other way.

No, not the play. Not the writer.

The actor.

It was John Wilkes Booth.

Somehow he held the key. *Was* the key.

* * *

Our American Cousin did make him laugh. Ms. Keane was delightful in her role, perhaps challenged all the more by having an actor of Booth's caliber to play off of. Lincoln and Mary laughed, squeezed each other's hands, relaxed a bit in the private balcony the theater had arranged for them.

Wilkes, cast in the role of the titular cousin Asa Trenchard, was not quite as believable, though. Here, Wilkes' classical training betrayed him, and Trenchard managed to come off less an entertaining American bumpkin than a bitter, down-on-his-luck Shakespearean actor. Still, the audience forgave him, laughed with him.

Halfway through the second scene of the third act, though, Booth watched Keane's character flounce off stage.

"Don't know the manners of good society, eh? Well, I guess I know enough to turn you inside out, old gal. You sockdologizing old man-trap," Booth leered after her.

At those words, Lincoln's left hand fluttered to his temple, his right tightened convulsively on Mary's, and he slumped forward in his chair.

The hissing gaslight squeezed down into a narrow funnel of light, and the pain in his head cycled up and up until it became a thin, keening vibration in his skull that carried him into darkness.

He didn't see Mary kneel down to him, cradling his head, didn't hear her call out to those around that the president—*the president!*—was stricken and required assistance.

Didn't see, at the moment his world went black, Booth on stage below, turning to see what had caused the commotion, catching his boot on the floorboard, twisting it roughly, falling to the floor himself.

* * *

He awoke in a bed, a thin wedge of hot sunlight squeezing through a gap in the heavy curtains.

Blinking, he tried to figure out where he was, what had happened.

In an instant, he remembered himself seated, a balcony draped in red, white and blue bunting, watching a play, a burst of incandescent pain in his head, falling, falling, darkness.

Had that happened, really *happened*? It was so much like his dreams that he was unsure.

But there was something, something that was different now.

It took him a moment to put his finger on precisely what it was.

His head didn't hurt any more.

The door to the bedroom opened, and it was only then that Lincoln remembered he was in a hotel room in San Francisco. As this reality settled over him, Mary bustled through the doorway, nearly elbowing a gentleman aside in her haste.

She fell to her knees beside the bed, the black crinoline of her dress like a chorus of low whispers. Grabbing his hand in hers, now gloveless, she covered it with teary kisses.

"Oh, Father, dearest," she wept. "I was so worried. So worried lest you leave me here all alone."

Momentarily irritated, Lincoln let it pass, reached down to gently stroke his wife's hair.

"Mary, dear," he said, finding his voice. "I am well now. Whatever happened, it has passed."

The man Mary had elbowed past cleared his throat.

"I am Dr. Samuel Mudd, sir," he said, in a curiously flat voice. "I am the house doctor and oversaw your treatment last night and this morning."

"Ahh, doctor," Lincoln said, sitting up in bed. "Thank you for your care, but I feel well enough now. You say it is morning?"

"Oh, Father," Mary, almost forgotten, snuffled. "You fell insensible last night at the play. We brought you here, and here you have passed the night unconscious until this very minute."

"Morning," he repeated. "What time?"

The doctor fished a pocket watch out of his waistcoat.

"Seven twenty-two. No, twenty-three," he responded.

Lincoln rubbed his forehead, more out of habit than any other reason, as there was now no hint of any pain, not even a ghost.

"You have a guest, Mr. Lincoln," Mudd said, slipping the watch back into his waistcoat.

Lincoln saw Mary flash the doctor an annoyed look, as if she had— and probably had—warned the doctor about mentioning this.

"A visitor? At this hour? Who?"

"Mr. Booth," Mary said. "The actor from last night's play."

Mudd snapped his bag closed. "He injured his ankle right after you collapsed. I offered to take a look at it, but he waved me off."

Mary sniffed. "I asked him to leave several times, but he would not. He's been in the parlor all night."

Lincoln raised his eyebrow. "All night? Well, we must let him in, Mother, mustn't we? If he was concerned enough to wait all night..."

Mary frowned but said nothing. Instead she rose, smoothed her skirt and went to the door. The doctor lifted his bag and followed her.

Lincoln heard a few sharp, muffled words, then Mary flounced back into the room.

"Mr. Booth," she said, turning her head aside in disapproval.

Booth lurched into the room, a dark and rumpled presence, but a presence nonetheless. Lincoln rose up in the bed and offered his hand, noticing how Booth favored his left foot.

Doffing his slouch hat, Booth stepped toward the bed and took Lincoln's hand.

"I hope my presence is no inconvenience, sir," he said, the southerner in his blood taking over. "I had wanted to ensure you were recovering from your collapse last night."

"Of course," Lincoln said, smoothing his bed clothes. "And thank you for your concern. I hope I didn't ruin the performance for everyone."

Booth raised an eyebrow. "Ruin *that* play? It was ruined when word was first penned to page."

Lincoln began to demur, but Booth stopped him. "If it isn't too bold of me, did the doctor say what it was?"

"Oh, exhaustion. Nervousness. Stress. Take your pick. I see, though, that you have suffered some injury of your own since last I saw you."

Booth frowned, not as if annoyed that Lincoln had noticed, but rather more in confusion. Then he remembered.

"Ah, the ankle," he said, looking down at it. "Yes, well, in my attempt to see what was happening in the balcony, I twisted my ankle a bit. Nothing more."

"I had noticed the other evening that you seemed to be favoring that very foot."

Booth smiled, but it was transparent and theatrical.

"Why, yes, interesting you should notice. This ankle has been bothering me for quite some time, really. The twist last night seems to have aggravated it."

"You should have had the doctor attend to it while he was here."

Booth waved a hand dramatically through the air. "It is nothing."

Lincoln considered this for a moment in silence, then turned to Mary. "Mother, would you mind leaving us for a moment?"

Mary turned a blank face to her husband, blinked several times.

"I have some private words for Mr. Booth."

Mary pursed her lips and a slight flush came to her face.

"Very well," she said, flashing a distinctly unfriendly look at the actor before leaving the room and drawing the door shut behind her.

Lincoln rubbed at his head. There was a slight, just a slight pulse of pain in his temple now, but growing, cycling up.

"You've had that pain in your ankle for a while, haven't you?" he asked, not opening his eyes, his voice quiet.

There was a pause of a few seconds.

"Yes, I have.

Lincoln nodded.

"As have I this infernal headache," he answered. "And your ankle, its pain trebles when I am near, doesn't it?"

"Yes."

Lincoln nodded, let his long arms rest at his sides. He looked up at Booth, who stared at him with wide, dark eyes.

"As my pain does when you are near."

"What are you suggesting, Mr. Lincoln?"

"*Suggesting*," Lincoln laughed, drawing himself up on his bed. "I scarcely know. But let me ask you, Mr. Booth. Do things feel right in your life? Do things feel…as they should be?"

Booth walked to the room's window, drew the heavy curtains apart. The day was overcast, and a cold, grey rain fell outside.

"No. They do not. Nothing has seemed right since…since…"

"Since the war was lost."

"Won, you mean."

"Yes, of course."

"No. It seems off-kilter, like the whole world has taken the wrong path, except…"

"Us two."

Booth turned from the window with a curious look. Lincoln's comment had been a statement, not a question.

"Us two?" he whispered. "But how can that be? I've had dreams. Nightmares."

"I, too, have had my share of nightmares," Lincoln responded.

Booth laughed. "I would dare say, Mr. Lincoln, that my nightmares are *not* shared by you. You shall have to take my word on this."

Lincoln considered this for a moment as Booth turned back to the window.

"I would not be too sure, Mr. Booth. Somehow you and I, your nightmares and mine, are tied together in this."

"Not to be rude, to be sure, but you and I share nothing," Booth said, turned back to Lincoln. "You stand for everything I hate. Or should I say *stood*? We share nothing, sir. Nothing," he repeated.

"Were it not for the nightmares, the strange pains that seem to amplify in each other's presence, I would agree with you," Lincoln said. "But faced with this, there is something. I don't know what it is, but I feel it. And I believe that you feel it, too."

Lincoln waited for this to sink in, then pressed on.

"Something has gone wrong, something involving the two of us," he explained. "And because of it, things are not right."

Booth shook his head.

"Madness," he sneered. "I thought you mad during your presidency, but this, this is *extraordinary.*"

"There's something about the play, too. Something that ties us together."

Booth burst out laughing, but Lincoln heard the laughter float on a stronger wave of anger and bitterness—and fear. His laughter was thick with fear, and Lincoln recoiled from the force of it.

"The play?" Booth hissed. "*Our American Cousin*? That piece of tripe? That somehow ties us together, eh? The former president of the United States of America and the man who wanted to…"

Booth trailed off, his hands flexing and unflexing at his side, the color draining from his cheeks.

"Are you all right?" Lincoln asked.

"Stay away," Booth said, placing his hat back atop his head. "Stay away from the theater, from *me*. You ruined my performance last night, and I can't afford that. I can't lose this role."

"I can't stay away," Lincoln said. "This must be put right. We have to figure out how—"

"There is no 'how!'" Booth shouted. "No 'why!' Leave it be, sir. I pray you, leave it be. You have no idea of what you are meddling with, what you're questioning. *What you want.* Let things be as they are."

Booth took hold of the doorknob, twisted it.

"I cannot," Lincoln said.

"You *must.* Don't come back to the theater."

Booth drew the door open.

"Mr. Booth, there is something I have learned from my years of enjoying the theater," Lincoln said.

Booth half turned, the door partially open. Through it, Lincoln could see his wife, eyes wide at the shouting.

"Yes?"

"It is that, in every performance, though lines are forgotten or otherwise altered, though the actors miss their cues or stand in the wrong places, or one actor is replaced by another, the play proceeds apace, always to the same end."

Booth stiffened, went through the door, closed it behind him.

"Always to the same end."

* * *

After Booth left, Lincoln rose and dressed, slowly at first, but then realizing that he felt reasonably well, he quickened his pace. Though Mary voiced her concern, they took an early lunch in the hotel's dining room, and Lincoln felt his appetite was large for the first time in years.

When they were finished with lunch, Lincoln and Mary walked, arm in arm, along the streets of San Francisco. Lincoln, ordinarily not a shopper, indulged Mary and went with her into an endless procession of shops. She purchased a new dress, a parasol, several pairs of gloves, and an expensive pair of kid leather shoes. For his part, he allowed her to pick out the material for a new suit for him, as well as a new stovepipe hat and a simple walking stick.

They returned to the hotel, unloaded their purchases, and took dinner in the dining room. Over dinner, Lincoln told Mary that he had a surprise for her.

Two tickets to see *Our American Cousin* at The Orpheum.

Dubious, she agreed to go because he told her a simple thing.

He had to see the end of the play.

* * *

They went that night, and the next, and the next. The following night, confused and concerned, Mary begged off, telling her husband that she had a headache and didn't feel well. She had hoped that he would stay with her, reading from the Bible or Shakespeare, as she did some needlepoint. She was cross when he didn't offer to do so, just quickly kissed her forehead and told her not to stay up too late.

He took a carriage to the theater, bought a single ticket, and watched from the main floor this time.

Lincoln didn't think that Booth noticed him in the audience any of these times.

But Booth did notice, each and every time.

And it began to weigh heavily on him.

* * *

Tuesday evening, and the performance seemed a bit off to Lincoln. Of course, unlike other members of the audience, he'd already seen the play eight times. Tonight, though unnoticed by his fellow patrons, Laura Keane's performance seemed superficial and bored, and her lethargy affected how much energy the other actors exerted.

Except Booth.

His performance seemed sharp and electric, his body as taut as a piece of rope pulled in two directions. The audience, at first unsure of the ferocity he threw into his performance as the American hayseed Asa Trenchard, eventually settled down and matched his vehemence with exaggerated laughter.

"Mr. Trenchard, you will please recollect you are addressing my daughter, and in my presence," said Mrs. Mountchessington.

"Yes, I'm offering her my heart and hand just as she wants them. With nothing in 'em," Booth's Trenchard said.

Laughter. Even Lincoln chuckled a bit.

But the laughter died fitfully as the audience recovered, saw that the play had stalled, with Booth staring out into the audience.

"August, dear, to your—" Mrs. Mountchessington continued.

"*You,*" Booth whispered, and the actress playing Mrs. Mountchessington paused and blinked furiously as she tried to figure out exactly whom Booth was addressing.

But Lincoln knew.

They locked eyes, Booth leaning down a little to get a straight line of sight.

"*You again,*" he repeated, this time a bit louder.

The audience looked around, tried to find the object of Booth's frustration.

As heads turned, they, too, found Lincoln, sitting ramrod straight in his chair, looking directly back at Booth.

"You!" Booth roared. "I warned you, I *begged* you not to come here anymore. But you won't listen, will you? You persist in coming here each evening and driving me mad! You have no idea, sir. None! No idea what you ask of me!"

Sighing, Lincoln rose from his seat, smoothed his jacket, bowed slightly to Booth, then excused himself as he left the row, departed the theater.

"Lincoln!" Booth shouted after him. "Lincoln! Don't come back. Don't come back to this damned theater anymore. Leave me be! *Leave it be!*"

The tall, somber figure continued up the aisle and out the doors, never turning back, never answering the actor raving from the stage.

"This play will not go on to the same end!" he screamed as the door closed behind Lincoln.

* * *

After that evening's performance, Lincoln returned to the hotel and was able to slip into bed without awakening Mary.

Booth slumped in his dressing room for two hours after the play ended, taking off his makeup in a desultory fashion, a bottle of whiskey and a half-filled tumbler at his elbow. People didn't knock this evening, to invite him to parties, to catch a late dinner, to have a few drinks. But Booth didn't miss them at all.

As the owner came to close the theater, Booth donned his jacket and slouch hat, grabbed the bottle and left his dressing room, pushing past the man with a muttered, "Good evening." He burst out the rear door of the theater into a dark alley.

A man leaning up against the building held the reins of a horse. When he saw Booth, he straightened, tugged at the reins to liven the animal.

Booth snatched the reins from the man, thanked him and tossed him a coin.

Jumping into the saddle, he gave the horse's side a quick kick, spurred it out onto the main street.

A brief ride along mostly dirt streets brought him to the saloon he was looking for, a run down and unsavory place he'd found his first night in San Francisco. It was far enough from the theater and disreputable enough for few there to recognize him or pay him any attention.

He made his way through the throng of people to a deserted table near the rear of the place. There, he took a long pull directly from his bottle, plunked it onto the table, eyed it suspiciously.

A woman came and asked him what he wanted, eyeing the bottle herself, but saying nothing. He asked for another bottle of the same and a glass. And then he asked to be left alone. She laughed at that but went away, coming back with the single bottle and the single glass. In the time since she'd left, he'd drained the first bottle. He pushed it across the table, and she took it with a rueful smile.

Uncorking the second, he splashed some into the glass, sighed, drained it. He waved off the advances of one of the establishment's paid ladies, a patron who recognized him from earlier performances and a drunkard who was looking for donations to continue the evening's work.

Glass after glass, the second bottle of whiskey went into him. Rather than calming his mind or, better yet, rendering him senseless, though, the alcohol seemed to fuel the flames that already burned inside him.

The bar, the life around him faded into the background, and the dreams, the infernal dreams came forward into sharp focus.

If Lincoln only knew, he would surely stop coming to the performances, surely stop harassing Booth with his presence. But, he feared, even the knowledge of Booth's dreams would not keep Lincoln away. Even the outburst he'd had tonight would not keep him away.

Because there was something, just as Lincoln said, something that drew the two together, though Booth found the idea repellant and somehow discomfiting. But there was something, and it plagued his mind, plagued his dreams.

Because he, too, had dreams.

They were unpleasant, murderous, streaked with blood, slopped with it.

At the end, the blood was his. Shot. To die in a barn.

Always to the same end.

It was the "always" that dogged him, frustrated him, scared him.

Because Lincoln could not possibly know, in the way Booth knew, what that end was.

* * *

"Father," Mary said, quietly drawing an evening glove up her plump forearm. "Must we see that play again tonight?"

Lincoln sat on a small divan near the foot of the bed, drawing on his boots.

"The play amuses me," he said, a little more crossly than he'd intended. "There have been so few amusements in our life as of late."

"But you've seen it a dozen times already."

Lincoln pulled the cuffs of his dark trousers down over the tops of his boots, wiped absently at a scuff.

"It makes me laugh, Mother."

Mary came to him, placed a hand on his shoulder.

"But you don't laugh," she said. "I watch you, Father. You don't even smile."

Lincoln lifted his face to hers and sighed, deeply.

"I may not be the smartest or loveliest woman you know, but I know you better than anyone. This play doesn't amuse you at all. There's something else. I don't know what, but I know that much. And it frightens me," Mary said.

Lincoln sighed again. "Yes, there is something. That much I admit. But what it is, I don't know quite yet."

"Your dreams?"

Lincoln nodded, silently and solemnly. She'd heard him cry out in the middle of the night, eyes wide, hands clenched, awaken with his bedclothes soaked with sweat.

"Oh, Abraham," she said, burying her face in the tangle of hair on the top of his head. "You are keeping something from me. *Something bad.* I just know it. I feel it. I feel that you're going to leave me alone."

Lincoln stiffened at this, but gently pushed her away so that he could stand, enfold her in his arms.

"Mother," he breathed. "The only one who can take me from you is

God. And despite what He may feel, my feelings on the subject should be quite clear to you."

He lifted her head to look up at him, kissed her cheek.

She relaxed a little, managed a blush.

"Well, they had better be," she said, in a mock-scolding tone of voice. "My father will not appreciate you leading me on for so long if your feelings for me aren't clear."

Lincoln smiled, an open and uncomplicated smile. "Well, I would be foolish to disregard the anger of your father, even though long dead."

He kissed her again, and they drew apart, smiled at each other.

Lincoln offered his arm, and she took it. They left their hotel room, arm in arm, and made their way down to the waiting carriage.

In the lobby, they glided through the early evening crowd, some eyes on them as they always were, assessing, judging, hating, feeling pity or disregard. Lincoln simply ignored them, and Mary did her best to hold her head up and focus on what was immediately before her.

"President Lincoln!" came a shout from nearby.

Instinctually, Lincoln jerked as he heard his name, quickened his already lengthy pace.

"Sir!" came the voice again, and two people nearly dashed before him to cut him off.

"Major Rathbone," Lincoln said, relaxing and squeezing Mary's hand as he recognized the man.

Rathbone was dressed in his military uniform, his dark hair and mustache gleaming. On his arm, a beautiful, fashionably dressed woman looked upon the Lincolns with bright, wide eyes.

Lincoln shook the officer's outstretched hand gratefully. Rathbone bowed to Mary as Lincoln took the other woman's hand and gently shook it.

"Is it still *Miss* Harris?" he asked with a slight smile. "Really, Major, how long will you make this beautiful young woman wait?"

Miss Harris's smiled beamed, and she turned to look at her date.

"Not much longer to be sure, Mr. President," he answered.

Lincoln shushed him gently. "Best to leave that title where I left it, back in Washington. What are you doing all the way out here?"

"You shall always be a president to me, sir," he said. Then Rathbone looked around, turned back to Lincoln. "I am taking a brief respite from planning."

Lincoln's eyebrows raised, but he said nothing.

"It is not over, sir," Rathbone whispered. "President Greeley has made it quietly known, after all, that he does not believe the Union can survive much longer without the South restored. Plans are afoot—"

"Major, Major," Lincoln chided, brushing the air with a hand. "Surely this is neither the time nor the place to discuss this. And surely I am not the person to discuss it with."

"I only meant, sir—" the young man said, blushing extravagantly.

"We were just leaving to take in *Our American Cousin* at the theater," Lincoln said. "We would be delighted if you joined us, right, Mother?"

"Excellent, sir!" Rathbone said. "We, too, were on our way there, having tickets for tonight's performance!"

"But we couldn't possibly intrude," Miss Harris protested.

Mary, facing an uneasy evening with her husband's mysteries, agreed wholeheartedly with this arrangement. She took the young woman's hand in hers and smiled.

"We will not hear of it," Mary said. "Of course you shall join us in our box. Two additional chairs will be no imposition at all. Besides, while the gentlemen watch the play, we can discuss how best to speed up Major Rathbone's request for your hand."

Mary drew Miss Harris near, where they began speaking and laughing almost immediately.

Lincoln looked at Rathbone, shrugged, and the party made its way to the carriage.

* * *

The carriage pulled to a sharp stop at the front of The Orpheum, and the driver hopped down, put a step out, drew the door open and helped the women out.

Lincoln stepped out of the carriage last, unfolding his lanky form onto the dirt street and placing his hat atop his head.

He breathed in the cool, night air, took Mary's arm and proceeded up the steps to the theater's entrance. As they mounted the steps, Lincoln saw the playbill posted outside the doors; the same playbill he'd seen countless times.

But this time, not the same.

"They've replaced Booth," he said to no one in particular.

"Good," Mary said. "Horrid man."

Lincoln allowed himself to be drawn past the sign and into the theater's lobby.

As Mary spoke with an usher about being escorted to the balcony, Lincoln saw the theater's owner walking across the lobby.

"Sir," Lincoln said to his passing form. "The playbill outside? Booth. Is he no longer performing?"

The owner jerked once at Lincoln's voice, then stared at him harshly.

"Mr. Lincoln," the man snapped. "I would have thought you of all people would know exactly why Mr. Booth is no longer appearing here. After the ruckus the night before, I had to let him go. His understudy, Mr. Harry Hawk, will play the part until the run ends, sir."

The man pursed his thin lips, looked as if he might say something else, then walked away through the crowd.

Mary was tugging at his arm, looking at him curiously as he turned back to his group.

* * *

Outside, John Wilkes Booth sat on a rickety wooden bench in front of the theater. His brooding, black eyes watched as Lincoln and his guests stepped out of the carriage. He watched them ascend the steps, saw Lincoln stop as he noticed the playbill with Hawk's name replacing his own.

As Lincoln went inside, Booth took another deep draw from the silver flask he held. Capping it, he slipped it inside his vest, stood, and walked quickly down the alley to the back of the theater.

His hand went to his coat pocket, touched the cold metal that lay there like an affirmation that this wasn't a dream. Not yet.

* * *

Lincoln noticed the difference in the atmosphere as soon as the play began. Hawk's portrayal of Asa Trenchard was broader, lighter, more comic and less florid than Booth's. More deft and confident, and less as if the character were a slight or an unfairness thrust upon the actor.

But there was more.

Booth's absence made the play itself, not just the character of Asa, more fluid and contagiously funny. Though he'd seen it a dozen times thus far, Lincoln found himself laughing more than he could remember at any other performance. He remembered that this was a comedy, something that hadn't really struck him before.

Mary, too, could feel it, Lincoln sensed. Her grasp on his hand was lighter, less stressed than usual, and she paid more attention to the play than to him, smiling whenever she did glance over at him.

Major Rathbone and Miss Harris, too, seemed to be enjoying the play, and Lincoln relaxed in his chair.

He realized that his headache was gone, gone for the first time in weeks.

Sighing, he squeezed Mary's hand, smiled at her.

Behind him, there was a grating sound, as wood upon wood, and the door burst open.

Lincoln did not notice. He had leaned forward in his chair, looked down upon the smiling faces of the audience.

A figure entered the box, and Major Rathbone turned to see who it was, started to stand.

Booth pulled the pistol from his pocket and aimed it directly at the back of Lincoln's head.

He pulled the trigger, and Lincoln slumped forward.

The rest was a blur.

The noise of the gun, though rather small, caused everyone, even those on stage to look up. For a single, fierce moment, Booth was glad he'd ruined Hawk's line, as Lincoln had ruined it for Booth.

Then, Rathbone was upon him, but Booth slashed at him with a knife held in his other hand.

He set his foot on the edge of the box, looked down to the stage, leapt.

The other actors scattered.

His ankle, the one that had been giving him trouble now for the last several years, snapped beneath his weight. Collapsing to one knee, he wobbled, produced the pistol, brought it to his own head.

"*Sic semper actores!*" he shouted.

For a moment, he stared out at the audience as they tried to comprehend what had happened, what he meant.

"*Not to the same end*," he whispered.

The pistol spoke the last line.

* * *

In another place, another time, nearby but not too much so, Lincoln lay diagonally across a narrow, rickety bed. His coat and boots had been removed. His injured head propped carefully atop a pillow onto which his life had ebbed out over the last several hours. His breathing, which had slowly risen and receded throughout the night, finally paused.

One last whistling inhalation, one last rattling exhalation.

Then silence.

The group of men that has crowded near his bed throughout the night stood on in silence, their own breathing stopped. Then one, a man with a long beard whose eyes were red-rimmed behind his glasses, stepped forward, placed his hand gently on the dead man's shoulder.

"He saved the Union. Now he belongs to the ages."

And somewhere near, but not too near, another man raced away on horseback, a broken ankle jammed into a stirrup, toward an end in a burning barn.

AFTERWORD

I GUESS I SHOULD SAY SOMETHING HERE at the outset about that title, *Little Black Spots*.

A few years ago, Tony Rivera at Grey Matter Press dubbed me the "King of Pain" for the emotional resonance my stories have. It was a goofy little marketing moniker, and it stuck. When we realized it was bouncing around in the marketplace, I was a little embarrassed.

King? *Really?* I found it a little too full of hubris and chest-puffing. But, pain? Yes. Absolutely. I fully admit I try to imbue my stories with some kind of emotional punch, because as I've said numerous times it makes the horrors so much worse.

So, *Little Black Spots*, from the song "King of Pain," on the sublime Police album *Synchronicity*. If that doesn't say I've come to embrace this title, nothing does or will. Not because I see myself as a "king" of anything, certainly not writing, much less any aspect of horror. But because it helps set my work apart in a sea of other writers—some awesome, some who might need more time to get there. It also, hopefully, draws some subliminal ties to two things I like very much: the music of The Police and Clive Barker, whose work I respect tremendously. "Dread" is one of my very favorite short stories ever. *Ever.*

That out of the way, here we are again.

I'm still where I was last time we chatted, plunking on the keyboard, churning out stories, making shit up. Still not earning millions, but following my call. I've done a lot in my fifty-four years—my age as I write this, anyway. I've been a professional marionettist—yes, really—and a publishing executive. I've worked at an ad/PR agency, a haunted house, and a science museum. I've swept out a factory at night, bussed tables and done territory ad sales. I've written for newspapers and magazines, edited other writers' work, marketed trade shows and helped non-profits raise money.

Through it all, even back when I was too young to be employable, I wrote. I started writing stuff, oh, let's see, when I was in fourth or fifth grade. I was pretty into Sherlock Holmes and Ellery Queen and mysteries back then, and I wrote a lot of little short stories, pastiches of things I'd read and liked. As I got older—and, of course, the more I read—the more I practiced. Most of it was just scribbling, but I learned that people around me wanted to read what I'd written. Or at least they were willing.

The first short story that sold, which isn't collected here—you'll have to wait for *Untitled John F.D. Taff Collection #3*, no doubt in a year with at least two 2s in it—was called "The Two of Guns." I wrote it around '87 or '88, basically for my grandfather, who loved westerns. It sat in a drawer for a couple of years, until I got the nerve to submit it to a now deceased—like my grandfather—little horror publication called *Eldritch Tales*. They bought it for about fifteen dollars.

I still remember, vividly, opening that envelope, the feeling of anticipation slowly turning into elation. I'd sold my first story! I remember calling my mother and telling her the great news.

"Mom, I sold my first short story."

"That's fantastic, dear. How much?"

"About fifteen."

"Fifteen hundred dollars! That's great."

"No, mom. Fifteen dollars."

"Oh…well…that's…errr…still…umm…great."

Okay, so I didn't do it for the money then, and I'm not doing it for the money now.

Then, why, you might ask.

Short story writing, and let's be charitable here, is as poor a career move as writing poetry. Don't let my wife read that last statement. Yes, there are a lot of markets for short stories, but few really pay anything. And—here's the real sucker punch—few people show much interest in short stories these days. Even big authors who put out short story collections see a dip in sales from their novels.

So, again, why?

Make no mistake, in addition to a waning audience and not much hope of pay, short stories also take some definite time to craft properly. A short story doesn't suffer foolish writers very well, though the world is filled with huge amounts of poorly crafted ones. Stories, not writers. No, its very brevity seems to shine a glaring, unflattering light on poor construction, bad word choices, flat characters.

So, again, why?

Love.

Love of the form. Love of the brevity, the enclosed nature of the short story. The compactness of it, the ability to read a carefully constructed short story in, say, less than half an hour and have it affect you for days and days.

I love the novella form, too, really just the bigger brother of the short story. And while I also like the expanse of a novel, the room to move and spread your wings. Ahhh, well, the short story will always be my true writing love. I think of those that have affected me most—"The Star" by Arthur C. Clarke, anything Sherlock Holmes related, "The Mangler" by Stephen King, "The Box" by Jack Ketchum, "The Juniper Tree" by Peter Straub, the aforementioned "Dread" by Clive Barker and, well, too many to talk about here.

What we can talk a little more about here are the stories themselves, my stories, featured in this new collection. About half of them have been previously published somewhere else; the other half are new, at least in terms of never having been seen in print before. Indeed, some of them are very old, stretching back, oh, nearly twenty-five years.

Again, these notes represent the how and the why of the stories, and if that's not your thing, then by all means, skip this section.

The Immolation Scene —

Did you ever read those Time-Life series of books on the occult? I think there were actually several, like *Mysteries of the Unknown.* You know what I mean? They were slick, slim, hardbound volumes that showed up in the mail once a month for $19.95, dealing with subjects ranging from UFOs to disappearances, from Sasquatch to the Bermuda Triangle.

These books, I must admit, have fueled many of my stories. In fact, now that you're here, would you like to know the recipe for making one John F. D. Taff? It includes:

Marvel comic books—particularly *The Amazing Spider-Man, The Immortal Iron Fist, Kung-Fu, Dr. Strange, Captain America & The Falcon,* and *The Avengers.*

Books like Edward Lear's *Book of Nonsense*, D'Aulaires' *Book of Greek Myths* and *Book of Norse Myths*, *The Lord of the Rings*, Stephen R. Donaldson's *The Chronicles of Thomas Covenant, the Unbeliever*, Roger Zelazny's Amber Series, Jack Vance's Lyonesse Series, Stephen King, Peter Straub, Clive Barker, Ray Garton, Jack Ketchum, anything Sherlock Holmes. Oh, and maybe stir in some Bill Bryson and Whitley Strieber.

Television like *Star Trek* (any version), *Monty Python's Flying Circus*, *The Twilight Zone*, *The Outer Limits*, *Night Gallery*, Leonard Nimoy's *In Search Of* (I now own the entire DVD set), Robert Stack's *Unsolved Mysteries*, *Battlestar Galactica* (new), and *Game of Thrones*. And while not TV, Coast to Coast AM.

Music like the Alan Parsons Project, the Police, Oingo Boingo, Duran Duran, Tom Petty, Don Henley, Hall & Oates, INXS, The Monkees, classical composers like Debussy, Ravel, Respighi, Mozart, Berlioz, Delius, Saint-Saëns, heaps and heaps of movie soundtracks, and (yes, Tony) Guster.

Anyway, somewhere, at some time, from one of these sources, I learned of spontaneous human combustion. I remember a black-and-white photo of the charred stump of a woman's leg, still in its stockings, lying beside a chair. Wow! That got to me. The whole rest of that lady having evidently burned up for no good reason. She just up and burst into flames, perhaps sitting with her cat and sipping tea, and that was that.

It took me a good forty years or so to process this, but I finally got around to it. And this story is the result.

The Bunny Suit —

This is the only story here I have no clear idea concerning where it came from. I remember being downstairs in our living room sometime around Halloween. I remember putting on my shoes, and I remember watching the news. Something about a Halloween costume or a commercial or something I've buried deep in my subconscious triggered a thought process that got me to this story, but I can no longer follow the breadcrumbs back. Sorry. Hmmm… Seems a strange intro to a Notes section, doesn't it?

The heart of this story is all those serial killers you read about and how many of them had people in their lives, people who had no idea what their friends or spouses were doing—or at least claim that. My question has always been if the killer saw everyone as prey, why didn't they kill those around them, too? What was it that set those people apart from those the killer killed? Which then led me to ask what happens when whatever that thing is changes? What happens when the killer begins to see someone close as prey, too? Story!

The Depravity of Inanimate Things —

Sold this to the charity anthology *Horror for Good*. Wrote it for a friend of mine, T.J. Lewis, who told me his deepest fear was accidentally hurting someone. The story didn't turn out exactly as planned, but as I rolled it over and over in my mind, the voice of the main character came to me—*forcefully*—while driving home from a movie. I often do my best thinking in the car. And I mean *forcefully*. I think, in this instance, and at least for me, the voice is what makes the story work.

I often think writing is very similar to acting, in that to do either successfully you sort of have to find the right *voice*. Whether you write a character or play a character on stage, you've got to explore what it is that makes that character who he or she is—what drives them, what motivates them. Once you find how the character *speaks*, it usually tells you—the writer or the actor, or for that matter the reader or viewer—exactly who that character is. That's why dialogue is often the most important part of a story for me. Nothing pulls me out of a story quicker than bad dialogue. Good dialogue, though, can tell you so much about characters, not just in what it is they say, but in how it's said. And what they *don't* say.

And, at least in the case of this story, what they hear.

A Winter's Tale —

You might have heard me say I'm not that big a fan of H.P. Lovecraft. Go ahead, gasp, clutch your pearls, I'll wait. Seems like today's Powers That Be have anointed Howard as the steward of modern horror. Oh well, I don't like Hemingway either, an opinion that was greeted by my college professors similarly to that of a seminarian opining that he didn't really like this Jesus guy.

Sure, I like some of Lovecraft's work. *At the Mountains of Madness* comes to mind, but even that's kind of a retread of Poe's infinitely better *The Narrative of Arthur Gordon Pym of Nantucket*. Most of H.P.'s stuff has an arid, humorless quality to it that I don't find appealing. I know, what a philistine, right?

I tell you this even though I've written several pieces with a Lovecraftian edge, this one included. I try not to edit the ideas that come knocking on the door of my mind. I don't try to size them up or make them wipe their shoes on the mat. I tend to just let them in, let them speak their peace, and make sure I write them down as clearly as they're dictating the stuff. Because I've come to believe more every day, writing fiction is like automatic writing. You just listen really, really well, and you're able to hear the dictation coming through the ether.

I begin to think that I doth protest too much, though. I've written a few that could be called Lovecraftian stories over the years, so something, on some level, must interest me. In this one, though, it's more about being an absent parent and trying to do right by your children, in whatever form that entails.

Their Hands —

Whatever you call it—micro fiction, flash fiction, etc.—I'm not that big a fan of the format. Yes, you can tell a *kind* of story in that limited amount of space. Yes, it can pack a punch. But, I mean, when you pare it down to this level, it becomes more of a synopsis than a story. Whatevs. But I've tried the format several times. This one's the best I got.

Just a Phone Call Away —

In my early writing days, there was a popular subgenre called "erotic horror" that had a brief, shining moment in the sun. And I succeeded in selling two stories to *the* popular anthology series in this genre, the aptly named *Hot Blood* books, edited by Jeff Gelb and Lonn Friend/Michael Garrett. One of these stories, "Orifice," was a strange little body horror piece collected in *Little Deaths: The Definitive Edition*. This is the other. It's perhaps body horror, too, or perhaps just a bit of uncomfortable grossness.

One thing about this: the story was written before the Internet was in full swing. The Internet has changed just about everything, as I would imagine it has the phone sex trade. I thought briefly about updating it, but decided against it. I mean, stories are meant to represent a sliver of time—some specific era or place or event—where moving the story or altering its details makes an intrinsic change to the story itself. I'm not—not at all!—saying that this story is some timeless short story for the ages. But to me, it just seemed better to leave it be, as it was written, to represent the period it was written for.

The Dark Level —

This one is a reprint, having appeared in the now-defunct magazine *Deathrealm*. I wrote it at a time when I was working in downtown St. Louis, having to park in one of those massive subterranean parking structures. They're kind of creepy, aren't they? Dim, dank, endless concrete corridors and spiraling ramps. I often thought of all the things that could be lurking in the shadows: thieves, murderers, troglodytes of every shape and kind. But it also got me thinking about the structure itself. And that, my friends, equaled a story.

This was also the story I experimented with years later by self-publishing a reprint on Amazon in those heady, early days of e-reading. It did very, very well, and made me realize I had an audience out there, which in turn led to *Little Deaths*, my first short story collection, originally published in 2012 and now available in a glorious fifth-anniversary Definitive Edition from Grey Matter Press!

Everything Must Go —

Let me begin by saying that Tony Rivera didn't like this one. Not. A. Bit. Didn't want it in here. But I finally convinced him. Not to like it, mind you, just to accept it. I do like this tale of a man who sees something others don't. What is it? To me, it's pulling the curtain back and getting a glimpse backstage. Of the fly system, the sets, the cogs and gears that move the machine. Stuff that we're not supposed to see, until it's our time, that is. And a horrifying reminder that going unnoticed by the universe might not be such a bad thing.

Purple Soda Hand —

Okay, well, that was a weird one.

I actually did write this for Josh Malerman, author of *Bird Box, Black Mad Wheel, Goblin* and *Unbury Carol*. I love Josh's writing, and Josh!, a lot. It, and he, are odd and endearing, creepy and deeply weird and unsettling, all in a good way.

When I first read his novella *A House at the Bottom of a Lake*, I fell in love with it. Its characters are heartbreakingly young and in love, and the story is lyrical and eerie. Its central conceit—the eponymous house at the bottom of the lake—is offputtingly askew, yet it's accepted in the story, addressed as if these kinds of things are found all the time. And the story precedes from it without looking back. I frakkin' love that.

Now, I didn't have Josh's story in mind when I sat down to write "Purple Soda Hand," but that idea—that something so arrestingly odd and disturbing is just accepted within the frame of the story—appealed to me the instant I landed upon that image of the soda bottle nestled in the weeds, with its purple liquid and tiny, amputated hand. How do characters deal with something so odd? How does that drive the story?

So, I let my inner Josh go, and "Purple Soda Hand" came pretty easily, all things considered. I should point out that the original title for this story was "No Deposit, No Return." Okay, decent title. I think it would have worked well. But "Purple Soda Hand" seemed much more in keeping with the tone of the story, so I went with it instead.

A Kiss from the Sun for Pardon —

Love them or hate them, this one's about vampires. For me, vampires have seen their fictional fortunes sputter, denatured by their over-familiarity. Each author who's used this trope over the years has felt the need to add something to the lore. Which has brought us to where we are today: sparkly vampires. I can count the stories I've written about vampires on exactly three fingers. I don't particularly think they're very interesting anymore, like zombies or the Kardashians. But this one, well, it's a reverse-vampire story, so that's different? Right?

The Bitches of Madison County —

I spend a lot of time on the titles of my stories. They're important to me. They say something about the story. They illuminate some aspect of it, even if it's just where my mind was when it was written. Sometimes they're playful, sometimes they're very serious. Sometimes they are double or even triple entendres. Sometimes, though, they're a joke.

I wrote this story a while back, and the title wasn't there until the very end. Once the details of this clicked—nature magazine photographer goes buggy and starts filming women around him—the title came naturally. And really, in this case, the title says more about the main character's frame of mind than it does mine. Just sayin'!

The Night Moves —

Another kind of experimental piece. I like its poeticism, its ebbing and spiraling and building to its final point. This story might be more of an acquired taste than most of my pieces, but I think there's a certain harsh elegance to it that appeals to me.

Gethsemane, In Rain —

I've spoken before about my erstwhile desire to write a literary volume of short stories, and all the angst that created in me as a writer. Bollocks! Write what you know, as they say, and the rest will follow.

But I think literariness, if you will, has informed my short story writing, for the good I think. I give you both "The Night Moves" and this offering as proof. I like the tissue that connects each of these stories to the next, and the hidden, subdued, subtle horror at its core.

The Coriolis Effect (Or, Chiromancy for Beginners) —

Okay, I'm kinda feeling that this is some strange therapy session for me. If you've read my stories elsewhere—in *Little Deaths* and perhaps especially in *The End in All Beginnings*—you're getting to know waaayyy too much about me as a child. I figured out recently (yes, I'm slow, thanks) that strip-mining my childhood was a great way to bring a gleam of realness to my stories. And I think that has worked well for me.

The center of this story, the bit about the naked man, really happened. *I think*. Well, I should say that both me and my brother think. My brother Robert, whom I've written this story for (and also two others, "Planting Robert" and "The Mellified Man," both in the recently published *Little Deaths: The Definitive Edition*) also thinks that this happened to us.

At some point in our early childhood, we each remember going to bed somewhat early on a summer evening, early enough for that actual episode of *The Carol Burnett Show* to be on. We both remember this, well, naked man coming to our open window and getting me to agree to open it, whereupon he tried to yank me through. He didn't succeed and was somehow scared away. I remember this vividly.

Robert remembers this vividly exactly as I do, and my mother remembers coming into our room after he ran off and us telling her about it. So, either it happened (Yikes!) or it's part of an elaborate shared hallucination. I choose to believe the former, and this is the story I wrote with this mysterious little gem of my childhood.

I wanted to examine this fictionally in terms of what might have caused such an experience, and the fallout it might have brought among the members of this family. I think my dad gets freaked out when I fictionalize parts of my childhood into stories that involve fathers. He's read other stories of mine and wondered if that's him, if that's what I think of him as a father. No, Dad, that's not you in this story or in any of those other stories.

Lincoln and Booth at the Orpheum —

I read a lot of non-fiction these days. It doesn't gum up the monkey-works, as my wife says. By that, I mean that non-fiction doesn't float around in my brain affecting my fiction writing. Or in other words, I don't have to worry about ideas being my own when I sit down to write. Cop-out? Whatever.

All that said, I read mostly science and history, and within the broader realm of history, I read a lot about the Civil War. I find that period ineffably sad, for obvious reasons, sure, but also for reasons that are harder to put my finger on. There seems to be a streak of inevitability to some moments in history. It's almost if some moments were changed, didn't happen as they did, that certain things would happen anyway. That they were destined to happen. The assassination of Abraham Lincoln always struck me as one of those events, so this little alternate history explores that idea.

So, that wraps up another batch of short stories. I think my next collection, probably published in a year with at least two 2s in it, will involve mostly stories I haven't even written yet. I find that an exciting, if slightly daunting, thing to think about.

I think what might be next for me, at least in terms of collections of short fiction, will be a follow up to *The End in All Beginnings*. Some kind of novella collection. I already have the stories outlined and an overall title picked out: *All We Leave Behind*. I obviously don't know much more about this next unpublished, mostly unwritten collection, but I do have one hope. That you'll be here when I get back, eager to see what I have for you.

Until then…

John F. D. Taff
Southern Illinois
Summer 2018

ACKNOWLEDGEMENTS

No book would—or should!—be complete with thanking those who've helped make it possible. No matter how much you might think of a book as being the product of one person, it isn't necessarily true.

Here are some of the people I'd like to thank: Joe Schwartz, Josh Malerman, Erik T. Johnson and J. Daniel Stone. My fantastic wife, Deb, who generally reads everything I write, even though she is pretty much not a fan of horror. Ahh, the love! Thanks also to my parents, Denny and Kathy Taff, who also, generally, read everything I write. And my kids—Harry, Sam and Molly. I love you dearly.

Thanks also to Tony Rivera at Grey Matter Press. Grey Matter has been an important, vital force in my creative life. They are now the publisher of pretty much my entire professional catalog. That's a huge vote of confidence in my work, and I am very proud to be associated with them. Tony is an absolute mensch, and produces wonderful books. I'd like to tell you that you should work with Grey Matter Press if you can. But frankly, I can do without the competition.

Thanks go to my group of beta readers, who've read many of these stories and offered cogent criticism: Lenny and Lori Lake, James Sabata, Brian Matthews, Kim Sofia, Aine Leicht, Joe Mercer, and Shelley Milligan. And particularly Marcus Draven, my man!

And finally, thanks to all of my fans, who've gotten too numerous to call out personally anymore in the back of a book. It's weird to think that, through my writing, I've made friends across the entire United States, Canada, Scotland, Great Britain, Finland, Australia and other countries all over the world. You know who you are. I appreciate your support more than I can say.

ABOUT THE AUTHOR

JOHN F.D. TAFF HAS BEEN WRITING for nearly 30 years, with more than 90 short stories and five novels in print.

His collection *Little Deaths* was named the best horror fiction collection of 2012 by *HorrorTalk*. His collection of novellas, *The End in All Beginnings*, was published by Grey Matter Press in 2014. Jack Ketchum called it "the best novella collection I've read in years," and it was a finalist for a Bram Stoker Award® for Superior Achievement in a Fiction Collection.

Taff's work also appears in *Dark Visions I, Ominous Realities, Death's Realm, Savage Beasts, Gutted, Behold* & *Shadows Over Main Street 2* among many others.

He lives in the wilds of Illinois with a wife, two cats and three pugs.

COPYRIGHT INFORMATION

"*The Fearing* isn't only John Taff's best book to date,
it's the kind you put on the shelf reserved for the ones
that really did something to you, emotionally, intellectually, physically.
A modern master at play."

**– Josh Malerman, internationally bestselling author
of *Bird Box*, *Black Mad Wheel* and *Unbury Carol***

THE FEARING
A SPECIAL PREVIEW OF THE NEXT NOVEL
FROM JOHN.F.D. TAFF

CHAPTER 1
THE MAN OF FEAR. LUNCH AT THE DINER. LIGHTENING THE LOAD.

THE END. IT BEGAN WITH ADAM SIGEL.

Because the end always begins in fear, and Adam was afraid of everything.

Everything.

He was too much of the world, and the world was too much of him.

Adam spent most of his time curled into a tight ball atop his bare bed in his small, spartan apartment in Brooklyn. Too afraid of people to leave its confines often, he dared going out only when he needed something badly—generally food or toilet paper.

He'd stopped refilling the prescriptions for his anti-anxiety medications months ago. His fear of doctors and needles had trumped what little benefit he received from the mysterious, generic pills they prescribed.

What good did they do? Adam was still afraid of people breaking and entering when he stayed inside, afraid of people mugging him when he went outside. He was afraid of germs and terrorist attacks and getting hit by a taxi. He was afraid of poison in his food, in the air, in the water. He was afraid of alligators in the sewers and rats in the plumbing and a million other things, rational and irrational.

He was absolutely glutted with fears, every niche and hidey-hole crammed full of them. They floated just under the surface of his subconscious, like bubbles filled with toxic gas. Some of them—a group of fears that seemed central to Adam, to who he was at the very core of his being—floated atop this pool, always there, always nattering at him to *watch, to beware!*

Because of this he usually spent his days, as he did this day, stretched atop his unmade bed, biting his lips and fingernails, sometimes until they bled.

The lights were on in Adam's apartment twenty-four seven. As silly as it seemed—and it did seem silly, even to him—he was afraid of the dark, the small scurryings and scuttlings concealed by the absence of light, the creaks and groans, how the traffic down on the street sounded angrier in the night.

Darkness was, of course, at the very center of his fears, this one, primal, all-encompassing dread.

He might get up and eat some cereal or perhaps a Pop-Tart. He didn't cook much, indeed didn't use much electricity, or even water. He was afraid of the possibility of electrical fires, so he kept only a small refrigerator plugged in. And the water? Well, who knew what they hid in New York's heavily treated and chlorinated water supply?

Today, though, there was no food in the apartment. He'd looked inside the little fridge earlier and saw only a small tub of margarine and a single slice of American cheese, curled and cracked within its plastic film like a great, yellowed toenail.

He would have to go out.

That thought brought to mind all the things he would have to do to leave the apartment, which in turn brought about a cascade of fears, each bubbling through Adam's mind in quick succession.

He would have to find clean clothes. If not, he'd have to do laundry, which involved getting into the rickety elevator to go to the basement of his building. There, in a cramped, damp and shadowy room, he would have to place his clothing into the communal washers, which might at one time have held shit-stained diapers or even women's panties flecked with menstrual blood.

Then there was the little market where he bought his food. He'd have to go inside, brush against more strangers, buy food that was perhaps poisoned or tainted in ways unknowable until he put it in his mouth, in his body. He'd have to handle money again, deal with the shopkeeper with his ill-defined accent and bothersome, unplaceable *foreignness*.

Adam drifted back to his bed. Too much, too many things to think about. He sprawled there for a while, until his stomach growled angrily. He was hungry, *very* hungry. The mere realization made his mouth water.

Ultimately, hunger trumped his fear. But he couldn't do the grocery store today. *No.* Today he would do the easier thing, face the easier fear. He'd go downstairs to the diner on the corner and eat among strangers. He settled on this compromise, putting the dreaded trip to the store off for another day.

But he still wept, wept just a little realizing what he had to do.

And how afraid he was of doing it.

* * *

The Minute Man Diner was crowded, of course. It was a little past one o'clock, and the lunch crowd was pressed cheek by jowl inside. It was a hot, muggy New York summer afternoon, and the little diner's air conditioning was turned so far up it fogged the windows. It was better advertising than a sign.

Denise backed to the front counter, turned and leaned into it, lifted one sore foot and spun it in the air, then the other. She raised her head and looked at the clock: 1:16.

She'd been on shift since 5:30 a.m. But at two she'd be out the door for a quick bus ride through the city to her small duplex, where she'd kiss her kids, change her clothes and report for the early evening shift at the laundry plant. She'd work from four to eleven at the plant, come home, stand in the shower for half an hour, drop into bed, wake up and do it all again in the morning.

Denise arched her back, felt it crack in two places, and something like relief washed momentarily through her.

Turning, she saw a young man, maybe thirty, shrug his way into the restaurant, as if apologizing for his entrance. His dark T-shirt was rumpled. He was of average height, perhaps an inch or so taller than her, and his frame was slim and willowy, compact and whippishly muscled. His features were dark, his eyes were dark, his curly hair was dark, as were the hollows of his cheeks, his eyes.

She grabbed a slick and greasy plastic menu from the rack by the door before making her way to him.

"One?"

The man, who possessed as boyish a face as Denise had ever seen on a man, smiled at her. "Ummm, yeah, just me," he responded in a voice that was low and shy.

She noticed he was wringing his hands, saw the twists in the thin fabric of his shirt where he had been worrying it, too. She'd seen him here before, not often, but enough to recognize his face.

"Sure thing," she said, turning to lead him to his table.

He slid easily into the booth, and she handed him the menu. Their fingers brushed briefly, and she jerked her hand away, her cheeks heating. She muttered something about letting him have a moment to look at the menu. Retreating to her position at the counter, she took great pains to avoid him.

When Denise returned to the table, the man ordered the all-day breakfast special—two eggs, bacon, hash browns, toast. He asked for his eggs to be cooked hard and his toast to be rye. She filled his coffee cup without asking, retreated again until the cook handed his order through the window.

The young man lifted his hands from the table as Denise set down his plate, refilled his coffee. With his hands still raised, he looked at her, and she thought there was a silent question in his look.

"Can I get you anything else?" she asked, and he shook his head before he turned his attention to the plate.

He ate slowly, methodically, she saw, cutting the eggs into a kind of yellow confetti, mixing it with the hash browns with each bite. He didn't touch the bacon at all, except to move it aside, even though he could have asked for sausage or ham instead. He ate all of this, then started on the toast, each bite of which he followed with black coffee.

He didn't look at her throughout the meal, yet she was very aware he knew she was studying him.

In between service at her other tables, she refilled his coffee cup four times. Each of these times, he raised his head, said a few quiet words.

* * *

Thirty minutes after he walked in, Adam lifted his head and looked at Denise, signaling he was finished. He watched her take out her pad and scribble on it. Her hands were very definitely shaking.

"What's the matter, miss?" he asked.

"I don't know…it's… I feel weird, that's all. Just a little weird. Probably been on my feet too long."

She tore the paper off, placed it atop the table.

Adam could see she wanted to drop it and leave with no further conversation, but he was ready with his money, pressed it into her hand.

"You seem afraid of something," he said, careful to be quiet within this crowd of strangers, their fears pressing against him so hard he could scarcely find breath to speak.

"Yeah, I don't know…I feel funny… Just thinking," she said, his hand still inside hers, curled around the money. "Strange…I was just thinking how afraid I am of heights. Why would I be thinking that now?"

"Sometimes the best thing to do with fear is confront it."

He watched her reaction intently. She seemed caught in some fugue state, dreamy and detached. "Yeah…"

"There's probably roof access somewhere in the building," he prompted.

"Sure. We go up sometimes for a smoke break. I don't like to get near the edge, though."

"Well, maybe this time you should," Adam whispered.

Inside the starched pink of her uniform, Denise's back accordioned as if someone had removed a critical support.

Adam heard—*thought* he heard—her utter a small squeak, and then she dropped his hand, ran through the kitchen door and disappeared.

A spasm rippled through Adam, shook his thin frame, and he uttered a low, almost sexual moan. His eyes fluttered, and he took a deep breath, overwhelmed and confused about what had just come over him.

As Denise left, the cook sprang from the kitchen, skidded to a stop at Adam's table. Adam watched his face closely, half expecting—*fearing*—the larger man might hit him. He stood close to Adam, then stepped back. His face looked as if he had walked into a cloud of rank air, gummy and humid.

"What the hell was that all about?"

Adam unclenched his fist and let the moist, crumpled money and the check fall to the table.

"I just gave her a tip," he said. "That's all."

The cook looked at the wad of paper and change on the table. As he stood over Adam, trying to figure out what had upset Denise, there was a tremendous crash from outside the diner.

People screamed. Glass shattered. Car horns blatted.

Customers leapt to their feet. Dinnerware clattered to the floor. Glasses broke.

The cook craned his neck over Adam's head to see what had happened, but could see only a crush of people gathering on the sidewalk outside, hands over mouths.

Adam, his hands now empty, took one of the cook's in his own.

"Knives?" Adam asked. "A funny profession for someone afraid of sharp things, of being *cut*."

Adam sounded funny, even to himself. Somehow, his voice betrayed a degree of confidence hitherto unknown. As if under some geas, the cook turned, walked from the crowd gathered at the window, back into the kitchen.

Adam scooted from the booth, made his way through the throng. He pushed the door open onto air that was dense, so hot it seemed like a force field pressing against his skin.

People stepped away from him with nervous, sidelong glances, until the scene they gawped upon was revealed.

There, splayed onto the hot concrete before them was a twisted, broken thing, arms and legs bent at unnatural angles, encircled by a halo of spattered blood. The body had struck a car, whose roof had collapsed, sagged. Shards of shattered glass spilled onto the sidewalk, glittered like tears.

From there, the corpse had rebounded onto a parking meter, felled it. Its metal pole lay bent under the tumble of her body. The actual meter lay a few feet away, dented, broken open, spilling drops of its own glittering, silver blood across the pavement. And there were some in the crowd, so unaffected, so *unmoved* by the horrible scene before them, they took advantage of the chaos to bend and snatch that blood up furtively, like chickens pecking at feed.

A man knelt within the mess, all shimmering pinks and glistening reds and shining, unnatural whites. Adam watched as the man's shaking hand passed over what he realized were eyes—*her* eyes, wide open and glassy—and closed them.

The spray of the woman's blonde hair floated around the ruin of her shattered head as if she were underwater, the name tag hanging crooked from her pink uniform. Shielding his eyes from the sun, he looked up to the top of the building, some thirty stories above him.

Funny. It doesn't look all that high anymore.

Normally, even looking up at a building from the ground would set his heart to racing. He wondered where his familiar dizziness had gone, his fear of heights.

As he mulled this over, he heard more screams, this time from behind him, inside the diner.

He heard snatches of whispered conversation, passed from lip to lip, getting closer.

"…inside…the chef slit his throat…"

Adam heard sirens from a distance, their wailing growing closer.

He hesitated at the door to his apartment building.

Maybe I'll go to the market today after all.

Somehow lighter, he set off down the street.

Chapter II
Scenic Bus Tour. We're Gonna be Late. The Great Big One.

Marcia Schlimpert looked out the bus's tinted windows at the brown desert landscape whizzing by and glowered. "I think we're lost, and I think you should say something."

Marcia was a woman who didn't care if her voice was heard. Though this was meant for her long-suffering husband doing his crossword puzzle and trying hard to ignore her, she knew the bus driver heard her, too. And that was just fine.

"We're not lost, Marcia," Glen sighed, viewing her over the tops of his reading glasses. "And even if we were, how the hell would you know? I didn't realize I've been married all these years to the heir to the Rand McNally fortune."

"We're not lost, ma'am," came the driver's voice. "Trust me."

"Don't *ma'am*, me," she snapped, leaning out into the tour bus's aisle to get a better look at the driver's back. "You're older than I am."

The driver, who was a few years older than Marcia's sixty-four, laughed. "Yes, ma'am. I probably am at that."

"*Probably?*"

"Really, don't worry. Normally, I'd have taken I-10 back to Phoenix, but there was a lot of traffic backed up and looked to be lane closures or something. My TomTom here was saying delays of five or six hours were expected. So I'm detouring around the Salton Sea. Depending on how things shake out, we'll either backtrack up 78 or take the southern route up to Phoenix. Any way you slice it, we'll be three hours or so late, but we'll get there."

"Five or six hours? It's already after eight," Marcia protested, ignoring her husband's shushes. "We won't be back home until early evening."

"Well, as I said, with this detour hopefully only three or so hours. Should have us in around two p.m.," the driver laughed. "But we've got restrooms right here on the bus and plenty of food and drinks back in the coolers. Help yourself."

Unappeased, Marcia sat back and glared at the thin slice of the driver's silver-haired head. She stared at Glen, who was doing his best to ignore her, then turned away toward the couple in the seats directly across from them, the only other people still on the bus after the trip to Palm Springs.

Charles and Wanda Trammel were an active, attractive black couple in their early eighties. Charles, if Marcia's memory served, was a retired professor from some podunk Midwestern college and Wanda, also retired, had been a graphic designer at a small ad agency. They were friendly, gracious and Marcia found them annoyingly cute.

They were each reading Kindles, and lifted their gazes in unison when they felt Marcia's attention. She smiled sweetly at them.

"Mark my words," she said, this time whispering just to Glen. "We're lost as hell."

* * *

It was just after ten in the morning when the Sutherland Tours bus—*Going Where You Want to Go!*—reached the little city of Calipatria, California. The town was achingly flat, everything the same sere, brown color. A few haggard palm trees arced into the deepening blue of the sky, their fronds drooping in the heat. Beneath them, a random group of bland buildings were herded together like dozing cattle. They housed a few restaurants, liquor stores and all-night markets, all the color of dust.

Annoyed they weren't in Phoenix yet and more annoyed that no one else seemed to share her annoyance, Marcia walked to the front of the bus, sat in the row of seats catty-corner to the driver. He acknowledged her with a brief nod, then turned back to doing what he was doing, fiddling with the radio controls.

"Shouldn't you be paying attention to the road?"

He ignored her, continued to thumb the buttons.

"I was listening to the radio, and they broke in with news about something in New York," he said, his voice neutral but taut. "Then the radio went dead. I can't get anything."

Marcia leaned in toward him. "Anything more about what's happened?"

"No anything about *anything*. I can't find any stations on the dial at all."

"Well, the reception here must be bad. Or the radio must be broken. You broke it fiddling around with it like that."

The driver gave her a look she immediately recognized as the kind Glen often gave her. Before she could respond, though, two things happened.

A sound filled the bus, swelling in volume; a ratcheting, rumbling noise almost like an enormous, continuous rush of wind or a train passing very close by. It wasn't coming from the radio. It seemed to come from everywhere.

The second was movement.

The bus, everything in it and everything around it lurched. Marcia caught the metal railing in front of her, but found herself torn away, thrown across the cabin. The driver was tossed from his seat into the well of the doorway.

Marcia pulled herself to the windowsill, looked out.

The bland, flat landscape rippled, flexing like a dog's fur ruffed the wrong way. She watched the low silhouette of the strip mall seem to wrinkle, then collapse in a spurt of dust and flames, engulfing cars in the parking lot in an expanding, fiery cloud.

Her mouth open, she saw the driver pull himself from the door well, grab at the steering wheel. The bus was still moving, veering to the right. As the tires clipped a curb, the driver jumped into the seat and whipped the vehicle savagely to the left.

"Earthquake!" came her husband's voice from behind. Growing up in Southern California, she had been deathly afraid of earthquakes. It was one of the main reasons she and Glen had finally retired to the suburbs of Phoenix. Now here she was, in one again.

"Everyone sit down and buckle up!" the driver shouted. "I'm gonna keep driving and see if we can't get through this."

Around them buildings collapsed, frantic people were thrown off their feet, disappearing into sink holes and cracks that appeared in the streets, zig-zagging like ground lightning, widening into alarming chasms. A thick, brown haze hung in the sky, obliterated the sun. Even with the bus's filters, Marcia could taste grit on the air, feel it against her teeth.

The bus swung suddenly left and Marcia fell into her seat, Glen slapping the belt closed over her lap and encircling her with his arm.

"Oh, shit," the driver yelled. "Everyone hang on!"

Through the dusty windshield, Marcia saw an enormous pit had opened a few hundred feet in front of them. It grew as she watched, grew to impossible lengths, widening as it went. Its edges parted, gouts of steam and gases rushed upward, catching fire.

The driver turned sharply, the bus leaning away from the turn, threatening to roll. He righted the turn just as the bus jumped over a median, plowed down a few saplings and rose into the air like a rodeo bronco.

It crashed nose down into a gravel parking lot, scattering rocks as it skidded to a stop. White-grey powder swirled around the windows, blocking any view of the outside.

The driver, breathing heavily in the silent interior of the bus, stumbled from his seat, almost fell down the steps to the door, opened it. Thick, oppressive heat rolled in, accompanied by gravel dust and the smell of burning things.

Marcia undid her seatbelt, swatted absently at her husband's hands imploring her to remain seated. She lurched down the center aisle, absently patted the arm of Wanda Trammel as she passed. She toppled down the steps, almost fell onto the gravel lot below. She felt the earth shuddering beneath her feet, twitching like a horse ridden too long.

She went to stand beside the driver.

"What's your name anyway?"

"Rich," he breathed. "Rich Mason."

"Well, Rich, great job there."

Marcia followed his gaze, stood beside him in silence and tried to process what her eyes showed her. There was the sky, a brilliant band of blue that swept dizzyingly overhead. High up, too high up on the horizon, was a band of solid brown, not dust or smoke, but dense like rocks and soil, exploding upward. Below that, where the ground *should* be, was more blue, but a hazy, chaotic grey-blue, full of turmoil. And it surged forward. Where the brown ascended, pushing into the sky, the grey-blue rushed towards them. The longer she stared at it, the faster it moved.

"What is all that?" she finally asked from her dry, dust-choked throat.

Rich couldn't catch his breath, seemed on the brink of hyperventilation.

"Ahhh...the blue is water. Probably the Salton Sea. And it's coming this way. We gotta get out of here...*fast*." He stepped away from her, headed back for the bus.

"Wait...what's that brown stuff?"

"California, I think."

Marcia felt woozy. It might have been the heat, the dust, the ground that still vibrated with thousands of tiny, incipient tremors.

Or it might have been the second she understood what he said. What he *meant*.

Gathering herself, she drifted back to the bus, climbed the steps.

Rich followed her, snapped the doors closed and peeled out of the parking lot. Marcia found her seat, fell into it.

As the bus sped away, the earth quivered beneath them.

MORE DARK FICTION FROM
GREY MATTER PRESS

"Grey Matter Press has managed to establish itself as one of the premiere purveyors of horror fiction currently in existence via both a series of killer anthologies — *SPLATTERLANDS, OMINOUS REALITIES, EQUILIBRIUM OVERTURNED* — and John F.D. Taff's harrowing novella collection *THE END IN ALL BEGINNINGS.*"

- *FANGORIA Magazine*

GREY MATTER
P R E S S

JOHN F.D. TAFF

MODERN HORROR'S KING OF PAIN

"A compelling and frightening read!"
— AIN'T IT COOL NEWS

A LEGENDARY AMERICAN HAUNTING

THE BELL
WITCH

FEATURING "A SKEPTIC'S GUIDE TO THE BELL WITCH"
AN INTRODUCTION BY BRACKEN MacLEOD
AUTHOR OF STRANDED AND MOUNTAIN HOME

THE BELL WITCH
BY JOHN F.D. TAFF

It's 1817, and Tennessee is on the western frontier as America expands into the unknown. In idyllic Adams County, home of the Bell family, there exists a collection of tight-knit rural communities with deeply held beliefs. And even more deeply buried secrets.

Jack and Lucy Bell operate a prosperous family farm northwest of Nashville where life with their many children is peaceful. Simple country life. That is until those secrets take on a life of their own and refuse to remain unspoken.

Much has been written about the legend of the Bell Witch of Tennessee, but the details of the Bell family's terrifying experience with the supernatural have never been told in quite the way that Bram Stoker Award-nominated horror author John F.D. Taff has conceived. In his novel, for the first time, the Witch has her own say. And what she reveals about the incident and the dark motivations behind her appearance reaches way beyond a traditional haunting.

Forget what you've read about this wholly American legend. What you believe you know about the mysterious occurrences on the Bell farm are wrong. Uncover the long-hidden reality that's far more horrifying than any ghost story you've ever heard.

Because sometimes the scariest tales are true.

GREY MATTER
P R E S S

greymatterpress.com

KILL-OFF
BY JOHN F.D. TAFF

Would you kill someone — *anyone* — if you knew you could get away with it?

David Benning's life is unraveling. Unemployed, running low on cash and with the responsibility of caring for a father struggling with Alzheimer's, he finds himself blackmailed by a shadowy cabal with mysterious and deadly goals.

Known only as "The Group," David quickly learns they breed killers. Turning everyday people into accomplished assassins with unusual targets. As he's dragged farther down into this dangerous world of secrets, guns and payoffs, their true motives are slowly, chillingly revealed.

With nowhere to run, David can trust no one, not even the woman he's been sent to kill...and has grown to love. Can they work together to free each other from the deadly grip of this lethal game?

Kill-Off is a tough, no-nonsense and inescapable thriller in the vein of Richard Stark's *The Hunter* or James Cain's *The Postman Always Rings Twice*.

In *Kill-Off* death is a way of life.

GREY MATTER
P R E S S

greymatterpress.com

JOHN F.D. TAFF

MODERN HORROR'S KING OF PAIN

"Accomplished, complex, heartfelt.
The best novella collection in years!"
— JACK KETCHUM

THE END
IN BEGINNINGS
ALL

INTRODUCTION BY SHANE DOUGLAS KEENE

THE END IN ALL BEGINNINGS
BY JOHN F.D. TAFF

The Bram Stoker Award-nominated *The End in All Beginnings* is a tour de force through the emotional pain and anguish of the human condition. Hailed as one of the best volumes of heartfelt and gut-wrenching horror in recent history, *The End in All Beginnings* is a disturbing trip through the ages exploring the painful tragedies of life, love and loss.

Exploring complex themes that run the gamut from loss of childhood innocence, to the dreadful reality of survival after everything we hold dear is gone, to some of the most profound aspects of human tragedy, author John F.D. Taff takes readers on a skillfully balanced emotional journey through everyday terrors that are uncomfortably real over the course of the human lifetime. Taff's highly nuanced writing style is at times darkly comedic, often deeply poetic and always devastatingly accurate in the most terrifying of ways.

Evoking the literary styles of horror legends Mary Shelley, Edgar Allen Poe and Bram Stoker, *The End in All Beginnings* pays homage to modern masters Stephen King, Ramsey Campbell, Ray Bradbury and Clive Barker.

"Taff brings the pain in five damaged and disturbing tales of love gone horribly wrong. This collection is like a knife in the heart. Highly recommended!" — Jonathan Maberry, *New York Times* bestselling author of *Code Zero* and *Fall of Night*

GREY MATTER
P R E S S

greymatterpress.com

JOHN F.D. TAFF

MODERN HORROR'S KING OF PAIN

"The dazzling array of themes...
has something for everyone."
— GABINO IGLESIAS

LITTLE
DEATHS

THE DEFINITIVE COLLECTION

INTRODUCTION BY JOSH MALERMAN
AUTHOR OF BIRD BOX AND MAD BLACK WHEEL

LITTLE DEATHS
BY JOHN F.D. TAFF

Step into new rooms of absolute terror.

Five years ago, Bram Stoker Award-nominated author John F.D. Taff welcomed you into the darkest recesses of his mind. Today, he returns to where it all began…opening doors to new rooms of abject horror. Disturbing rooms. Darker rooms.

Rooms where a farmer awakens to find a gigantic tentacle writhing in his fields. Where the desiccated mummy of a young girl wants nothing more than something warm to drink. Where a memorabilia collector resurrects his dead girlfriend with the prop neck bolts from the 1931 movie Frankenstein. And where the sweetest candy of all is a dead man's flesh.

Little Deaths: The Definitive Collection features 24 stories, five of them new to this edition, plus expanded notes for each tale, a new afterword by the author and a new foreword by Josh Malerman, author of *Bird Box* and *Black Mad Wheel*.

"Little Deaths is dark magic! Taff's incredible talent washes over you and you know you're in masterful hands and have a book that can reach that spot: the reason we all love reading to begin with." — Josh Malerman

GREY MATTER
P R E S S

greymatterpress.com

AVAILABLE NOW
FROM GREY MATTER PRESS

Made in the USA
Lexington, KY
13 July 2019